On
LIVING
STONE

Books by Heather Kaufman

WOMEN OF THE WAY

Up from Dust
Before the King
On Living Stone

Praise for *Before the King*

A beautifully told and imagined story of secrets, faith, love, and devotion. With a compelling plot and cast of characters, *Before the King* is a tale not to be missed.

Tosca Lee, *New York Times* bestselling author of *Iscariot*

In *Before the King*, Heather Kaufman presents a moving tale of two sisters, one of whom has a front-row view of Jesus' ministry and crucifixion. Joanna's story is a reminder that God does use ordinary people in extraordinary ways . . . if they are willing.

Angela Hunt, *New York Times* bestselling author

Heather Kaufman's characters are intricately crafted; they vibrantly reflect the fears, struggles, and hope of the period. . . . Kaufman has a talent in bringing Biblical times to life in a way that's accessible to modern readers.

Historical Novels Review

Praise for *Up from Dust*

Kaufman's biblical tale is based on the scriptural account of Martha, the sister of Lazarus and Mary . . . a novel that will be greatly appreciated by readers who enjoy Christian fiction. . . . Kaufman's writing is skillful and compelling, conveying Martha's deep emotions and inner conflicts.

Booklist

Heather Kaufman gives us a biblical story with a heart for today's world, pulling out an array of joy and hope, sorrow and loss. Ultimately, this book consumed me with absolute delight. . . . *Up from Dust* is a ray of hope for every Martha who seeks and follows Jesus.

Mesu Andrews, Christy Award–winning author

Up from Dust invites us into Jesus' inner circle with fresh insight on the life of Martha of Bethany. Taking us on an intriguing journey through heartbreak and healing, this strong debut from Heather Kaufman leads readers directly to the joy of the empty tomb.

Connilyn Cossette, Christy Award winner and
ECPA bestselling author

A heartfelt story of faith . . . Through Heather Kaufman's gorgeous and masterful writing, the world of first-century Judea comes to life. . . . To say that I fell in love with Martha is an understatement. This was Kaufman's debut novel, and I look forward to what she writes in the future!

Historical Novels Review

Up from Dust is a story of struggle, of old family hurts that haunt life for aching years. Ultimately, this novel pits our unhealed wounds against the hope that only Jesus can offer. Heather Kaufman is a truly fresh voice in biblical fiction with great promise.

Tessa Afshar, *Publishers Weekly* bestselling author of
The Hidden Prince and *The Peasant King*

WOMEN OF THE WAY

3

On LIVING STONE

SALOME'S STORY

HEATHER KAUFMAN

BETHANYHOUSE

a division of Baker Publishing Group
Minneapolis, Minnesota

Published by Bethany House Publishers
Minneapolis, Minnesota
BethanyHouse.com

Bethany House Publishers is a division of
Baker Publishing Group, Grand Rapids, Michigan

Printed in the United States of America

Library of Congress Cataloging-in-Publication Data
Names: Kaufman, Heather (Heather M.), author
Title: On Living Stone: Salome's story / Heather Kaufman.
Description: Minneapolis, Minnesota: Bethany House, a division of Baker Publishing Group, 2026. | Series: Women of the Way
Identifiers: LCCN 2025029623 | ISBN 9781540903587 (paperback) | ISBN 9780764246135 (casebound) | ISBN 9781493452545 (ebook)
Subjects: LCSH: Salome (Biblical figure)—Fiction | LCGFT: Bible fiction | Fiction | Novels
Classification: LCC PS3611.A8277 O5 2026
LC record available at https://lccn.loc.gov/2025029623

This is a work of historical reconstruction; the appearances of certain historical figures are therefore inevitable. All other characters, however, are products of the author's imagination, and any resemblance to actual persons, living or dead, is coincidental.

Cover design by Jennifer Parker

Published in association with Books & Such Literary Management, BooksAndSuch.com.

Baker Publishing Group publications use paper produced from sustainable forestry practices and postconsumer waste whenever possible.

26 27 28 29 30 31 32   7 6 5 4 3 2 1

For all the thunderous boys God is growing into men.
And for the mothers who love them.

Consider me and answer, LORD my God.
Restore brightness to my eyes;
otherwise, I will sleep in death.
My enemy will say, "I have triumphed over
    him,"
and my foes will rejoice because I am
    shaken.

Psalm 13:3–4 CSB

prologue

44 AD
Capernaum, Israel

Their footsteps are slow, sluggish—like the steps of my children after blundering a task, coming to me with half-frightened eyes. I lift my hands from the dough, pluck sticky pieces from between my fingers, and turn to face them.

Two young men enter, bearing sorrow on their shoulders, carrying news that cannot be good, for their gazes refuse to meet mine. I fuss over them, tell them to sit, fear lurching in my chest as I push food upon these sojourners from Jerusalem. They stop me with a kind word and firm hands. Now they are the ones urging me to sit, but I refuse.

"My boys—how are they?" I speak the question, forcing it around the lump in my throat. I am journeying to the Holy City soon. I have finished two warm cloaks for my two strong sons and will bring them with me when I come. "How are my boys?"

Sit. They insist, and so I do, trembling entering these aging bones. With soft voices they give me the hard words. In my heart, I already knew. I bow my head as they say it.

My eldest son—my bold boy grown into a passionate man—he ignited the wrath of Herod Agrippa I. He refused to be silent, refused to draw back even when urged to be cautious. Such was his passion and impact that Herod's only solution was to silence him for good. He faced death by the sword with a song of praise upon his lips.

He is the first of the apostles to die.

Sorrow enters my being—a blade embedded deep. I hold the pain close in trembling hands.

They note my distress and reach to brace me, but I push aside their steady grip, push past their worried faces, and walk out into the night to stand beneath God's stars.

I birthed my boy and taught him to walk along the shores of this lake, catching and righting each bumbling step. In this very home, I kissed him, sweaty from his labors, eyes gleaming into mine with that impish half grin.

Oh, but I am proud of him, my unfaltering, unshakable son.

I stand beneath the stars and blink up into their brilliance, feel the smooth black stones firm beneath my feet. There is rain on this air. I can smell it.

With a shuddering breath, I pull the pregnant air into my lungs and hold it next to the pain, moisture lining my cheeks.

There will be numerous nights in which I give myself over to this grief, tracing the story of our lives along the shores of Gennesaret. But right now, a singular, startling truth pushes up against the pain, both confronting and comforting me.

This moment is not an undoing, not an ending.

We follow a rabbi whose steps extend beyond the grave.

I lift my face to the sky as the first drops come and open my hands. I haven't always understood. I haven't always listened, but I am doing so now, and I hear it.

My boy, his life—

It is singing.

PART
ONE

ONE

"Listen, child—right here." Abba pressed my smooth cheek against the rough black stone on his workbench. "What do you hear?"

I grinned, raising a skeptical brow. "I hear Noy outside whining to be let in."

Abba released a hearty laugh. "The dog can wait. I meant in here." He tapped the slab of basalt with his chisel.

Pursing my lips, I pretended to listen, brow furrowing in concentration. With a small huff, I straightened. "Nothing."

"Ah, you don't have the ear for it yet." Abba leaned over the ordinary stone, one hand cupping it reverently while he listened. "Adonai built potential into the very rock of the earth. It is the stonemason's job to call that rock out of the ground, shape it with care, give it over to its purpose. When I still myself to listen, that is what I hear—a faint echo as the stone searches for its new place."

"You hear all of *that*?" I snorted, shifting restless feet.

Abba chuckled as he shuffled to the door to let Noy inside. "It takes time and patience to hear what is unspoken, *Zohar*."

Zohar—not my given name, but the one he used to show tenderness. Zohar—light, brilliance.

As Abba continued his halting way to the door, I scrambled to gather his cane from where it rested against the workbench, bringing it to his side.

With a gentle smile, he accepted the cane, easing his weight off the ruined foot as he unbarred the door. Noy tore into the room, knocking me onto my backside and eliciting a yelp of surprise.

Noy was more wolf than dog. Lean and ragged, he boasted a mangled ear and not a few missing teeth. A few years ago, I'd found him alone and starving, had fed him pieces of fish and bread, and he'd remained by my side ever since. I'd named him Noy, beautiful, for so he was—on the inside.

"Bah, this dog," Abba grunted, but there was no true anger in his tone. "Better take him back outside before he sets the whole shop in disarray."

Our home was located on the northern outskirts of the village, farthest from the Sea of Galilee—or as we called it, the Lake of Gennesaret—and closest to the basalt plateaus of the Golan Heights. With Abba's workshop in the front and our living quarters in the back, it was a humble arrangement, small and quiet.

"I need to begin on this piece." Abba shuffled back to the workbench. "Go feed Noy—outside," he clarified with a lift to his brow. "And then go find Naysa and make yourself useful."

A groan slipped past my lips before I could catch it. "She has two daughters, Abba. She doesn't *need* me."

"Perhaps, but *you* need *her*, so go."

I wanted to keep protesting. I did *not* need the woman with the shrewd eyes that too easily saw my flaws. But I loved Abba and would not continue to press him. "Come, Noy." With a cluck of my tongue and a firm hand on his scruff, I led him back outside, sneaking him a bit of bread I'd been saving for later.

Obediently, I wended my way to Naysa's family compound

on the southern border of the village. They were a family of fishermen, making their living off the abundance of the lake. I shouldn't complain so much, for their family was more than generous to us. After Ima's death and Abba's accident, they had kept our table full of fresh fish.

"It's the very least I can do," Naysa had insisted.

Naysa had been my mother's closest friend—so close that she'd been present for my birth, there to wrap my squalling body in linen. Ima had been softspoken and gentle, a stark contrast to Naysa's blunt temperament, but the two had forged an unbreakable bond.

Nearing my destination, I kicked at a rock, watching it skitter across the uneven dirt road. I knew what everyone said about me. The only child of the stonemason with the one good foot. The wild girl with startling, unusual eyes, more at ease with animals than with people.

The girl with no future.

"Jacob, I worry." The other day, I'd overheard Naysa talking with Abba. "I fear that you indulge her too much. She's twelve and needs to be trained to keep her own home. It's what Miriam would have wanted. You know that. Many girls her age are betrothed. How can she grow into womanhood when you let her crawl all over these hills like an untamed creature?"

"She will learn in time" came Abba's soft reply. "She's lost so much and grieves in her own way."

It'd been a full three years since Ima's passing. Sickness had gripped her suddenly, and when it took her, we were left reeling and confused. The warm, wide world had darkened and grown cold, narrow, quiet. Ima had filled our home with song, steady as a heartbeat, a constant presence whose absence was so jarring that our four walls became foreign. Abba had turned to drink until the accident happened and he put it away for good. And me? I'd turned to the fields and hills.

Abba and I had each other, and some days it was enough. But then there were days when my life folded in upon itself, squeezed and confined until I could scarcely breathe. At such times, I needed to be outdoors, away from the village. Only then, when there was nothing between me and the wild, did the air return to my lungs and the fist loosen in my chest.

Naysa's home sprawled before me, and beyond it was the lake, teeming with its fish. In the central courtyard, Naysa's daughters, Deborah and Leah, were surely busy at the loom or millstone. As soon as Naysa saw me, she'd comment on the state of my hair and put me to work. The thought of sitting in one spot carding wool for hours sparked panic.

Noy panted patiently, attention pinned to my hand as he awaited another morsel of food.

"Abba doesn't have to know if I don't *fully* obey, does he?" I scratched behind Noy's good ear as he moaned in agreement. "Naysa means well, but I can't bear it, not today." Not when we'd just passed the date of Ima's death. Instead, I headed swiftly toward the water before anyone in the family saw me.

Bethsaida stretched along the northeastern shore of the Lake of Gennesaret, on land wedged between the lake and the Jordan River, which poured into it from the north and cut us off from the western Galilean villages. Instead of heading down to the banks of the lake as I was prone to do, I turned east into a wheat field, Noy trotting at my heels. They wouldn't miss me. Well, at least Deborah wouldn't. She was fifteen, recently betrothed, and had little interest or time for me.

A sprawling carob tree loomed above the wheat. I hitched up my tunic and ran toward it. Leah used to join me in seeking out adventure. Two years younger than me, she was sweet and lovely, everything I wasn't. For a while, we were the best of friends, but the longer Abba let me roam free, the tighter Naysa seemed to hold on to Leah. Now, when we were together, there was a new strangeness as memory mixed with distance.

Reaching the tree, I grabbed at a low branch and hauled myself up. "Sit and stay, Noy! I'll throw some down."

Bethsaida housed fishermen, craftsmen, farmers, and merchants, with this particular field belonging to Ephraim, a merchant and one of Bethsaida's more prosperous residents. I shouldn't help myself, but surely he wouldn't miss a handful of carob pods. It was late summer, and they were ripe and ready for the tongue.

The thick foliage was evergreen and easily hid my thin frame as I pulled myself from branch to branch. Plucking a long, dark pod, I snapped it in half, tossing one piece down to Noy and tearing into the other with eager teeth, spitting out the small, hard seeds as I found them. The nutty, sweet flavor flooded my mouth, and my belly rumbled its welcome.

When I was younger, our table had never lacked for provision. Abba had spent long days away from home, pulling stone from the earth all throughout the Golan Heights. He'd worked in both basalt and limestone quarries, and even though we saw much less of him, Ima and I had never gone without. When he wasn't digging for the stone, he was building with it, helping to construct many of the black basalt buildings in the region.

With the injury to his foot, however, Abba had lost the ability to travel long distances, lost the surefootedness that was so necessary for his former work. Now he spent his days dressing stone, turning the raw product into millstones for grinding or dinnerware for serving. He managed to keep us fed, for others in his guild ensured that he never lacked for work. Sometimes, however, there were hungry days, and in such times, I hid my rumbling belly from his distraught ears.

Plucking another pod, I threw the whole thing down to Noy, who snatched it right out of the air. I chuckled and had just taken another bite when raucous voices carried on the wind. Peering through the leaves, I saw a group of five boys crossing the field from the north. Unease flared at the sight of Deborah's betrothed, Elazar, at the front. At eighteen, he was broad-shouldered and strong, with an imposing presence and unyielding arrogance. He was also the son of Ephraim, whose carobs I'd enjoyed.

My relief that I was safely hidden was soon destroyed by Noy's yelping declaration of my presence as he pranced beneath the tree, awaiting more pods. Five heads swiveled in my direction.

"Shush, Noy! Shush!" But it was too late. Elazar turned toward the tree, the other four dutifully trailing after him.

Gritting my teeth, I curled into a tight ball. "No, no, no," I muttered. Not these boys. Not these boys.

"This mutt has something caught in the tree," Elazar shouted.

Pieces of pod stuck in my throat, and I gagged, spitting out flecks of the fruit as I clung to a branch.

Gideon, the blacksmith's son, poked his head beneath the tree's canopy. "Ha! Look, it's the girl with the glowing eyes stuck up a tree!"

"Go away, Gideon!" I hissed down the length of the trunk. Unease threatened to turn into fear, but I pushed it aside.

Several other faces joined him, gazing up and snickering. Elazar, however, wasn't laughing. "This is our property. You're stealing, and I'm going to tell my father."

"Shouldn't you all be working and not idling in a field?" I accused. "It's the middle of the day. Perhaps *I* should be the one telling on *you*!"

"Fine words coming from the girl who's never where she's supposed to be." Elazar snorted.

"You're more dog than girl." Gideon laughed. "Do you roam with the wildlife at night too?"

"With those eyes, she can probably see in the dark." Another boy smirked.

"Be careful of the company you keep, Jonah," I warned, recognizing the gangly youth. "Since when did you become so *mean*?"

The taunts had increased after Ima's death. I went to the well in the middle of the day to avoid the hurtful words and glances. I was "unmarriageable," according to the other girls. But what did I care? I had Abba, and he was more than enough.

"*You are wearing armor, my child. Words cannot touch you.*" Abba had taught me what to do when mean words came my way. Even so, an uneasy swirl entered my stomach—round and round it spun as the boys circled the tree, Noy barking with confused energy.

Heart thundering, I willed them to leave. "Get out of here!" I demanded.

"Make us!" Gideon cried.

I had no intention of leaving the tree, but then Gideon plucked a carob and held it out to Noy, who stopped barking to snap at it eagerly. With a swift jerk of the hand, Gideon swept the carob out of reach and tossed it to Elazar, who waggled it in Noy's sight. One after another, the boys tossed the carob, relentlessly teasing Noy, who yelped and dashed between them.

Rough bark scraped at my legs as I slithered down the trunk. "Stop it! You're being hateful and cruel. Stop it!" Feet touching ground, I flung myself at Jonah, snatching the carob from his hand. "You're better than this, Jonah! I know you, and you're better than this."

Elazar plucked the carob back out of my fingers. "This is my property to do with as I please." He tore off a bite with his teeth and spat it on the ground. As Noy jumped upon it, Elazar landed a kick to his side.

With a shout, I was upon Elazar with my fists, pounding at his chest, face, anything I could reach. "Wait until I tell Deborah! You aren't worthy to be a part of their family, hurting a helpless dog." Fury clouded all judgment as I flung my fists and words at Elazar.

"You're an animal! Get off me!" Elazar captured my wrists and when I still struggled, shoved me hard. I stumbled back, tripping over a root and crashing to the ground, scraping my head on a rock.

For a moment, I lay dazed and panting as searing pain flashed through my head. Gingerly, I placed fingers to my temple. They left sticky with blood.

"What did you *do*?" Jonah squeaked.

Elazar loomed above me with a large stone in a raised hand, nostrils flaring.

"Put the stone down," Jonah urged. All fun drained from his voice.

Fear—I could suppress it no longer. Panicked, I searched for Noy. He was growling and pacing, all thoughts of food gone as he snapped at two boys who held him at bay with large sticks.

"Put it down, Elazar!" one of the boys echoed, throwing the words over his shoulder, attention never leaving Noy.

With a mighty snarl, Noy lunged. The boy whacked him in the neck with his stick, and Noy yelped, circling back with bared teeth before making another rapid lunge.

The stone flew through the air, heavy and sure, meeting the side of Noy's head with a dull thump. He fell to the ground mid-leap and lay still.

I screamed—the sound shrill and cracking in the hot summer air, while Elazar stood empty-handed and tense.

"Y-you've killed him!" On trembling legs, I scrambled to my feet, grasping at the trunk as my head swam and blood pooled in my ear and dribbled down the side of my neck.

"He didn't have a choice." Gideon scowled. "Your mangy animal would have killed someone."

Elazar was staring at me. "*I'm* unworthy of Deborah's family?" He shook his head. "*You're* the unworthy one. I come from a respected family. Your family is cursed. I've conducted business with my father from here to Joppa, while you—" His thin lips curled into a sneer. "While you haunt quarries at night like a she-wolf."

"It's been a long time since I've . . . I don't go to the quarry . . . I don't do that anymore." I was afraid and babbling, offering useless explanations to a boy who didn't deserve them. Swiftly, I shut my mouth before I further humiliated myself.

Abba had said words couldn't hurt me, but these words had found cracks in the armor. Trembling rose up my legs and to my arms, spreading to my chin. I hated to look weak! These empty-headed boys with their spiteful words and small hearts shriveled like raisins in their chests—I despised them.

Elazar took a step toward me, and I drew back. His words had landed hard, but rocks would land harder. Blindly I fled, sandaled feet kicking up dirt as I scrambled away from the tree and toward the village. As I ran, I wept angry tears, overcome by my own powerlessness.

Footfalls sounded behind me, and I threw a wild look over my shoulder. They were coming for me, and the village was too far away. I turned and made for the lake instead.

The bank was steep, but I flung myself downward anyway, the brush tugging at my hair and the rocks biting at my flesh as I tumbled into the cold water. Shouts sounded from above, but I didn't stop to look. I tore into the lake—one stroke and then two—pulling myself deeper into its glinting blue arms.

I was unafraid of the waves, for Ima had taught me to swim from an early age. When only the very tips of my toes could touch bottom, I turned. Four boys stood on the embankment. Only Jonah was pursuing me. Already he was thigh-deep in the water. He shouted and waved, but his words were whipped away by a strong gust of wind.

My toes parted from the ground as a wave swelled beneath me. I rocked in a momentary lapping embrace before the wave set my feet back onto the pebbled lakebed. I pushed off hard and swam parallel to the shore. Jonah came from a fishing family and was more at ease in the water than I was. Panicked, I swam faster, catching glimpses of the boys running along the shore.

The wind on Lake Gennesaret was unpredictable. I knew this and usually didn't swim so far from shore, but desperation to rid myself of the boys overwhelmed caution. An uncomfortable hitch in my chest finally stopped me. My toes sought ground but found water. As I spluttered and paddled, a wave rose high and plummeted down, crushing me like olives in the press. A swift current grasped my legs from below and then I was tumbling, disoriented and wide-eyed with burning lungs.

"Don't fight the water or try to swim back to shore." Ima's instruction sounded in my mind. *"Let go and relax into the waves."*

But that couldn't be right. If I stopped fighting, I'd be overwhelmed and carried off. My mind told me to obey Ima's words, but my body strained against the current, which pulled at me harder.

Soon it became clear that fighting wasn't working, so with every last bit of effort, I relaxed my body and let the waves take me where they would. With a gasp, I sucked in air as my head broke through the water.

Another wave swelled beneath me, spitting me to shore like the prophet from the great fish. I landed hard on the rocky bed, the receding waves sucking at my legs. Coughing and gagging, I struggled to my feet and stumbled to shore. How far had the current taken me? Hopefully far enough that the boys wouldn't find me. I'd lost my sandals to the waves and waded to shore on cut and battered feet, tensing as I saw figures in the shallows.

Two bare-chested boys crouched among the reeds with spears at the ready, hunting for fish and finding me instead. Our eyes locked, and I tensed, readying myself to fight, hands balling into fists.

"Salome?"

Recognition weakened my legs, and I sank to my knees.

"Salome!" the taller of the two repeated, dropping his spear to run toward me. I let him come, let him pull me back to my feet.

"What happened? Are you okay?"

"Th-they killed him," I cried. "With a rock. They killed him with a rock." I blinked up into Zeb's worried face, barely seeing him for the water obscuring my eyes . . . or was it tears?

Zeb was Naysa's eldest child and only son. Five years my senior, he was typically out fishing with his father, but when I saw him, he always had a ready word of welcome or teasing for me.

At my dire announcement, his face lost color. "Who has been killed?"

"Someone's dead?" The second boy splashed toward us— Kadmiel, the eldest son of the synagogue ruler, Baruch.

I bowed my head. "Noy. A bunch of boys were mocking me, and Elazar hit him in the head with a rock."

"Is that how you received this?" Zeb's long fingers gently brushed my temple.

"I . . . I fell."

Distant shouts jerked everyone's attention back to the bank.

"They're searching for me!" I cried.

With a grunt, Zeb thrust me into Kadmiel's arms. "Watch over her. Make sure she gets home to her father."

Snagging his spear from the bank, he ran off with an easy, loping gait.

Alone with Kadmiel, I found I could muster up no more strength. With a strangled gasp, I sat down right in the water and buried my face in my hands. Was our family indeed cursed? Was that why Ima had died, and now Noy?

Kadmiel extended a hand to pull me up. "Don't cry. Everything will be all right."

"I'm not crying!" I shoved his hand away, lurching to my feet and staggering toward land. "And I don't need your help!"

Fear and sorrow were making me insolent. Regret nipped at my heels as I clambered onto the bank.

Kadmiel hurried after me. "Wait a moment. You're bleeding! The water must have stemmed the flow for a while, but you're losing more blood. Here—" Withdrawing a knife, he grabbed his outer garment from the bank and cut off a length of fabric.

"Your mantle!"

"Never mind that." Swiftly he wrapped the fabric around my head, applying firm pressure and tying a secure knot.

I touched the bandage and found blood already seeping through the cloth. At the feel of the sticky substance, my head went so light a puff of wind would have knocked me sideways.

Kadmiel braced my slumping form. "You're all right. Steady now. Hold my hand."

"I don't need—"

"Just hold my hand, Salome!"

Mutely, I took his offered hand, every scrap of pride balking as he placed a strong arm about my shoulders and guided me toward the village. After a few paces, my narrowing vision cleared, strength returning to my limbs.

"I'm fine now. I'll be fine." I dropped his hand, but he kept an arm about my shoulders until I wrenched myself free and moved a few paces ahead of him.

"I see the rumors are true. You're as obstinate as a mule."

Rumors? What else had he heard?

Whirling, I gaped at him, lips ready to utter a defense, but the mocking disdain so evident on Elazar's face was nowhere to be found in Kadmiel's expression.

"There's no shame in needing help." He raised a brow.

"I know. I'm . . . sorry." Swallowing hard, I turned away. "I'm accustomed to taking care of myself."

I also disliked appearing weak in front of anyone—especially someone like Kadmiel, someone prominent and praised.

Long after other boys had left school to learn their fathers' trades, Kadmiel had continued in his studies. *"Exceptionally bright,"* his teacher said. So bright, in fact, that at fifteen years of age, he was soon to enter the tutelage of a rabbi. He hurried now to catch up to me.

"I'm fine," I protested. "I don't need—"

"I'll walk with you anyway."

With a huff, I resigned myself to his presence. In truth, I was anything but fine, for the image of Noy lying limp on the ground was haunting me. My hands trembled at the memory. I clasped them together and glanced at Kadmiel to find him studying my face, gaze snagging on my eyes. He must think them unsettling the way so many others did.

"Why were those boys mocking you?" The question was gentle, but I winced.

"I'm sorry. You don't have to talk if you don't want to."

I paused, but the words gushed out anyway. "I'm not like other girls, and that upsets them for some reason."

Kadmiel didn't say anything, and for a while we walked along in silence.

"I'm sorry they were mean to you," he finally said. "Sometimes boys poke fun because they don't know how to say what they really feel."

"They were clear about how they really feel," I muttered. "This isn't the first time they've mocked me. They were hateful."

"There's no excuse for hatred. I'm sorry."

Kadmiel's soothing words continued to loosen my tongue. "The other day a woman at the well said I was far too wild and would never secure a husband. When boys run off, climb trees, and pick fights no one calls *them* animals, and yet when I—"

"I'm not sure boys *or* girls should be shirking duties and picking fights," Kadmiel interrupted.

"I'm not picking fights!"

Kadmiel spread his hands wide in a wordless defense.

"Well, yes . . . I suppose I'm picking a fight right now," I admitted.

Kadmiel laughed, and then I was laughing too, and the tenseness between us lifted.

"I know I can be quick-tempered. When people poke and prod without cause, you learn to fight back in order to survive." I hugged myself.

"That sounds lonely."

"It's necessary."

"You stand out because you're different." Kadmiel paused to scrape a rock loose from the ground, then tossed it from one palm to another. "I know what that's like."

"You?" I couldn't help the surprise that tilted my tone into a squeak.

Kadmiel grinned, casting a sidelong glance at me. "How many great scholars do you know from Bethsaida, hmm? How many esteemed rabbis come from Galilee? Especially now, after the rebellion and with Sepphoris still wreathed in smoke—" His grin disappeared as his gaze dropped to the rock. Abruptly, he chucked it, and we watched it cut through the air in a wide arc.

No one looked to our region for learned men, not with the rise of Judas of Galilee and his bandits. With the death of Herod the Great, Judas, son of the famed insurrectionist Hezekiah, had seized control of the large Galilean city of Sepphoris until Rome had marched in and burned it to the ground. Two thousand crucifixions had followed. No one had forgotten it. How could we? Judas certainly hadn't, for he still roamed Galilee, inciting unrest.

"We are nothing but ignorant revolutionaries in Rome's eyes and in the eyes of our own brethren. But I can prove their assessment of us wrong." Breathless, Kadmiel bent to scrape another rock free. "Why shouldn't I aim high?" He let the second rock loose in an even longer arc. "It's those who are different who will leave a mark upon our world." Kadmiel turned to me, and a frightening thought tore through my mind.

He's beautiful.

Jerking away from his gaze, I focused on the ground, startling when he lightly tapped my shoulder. "I didn't intend to chastise you."

"It's okay." I shrugged, still unwilling to meet his gaze.

"I'm sure you'll make a fine wife and mother someday, no matter what anyone else says. Even if you *are* as stubborn as a mule."

My face was blooming into a flush that I quickly hid behind grimy hands, embarrassment bubbling up as laughter. "I doubt that very much, but thank you."

He was being kind, and I didn't have the heart to tell him that motherhood was someone else's future—not the destiny of the wild girl with the glowing eyes. A lump swelled in my throat and stuck. We were close to the village now, and all I wanted to do was run across the remaining distance.

Kadmiel had gone still, eyes peering forcefully into mine. "You really do have . . . unusual eyes." His gaze deepened.

My already-warm cheeks burned even hotter as my throat dried out and a tickle formed, causing my "unusual eyes" to water. "I can go the rest of the way alone."

Before he could detain me, I fled. Lifting my sopping wet tunic in both hands, I tore through the field on bare feet, toward home and away from this confusing boy.

Two

My head needed stiches—just a few, but it hurt, and I bit the inside of my cheek until it bled to keep from crying aloud. I sat on the workshop roof with knees tucked beneath my chin and allowed Naysa to minister to my needs.

With pinched lips, Naysa applied a poultice to my stitched head, fingers lingering at my temple before slipping to my face, where she cupped my cheek with a weathered hand. Her sigh was long and deep. "Jacob." She pushed to standing, nodding for Abba to follow her downstairs into the workshop. She kept her voice low, but my ears were sharp.

"I've offered before, but now I insist. She's getting out of control. Surely this isn't what Miriam would have wanted. Please, Jacob. Let me take her in. Let me raise her alongside my Leah."

Abba was responding, but I didn't want to listen. I scrunched my eyes tight, ducked my head between my knees, and hummed one of Ima's songs.

After what seemed an eternity, the front door groaned shut. Abba's uneven tread sounded on the stairs and then his fingers were slipping into my hair, which was still tangled and damp from the lake. "My daughter." His voice caught, squeezed into silence. I dared to look up at him and saw tears.

"I'm sorry, Abba."

"You could have been killed."

"It's only a scratch. . . ."

"This time, but what if you'd landed directly on that rock? Or the current had taken you out deep into the lake and you drowned?"

Sniffing hard, I blinked at the ground, registering my filthy feet and dirt-encrusted fingernails. Elazar's words landed upon me in a new way. *You're an animal!*

"Here, drink this. It will soothe some of the ache." Abba slipped a fragrant cup into my hands. Fennel—the tea he often drank after a long day on his feet.

I took a tentative sip, allowing the earthy scent to envelop me. He'd cut the bitter edge with honey, a special treat and one he never enjoyed himself. A lump formed in my throat at the small gift.

With a groan, Abba sat by my side, which wasn't easy with his foot. I gave him a steadying hand as he settled on the ground and stretched out his leg.

"When your mother died, it nearly destroyed us both." He held my hand, squeezed it. "I'm afraid that I've allowed you too much freedom in your grief."

"You sound like Naysa."

"She isn't *always* wrong." He smiled. "Only sometimes," he added with a laugh. "In this, I think she might be right. You're twelve, Salome, and must prepare for womanhood."

"Naysa sees everything I'm not."

"She sees everything you could be, all the big things bundled up in here." Abba pressed a finger to my chest.

I studied the cup. Abba had made it from limestone he quarried himself. Tracing its smooth edge, I considered his words.

"It wouldn't be *so* bad, would it?" Abba bumped a shoulder against mine. "You could still spend your nights here with me but spend your days with Naysa's family."

This conversation—we'd had it on and off for years. Abba would gently push, and I would harden like stone, immovable. This time, however, something in me shifted as I recalled the boys' mocking words and Kadmiel's kind ones. *"I'm sure you'll make a fine wife and mother someday."*

"Maybe you're right," I whispered.

Abba relaxed at my admission. "You've been cut from the mother rock and are searching for your new place." He tucked my hair behind an ear, thumb rubbing a loving pattern on my cheek.

"I think I'm scared." My own words surprised me. Yes, I was scared, terrified that I couldn't become what I needed to be—not without Ima. This confession of fear would have shamed me had it been delivered to anyone other than Abba.

"I understand the future feels bleak and uncertain without your mother. But you and I must trust the future to Adonai." Abba moved his hand to my chin, catching it between finger and thumb. "You can trust Adonai to form you into who you need to be."

I set down the cup and buried my face in his shoulder. He shifted and, with great effort, scooped me into his lap, even though I was far too large for such things anymore. I melted against the broad expanse of his chest and sighed with deep contentment. Oh, I loved him. I *loved* him.

◆

After an exhausted nap, I felt much better. Abba had left a pitcher of water by my side as I slept, and I was finishing a makeshift bath when someone pounded on the door. A masculine voice mixed with Abba's, but it was the sharp, distinctive whine that stopped me.

"Noy!" I was barefoot with undone hair and clad in nothing but a tunic, but I hardly cared as I flew down the steps and into the cramped workshop.

"Look who found and returned Noy." Abba stepped aside to

reveal Zeb in the doorway with Noy in his arms. "Zebedee, you are a good man." Abba clapped a hand on his shoulder.

"I thought he was dead!" Tearing across the workshop, I cupped Noy's ragged face in my hands.

"Let him inside." Abba chuckled.

Zeb entered the room with stumbling steps, lowering Noy onto the ground, where I crooned and fussed over him.

"He must have come to and staggered off," Zeb explained. "I found him roaming the field north of town."

"And those boys?" I asked.

"They won't be bothering you—at least not for a while."

Only then did I notice the bruise that darkened his jaw. This wasn't the first time Zeb had stepped in when hurtful words flew my way. Gratitude overwhelmed me as I surged to my feet and launched myself at him. "Thank you!"

Zeb grunted as I made contact. He was tall and thin, and my head barely reached the middle of his chest as I squeezed him hard, pinning his arms to his sides.

"Don't crush the man." Abba laughed.

"I'm glad you're all right." Zeb attempted to pat my back, but I squeezed him so tightly he couldn't move. "You're strong." He shifted his feet. "You could haul in a dragnet full of fish with these arms! Here—I brought you something."

With great exaggeration, Zeb wriggled free and pulled a handful of almonds from the pouch at his waist. "I know how you like them. Thought it would distract you from . . ." He glanced at my head and suppressed a grimace. "Ah, Salome, I'm sorry."

"I'm fine." I waved a hand.

"Of course you are." He grinned and yanked on a tendril of my hair as he often did. "It would take more than one tumble to crack that hard head of yours."

"A gift *and* an insult." I shot him a glare as I nabbed the almonds from his hand.

He chucked my chin, and I couldn't help the resulting smile that spread my lips wide. "Thank you."

Zeb scrubbed a large hand behind his neck. "Promise me you'll be careful whose tree you climb next time."

"I will. I promise." I nestled some of the almonds back into his palm. When he made no move to accept them, I plucked them up and popped them into his mouth. "You worry too much."

Shifting the almonds into his cheek, Zeb gave me a lopsided grin. "You're worth worrying over, Salome." He tapped me lightly on the nose. "Let me know how Noy recovers."

Tossing an almond into my own mouth, I promised him that I would before returning to Noy, who was resting comfortably. I would nurse him back to full health and make sure that he stayed far away from boys with sticks, rocks, and spiteful words.

———◆———

On hot summer nights, Abba and I spread our pallets on the roof, with nothing between us and God's stars. I loved falling asleep in the night air beneath the sound of Abba's voice as he recited portions of the Torah. Tonight, however, I was determined to sleep by Noy's side in the workshop.

"Are you sure you won't be too warm?" Abba questioned as he draped a thin blanket over me.

"I'm sure." I yawned. "I want to be close in case he needs me."

"I'm thankful Zebedee found him. He's a good boy—already more of a man than his father."

"What do you mean?" I frowned. "Because of Jonathan's temper?" Zeb's father was a burly man with a loud presence and a demanding nature.

Abba sighed. "I shouldn't have said that. It does me good to see a young man like Zeb, especially after how those other boys treated you."

I quieted, thinking of the latest painful blows that had found chinks in my armor.

"Those boys were cruel," I whispered.

Abba grew still. "How so?"

I laced fingers through Noy's matted fur, focused on working loose a stubborn knot. "They called me an animal. They made fun of my eyes. . . . People often do so as if I'm something . . . unnatural."

Abba groaned and settled onto a nearby stool. His foot was bothering him, but he hid the wince by running a large hand across his face. "I didn't realize you were still taunted so much over your eyes."

"They said our family was cursed. Do you think they're right? Ima's death and your accident and my eyes . . . like an evil mark . . ."

"No!" Abba's resounding reply was chisel to stone, driving hard to release the truth. "No, my child. Adonai taught us to trust His words and works alone—not to be ensnared by superstition. We are not cursed, but . . ." His face twisted with regret. "But our actions do come with consequences. Look at our own King David, a man after God's own heart, who, although forgiven, reaped the consequences of sin for the rest of his life. If there is blame to be shouldered, it is mine alone."

Swallowing hard, I glanced at his foot, remembering it too clearly—how he'd started every day bleary and angry, returning late at night, intoxicated, stumbling through the door and onto his bed, rising the next day mad at the world once again. That's when I'd started to run, to stay far away from the man I no longer recognized.

There was an abandoned quarry not far from Bethsaida. I'd begun going there at night. It was far from safe, but the danger soothed my scattered mind. The external fear of dark rocks and night animals quieted the internal fear—for a moment.

In the end, Abba's carelessness had cost him his foot. While cutting a large ashlar from limestone, he'd fallen along with the loosened stone, which crushed him. The man who'd risen afterward was humble and kind, quietly shaping black stone in his workshop, providing for his daughter, who was still prone to run. I'd never once heard him complain.

"Abba." Love swelled like a current, lifting me up to his side, where I laid my head on his knee. "You know I don't blame you. The accident doesn't change how I see you."

"Neither do these"—he lifted my head and rested his fingers at the corners of my eyes—"define you."

When I was six months old, my true eye color had shown—a golden yellow that contrasted sharply with my dark hair and skin. Some days I convinced myself it was a warm brown, but then someone would stare, point, or mutter, and I knew how unusual the color was. What I wouldn't give for Leah's deep brown eyes or even Deborah's lighter ones. Anything but my bright and glowing eyes that I couldn't change or hide.

"Did I ever tell you what your mother said when this color first emerged?"

I settled my head back against his knee and peeked up at him. "Yes. Many times, in fact."

He chuckled. "Well, let me tell you again. She took one look at you and gasped with delight. She said, 'Look at this, Jacob! She has paradise in her eyes!'"

A sigh eased from my body as I relaxed into the familiar story. Ima had indeed loved my eyes. Had loved every part of me.

"Salome." Abba lifted my chin to study my face. "An ordinary name for an extraordinary girl. Adonai has good things in store for you, never doubt it."

He'd said similar things to me before, which I'd always brushed aside. But something in his face tonight checked my usual response. He was so serious. So . . . *certain.*

"I thank God for you, daughter." His voice shook. "I don't think I would have survived—" He coughed, tears lodging in his throat. "You are full of passion and hungry for justice. These are good things when placed under Adonai's control. Receive my words over you and release the hateful words of those boys who cannot see what a gift you are."

He held back tears, but mine dripped off my chin and into his cracked hands as I allowed his words to seep into my battered heart. His face was blurry behind my tears, but I could still see his smile as he gently tapped the corner of one eye and then the next.

"Your mother was right. You have paradise in your eyes. As if you've seen God's very glory."

THREE

Spring 3 AD
Bethsaida, Israel
Five Years Later

The sun was still abed as I entered Naysa's courtyard with eager steps. I was earlier than usual, the stars faintly visible as I slipped into a storage room to collect the ingredients I'd need: red lentils, honey, cinnamon, and oil. As I settled into a corner and began grinding the lentils into a powder, a nearby voice made me jump.

"You're early." Naysa stood in a doorway with a bag of grain perched on her hip.

"I'm making *ashishot*."

Naysa cocked her head as she knelt nearby and poured the grain into the millstone to begin grinding flour for the day's bread. "What's the occasion?"

"Kadmiel is home," I murmured and ducked my head.

"And this warrants ashishot?"

I worked the pestle harder. "He loves this sweet and is so rarely home."

The harsh scrape of stone against basalt filled the air as Naysa methodically worked the millstone without further comment. I risked a glance. Her features were barely visible in the lamplight,

36

but even so, I saw the purse of her lips that said, *What are you about, girl?*

What *was* I about? It was unlike me . . . making sweets for a man, spending too much time on my hair this morning. But I was seventeen with no suitor, and a girl could only go so long before fear came roaring in.

With the lentils ground into a fine flour, I added olive oil, honey, and cinnamon and then kneaded the mixture into a sticky dough, shifting my body away from Naysa's shrewd eyes.

Time had given me a curvy and appealing form, but despite this, I was no great beauty. My ordinary features made my eyes more unsettling, and as hard as I tried, I couldn't seem to tame my nature into the modest demeanor that was the most desirable trait for a woman.

"Your mother always said you had a large spirit," Naysa had told me. *"When you were little, your antics could be more easily forgiven, but see to it that you get ahold of your tongue. Too many sharp edges will drive people away."*

Why did Naysa insist on bringing up my mother? Over and over again I felt the undercurrent to her words: *You are not like Miriam.*

It was true. I was not like the mother whose lilting song still sounded in my ears on sleepless nights. But I tried to be. In the years beneath Naysa's roof, I tried to be like the mother from my memory.

The spitefulness I'd endured as a child had mellowed but was still alive in some. My presence in Naysa's home meant I encountered her son-in-law more times than I'd like. Recently, I'd caught Elazar's infuriating smirk—a look that drove home his words from the past: *"You're the unworthy one."* By now he had two young children with Deborah, providing Naysa and Jonathan with beautiful granddaughters. His look the other day had asked, *And what have you to offer?*

Fury had thumped in my body. Five years under Naysa's care, five years of learning by her side, and yet that look said Elazar still saw me as a wild girl. I no longer came at him with fists and shouts, not anymore. Instead, I'd waited for him to turn before spitting on the ground.

My eyes meant people looked at me all the time, but no one truly *saw* me. There was an ancient ache in my breast that said I had dignity no one could touch, but year stretched into year and all the girls my age dandled babes on their knees, while I remained the wild girl with no future.

"Why shouldn't I aim high?" Kadmiel's own words returned, heating my cheeks as I worked the dough.

Abba deserved a legacy—deserved grandchildren—and so I would make Kadmiel his favorite sweet. Perhaps he would look up from the gift and see the woman behind it, and perhaps he would like what he saw.

Forming the dough into balls, I flattened each one and slid them onto a heated oiled stone. A harsh hiss rose from the dough, and I watched for burning.

For the last five years, Kadmiel had lived and traveled with his rabbi all around upper Galilee, seeing for himself the general unrest in the region. There were rumors that Rome might supplant the incompetent rule of Herod Archelaus in Judea, and resistance was rumbling throughout Galilee and beyond.

"Zeal for Adonai is good and righteous, but Judas of Galilee has married banditry and zealotry into a new movement whose claws are strong in this region," he had said once while visiting home.

The life of a disciple was rigorous, meaning many young men put off marriage until later, but gossip flowed freely at the village well, and some said Bethsaida's brilliant scholar was looking to take a wife. That, in fact, his trip home was for that very purpose.

He won't choose you, Salome. Doubt rang through my head.

Perhaps not, but I can try. I can aim high. I talked back to my own stubborn thoughts, clenching my jaw with resolve. Being the wife of a disciple meant honor for my father and the definitive silencing of Elazar's churlish looks.

Salome—I was as plain as my name but with a beat in my heart that felt anything but commonplace. At night, the sigh of the wind beckoned me, and sometimes I still answered, running to the lake, standing ankle-deep in the water, ears open to the night sounds.

With a swift hand, I flipped the ashishot. A perfect golden brown. I sighed with satisfaction and swept a wisp of hair from my sweaty brow.

Once they were done, I turned each sweet over before sliding them onto a dish to cool. With a tsk of the tongue, I noted the one that was burnt and set it aside for Noy as Eli came bursting into the courtyard.

"Master Jonathan says to hurry! The catch is huge and he needs more baskets to hold the fish, but I don't know where they are!" He danced from foot to foot.

Naysa sighed as she gazed at the jittery neighbor boy. "Salome, you go. This bread won't make itself, and I'm already behind."

I caught a retort before it fell off my tongue and cast a worried gaze to the sky, which was now streaked with hints of daylight. Could I be there and back before Kadmiel arrived? Yes, I decided, I could. I *would*.

Wiping the lingering oil from my hands, I led Eli from the courtyard into the storage room that housed the extra baskets. I stacked as many as he could manage into his thin arms before shouldering the rest myself and letting us out into the growing sunlight.

The family compound boasted a large interior courtyard surrounded by rooms and an exterior courtyard that fronted the lake. A handful of men at the shore were in the process of hauling in hundreds of feet of dragnet, which were teeming with fish.

Eli and I scurried down the embankment to the rocky shore, where a bare-chested Zeb was dragging in the last of the net with long arms. He was impressively tall, surpassing even his towering father. The height, however, was not paired with bulk. Rather, he was as thin and sinewy as a length of sturdy rope.

"I see it was a good night!" I called out the greeting as I approached.

Zeb flicked a grin at me, shaggy hair falling into his brown eyes. "And thank God for it! We've had too many scarce nights lately."

The men often worked throughout the night, since that's when the fish were most active, but Zeb was always out on the water. Whether in a boat or casting a net from the shore, he lived to fish. His bright and open greeting this morning stirred hope. In the last few years, Zeb had quieted, more dedicated to his profession than anything else. The comradery that had always flourished between us was all but gone as he kept himself furiously busy.

"Surely you've worked up an appetite," I quipped as Zeb finished with the net and took the baskets from my arms. "You need to put more flesh on these bones." I snagged a pinch of skin at his ribs.

"Stop that!" He jerked away, smile slipping right off his flushed face.

Dismay and embarrassment overshadowed my earlier spark of fun. "I'm sorry. I was just . . . playing."

"You're always playing. But I'm a grown man, Salome." He was agitated, eyes jerking quickly from mine as the flush spread down his neck.

I stared at my hands, properly rebuked.

"And you . . . you're . . ." He was stuttering now, face growing a deeper red by the second as he looked me up and down.

Defensiveness flared, snuffing out the dismay. "I'm what, Zeb?" I snapped, eyes jumping to his. "An annoying scrap of a girl?"

"No!" He swallowed hard, the bump in his throat wobbling.

"Salome, good!" Jonathan's greeting cut through the morning air and tore my frustrated gaze from Zeb to his father. "Help us sort the catch."

"I was told to deliver baskets. I need to get back to—" I bit off the rest of my words—*to be there when Kadmiel comes.*

They'd solicited the help of another family to bring in this catch, for I saw Jonah and his father already sorting fish with Eli. "It looks like you have enough help at the moment."

"Salome." Jonathan's firm voice cut me off. He stood before me with a broad and hairy chest that glistened with sweat in the morning light, which was now making a decided entrance. As long as everyone did Jonathan's bidding, he kept his temper at bay. But I had seen anger flash from him like lightning and knew better than to openly disobey him.

Worry clutched tight as I cast a glance back the way I'd come. Maybe I could finish in time. Maybe.

With a resigned sigh, I settled onto a large rock near Zeb, drew a basket to my knee, and picked up a wriggling fish.

There was an abundance of small fish, no longer than the length of my hand, but with this catch came a quantity of larger fish—barbels and musht, some over a foot long and hefty. As I sorted, my discontentment grew. Even if I did make it back in time, now I would stink of fish. Gritting my teeth, I cast a look to Zeb. He sat merely three feet away, but kept his face averted, working silently and steadily. Ignoring me.

I watched him with hidden glances, my irritation mounting the longer he remained quiet. Had I been wrong to jest with him? Why wouldn't he engage in the easy banter that we used to enjoy? With a grunt, I threw a barbel into a basket. He used to bring me gifts—pressed flowers or pieces of driftwood gnarled into unusual shapes. He used to yank tendrils of my hair loose and welcome my teasing with good-natured smiles. But no longer.

Without warning, he'd become withdrawn, increasingly committed to his work. His aloofness chafed. But it wasn't until recently that his tone had shifted into open rebuke. Zeb had lost patience with me, his tongue ready to criticize as though he could no longer tolerate my presence.

I threw another barbel into a basket and shot Zeb a look, which he ignored. Why wouldn't he look at me? Hands slick with water, I flicked some at him and missed. Tried again, and got him squarely in the eye. I gulped, muscles tightening with surprise at my own accuracy.

He froze, blinked rapidly, then slowly turned to face me, resting a strong forearm on his thigh.

I forced myself to meet his gaze.

Without breaking eye contact, he cupped his large hands, drew water from the lake at our feet, and flung it directly into my startled face.

With a yelp, I stood, blinking hard and gasping, "How *dare* you!"

"Isn't that what you wanted? To play?" he asked quietly, no fun in his voice, only a sadness that I didn't understand.

Now I would stink of fish *and* be sopping wet. My hands shook as I snatched at my tunic and took a step away from him, chin trembling with a surge of emotion. I was shocked to feel tears welling. Zeb must have noted them too, for regret crossed his face.

"Salome, I'm sorry—" He rose to standing, words rushed as he reached for me, but I was already gone.

The catch was far from sorted, and I would certainly receive Jonathan's wrath later, but I didn't care. I didn't want to be there. Didn't want to be around *him*.

I ran back up the bank, swiping angrily at my face and muttering under my breath. I would change my headdress and dab scented oil to my neck to hide the fish. If I hurried, everything would be fine.

As I entered the inner courtyard, my steps came to a ragged stop, lips parting with surprise.

In the center of the courtyard, Leah was standing with Kadmiel, the full plate of ashishot in her hands. He had one to his lips, had just taken a bite, face flooding with pleasure. I watched silent and alone as he slid a hand to her arm and squeezed. She gazed up at him with a shy, radiant look I'd never seen on her before.

"Salome, there you are." Naysa hurried to my side. "Where's Jonathan? They're looking for him."

They? Kadmiel stepped to the side—closer to Leah—revealing Baruch, standing behind him. Why was his father here?

I blinked stupidly into Kadmiel's face as his hand brushed Leah's and his father announced, "Will someone fetch Jonathan? We have business to discuss."

FOUR

My bones were about to break apart from this deep and terrible ache that rattled throughout my body. Agitation jerked me about the cramped storage room as I tried to untangle my emotions.

Even now the fathers were sitting down to negotiate the *ketubah*, the marriage contract. As soon as Kadmiel's eyes had landed upon me, I'd ducked through the first doorway I'd found, unwilling for him or anyone to see my face. And now I was stuck in this room with my own racing thoughts.

Of course he wouldn't choose you! Doubt screeched as loneliness yawned open in my chest. It shouldn't matter that the younger Leah would be married first. I should be happy for her, not sitting alone in a storage room with this howling, growing humiliation.

Groaning, I sank onto a low stool and hunched over my knees, but that made the restlessness worse, and so I stood again and paced. My hands were shaking. I held them out before me, stared at them, and wondered at my own strong reaction.

I didn't *love* him, did I?

No, not love, but hope. Kadmiel had become tangled up with hope for the future—with proof that I had one. If that future was given to Leah, what was left for me?

My fingers tingled, and my lips were numb as my chest

squeezed impossibly tight. This room was too small. This home was too small. This village was too small.

Bursting from the room with chattering teeth, I tore out of the home, toward the lake, where I caught sight of Zeb with Jonah. The two were spreading the dragnet out along the shore for cleaning. Fresh mortification washed over me. Zeb now viewed me with impatience, had outgrown me and my playful ways, and surely I'd proven his assessment right.

I veered sharply to the right to bypass the lake, running hard and fast and far, far away.

❖

Dusk was upon Bethsaida by the time I could breathe again. It had taken longer this time, longer to find the peace I needed in order to come back. I'd stood on the ridge of the abandoned quarry, eyes tracing the paths I'd taken as a girl. For long hours, I'd stood there, moving once to heft a stone into my hand and throw it with all my strength into the deep with a single, piercing shout.

I'd lost my veil in my flight. Alone with uncovered hair, I approached the village from the north to avoid the lake. The men would be preparing to fish, and I didn't want Zeb to see me.

Coiling my hair into a knot at the side of my neck, I entered the village swiftly, ignoring the shocked stares at my uncovered hair from those in the streets. I was calmer now, and the embarrassment had subsided to a manageable pang as I neared home.

Abba was preparing for bed when I arrived, outer garment carefully folded by his pallet, a cup of tea waiting on a table, Noy asleep in the corner.

"*There* you are." He leaned heavily on his cane.

At the sight of him, something small and scared released within me. I pushed through the door and into his arms, bracing him even as I clung to him.

"Abba—" My words broke apart as the tears I'd so stubbornly resisted all day finally came.

Gently he pressed me for answers. "You're holding such sadness in your eyes, Zohar. What has dimmed your light?"

What could I say? *Abba, young men don't see me as a desirable wife. I will forever be overlooked, and your good name will end with me.*

I kept the source of my sorrow to myself while Abba sat by my side, one hand on my back until I fell into an exhausted sleep.

The next morning, I returned to Naysa's home on reluctant feet. She met me at the door, clearly waiting for me. Averting my face, I tried to hurry past, but her words snagged me.

"Salome, wait."

I didn't recognize this tone from her. Overt tenderness mixed with worry—it was the special tone of a mother.

She padded to my side, hand fluttering over my shoulder before deciding to land and squeeze. "Are you all right?"

"I'm fine," I answered brightly.

She studied me, lines evident on her brow. "I thought perhaps you might be suffering . . . with Leah betrothed before you."

I studied my hands, picked at a fingernail.

"It will be a short betrothal. They'll be married and away come winter, so perhaps that is a blessing."

A blessing indeed, for I would not have to witness Leah's flushed and happy face for too much longer.

"You had a doll as a child. You named her . . . Yanira?"

"Yakira," I corrected. "You remember her?"

"I remember how you loved on that doll like it was a living thing." Naysa smiled. "There you were, toddling after Miriam with Yakira strapped to your small back, and I thought to myself, 'What a little mother she is, so attentive.'"

Fresh pain twisted me away from Naysa, but she pulled me back.

"There's a fire that leaks out of you. It frustrates me at times, but . . . well, that fire also makes you strong. Resilient." Naysa leaned close. "A woman needs to be resilient in this world. Believe me." She placed her hand over mine. "You will be fine, Salome. You *will*."

As I stared at our clasped hands, love sprang open and surprised me. I'd known this woman my entire life, but in all that time had not experienced this spread of warmth that now blanketed my body, cozy and new. Swallowing hard, I allowed my eyes to join with hers and for once to linger there. Naysa had poked and fussed at me for years, but in the prodding, I now realized there was love.

The quarry held so many painful memories that I needed a new place to bring this fresh hurt. There was a large stone that jutted into the water from a desolate stretch of shoreline, and nightly I ran to that rock, tucked my knees up beneath my chin, and stared out across the lake.

"Adonai has good things in store for you, never doubt it." Abba's words, so calm and firm, stuck in my mind like a burr.

"What is Your purpose for me?" I whispered the question into the night, voicing my deepest fear to Adonai—that there was no place for me to flourish, that I would always and forever feel this restless shifting in my soul. "What good things do You have in store for me?" I laid the question out for His inspection, awaited His answer.

Nightly, I stretched my heart wide to Adonai. Night after night, there were no direct answers other than a gradual loosening in my chest, which I accepted as a gift.

And then one day I laughed, loud and open in Leah's presence, a genuine laugh from the bottom of my stomach, the kind that made my cheeks ache. I was watching Deborah's two small children while she assisted Leah in embroidering her wedding garments. Soon Leah was laughing too while Deborah scolded her little girls for their antics, and Naysa smiled, wide and unhindered, as she watched me with a careful eye.

✦

Winter 3 AD

On the night of Leah's wedding, I put on a happy face. With great care, Naysa combed my hair, lingering in a way that surprised me. "You are . . . beautiful, Salome," she whispered. "Just like your mother."

Her tongue was unused to compliments, and this one sounded halting and strange, but it was also heartfelt and opened the door to new thoughts. *Am I? Am I beautiful like my mother?*

Kadmiel came for his bride with a radiant face, and I, along with many others, accompanied Leah to his father's home in the center of the village, where they were joined as husband and wife beneath a canopy.

"May you become thousands of ten thousands, and may your offspring possess the gate of those who hate him!" Jonathan spoke the traditional words of blessing over his daughter, the words of Laban over Rebekah, the words spoken over women for generations. It was every woman's desire to be the mother of many, to build up the house of Israel.

I drank to the couple but did not join in the dance. Instead, I stood to the side with my happy face firmly in place. As the synagogue ruler, Baruch was one of the more prosperous citizens and had roasted a fatted calf for the occasion. I took a small nibble of the succulent meat with the sesame paste but found I could eat no more without tempting my stomach to rebellion.

"You're quiet tonight. You don't wish to dance?"

A genuine smile spread across my face as Jonah settled by my side. I'd known him as a scrappy youth hanging on the heels of Elazar, but he'd since filled out his scrawny form and grown into a thoughtful young man with a proven character.

"Maybe later. I don't see you dancing either."

"Keturah is too uncomfortable to dance, and so I promised to keep her company." Jonah cast a loving gaze to his wife, who was large with child.

"I haven't congratulated you yet . . . on the babe." My smile was slipping. With effort, I held it in place. "So many weddings and new babies. I hear your friend is expecting his second."

"Gideon?" Jonah's tone soured as he glanced in the large man's direction. The quick-tempered boy who'd joined Elazar in taunting me had become a brooding man who'd recently taken over his father's smithery. "I don't count him as a friend. Not anymore, Salome."

I raised a brow, surprised at the vehemence in Jonah's voice. "I didn't realize. You still seemed friendly with him."

"That was before—" Jonah broke off, bit his lip. "Before I saw how he treats his poor wife. Gideon is harsh, brash, and already his eldest is showing the tendencies of his father."

"Philip is only two," I assured him. "All children that age are brash."

"Even so . . . you cautioned me more than once to be careful of the company I keep." Jonah quieted, voice lowering for my ears alone. "I'm ashamed of the part I used to play in taunting you, and I don't think I've ever told you so directly. I'm sorry, Salome."

Surprise clogged my throat. "I forgive you. It was years ago."

"And the apology is years overdue. But I listened to your advice." His easy smile returned, dimples forming in his cheeks. "And Zeb has proven to be good company—a true and loyal friend."

"You're close to him, and I'm glad for that. Leah has been a good companion to me. I suppose now I will have to find a new friend."

"Keturah would welcome your friendship," Jonah stated. "Especially as her time approaches and seeing as her family and friends are all back in Magadan. She's nervous . . . this being our first babe."

At the edge of the courtyard, Keturah stood alone, hands to her stomach, a tight expression on her face.

"I won't have any wisdom from personal experience to give her." I grimaced, each word a heavy stone that I tried to deliver lightly.

Jonah noted the weight of my words and furrowed his brow. "That could change, you know. Perhaps this time next year, it will be you." Jonah nodded to the center of the courtyard, where Leah danced with her groom.

He'd meant his words as kindness, but they landed hard and mocking. My eighteenth birthday was fast approaching. Surely no one expected me to marry anymore. I had no dowry to speak of and no beauty to praise. My earlier, hopeful response to Naysa's kind words had diminished the longer I'd observed Leah's true beauty tonight.

As Jonah returned to his wife, I blinked rapidly to dispel the hot press of tears. Averting my face from the dancers, my gaze landed upon Zeb. I was used to seeing him sweaty, with hands full of fish, but here he was, scrubbed clean of the lake and with his wiry hair oiled into submission. He wore a blue mantle with a yellow sash cinched tightly at his trim waist. I'd never seen him so well-groomed in my life. Most likely it would be *him* next year under the marriage canopy and not me. And then I would be truly alone.

He turned, gaze locking with mine, eyes gentling and then darkening in a frown. My throat dried out as he shouldered his way to me with such intentional effort that I impulsively began backing away. I couldn't bear a conversation with him right now, couldn't handle his rebuke—not with his sister glowing as the epitome of womanhood and highlighting my own lack.

I tripped, righted myself, and threw a panicked look at Zeb, who'd stopped short. He let me go, large hands hanging limp at his sides, shoulders drooped while I skittered away, both missing and dreading his presence.

The feasting would last a week, but already I sensed my happy face faltering beyond my ability to control it. That night I went to my rock. Without bothering to take off my wedding garment, I splashed through the shallow water, soaking my perfumed slippers. The moon was hidden by a gathering of clouds, but I detected a small object in the center of the rock as if set there for me. Frowning, I probed it with a toe before scooping it up.

In my hands was a lovely piece of driftwood, gnarled and smooth from the waves.

FIVE

The sky was beginning to lighten and the fishermen were bringing their catches to shore as I slipped out the door and into the street, arms full of treats for Deborah's children. I left a whining Noy behind. As much as the girls loved him, Deborah would not allow a dog to step foot within her home.

Rounding the corner of Abba's workshop, I squealed as a dark form emerged from the shadows. "It's me, Salome."

"Were you waiting for me?" I stammered as Naysa neared. "I was going to spend the day at Deborah's."

After Leah's wedding, I had begun spending more time with Deborah, who was expecting her third child. Even though I loved her young girls, I usually avoided their home, having no desire to be under Elazar's roof. But with his father recently deceased, Elazar had taken over the family business and was often away, traveling to ports along the Great Sea or as far north as Damascus. This current trip would keep him away for months.

"Salome, we need to talk." Taking the gifts from my hands, Naysa threaded an arm through mine. "I'll walk with you."

The dusty streets of Bethsaida were beginning to fill as we

wended our way to Deborah's. I glanced at Naysa's hand tucked intimately into the crook of my arm.

"I've been holding on to information, unsure what to do with it," Naysa admitted as Gideon's smithery came into view. "Your father approached me with a request several years ago."

I stilled to face her. "Abba spoke to you? About what?"

"About you." Naysa cleared her throat. "He asked about betrothing you to . . . Zeb."

A laugh poured from my lips before my mind could comprehend her words. "Zebedee?" I squeaked.

Naysa's mouth worked as she struggled to find the right words. When she did, they came gushing out like water. "Haven't you wondered why my son remains unmarried? When most men his age have several babes to tend by now? My eldest and only boy, who bears the sole responsibility for carrying on this family's line?"

My mind spun beneath her direct questions.

Naysa pinched the bridge of her nose. "Salome, open those bright eyes and see what is right in front of you. My son loves you."

No, this couldn't be right. Zeb viewed me as a pesky girl.

"Breathe, child. You're as white as a cloud."

"You're mistaken." I tried to laugh, but the mirth had dried up inside me. "He's always been like a brother toward me. And lately not even that. He never said anything, never approached Abba, or—"

"Perhaps he viewed you as a sister . . . once." Naysa tilted her head. "But trust me, that time has long since passed."

Everything drained from my head—blood, feeling, thought.

"Perhaps his silence is because you continue to treat him as a brother."

Heat seared my cheeks with such force that I covered them with my hands.

"Your father admires Zeb and talked with me instead of Jonathan. He sensed that I would be more amenable to the idea, and I was—I . . . am." Shyness peeked through Naysa's lowered voice. "Miriam and I used to talk about it—her daughter and my son. And the two of you have always been friends."

My lips were numb. Was I even breathing? I sucked in a stream of air.

"After your father talked with me, I approached Jonathan with the idea, but he was resistant. My husband still sees you as a little lost girl, not the strong woman that you have become."

There were so many layers to Naysa's words that I didn't know what to feel—anger, defensiveness, gratification? Shock won, suppressing all else.

"And so I told your father no, even though my heart said yes. I've sat here, watching as Zeb's love for you consumes him."

My vision was narrowing. I instructed myself to take another breath.

"Jonathan has pushed Zeb hard about taking a wife and has viewed his reluctance as bullheadedness, but I know the truth. My son resists because he doesn't want anyone but you."

I hunched over to hide my face from Naysa, the new image of Zeb too much to take in all at once. My heart was fluttering in a strange pattern, as if someone held it in their hand and was squeezing on and off.

"Jonathan has a way of cutting Zeb down with his words." Pain surfaced in Naysa's face. "My boy doesn't see his own worth, and so I fear he'll never say a thing to anyone, never stand up to his father, and the family line will die with him."

Zeb, my own dear, infuriating Zeb, whom I'd always viewed as a brother. Had I ever considered him as more?

A sinking began in my chest as I recalled how he'd looked at the wedding. There had been moments, small flashes of awareness that I hadn't been able to name. The sinking in my chest reversed, throwing blood up into my head in a painful, surging wave.

This couldn't be normal. Was my heart going to burst from shock right here in front of the blacksmith's shop? I placed a hand over its erratic beat, attempting to press it back into a steadier pattern.

"I've kept quiet out of deference to Jonathan's wishes, but I cannot bear to continue watching Zeb struggle, and you—" With a firm hand, Naysa grasped my chin, tugging my face close. "I know I've been hard on you. But I've been hoping . . . all these years, hoping . . ."

"Hoping what?" I gasped.

Naysa released my chin to yank me into her arms. We had never embraced like this—in a crashing, crushing blow that was more desperation than love. "That one day I could claim Miriam's daughter as my own!"

I trembled in her arms and clung to her. Naysa as my mother-in-law, a permanent place within her household, a life and a future.

A beam of happiness cut through the shock.

"Zeb will not speak to Jonathan, so I will speak to Zeb. In truth, I should have done so long before now."

"Don't say anything to anyone, please!" I lurched from her embrace, doubt clawing up my throat.

Naysa quieted at my outburst. "Perhaps you don't want my son?"

"I-I don't know what I want." All I knew was that I couldn't bear the ensuing humiliation should Zeb scoff at Naysa's request.

The harsh clang of Gideon's hammer rang out, its piercing clamor pounding in time with my thoughts.

"My son is a good man, Salome." Naysa transferred my bundle back into my slack arms. "Adonai knows what we need, what is best for us, and He will give it to us in His time. Be open to His provision."

———— ◆ ————

I couldn't eat, couldn't sleep, could barely think straight, and most days went through my tasks in a daze. The suggestion of Zeb's admiration was all I could think about, and my memories of him took on fresh meaning that left me flushed and confused.

With shaking hands, I withdrew the wooden box I kept in my room and opened the worn lid to uncover the small gifts Zeb had given me. I removed them, tracing crumbling flower petals and sliding fingers over gnarled wood as I allowed the new image of Zeb to take shape in my mind. When had he stopped viewing me as a sister? Maybe Naysa was wrong. How could Zeb love me when he avoided me?

I began watching Zeb in disbelief as my heart hammered hard in my chest in that new, uncomfortable way. Things I'd noted before grew more textured with meaning and illuminated his character, such as the way he interacted with Jonah. The two talked closely while they worked, and in Jonah's expression was a deepening respect.

Even more telling was how he responded to his father. I'd known that Zeb often took the brunt of Jonathan's harsh nature. He was quick to find fault in his son. No matter how diligently Zeb worked, Jonathan would find at least one flaw and bring it to Zeb's attention. But now I observed how Zeb shouldered the criticism with quiet steadiness. It wasn't his reserved nature that made him respond so, but control. He was stronger than I'd realized and kept his strength tightly within hand.

A slow burn began in my chest, spreading from my uneven heart outward. Zeb indeed remained unattached with no signs of changing that fact. And then there was the matter of my own father's wishes. He'd never spoken of Zeb to me, but why would he when Jonathan had disapproved?

I considered confiding in Keturah. Despite my doubts that

she'd welcome my friendship, I'd taken Jonah's advice and reached out to her. Even though we were now friendly, I was hesitant to share something so personal with her and so resigned myself to holding this secret alone.

Months passed as I circled Zeb in an agonizing dance of watchfulness and avoidance. The banks of the lake swelled as snow melted from the mountain heights and the early spring rains descended upon the land.

When Keturah's time came, she gave birth to a large, bawling boy with an abundance of black hair. The midwife said his full head and lusty cry meant he would be a forceful son. With a lump in my throat, I congratulated the new mother and asked what she would name him.

Her face was tired and filled with so much joy that I nearly looked away. "His name is Simon."

Later I came across Zeb congratulating Jonah with an enthusiasm that grated on me. Naysa claimed Zeb avoided marriage because he wanted no one but me, but how could that be when he made no sign of approaching my father? Did he experience no jealousy over Jonah's good fortune? I gritted my teeth as Zeb clapped a strong hand on the younger man's shoulder, face open and unaffected.

That night I shoved the box of gifts into a corner and out of sight.

◆

Early spring was the height of the sardine fishing season. So many landed in our nets that we took to drying and salting them. The catch had been plentiful the night before, which meant I had a full day of salting ahead of me. With a short knife, I scraped the small fish, removing the scales before slicing into the gill to remove it. Once I was finished gutting, I would rub the fish with coarse salt and layer them with reed mats to dry.

Naysa was visiting Deborah, who was due any day, leaving me to work alone.

A step sounded behind me, and then Zeb was by my side, dipping his large hand into a basket to remove a fish and join me in the gutting process.

"Put that away," I chided. "Your mother will be back soon, and I'll have plenty of help."

Zeb worked his knife with quick, expert fingers. "I'll stay until she comes, then."

"You should be abed." I realized belatedly how harsh I sounded. I tried to soften my tone. "You've been up all night bringing in this catch, so let me work while you sleep."

"You are not my mother, Salome, so stop scolding me."

I quieted at that. No, I was not his mother. And I most certainly was *not* his sister.

He stood too close as he sliced into a fish, still bare-chested from a long night of work. How many countless times had I seen him this way? And yet the sight of his wiry frame and the gentle brushing of his arm against mine was unbearable, the small flickers of awareness I had long overlooked now sparking with noticeable heat. Discreetly I stepped away and continued working, eyes finding every possible reason to jump to him.

Zeb's quiet nature found a suitable home in his lanky build. Everything about him was unassuming, but that didn't mean he was unimpressive. I sliced into another fish and risked a glance at the firm curve of his muscles. No, this was ridiculous. I pulled out the gut and grabbed another fish.

"Perhaps his silence is because you continue to treat him as a brother." Of course I'd treated him as a brother. More than once, he'd chased off mocking boys with hurtful tongues. More than once, he'd caught me crying angry tears and had extended comfort. He'd been a dear brother—until he wasn't. Until he'd begun

responding to me with a mounting irritation that Naysa would have me believe was love.

"Be open to His provision." Naysa's exhortation resounded in my head as I agitatedly ripped another gut from another fish.

He wasn't my brother, and he wasn't a boy. He was a man. My throat ran dry as I risked another peek.

He was watching me.

Embarrassment flooded my cheeks with color as I jerked my gaze back to the gutted fish in my hand.

What was wrong with me? Did I . . . love him? I'd been speaking ragged prayers into the night, pleading with Adonai to give me a place to flourish. Had His answer been staring me in the face for years?

My basket was empty, and so I stretched across Zeb to grab another fish, arm brushing against his taut stomach. I thumped the fish down and began drawing my blade across its scales a bit too aggressively, for the blade went too far and scraped up onto my hand.

With a yelp, I dropped the fish and the bloody knife and clapped a hand over the wound.

Immediately, Zeb turned and was prying my hand off, his brow creased. "What did you do to yourself? Here, let me look."

I couldn't bear to see the damage and so stared at Zeb instead. He cradled my injured hand in both his own, dark eyes assessing the wound. I hadn't realized how long his lashes were. Shaggy hair spilled about his ears and framed his narrow face in an endearing way. He wasn't particularly handsome. His ears were too large, and his lips were too thin. And yet my stomach flopped free of the rest of me as I watched him.

"You took the skin off your hand," Zeb observed.

I risked a glance. Sure enough, I'd pulled a layer of skin right off. The tender flesh beneath glistened red in the early morning sun.

"We need to clean this. You'll have to wear a bandage until the new skin comes in." Zeb began washing my hand. "Where was your head at, Salome? You're nearly as good with a knife as I am." His rebuke was soft as he bound my hand. When I didn't answer, he looked up and stilled, eyes widening as they held mine.

What was in my face? Whatever it was, it was causing Zeb to grow serious.

Say something. The urge fell forcefully upon me, and my lips parted. I couldn't go on like this. *Say something.*

"Zeb?"

"Yes?" He'd stilled completely, my half-bandaged hand captured between his own.

"Zeb?"

"Yes, Salome?" Understanding flickered in his face.

"Do you—? I mean . . . I . . ."

He was smiling now, and my hand was awfully close to his heart. Oh, but his smile went on forever. Like ripples of water after throwing a stone, creases wreathed his lips and went on and on.

Blinking up into his face, I tried to read his expression. I was used to being ridiculed or disregarded. Being desired was something new, and I didn't know what it looked like. Was it this? A melting softness in the eyes? A firm pressure on my hand that drew me close?

And now I realized I was indeed close, so close to him. His chest was still damp from the lake and now my hand was crushed to his breast and the bandage was getting wet and his gaze was still upon me and I didn't know what to say.

What if Zeb laughed at the very idea of me as a wife? Me, the girl who'd teased and goaded him and accepted his attention while never truly *seeing* him? To be rejected by Zeb would be devastating.

"Salome, what is it? You're trembling." Concern eased the smile from Zeb's face the longer I remained silent.

With a sharp intake of breath, I pulled my hand from his and took a large step back. Pain flashed in his eyes. *Say something.* I opened my mouth, but all that released was a strangled squeak as I ducked my head and ran.

❖

After my careless blunder with the knife, I avoided Zeb. With such a clouded head, I'd likely take a finger off next time, and so I kept my distance. My thoughts, however, refused to be parted from him, and my bandaged hand served as a daily reminder of how it'd felt to be tended by him.

My hand was still healing when Abba settled beside me one evening. "I have news, daughter. I knew this day would come, and here it is. I've received a request for your hand in marriage."

Zeb.

My hands began to shake. "W-who?"

"Matthias. Now, I know he's older than you and recently widowed with three children to care for. Perhaps not the match you would have imagined, but he seems to be a righteous man . . ."

I couldn't hear the rest of what Abba said through the intensity of my disappointment.

"Salome?" Abba inspected my face. "Do you want me to begin the negotiations? To—"

I shook my head before Abba could continue.

Tension eased from Abba's shoulders. "Are you sure?"

Quite sure. The heart had a way of showing what the mind had yet to embrace. This unbearable dismay was casting fire into my bones, urgency into my breast, and clarity into my tangled thoughts.

I wasn't going to marry Matthias. I couldn't.

I was going to marry Zebedee.

Six

I acted before I could think too hard and talk myself out of it. Birds chattered in the trees, chastising my brashness. Brush scraped at my legs, attempting to pull me back. My own thoughts whirled within, begging me to reconsider. But down to the shore I stomped anyway in search of him.

He was sitting alone, cleaning a net in the heat of the afternoon, when I found him. With concentrated effort, he bent over his work, long fingers plucking out debris and repairing holes. My head grew light, my legs weighted as I approached, hand on hip, waiting for him to look up.

He squinted at me and gestured to the net. "Did you come to help? How's your hand?"

I remained still, hiding my nervousness with irritation. This man was infuriating, making *me* come to *him*.

He scooted on the rock to make room for me and lifted a portion of the net. I didn't take it.

"When are you going to approach my father, Zebedee bar Jonathan?" The words leapt from my tongue as my insides swirled.

Zeb froze, fingers tangled in the net. For a long moment, he wouldn't look at me. When he did, his eyes were narrowed. "Approach him about . . . what exactly?"

If Naysa was wrong, then I would never live this moment down. I thrust my other hand onto my hip, elbows askew as I tried not to break apart from embarrassment. I was scowling now—hardly the expression I'd hoped to wear, but I was powerless to change it as my insides continued to quake.

"You know," I stated quietly, evenly. "Or are you going to make me wait forever?"

Something sleepy in his face woke right up. Roughly, he shoved the net aside, tripping on it in his haste to stand. I scuttled backward as he stumbled to his feet and reached for me.

"You can't run away again." He was breathless, happy.

Oh, but I could, and I would. Lifting my tunic, I turned, but he nabbed me and spun me back around. I stared up into his endless smile.

"You *want* me to talk to your father?"

Swiftly, I nodded, too overcome to speak.

"I didn't think . . . are you sure?"

"*My boy doesn't see his own worth.*" The truth of Naysa's words was evident in Zeb's disbelieving eyes. With careful fingers, I brushed the hair from his face and nodded again, slowly this time. My touch was gentle rather than jesting. Zeb's smile spread even wider as he stilled my hand in his own.

"I would have talked with your father a long time ago, but I didn't think you wanted me. Didn't think you could ever view me that way."

"And you didn't look to someone else? Someone more suitable than me, someone—"

"I couldn't. Other women pale in comparison to you."

The air left my body in a rush as I studied him. "But I—I don't have much of a dowry."

"And you think that bothers me?"

"I'm not beautiful, not—"

"Not beautiful?" His voice was so incredulous, I began to

shake. He tipped my chin up with a knuckle, eyes roaming my features. "Salome, you are stunning."

A hungry corner of my heart that I'd long dismissed leapt at his words, and then I saw it—the undeniable love in his face. He was no longer trying to hide it, and the sight overwhelmed me so much that I ducked my head, touched my forehead to his chest, and blinked back tears.

He wrapped long arms around me until I was completely surrounded by his sturdy embrace. He was the steady beat of a drum, a warm cloak on a dark night, a spoken word of comfort into a lonely heart.

Relief flooded me. I leaned into him, and he responded by tightening his arms. When he spoke again, his voice was husky. "I'll go to your father now—right now—as long as this is what you truly want."

It was. Joy sang the undeniable truth within me. Yes—this was what I wanted. I'd looked to Kadmiel, thinking he was the answer to securing a future, when all along there was goodness to be had in the form of a lanky fisherman.

Zeb was looking at me like I held the world in my hands and was giving it to him. I shivered and couldn't stop. I'd have to say some of my giddy thoughts out loud. A blush crept up my neck. He noted it and beamed.

"Salome." His hand hovered at my temple, fingers lightly tracing my hairline. "Is this what you want?" He was certain now that it was but clearly wanted me to say it. He grinned wider, deeper, the love in his face mixing with a mischievous delight that made my heart thump even harder.

"Oh, *you*—" I took his familiar face in my hands. "Yes, it's what I want, Zebedee." My heart dipped, fluttered. "Y-you are what I want."

His hands slid to my waist, and now his eyes fell upon my lips and a new emotion sprang up and startled me straight into silence. With my declaration and his searing look, the old relationship had been stripped from between us. What was left was so vulnerable, I didn't know what to do, how to be.

He was ducking his head, intention in his features as he studied my lips. If I let him kiss me, I might come undone, and so I twisted from his grasp. He snagged a corner of my mantle before I could flee completely, eyes dancing with eagerness.

"When are you going to stop running away from me?"

"I suppose when you marry me," I quipped with a raised brow.

A determined look entered his face as he set his jaw and pulled on my mantle, hand over hand, as if I were a dragnet full of fish.

I yanked my mantle free, smacked at his reaching hands, and fled back the way I'd come.

Behind me he laughed, exultant and satisfied.

Emboldened by my desire for the union and armed with Abba's wholehearted approval, Zeb confronted his father for the first time in his life. Jonathan finally agreed to the match, although his approval certainly had less to do with me and more to do with the continuation of the family line and Zeb's own stubbornness.

"You're the unworthy one." Now that I was to become Zebedee's wife, I realized how deeply I'd taken Elazar's words to heart. My future father-in-law's reticence added to that hurt, but Naysa's joy was a balm that soothed any incurred wounds.

"Our children will be cousins." Deborah bounced her new babe wearily.

"I haven't allowed myself to think about being a mother." I breathed the last word. Motherhood was a joy I'd been certain I wouldn't experience, but now the world had opened up at my feet. Did I have the means to navigate it?

"I'm not sure I can be as good a mother as my own." I bit down on the spoken fear. Why had I admitted this out loud?

Deborah turned a conflicted gaze upon her babe—a third girl, much to Elazar's dismay. "What constitutes a *good* mother?" She left the question dangling between us, hovering with no answer.

"I . . . I'm not sure." The words stretched slowly from my lips, pulling and resistant like dough. "I suppose . . . a good mother is the one who would do anything for her child."

Instead of responding, Deborah merely quirked her lips. Was she testing me? Judging whether I was worthy of her brother?

A determined fire ignited within. "Ima used to say that a mother is like a lioness guarding her young to the death. She taught me that love is fierce."

The fire flickered as I recalled Ima's final moments, when she'd left this world for the next, so reluctant to go, hand clasping my face to the end. Her last word had been my tender name—*Zohar*.

"There is nothing stronger than a mother's love." The observation scraped across my tongue in a broken whisper.

"A mother's love," Deborah muttered, conflict once again evident upon her face. Extending her arms, she offered me the babe, who was swaddled into a cozy bundle.

I lifted her to my face and inhaled her scent—a mixture of soured milk and fresh linen.

"Love is a strange creature," Deborah mused. "Sometimes it chooses you. And sometimes you have to choose it. Motherhood can be a joy, although some days it can feel like a burden. It's not surprising you harbor uncertainty, since you lost your mother at a young age. You're very strong, Salome, but also incredibly frightened."

My eyes flew wide, arms tightening about the babe, lips parting to refute Deborah's direct and infuriating words, but doubt silenced me.

Yes, you're frightened. You're terrified and don't want anyone to know it. But she knows it.

I clenched my jaw at the thought, nostrils flaring.

"You're offended." Deborah raised a brow. "But you shouldn't be. You use fear as fuel. It's the ones who let fear paralyze them who should be ashamed."

Frowning, I cocked my head to assess this woman who would soon be my sister-in-law. I did not know what to make of her. She had never used her words to wound me the way others had, and even now I sensed no ill intent. Yet the hair on my arms rose.

"I think that's why my own mother was so taken with you," Deborah continued. "You had strength that needed tending, and she enjoys being . . . needed."

Catching my lip between my teeth, I matched her directness with my own. "And do you resent me for that?"

We stared at each other for a long, tense moment before Deborah finally answered. "At times, yes."

Her blunt admission illuminated something murky between us, naming it before releasing it into the light.

The babe squirmed in my arms, perfect lips moving in and out, searching for milk I couldn't give. "Here. She needs you."

As I deposited the bundle back into Deborah's arms, I examined her eyes. Yes, there was a touch of bitterness within their brown depths, but also something else, something kinder.

The babe smelled her mother and squirmed. Deborah settled her with a bouncing motion. "When you decide to do something, Salome, you do it body, mind, and soul. When motherhood comes, I'm sure you will lay hold of it like a lioness."

------◆------

On the night I married Zebedee, Abba raised joyful hands to bless me as Naysa supported his weak side. "Blessed are you among women!"

I stood beneath the bridal canopy next to my groom, hair flowing in luxurious waves beneath my veil. Zeb's eyes never left me, but I was having trouble meeting his earnest gaze. He was magnificent in his wedding garments. Every time my eyes lingered on him, something so wide, wonderful, and terrifying opened up inside that I had to look away.

Later that evening, several women escorted me to the bridal chamber. I waited in the middle of the room, shaking, rooted to the spot, until a knock sounded on the door, and then Zeb was present, stumbling inside, pushed from behind by eager hands that pulled the door closed after him. He stood there with a sloppy smile on his face that shifted as he noted my demeanor. Silently, he extended a hand.

The stiffness in my legs loosened, all of my suspended emotion hurrying my feet. I buried myself within his arms and clung to him.

He pulled the veil from my head, sliding large hands through my tresses. "You're crying," he murmured. "Why?"

Was I? Lifting fingers to my face, I noted the wetness on my cheeks. "I don't know." I sniffed hard.

Gently he tipped my face to his. There was no other place to look now but directly into his eyes. What I found was all love and invitation.

"I . . . I suppose I'm used to feeling out of place." My lips trembled, eyes falling to his collarbone.

Zeb slid his hand back into my hair, tangling long fingers in its folds, anchoring my face so it remained open to him. "Look at me, Salome."

My gaze shifted to his nose, his brow, his hair, finally resting upon his eyes. He stared at me for a long time. I made myself do the same.

"You have a place." Dipping his head, he brushed his lips against my ear. "Or do you still doubt it?"

His breath sent shivers down my back. "I *have* doubted it . . . for too long," I admitted.

"You have a place by my side, and I have a place by yours,"

he whispered, pulling back, holding me at arm's length to take all of me in.

Desire dropped my gaze to his lips, but embarrassment returned them to his eyes, which were now regarding me with a decided gleam.

"You . . . you don't think I'm too wild, too stubborn?" I prodded.

"No, you're just right." His answer was immediate as he tugged me against him. "I want daughters with your spirit, with that tenacity you call stubbornness."

He pecked a kiss upon my nose, and I laughed shakily. "I hope not! We will drive your mother to an early grave if we fill this home with miniatures of me."

"Sons, then." He kissed the corner of one eye and then the other. As his lips moved to my cheek and then down to my throat, something unfolded in my chest that promised to be stronger than my nervousness.

"Sons as kind as you," I whispered.

"And as strong as you," he answered.

I buried a smile into his breast, happiness pounding down the door to my heart. "What have you gotten yourself into, Zebedee bar Jonathan?" Teasing trickled into my tone.

"Something wonderful." His voice was serious as he cupped my face in his hands and gazed into my stubbornly brilliant eyes. "Salome, you are fire and stone, ice and heat. I confess, you—you overwhelm me."

At his words, the shy twist in my spirit released. He bent to finally kiss me, but I was already pulling him down. As his kisses came, soft at first and then searing, I found that I was coming undone . . . and coming home all at once.

Seven

Summer 5 AD

Most grooms enjoyed a respite from duties and extended time at home with their new wife, but this was not to be the case for Zeb. There was a new tension in Bethsaida that set Jonathan on edge. He kept Zeb out on the water for longer stretches, attempting to increase production and offset the loss of profit due to steeper taxes and dwindling trade options.

"It's now impossible to send our fish to Magadan," Jonathan groused to Naysa.

On the western shore of Lake Gennesaret, Magadan boasted a large fish-processing factory. It was, however, under the territory of Herod Antipas in Galilee, while Bethsaida was in Gaulanitis under Herod's brother, Philip. Since he'd come into power less than ten years ago, Herod Antipas had steadily raised the taxation of imported goods in order to fund his reconstruction of Sepphoris. Fishermen from Bethsaida paid increasingly steep fees as they transferred goods into Galilee.

"A tax to export from Gaulanitis, another to import into Galilee, and the sales tax on top of it all. We may have to withdraw completely from Galilee," Jonathan muttered.

"And keep our trade in Gaulanitis alone?" Naysa questioned. "Do you think it wise to cut ourselves off so thoroughly from other regions? If we could branch out into the Jerusalem marketplace, then—"

"And pay an additional customs tax in Judea?" Jonathan thundered. "The fight for footing in the Jerusalem marketplace is fierce, and we are not at the scale to compete. The royal family has enough of my coin as it is. I will not give them any more than is strictly necessary."

And so Jonathan kept Zeb busy nearly every night and sometimes well into the morning, which meant most days Zeb was exhausted and half asleep.

"Allow the boy to enjoy his new wife," Naysa cautiously exhorted. "I need grandsons, and you are keeping him so occupied he won't have the chance to give me any."

"What good are grandsons if they starve?" Jonathan grunted.

Each morning, I rose extra early to run to the lake. It was a familiar path, but now an entirely new desire paved the way for my eager feet. Before the sun even teased the night sky, I stood on the shore, watchful and alert.

When his boat came into view, I ran into the water up to my knees, tunic pooling about my legs. His shout announced the moment he saw me, his lithe frame perched on the bow. With a splash he was in the water, pulling himself through the lake, tearing toward the shore to meet me, catching me up into his embrace. I spluttered and clung to him, thoroughly soaked as he splashed back to shore with me in his arms and his kisses on my laughing lips.

I held happiness like a secret, but no matter how I tried to hide my giddiness, it kept seeping from my skin, out onto my flushed and grinning face.

"*You overwhelm me,*" Zeb had told me, and I found that I liked being formidable.

◆

The blanket I'd draped over the high window had slipped, allowing sunbeams to filter into the small room. I pulled a stool to the wall, climbed up, and raised to tiptoe, maneuvering the blanket securely into place. Thankfully, Zeb had no problem sleeping in a brightened room after years of fishing each night. This morning, however, he hadn't done much sleeping.

With a grin, he tugged me back to his side, where I nestled against him for a brief moment before sitting up with a scowl. "You need to rest now." I swept the hair from his brow, trailing kisses behind my fingers.

He captured my hand in his own, drawing it to his lips. "I will, but . . . I've been pondering something for a while and want your thoughts on the matter."

"I have no problem giving you my thoughts."

"I know it." He chuckled, running the back of his finger along my arm. "Here it is, then. What do you think of moving?"

"Moving? Where?"

"Capernaum makes the most sense."

"Capernaum?" I squeaked, envisioning the larger village on the western banks of the lake. It sat along a major trade route and was home to not only a customs office but also a small garrison of Herod Antipas' troops. I'd been through Capernaum many times on my way to the Holy City. It was louder than Bethsaida, with Herod's soldiers serving as a somber backdrop to the bustle of commerce.

"You seem surprised. Hesitant?" Zeb frowned.

"I'm used to the quiet of Bethsaida. I'm not sure how I'd feel living in a village with a garrison. And to leave this land and home . . . It's been in your family for so long."

"I know, but—" Zeb interrupted himself with a giant yawn and a mighty stretch, the movement so reminiscent of a large cat that I giggled. At the sound of my mirth, his eyes grew alert, hand tangling in my tunic.

I pulled free with a smirk. "Where is this idea coming from? Your father would never agree to leave."

"My father might starve us with his stubbornness." Zeb propped himself up on an elbow. It was the first time I'd ever heard him criticize Jonathan. "If we move into Galilee, then we bypass the import tax and can begin processing our fish at Magadan again. If we hope to trade in larger quantities, then we *need* access to Magadan."

Zeb was adamant and growing more determined as he spoke. "We can't compete in the Jerusalem marketplace at the size we are now, but if we focus on increasing production and even partnering with another family, then why couldn't we trade in the Holy City?"

I couldn't deny that his words made good business sense. "But to leave family . . ."

"Your father might agree to come and live with us if it meant remaining with you. I'm going to talk to my father about it but wanted to get your thoughts first."

Leaning over him, I grazed his lips with my own, murmuring against his mouth, "My place is by your side, Zebedee. I'll go wherever you go."

He smiled, eased back, and took me with him, but I pushed away with a breathless laugh. "You must sleep, and I've lingered in here so long I'm embarrassed to show my face to your mother."

Chuckling, he let me go. He was asleep before I even left the room.

As determined as Zeb was to approach his father, he still tarried. Night after night he hesitated, and in his face, I saw the old uncertainty. When he finally did approach Jonathan, it was with a humility that no man could fault, and yet Jonathan immediately took offense.

"You would have us abandon this land and move to Capernaum with its military presence?" Jonathan's words were drenched in disbelief.

Quietly, Zeb communicated the benefits of his idea, but the more calmly he talked, the more enraged Jonathan became.

"I would rather die upon my own land than abandon it." His answer was firm, indicating that there would be no revisiting the discussion.

That afternoon, I tried to comfort Zeb, but he pushed away, face grim and closed off.

"Jonathan has a way of cutting Zeb down with his words." Naysa's dire observation was playing out before me, and I was powerless to stop it. *"My boy doesn't see his own worth."* I tried to communicate it to him in my touch and look, voice and action. I tried to extend what his father wouldn't give—approval and trust. But Zeb didn't seem able to receive it.

Anxiously, I began dreaming of a child, fervently monitoring my body for symptoms. Keturah was already expecting again, and Simon was only a year old, already toddling about after Jonah with dimpled cheeks and an abundance of black hair.

"If I could give Zeb a child, then perhaps he would feel Jonathan's rejection less keenly," I confided to Deborah. Since our direct conversation, I found myself returning to her, nearly against my will. Her unfiltered honesty was honey and I, the drunken fly. There was a delicate scale between us, precariously balanced between resentment and respect.

Propping Deborah's youngest on my hip, I tickled her chubby cheek until she shrieked with laughter. They had named her Abigail—father's joy. "You're going to be a great beauty, aren't you?" I nuzzled her nose with my own, eliciting a gurgle. Already she was a delightful child, well-tempered and sweet.

She was named "father's joy," but in truth, her father dismissed her—unable to forgive her for not being a boy. Even Deborah was slightly aloof toward the child, as though affection had dried up under the heat of her husband's disappointment.

I pressed a kiss into Abigail's neck and whispered the words I wanted her to remember all her life: "You are loved."

"You claim Abba is rejecting Zeb, but he's not really." Deborah shrugged a shoulder, hands busy at the loom. "He's rejecting his idea."

"It was the manner in which he did it," I stated, blood pounding in defense of my husband. I cradled Abigail close, burying my nose in her curls.

"Zeb takes things too personally."

"Zeb feels things deeply." My voice quavered with emotion, and I cleared my throat. "Jonathan sees this as weakness and is too dismissive of his son."

"Ah, you love my brother, don't you? Quite a bit, I see. And love is often blinding."

I clamped my lips tight. We were often like this, vying for the final word. But today I would let it go and focus instead on Abigail, who twisted in my arms and yanked triumphantly on a fistful of my hair.

Deborah was all practicality, without much softness. The observation made me smile as I recalled Naysa's exhortation to me: *"Too many sharp edges will drive people away."*

Zeb had softened me. We were so unalike—he with his quiet, steadfast nature and me with emotions that leapt straight off my lips. *A child for Zeb*, I prayed. *Adonai, he deserves a child. He would be an excellent father.*

We hadn't been married for that long, certainly not long enough to begin worrying about barrenness, but doubt still crept in: *Zeb would be an excellent father, but you would hardly make a good mother.* I shook my head to dislodge the thought.

That night I lay in bed alone and thought of my husband out upon the lake. I drew in a slow breath and held it, imagining a child within his arms. Placing my hands over my belly, I stared hard at the ceiling.

"You've given me a place by Zeb's side. Now hear my prayer and grant me a child. Worthy or not, suitable or not, I would do my best. I would try. Adonai, I would try to be a righteous mother. Please give Zeb a child." Over and over, I prayed until I fell asleep.

A hand on my hip jolted me awake, but before I could yelp with panic, Zeb was quieting me with a kiss.

"What are you doing here?" I threw a worried gaze to the window, which was still dark.

Zeb was fresh from the lake as he slid beneath the blanket to take me into his arms. He'd been tightly wound for weeks, bundled up and away from me as he held his hurt between us. But now he was here, legs tangling with mine, inviting me close again. Disregarding the smell, I held him, rested my cheek against his breast, and listened to the sound of his heart.

"I told my father I needed to be with my wife tonight. He didn't like it, but I didn't ask for his approval, and I don't need his permission to be with you."

There was a new decisiveness in his tone that was deeply appealing. I shivered and pressed myself up against him as he kissed my temple, ear, and throat.

Typically quiet and compliant, that night it was Zeb who was the formidable one.

Eight

AUTUMN 5 AD

"They will be living in the Holy City!" Jonathan's eyes were alight as he relayed the news to a neighbor. "My son-in-law is following his rabbi right into Jerusalem and taking my daughter with him."

Biting the inside of my cheek, I hauled a basket of fish onto my hip. Jonathan had never sounded this proud when speaking of his own son, who now sat two paces away, cleaning a net. An indignant huff left my lips, but no one noticed.

"To be the disciple of a member of the Sanhedrin . . ." Our neighbor clucked his tongue appreciatively.

Jonathan laughed, the sound reverberating off the water and scratching at my ears. I left before anyone saw my disgruntled face.

Kadmiel's aspirations were close to fulfillment. With clarity I recalled his young voice, cracking with earnestness as he'd asserted, *"I can prove their assessment of us wrong."* He'd always had his eye on Jerusalem. I'd be happy for him if it wasn't for the unbridled joy in Jonathan.

"This is the fifth time today he's told the story," I grumbled to Naysa as I thumped the basket on a table where she was gutting fish.

"Can you blame him?" Naysa cast her eyes down the shore to where Jonathan was assaulting yet another person with the news. "Good things can come from Bethsaida after all."

"With his rabbi in such a prominent position, do you think Kadmiel himself might someday sit on the council?"

Naysa slapped a fish onto the table and shrugged. "Perhaps. Who is to say what the future will hold?"

I tried to imagine it—a boy from this small village sitting as a revered member of the Sanhedrin. If Zeb envied Kadmiel and the stir he was causing, he wasn't showing it. I knew what it was to be overlooked and underestimated, and that knowledge bound me in this moment to my husband in a deeper way. Zeb bore his father's loud praise over Kadmiel with grace, with a humility I was sure no one else even noticed.

Warmth pooled in my belly. I gazed at my husband and placed a hand to my middle.

"Now if Adonai would see fit to give Leah a child," Naysa muttered. "Married for two years by now and no babe."

A slow smile parted my lips as I pressed my hand tighter against my womb. I had no mother to consult, had been too embarrassed to go to Naysa or Deborah, and so had gone to Keturah as soon as I'd suspected it.

"You're most certainly with child." Keturah's face had confirmed it even before she'd spoken the words.

I'd held myself tightly as awareness throbbed through my body. Adonai had heard me. Had seen me. *Knew* me. No sooner had I prayed than He had answered. This knowledge was too wonderful for me, too high. I could not begin to understand it.

Keturah was all delight, the friendship between us deepening in an instant. She'd bumped her rounded belly against my flat one, voice lifting in praise.

I searched the sky, aching for Adonai. I longed to see Him the way Moses had—a glimpse of His glory as He passed me by. *Thank You.*

"Take these to your father for his supper tonight." Naysa nudged me with a small basket of fish. "And tell him to stop being so stubborn!"

Abba had slowed this past year as his joints stiffened and yet he wouldn't come and live with us despite Naysa's insistence, wouldn't abandon the work that was becoming increasingly difficult. I accepted the basket and trekked to my childhood home, not bothering to knock, simply calling out a greeting as I entered.

Abba perched on a stool, chisel in hand, while Noy lay in his corner, gray in the face and half asleep. Upon my entrance, however, Noy perked up, straining to rise, twitching with excitement that his aging body could no longer accommodate.

"Hush, boy." I set the fish upon a table and knelt by Noy's side, fingers sliding to that secret spot behind his good ear.

Abba nodded at the basket. "Thank you, daughter."

"Thank Naysa." I grinned. "Who also passes along an admonition to stop being so stubborn."

Abba snorted. "How is Jonathan? Still crowing over Kadmiel?"

"He told five more people just this morning."

"And Zeb?" Love rounded the edges of Abba's voice. "How is my son-in-law? Recovering from his disappointment?"

"He is determined to move to Capernaum but holds that desire close—away from Jonathan. Would you . . . come with us if we did move one day?" I dared to ask.

Abba frowned and reached for a hammer, but it fell from his fingers with a clatter.

Moving quickly to ease his embarrassment, I retrieved the tool and repeated my question.

He squinted at the stone upon his workbench, gave one hesitant strike and then two, flecks of basalt falling away as the piece took shape. "Capernaum is in Galilee, and Galilee is still in turmoil. Rome has her eye on the region, even with Herod Antipas in control, and Judas is still stirring up unrest."

I bit my lip at the mention of the revolutionary figure.

"I'm an old man, Zohar, and have lived all my life beneath these quiet plateaus. Place has a profound pull upon people."

I stilled one of his hands, turned it palm up within my own. His fingers curled inward like talons. Gently I rubbed them. "Perhaps you could find a new place . . . with me, Zeb, and our child. . . ."

"Are you expecting?" His eyes searched mine, face brightening.

"Oh, I—" I hadn't told Zeb yet, hadn't intended to let this precious secret slip. My mind scrambled for an explanation. "I meant the children I'm sure we'll have someday."

But Abba was beaming, hand pulling from mine to lift upward in praise—tears forming, pooling, spilling. "Zohar . . . a child?"

His joy surpassed the midday sun, igniting my own, eliciting a trembling smile upon my lips. I beamed and allowed my tears to answer him.

"Praise Adonai!" Abba's worship pierced the air, up and out to God's throne. "For this child I prayed, and the Lord has granted my request."

The words of Hannah rejoicing over Samuel poured from Abba's lips, dripping down upon my head like oil.

"You prayed for this child?" I whispered.

Abba's eyes returned to me. "May your heart rejoice in the Lord. There is no one like Him. There is no rock like our God."

I held his hand as a new soaring hope formed into a prayer. *May this child be filled with Your Spirit.*

That very night, I took Zeb out to the rock—the one I'd run to after Leah's wedding, the spot where I'd learned to talk directly to Adonai. I threaded my fingers with his, heart too full to speak.

He knew before I said a word. Releasing my hand with a low cry, he dropped to his knees and pressed his face into my belly. I laughed and wept and laughed some more as he placed strong hands on my hips and spoke to our child as if he were there, right there, already in our arms.

❖

SPRING 6 AD

As I grew large with our child, troubling news swelled from the south. The tetrarch over Judea, Herod Archelaus, was being deposed and his former territory annexed and turned into a Roman province under the procurator Coponius. As the first step in taking over the territory, Coponius called for a census, which would lead to increased taxation.

For years, Judas of Galilee had been terrorizing the region as he plundered the Jewish aristocracy. His efforts in Sepphoris had been quelled, but now, with this newest development, his banditry turned once again into a more organized revolt.

"I know Judas," Elazar stated in the synagogue. "He grew up in Gamala, six miles north of here. We may doubt his methods, but his heart is righteous, attuned to God's Law."

"Then how do you explain his actions?" a man spat, face clouded with fury. "You saw the fruit of his efforts ten years ago. Sepphoris is still being rebuilt. Does he want another two thousand crucifixions? How many of our brethren must bleed for his cause?"

"He welcomes scoundrels and thieves, dredging up scum under the banner of resisting Rome when all he does is incite Rome's attention and wrath!" another man thundered.

"He targets his own people," Jonathan spoke up, subdued.

"He targets the aristocracy—those who have compromised their faith by bedding Rome," Elazar clarified.

But Jonathan was shaking his head. "Perhaps at first, but now he targets anyone—high or low—who promotes cooperation with the census."

"Are you certain of that?" Elazar asked, face ashen.

"Didn't you hear of the incident in Jericho?" Jonathan's brow lifted. "His followers killed at least a dozen men who were advocating for compliance—fellow Jews all of them, men who work the ground, like you, Simeon." Jonathan threw a hand in the farmer's direction. "Or you, Matthias." Another hand, another lift of the brow. "It's hard enough to live within the fist of Rome without our own brethren dispensing violence upon us."

Elazar's face went from gray to white. "His reasoning, though—"

"I know, I know." Baruch raised his hands. "Ideologically he is not far off from the Pharisees, but, Elazar . . . what good is solid ideology if it breaks down in practice?"

That night, Zeb stayed home from the lake. I lay on my side and held his hand, too mentally and physically uncomfortable for sleep. "What did Baruch mean when he said Judas' group was similar to the Pharisees?"

Zeb was quiet as he lay on his back. "Both are looking for the Messiah, someone to break the yoke of Rome and unite Israel under the reign of God. But they seem to differ on how to usher in this messianic age."

"The Pharisees believe adherence to the Law will bring the Messiah."

Zeb nodded. "Judas represents the growing number of Israelites who are tired of waiting—who see *themselves* as ushering in the Messiah through active resistance."

I shivered and placed a hand to my womb in time to catch a kick. "Here . . . here, he's active tonight." I guided Zeb's hand to where the babe moved within me.

"He?" Zeb asked, easing onto his side, large hand pressing back, teasing the babe with nudges. "Do you think it's a boy?"

"I just know. In this quiet place inside, I know." I rested a hand over Zeb's. "We will pour our love upon this child—boy or girl—but my heart keeps calling this babe *son*. I can't explain it."

Zeb framed my rounded belly in his calloused hands and placed a deep kiss to its center.

"I worry about the world he's coming into." I sighed. "Judas is drawing the nation's youth. Surely by the time our son is of age, this will all have died down." The thought of our child involved in active resistance to Rome was nearly enough to incite panic.

"God alone knows the future. He only asks that we walk uprightly in the present day." Zeb's words were calm and confident, but his eyes mirrored my worry.

✦

As my time drew closer, we received more news from the south, this time of a celebratory nature.

"Leah is expecting!" Naysa clapped her hands, face jubilant. "At last!"

"Of course Leah is pregnant now that I am," I complained to Keturah as she laid out wet garments to dry along the shore.

Keturah's second son, Andrew, was strapped to her back, where he flailed agitatedly, the longing to crawl and tumble evident on his scrunched face.

"Bitterness doesn't suit you, Salome."

"I know, but . . . Zeb's parents were exuberant at the news of our babe. For months, Jonathan has been looking at Zeb with such respect. I—"

"You don't want that look redirected." Keturah straightened, ignoring Andrew's indignant grunts.

I sighed. "Yes."

"Someone else's joy doesn't diminish our own. Good fortune is worth celebrating, no matter whose door it comes to."

"You're right. But I feel protective of Zeb." Uncomfortably protective, like someone had lit a fire beneath my feet.

Keturah wrung out another wet garment. "That's one of your good traits, friend. At least it's one of the traits that I admire. You are loyal and fight for your own to the end."

"Zeb says I'm formidable."

"In someone else's mouth, that would probably be a slight. Coming from Zeb, though? That's the highest of compliments."

I giggled, and Keturah huffed a laugh, eliciting more giggles from my lips and drowning out the sounds of Andrew, who saw nothing humorous about the situation.

That night, as I prepared for bed, I prayed, "Forgive me, Adonai. Help me rejoice with Leah."

It was in my nature to fight, but was this the message I wanted to send my child? That he must fight for every scrap of attention? As I tossed and turned in hunt of a favorable position for sleep, I prayed that when this babe finally arrived, he would find a suitable mother greeting him.

Nine

The labor pains began in the dead of night, weeks after I'd expected him to arrive. "The babe is large," Hadara muttered, practiced hands feeling my stomach as another spasm gripped me. "Babes who arrive this late are often so large they stick within the mother."

"But that will not happen to our Salome." Naysa scowled as she gripped my hand. The midwife in Bethsaida was known for her candor and less for her comforting manner, but she was also experienced, and I was in too much misery to care about bluntness.

Deborah placed a hand on my shoulder. Her babes had all arrived early and small. In her tight expression, I noted fear.

Even though men were never present for childbirth and Zeb was out on the lake, I longed for him with a fervency that poured from my lips in a moan.

"Zeb will be back by daybreak, and then you will have a healthy child to present to him," Naysa crooned, swiping the hair from my brow.

Hadara's pursed lips spoke otherwise, and as daylight

presented itself and I was no further along, her fears proved true. Outside the room, I could hear a panicked Zeb. Naysa went to him while I tossed upon my bed and bit back a moan.

All that day, I labored while Zeb waited in the courtyard, refusing to sleep or eat. That night, when the babe still hadn't arrived, Zeb wouldn't join his father on the lake, and for once Jonathan didn't push him.

In the early hours of the following morning, the babe finally began to move, and as daylight stretched into the window, Hadara settled me upon the birthing stool and instructed me to push.

With great difficulty, I delivered him, a ten-pound squalling son with a shock of hair, flailing fists, and a trembling, screeching cry.

"A son!" Naysa's joyful proclamation pierced the room as my head grew dangerously light. Hadara labored to stanch my bleeding while Naysa scrubbed her grandson with salt and wine, then washed him with warm water and rubbed him in olive oil.

"A son! A son! Adonai has gifted you a son!" She sang the words, pausing to release a joyous laugh. In the corner, Deborah watched her mother, arms folded across her chest.

As Naysa began wrapping him with strips of linen, I stopped her. "No," I rasped. "Let me see him. Give him to me."

Naysa began to ease him into my arms, but I snatched at him hungrily, sprawled him out upon my lap, and picked at his limbs, lifting one and then another. I ran fingers over his face, tracing his impossibly tiny fingernails and exploring his wriggling, chubby body.

"He looks like a child already months old!" Hadara cackled. "Large babes are contented babes. You are blessed."

Anxiously, I peered into his eyes—a murky gray. The true color would emerge later. *Adonai, please—*

Naysa tried to take him, but I pushed her away and stared at this, my beautiful child, my perfect son.

"Congratulations," Deborah stated from her corner, voice flat.

The babe wailed, and the sound burrowed straight to my heart. I lifted him to my face, touched my lips to his skin, let my tears fall upon his face, and breathed in long and deep.

Bone of my bone and flesh of my flesh.

———— ◆ ————

Keturah had described this moment to me. There was a moment, she said, once the babe had learned to suck and the pain of birth receded and your body had healed just enough. There was a small moment of time in which it was perfect—the babe, yourself, life.

It wouldn't last. The babe would go through crying stages, and your body would continue to go through painful and confusing changes, but there was a golden, glowing moment, and when it came, I was to hold on to it—suck it dry of the life it offered.

It was here, and I was gulping every bit of its joy.

Zeb rested an arm about my shoulders as his tired, red-rimmed eyes took in our son at my breast. "What will you name him?"

I leaned into his side and considered. "There *is* a name I've been holding on to. Could we name him . . ."

"Yes? Say it, love."

Oftentimes the eldest son was named after the father, and I didn't want to offend this dearest man. "I want to name him after Abba." I spoke the desire aloud.

"Jacob?"

"A variation of the name—James."

Zeb stroked our son's downy head with a long finger as he thought. Finally, he bent to press a kiss to his son's brow and then up to my waiting lips.

"Yes," he murmured, breath warm, lips warmer still. "James."

For the first time in my life, all doubt was shamed into silence under the brilliance of this great and overwhelming love. I could not recover from the gift of it—this big, beautiful boy in my arms. His presence solidified my place by Zeb's side and in his family. I was no longer wild, untamable Salome with the glowing eyes. I was Salome, the mother of a son.

When Jonathan first held James, his whole body stilled, transfixed. His strident voice dipped into gentleness as he addressed me, gaze never parting from his grandson. "Well done, Salome. Well done."

With those quiet words, joy and pride bloomed fiercely within.

As James grew, his eyes deepened into a lovely brown. *Praise You, God of mercy.* I sighed, not realizing how ardently I'd awaited this moment.

I kept James close, unwilling to be parted from him. *What have I done to deserve this?* He was all gift to me, God's grace in the form of a boy with curly black hair.

Even as my own arms were full, however, the arms of Israel's mothers were slowly being stripped of their sons as more and more men flocked to Judas of Galilee's growing movement. His influence extended across the lake, thrusting into Gaulanitis, breaking into Bethsaida. In the dead of night, a handful of our village youth ran off to join Judas—Elazar's younger brother among them. His mother mourned as though her son were already dead.

"He'd just turned thirteen," Deborah muttered. Since James' birth, she'd remained distant, and I wondered if the scale between us had irreparably tipped. I'd asked her as much and had received a veiled reply that suggested the honesty we'd once shared had soured.

"He was barely a man. Still so young." Deborah shook her

head. "He should be entering an apprenticeship under Elazar, not running away to join this dangerous group."

"Some have begun calling them Zealots," Jonathan relayed one night. "They agree with the Pharisees that we are forbidden to acknowledge any other Lord than Adonai, but they purport that violence is justified in keeping our land free of Roman control. Some have even begun calling Judas 'Messiah.'"

Messiah. I understood how fury over injustice could thump through one's body, a heartbeat compelling action. But when the Messiah came, would it be through the blood of our nation's sons?

"Do you think this man is the one we've been expecting?" I asked Zeb one morning as I helped him sort the night's catch, James strapped to my back.

Zeb frowned. "The Messiah will perform a great sign of his power, won't he? What power has this man demonstrated other than stirring up unrest and turning upon his own people through intimidation? And his lineage . . . the Messiah must be from the Davidic line."

And yet Bethsaida remained divided, as some took pride in their sons joining Judas, while others mourned with a sorrow that refused all comfort.

◆

The first winter after James' birth, Jonah's father unexpectedly died, leaving the family business to his grieving son. Quickly after, Jonah began making plans to move to Capernaum.

"So soon?" I worried to Keturah.

"Jonah handles grief by looking ahead," Keturah replied with a pinched face. "And he's always seen the wisdom of Zeb's idea to move."

"But I—" A sharp pang halted the remaining words. *I will miss you.*

I had hopes of our sons being raised together. Daily, Simon

fulfilled the midwife's prediction that he would be a forceful son. Robust and loud, he was angry and yelling one moment and showering Keturah with kisses the next. His brother, although quieter, was no less busy. Only a year older than James, Andrew had recently learned to walk. Keturah and I often laughed to see him toddling along the shore, tangled in his father's nets, knowing that one day he would be a strapping man wielding them instead. I did not want to give up this version of my future, the one with Keturah and her boys in it.

"Perhaps you will join us?" Her hope was almost more painful than her news.

I shook my head with a resigned sigh. "I'm afraid Jonathan sees the arrival of Rome in Judea as further proof that a move to Capernaum is unwise. Even though Herod Antipas is still in control of Galilee, if the influence of these Zealots continues to spread, Rome might direct her attention farther north."

"We can hardly remain untouched," Keturah mused. "Those young men running off proves it, and your father-in-law will see it. Bethsaida is no safer than Capernaum."

"At least here there is no garrison. Zeb claims his father is frightened of change, that he'd rather cling to what is familiar than take a risk."

Keturah lifted a shoulder. "And Jonah says that abundance never happens by accident, that he wants more for our sons than Bethsaida can offer."

Tears threatened, and I blinked hard before they could fall.

Keturah was quiet for a long moment before threading a slender hand through the crook of my arm with a whisper. "I'll miss you too."

❖

James sneezed into the nippy night air. I adjusted him on my hip as I sang the *Shema*, hoping the ancient words would soothe his restlessness. We'd recently passed his first birthday, and he was teething—about as irritable as a struck bee nest. Movement helped, and so most nights I walked him to sleep along the shoreline until my lower back ached and my voice grew hoarse from singing.

Tonight, however, I was tired and sat on my rock, legs dangling, toes dipping into the cold water. James wriggled and whined, so to distract him, I lay back, stretched us both out beneath the stars, and pointed.

"Look there and there. What shapes do the stars make when you string them together?"

James refused to lie down, choosing instead to sit on my stomach and smack at my face, slobber streaming down his chin. I tickled him until he shrieked, then nestled him up against me and quieted him with kisses.

Finally, he pointed a fat finger to the sky and attempted the word *star*. I captured that pointing finger with my lips, pretending to nibble it off.

"Not just one star, not just two, but millions of stars, too many to count. Adonai promised Abraham that his offspring would be as numerous as the stars, and look!" I eased upright and swept an arm across the lake to encompass the whole land. "Here we are—a multitude."

James stuck his fingers into my mouth. They were slick with his drool.

I laughed, then gagged, removing his grasping fingers and gazing across the dark water toward Capernaum. For months now our dear friends had lived *there* rather than *here*, and already it felt like a lifetime.

"They're not that far away." I attempted to laugh off my sorrow but still the tears came, lingering on my lashes. "But it *feels* like a great distance."

James slapped me across the face, laughing heartily as I startled.

"You mischievous boy. You deliciously horrible boy." I pulled up his shirt to expose his stomach and gobbled at the rolls of flesh before scooping him up and planting him on my hip. "It is well past your bedtime."

Often when I left the lake it was with a renewed peace, but this night thoughts of my friend left me as agitated as my son, who squirmed and shouted, "No!" protesting my every step toward home.

"We are a pair, are we not? You flailing on the outside and me on the inside." I pinned James' hand in my own to keep his fingers from poking my eyes. "We need to take a lesson from the stars. If Adonai knows each star by name, then He knows your name, sweet boy, as He knows mine. El Roi—the God who sees us."

As James finally settled, I prayed for my heart to do the same—to be quieted by Adonai's love.

TEN

Only a year after Elazar's brother ran off, he returned—wrapped in linen, prepared for burial. His mother screamed at those who delivered the body, tearing at them with her hands, collapsing at their feet, shoving aside all comfort. I trembled and wept at the burial, clinging fervently to James.

Judas' attempt to dissuade the people from submitting to the census had been undermined by the high priest, Joazar, who pacified the people into compliance. Rome—like they had years before—intervened, this time capturing and crucifying Judas. There was no more talk of him as the Messiah as the Syrian governor stepped in to conduct the census upon Judea. The passion behind Judas' movement, however, remained alive, leading many to believe that another would arise to continue what he'd begun.

At night, I ran fingers in soft patterns over James' slumbering face and smiled as he twitched in his sleep. "May Adonai shape you into who you're meant to be." Nightly, I prayed this benediction over my son, but lately it had morphed into a prayer with sharp edges of worry. "May Adonai keep you from danger and out of paths full of violence."

James, as he toddled about, carried my very soul along with him. Treasured by all, he was the only one who could soften Jonathan's lined face or make Naysa forget about household duties.

With a deepening quiet, Deborah observed her parents' joy. "It's as I said," she told me one day. "You are a lioness, Salome. A good mother to James." And the scale tipped toward respect.

James laughed upon sight of his father, reaching eager arms to him and pulling on his ears, but it was my own father who seemed to command his deepest affection. The two were so enamored with each other that James shrieked every time I had to pry him away. Every morning, we visited the workshop while Zeb slept. James would lie upon Noy or snuggle into Abba's arms, and I would hold these images in my heart.

As James' sturdy little body stretched into toddlerhood, I continued to experience a deep contentment coupled with a growing awareness that my womb remained empty. At night I sang James to sleep, his head nestled within my lap. I sang him the songs of my mother, less stunning from my lips than hers, but beautiful to my boy nonetheless.

"Again, Ima. Sing again."

And so I did, all the while wondering if Adonai's gift had begun and ended with this astonishing boy.

✦

One night, Zeb turned to me, breath feathering my cheek, words tumbling over themselves in a rush to get out.

"Do you suppose Adonai has closed your womb? That there will be no more children for us?"

I lay on my back, silent and wide-eyed until Zeb repeated his question.

"It's been three years, Salome—*three years*. Many conceive before then. We conceived James right away. It seems strange that we have yet to do so again." Zeb propped himself up on an elbow to peer into my face. "I've been praying ceaselessly for more children. It's become a burden too heavy to carry alone."

I closed my eyes and held myself still.

"Salome? Say something."

"I am content with James, aren't you?"

"Of course I am. Children are a blessing from the Lord that every man desires, so it's natural to want more than a single arrow in one's quiver."

There was an irritable edge to his voice that was unlike him. I shifted so that our legs were no longer touching.

"You are enraptured with James, as well you should be," Zeb whispered. "But at times . . . at times I wonder if it's become enough for you, if you even *want* more children as I do."

I twisted away to stare, unseeing, at the wall. His words were a lifted veil that I didn't want to confront, for I was indeed content with only my James. Hadn't I wondered at that contentment over the years? Shouldn't my heart mirror the longing on my husband's face? Shouldn't I want more than one arrow too?

"Certainly I-I want more children." I stammered the expected words, cheeks growing hot with the unbearable thought. *What is wrong with me?*

"You don't speak of it."

"Must I speak everything I'm thinking?"

"You've never hesitated before."

I scooted farther away, increasing the distance between us. "You're one to talk about speaking what's on the heart and mind! You who do so little of it yourself!"

A sharp huff of air left Zeb's lips. "I just . . . find it strange that you are so content without more children. Most mothers—"

I turned fully from him then and bit back a cry.

He's right. Most mothers would be praying for another child. You are not like most mothers. Fear crept into my head, filling it with unwelcome accusations.

"I-I am an *excellent* mother," I whispered fiercely, uttering it with force so that I would believe it. "That you would doubt—"

"I'm not! Salome, I'm not doubting you." Zeb scooted close,

wrapping his long frame around my back, arm draped over my waist. "You are the best mother to James, which makes me eager for another child to experience that love," he murmured, tone shifting from irritable to amorous in one swift movement.

Gritting my teeth, I held myself still, signaling that he could not make this right so easily. Unknowingly, he'd prodded at a hidden, hurting part of me that I thought had long healed.

Hot tears leaked from my golden eyes, but I kept them from Zeb, held myself tighter, and turned my face into the blanket.

His lips were at the hairline below my ear. Gooseflesh sprinkled across my skin as his hand kneaded the flesh at my waist. Finally, he seemed to note my demeanor and stopped.

I didn't need to look at him to know what expression he wore. Lips parted, throat bobbing like the words were caught there, eyes squinting, trying to see a way forward. With a frustrated groan, he flopped onto his back.

Neither of us spoke or moved toward the other for the rest of the night.

◆

"*Love is a strange creature. Sometimes it chooses you. And sometimes you have to choose it.*" For all her faults, Deborah had never spoken truer words. I observed my husband and knew I would choose love. Just not yet. Not when my heart wanted to hold on to offense a bit longer.

"Zeb longs for another child," I shared with Abba. He had James up on a stool and stood behind him, one arm on each side of his grandson as he guided his small hands.

"That stone, Saba! That one!" James pointed to a piece of white limestone.

Abba hesitated for a moment, considering James' expensive choice, but finally he chuckled and scraped the stone forward. "You know a good piece of earth when you see it, *Gibor*."

My heart settled at the use of James' nickname—Gibor, mighty hero.

"He's been praying for another child," I continued, guilt creeping into my voice.

"And you?" Abba flicked a glance my direction.

I studied a chisel upon the workbench, running a thumb along its worn edge. "Zeb thinks that I'm so full of love for James that there's no room for another child."

"Is that what he said?"

I worried my lip. "Well . . . no. Not in so many words."

"Hold the chisel like this, my boy." Abba turned the instrument around in James' determined fist, covering the chubby hand in his own gnarled one. "Hold it still. This hand is still while this is the one that strikes." He placed a small hammer in James' right hand and tried to carefully swing it down, but James pushed hard and the hammer missed the chisel, skimming off the stone.

"Again! Again!" James squealed.

Abba glanced at me. "Not every word is a strike, Zohar. You've been the recipient of harsh words before, so you are accustomed to pulling your armor tight, receiving each word as a blow. Can't say I blame you."

James wrested the hammer from Abba and swung wildly at the stone before Abba nabbed it from his hands and regained control. "There is wisdom in waiting before reacting."

Abba crouched, pressing his gray, stubbled cheek to James' smooth one. "Approach the stone intentionally, my boy. Not like a wild person but like a man willing to wait for the right moment. You must feel for that moment, like this."

Slowly he moved the chisel, angling it one way and then the other until settling upon a position, lifting the hammer, and striking. A sharp, ringing tone sounded throughout the workshop. More strikes, more ringing, intermingled with James' laughter.

"I like the sound," James shouted.

Abba smiled broadly at his namesake. "As do I. The stone is singing."

James chortled. "Rocks don't sing, Saba!"

"Maybe not the way you and I do, but all creation sings God's glory. Even the rocks cry out."

Sadness, inexplicable sadness snaked through me as my son squirmed on the stool, excitement oozing from his body, stirring his feet into an impatient dance.

"Zeb has prayed, but I have not." The confession fled my lips. There was no relief to be found in finally uttering the words, only an increasing urgency to say more, to finally confront what I'd left untended. "Abba . . . I prayed fervently for James but haven't uttered a single prayer for another child. What is wrong with me?"

"Nothing is wrong with you." Abba's answer was swift as he left James' side. "Zohar, you must stop looking within here." He placed a knuckle to my breastbone. "And start looking here." Moving his knuckle up, he tilted my chin to the ceiling. "Let your Maker tell you who you are."

His words were true. I knew this within my head but not within the part of me that *felt*. Not within that hidden place that kept me up at night. With great effort, I cracked that place open and allowed the fear there to be spoken.

"What if I can't do this again?" I rasped. "What if I can't be a good mother to another child? What if there *isn't* room in my heart?"

"Ah, Zohar, you don't have to worry about that. Love is an unlimited resource. It comes as it's needed. Your Maker knows the stone with which He works, and He does not make mistakes."

Three nights later, when Zeb remained home from the lake, I kept that hidden place open and turned to him, but he was already halfway to me, each of us moving back toward the other with intention.

ELEVEN

SUMMER 10 AD

Four years of beautiful James, a sunny boy beloved by all. Four years of nurturing and loving him before I knew that, at last, more love would be needed.

This time there was no trip to the rock. As soon as I was sure, I told him, knowing how much he desired it. I told him as he brought the night's catch to the open courtyard for me to sort.

He stopped and stared as though he'd misheard, made me repeat myself several times until I was shaking my head and laughing at the dumbfounded look splayed all over his face.

"You heard me correctly the first time, Zebedee bar Jonathan." I took the basket of fish from his arms and thrust it upon my hip with a smirk. "You're going to be a father once again."

A long, strained silence, and then he shoved the basket off my hip and lifted me with an exuberant whoop while freshly caught fish spilled about his legs. James laughed and clapped his hands, chasing after the fish and throwing them back into the basket while Zeb spun me in a circle. I was swept up in a whirl of his delight, laughing and nauseous as he spun me one more time before planting my feet back upon land. His eyes were bright with tears, and I thought, in that brief moment, that I had never seen him so happy.

◆

In the weeks after my announcement, Abba began experiencing greater discomfort in his joints and pains in his chest and shoulder that drove him to his bed and away from his beloved workbench. To cheer him, I began visiting multiple times a day with James, who enjoyed bringing little gifts to his saba and scraps of food to the aging Noy.

But one morning, Abba called out, stopping us before we could enter. "Send James home, Salome."

"I don't *want* to go home!" James stamped his foot with a defiant scowl.

"Saba might have a surprise," I soothed. "And he might not want you to see it yet."

Mollified, James returned the way we'd come while I entered.

Abba sat by Noy's quiet bed, one hand on his scruff, which was unnaturally still, the other covering his own face.

Understanding filled my heart, heavy and warm, pulling it down in my chest like a lead weight.

We buried him north of Bethsaida. With great care, Zeb wrapped him and carried him in his arms, even though this caused a stir among our neighbors, who did not understand such attention given to a dog.

Gideon vocalized disbelief to his customers, shaking his head with derisiveness. "So much grief over one animal. Then again, Zebedee has always been soft. Can you imagine? Holding a burial ceremony for a dog."

His son, Philip, followed our procession. A thin, scrappy boy of eight, Philip had indeed earned Jonah's description of "brash." Only a year into his schooling, and he was prone to run off, finding company with a handful of boys who stuck to his heels like burrs, all of them rude and insolent.

We buried Noy near the abandoned quarry I'd run to as a girl, in sight of the jagged ledges where I'd perched. I clasped James' small hand while supporting Abba on my other side. Together we watched Zeb lower Noy into the ground. When the earth covered him, I wept for my childhood companion. James pressed his face into my hand, dry-eyed and confused.

A shout came from the quarry. Philip stood on a large boulder, a gangly boy flanking him on either side while he pointed and laughed, all three reminiscent of birds of prey.

"Why is he doing that?" James' chin trembled as he gazed at the older boy.

I pressed a kiss to James' hand. "Because he's angry and lost."

Later that night, my son snuggled up against me and tapped my stomach, a gesture he often did, as if his hand were the hammer and he was attempting to unearth his sibling.

"Where did Noy go?" he whispered, voice small and squeaky, fingers tap, tap, tapping.

"He died, my love." I explained it yet again.

James sighed and wriggled. "Yes, but . . . when will he climb back out of the ground? Abba dug the hole so deep."

"Oh, my love . . ." My voice broke, and I simply held him.

All of us had seen death many times over, James included, but it was different when it was your own family, your own, beloved Noy. And then everything inside rose up in denial.

✦

"Kadmiel says the high priest is looking for a new supplier. He's gone through two in the past year and has been unsatisfied in terms of quality and price." Zeb followed at my heels, eager as a pup hunting for scraps.

The current high priest, Annas bar Seth, came from an

established Sadducean family who'd made their wealth by controlling the market on sacrificial animals within Jerusalem. Appointed four years ago by Quirinius, the Roman governor of Syria, Annas had already held his position longer than the previous five high priests before him.

"I've heard he is meticulous and demanding." I frowned, grunting as I lifted a vat of fermented fish onto the table.

"You shouldn't be doing that." Zeb's attention shifted to my rounded stomach, concern for me distracting him.

I waved a hand. "Okay, then, you get the next one."

Zeb hurried off and returned with another vat.

The process of making *garum* was one I abhorred, but I couldn't deny that the fish sauce was delicious. As most fishermen did, we mixed the fish too small for market with the entrails of our cleaned fish, heavily salting them and storing the concoction in a vat. We left these vats out in the sun for three months while the mixture inside fermented. As the final step, we skimmed the liquid off the top, bottling it for use as a condiment and dipping sauce.

"Annas may be selective, but Kadmiel managed to secure a trial order for us—a variety of fish and a bottle of our finest garum." Zeb tapped the vat with a knuckle.

We saw Kadmiel and Leah at least three times a year during the annual foot festivals. This last time, Zeb had remained holed up with Kadmiel, leaving me alone to navigate the uncomfortable situation with Leah.

Six months after James' birth, Leah had delivered twins—a boy and a girl whom they named Admon and Affera. During each visit to Jerusalem, James looked upon his cousins with skepticism, for they were so different in temperament from himself, content to remain indoors with their mother rather than tumble and tear around outside.

"They're intimidated by James," Leah had explained while both her children hid behind her tunic.

Defensiveness had flared, but I'd pushed it back. *"Not every word is a strike."* Time and time again, I'd returned to Abba's admonition.

Still, I was tense around Leah, who winced every time James was too loud, as though his exuberance gave her a headache. While Zeb had been making big plans with Kadmiel, I had been busy reining in James' big spirit in deference to Leah and her children.

"A trial order seems promising, but . . . the high priest, Zeb? The *high priest?*" I couldn't suppress my disbelief.

Zeb opened the vat, releasing a pungent smell. "Kadmiel has connections. Why not make use of them? If Annas likes what we bring, it could lead to a standing account."

"If Annas is so particular, what makes you believe that *you* can satisfy him? That you will be any different?"

"I will learn from their mistakes. I am confident in our quality and will keep our prices down."

I tried propping a hand on my hip, momentarily forgetting that I no longer had a defined waist. "How will you keep prices down as a fisherman from Gaulanitis selling in Judea?"

Zeb quieted, settling both hands on my stomach, searching for the kicks that came more frequently these days. "This could be big, Salome. Abba says if we secure a standing account, he will consider a move to Capernaum. Imagine it—"

He moved closer until our unborn child was pressed tightly between us. "Capernaum is not far from the garum factory in Magadan. We could hire others to do this work." He crinkled his nose, touched it playfully to mine. "No more shriveled fish hands for you." He lifted one of my hands to his lips for a kiss, but I pulled it free to smack his chest.

He laughed and kissed my pursed lips instead.

Zeb's kisses and laughter became common occurrences as he readied for his trip. I tried to match his happy anticipation, but increased worries over Abba clouded all joy. Before Noy's death, he'd groused against the pain that kept him from his workbench, but now he had no will to rise from his bed. Even walking the length of his workshop winded him.

"Your legs are about as swollen as my own, Abba." I tried to jest, but my words wobbled with worry.

"We are a pair, are we not?" Abba laughed weakly and then winced.

"You need to get better before your granddaughter arrives."

Abba squinted. "Granddaughter? You were convinced James was a boy. You have the same feeling this time for a girl?"

"Not so much a feeling but a hope," I confessed, running a hand over my stomach. "I've been praying for a girl as sweet as Abigail. I want to honor Ima by raising a daughter of my own."

Abba sank back down on his bed, hand searching for mine. "You honor her, Zohar. Never doubt that. Every day you bring her memory honor."

❖

Zeb's spirits remained high while mine sank lower the closer he came to leaving. Even though I was skeptical that this opportunity would prove profitable, I should have been happy for him, grateful for the brightness in his face and renewed vigor in his stride. But all I could think of was how I didn't want him to go.

Something deeper than worry plagued me—a dark certainty that something bad was going to happen. I held on to the slithering, awful feeling for as long as I could until I could bear it no more.

"Please don't go." I lumbered by Zeb's side as he strode through the marketplace on his way to Elazar's home.

"The preparations are all set. We leave in a few days. How can you ask this of me?" Zeb shot me a quick glance.

Huffing, I tried to keep up with his pace. "I-I don't know how to explain it. There's a heaviness I cannot shake. As if something bad will happen to you or to my father."

He stopped, and I bumped into his back. Turning, Zeb gripped my arms, sighing before looking me full in the face. "It's a feeling and will pass. It isn't truth."

"But Abba isn't himself, and it worries me."

"I know he's grown weaker."

"His light is all but gone," I choked out. "I don't know what's wrong with him, but he's so tired all the time, can hardly get out of bed."

"He is old, Salome." Zeb said the blunt words gently, but still I cringed. "He's been slowing down for years."

"This feels different," I whispered.

Zeb drew me into his arms. "What does Hadara say?"

"That he should rest and not exert himself."

"And he's doing that." Zeb kissed the top of my head. "He will regain strength the longer he rests. I understand your concern, but this trip is too important to postpone."

"Couldn't Jonah represent you? He's going with you, after all. Couldn't he stand in your stead?"

"And how would that look to the high priest's household? Annas' steward is expecting to meet with *me*."

"It's so far, and my time is drawing near, and I don't trust Elazar." The desperation in my voice grated on my pride.

We were now within sight of Elazar's fine home. Zeb glanced at the latticed windows and finely carved door before hooking a work-worn hand behind his neck. "I'm not overly fond of the man, but he's being more than generous. He's my brother-in-law, and it's about time he acted as such." Zeb slipped his hand from his neck to my arm. "And you are still months away from delivering our babe."

"I wish it was days instead of months!" I groaned. The veins in my legs were swollen and knotted into gnarly, unsightly masses that throbbed when I walked.

"I'm sorry this pregnancy has been harder than the first." Zeb's voice softened. "But I'll be back before the babe arrives, and I cannot delay the trip until your father is back on his feet. That could take months, and Annas will have found another supplier by then."

My gaze slid to Elazar's door. "If you must go, must you involve *him*?" When I'd learned that Elazar had offered Zeb and Jonah the use of carts and animals, even inviting them to journey in his own caravan to the Holy City, an alarm had sounded in my head.

"You have a hard history with him, I know." Zeb shook his head. "And you're not the only one. He grew up with a prideful streak that is still present. He's always been a shrewd man, but at least now he is using what he has to aid the family."

"I suppose." I chewed my lower lip.

Zeb's hands moved to my upper arms and squeezed. "Allow yourself to see what I see—this trip going well, my father viewing me with respect, an established life in Capernaum with friends we love." His easy smile returned, inviting me into his vision for our future.

"Very well." I sighed, long and shaky. "But hurry back before I burst with this babe of yours." I lightened my tone while suppressing the darker thought. *Hurry back before something horrible happens.*

TWELVE

The pain of Zeb's departure was offset by the fact that Jonah brought his entire family to Bethsaida for a visit before leaving with Zeb.

"Your boys are so large!" I squealed and clasped Simon in my arms.

He grunted. "You saw me at Passover, Doda."

Doda—how I loved hearing the cherished title from the lips of my friend's sons. "Be that as it may, you have grown!" I captured Simon's lean face within my hands, angling it this way and that. "Yes, your face is older, and you are taller."

He grinned good-naturedly and allowed me to rain kisses down upon his cheeks. "And you've turned seven since I've seen you last—seven!" I drew back with an exaggerated gasp. "Practically a man!"

He snorted a laugh and stood a bit taller.

By my side, James scowled, casting dark glances at Simon, clearly displeased by the outburst of my affection directed toward someone other than himself.

They stayed a week within our home, long enough for James' jealousy to thaw and his young face to break open with eagerness upon sight of Andrew, whom he began tackling with great relish.

A week of sweet fellowship that distracted me from my husband traveling so far away and my father lying so weak and worn.

———— ◆ ————

On the evening before their departure, Keturah was quiet. Naysa was putting the boys to bed, but James had fallen asleep by the fire and we had yet to move him. His head was nestled in Keturah's lap, lips parted to release a trail of drool across his cheek. She ran thin fingers through his curls and stared at the dancing flames. Above us, the sky was shot through with stars.

"You seem . . . tired," I whispered, watching her profile.

She smiled but didn't turn to me. "I'm tired after chasing these boys all day."

"That's not what I meant."

Keturah's gaze drifted to James. "I lost a baby a year after we arrived in Capernaum."

The upsetting news slid so simply over her tongue. I blinked, disoriented. "Why didn't you tell me?" I moved closer until we were hip to hip, James' curls spilling from her lap to mine. "Why didn't you share this with me sooner?"

"Holding something close is easier than sharing it." Keturah's eyes shimmered, reflecting the flames. "Even when you know in here"—she tapped her chest—"that healing happens when sharing a burden, sometimes it feels too hard. And it's simpler to . . . hold on to it." She dropped her hand limp at her side.

I snatched up that hand, threaded her fingers through mine. "Thank you for sharing it with me now. I am so sorry you had to walk that path."

"Me too. We named him Gabriel—God is my strength." She sighed, hand trembling in mine. "He was born too soon and only lived for one day."

Swallowing hard, I held her hand, staring at our entwined fingers against my rounded belly.

"Would you help watch over my boys should anything happen to me?" Her question was abrupt, urgent.

"Keturah—" Dismay stopped my words.

"I ask because . . . since Gabriel's death, I've been thinking about my own. Oh, it's not as morbid as it sounds, truly." She smiled gently at my horrified look. "When you lose a child, death becomes so intimate that you can't help but think about it. I know we no longer live close . . ."

"That could change."

"I pray it does." Keturah squeezed my hand. "I can think of no one else I'd rather entrust my boys to than you. From a distance or close, you would find a way to help my Jonah, wouldn't you?"

"Friend—" My skin flashed cold even with the fire so close. I rested a palm on her cheek, seriousness burrowing into my bones. "Look at me. *Look* at me." When Keturah's eyes met mine, I could barely speak. "Whatever the future brings for you and for me, we will be there, one for the other."

Keturah nodded her assent.

"I promise you I will treat those boys like my own should anything happen to you. I will never abandon your family—never."

Keturah's smile reached her eyes and eased the sadness from them as she tilted her head against mine. "Zeb has always been right about you. You're formidable in all the best ways."

◆

Week stretched to week with no word from Zeb, leaving me restless. Adding to my distress was the care of my father, who now left his bed only when aided. Rather than growing stronger with rest, he was declining rapidly.

"How is my son?" Daily he asked after Zeb as if I had new information to share since the day before.

"He's not home yet. Jonathan thinks the delay means good news."

Pride crossed Abba's features. "He is a good man."

"Yes. I know."

"And you are a woman of excellence, like Ruth."

I gave him an indulgent smile.

"It's true." Abba's voice was thin. "You will be a good mother to your sons."

"Sons? I've been praying for a daughter."

"I know you have." Abba quieted, a settled look upon his face. "This one is also a boy. Two strong sons. Salome, you are blessed indeed. The mother of mighty men. Mother of thousands, of ten thousands . . ." He muttered a portion of the traditional wedding blessing.

I placed a hand on my stomach. "May Adonai make me worthy of such a gift."

"You doubt yourself. You always have, but you are a woman worth emulating. I could have learned more from you."

"Surely not, Abba!" Bowing my head over his bed, I studied the frayed edge of his blanket, ran my thumb along the veins standing starkly from his hand.

"You embrace what life brings with readiness. I could have learned more from your spirit," Abba whispered, voice fading.

I held his hand loose within my own even as my heart grasped at him.

◆

When Abba left the world, he did so in peace, his hand in mine, a smile upon his lips. I pressed a deep kiss to one eye and then the other, blessing him as he'd blessed me. Years of his blessing upon my unruly head. I folded his hands upon his chest, exhaled long and slow, and held my tears tightly in check.

He was a man of the earth, and to the earth we returned him. In a great reverse, we nestled him among the rock he'd once pulled free, next to Ima, whose song had brightened his days. Was she singing now in welcome?

Everyone looked at me with confusion, for I shed no tears.

I thought that Noy's death might have prepared James for this moment, but nothing could prepare him for the loss of someone so necessary to him. Nothing made sense anymore. I could see it in James' wide, fathomless eyes. His world had been gutted as thoroughly as a fish.

Night after night, he clung to me, too confused for sleep. Nothing I could say would make this right, and so I offered very little by way of words and simply held him while he cried and listened while he asked question after question.

A week after the burial, Zeb returned. I left Bethsaida to meet him along the road, each ponderous step painful, one hand to my aching back. I stopped when he came within sight and stood still, allowing him to come to me where I stood blocking his way. When he was close enough for me to see his features, the control I had been holding on to loosened. Sinking onto my knees in the dusty road, I wept until my eyes swelled shut and my cheeks flushed with heat. Sorrow mixed with anger.

Zeb was by my side, pulling me up and into his arms, but I shoved at him and spat out hard and horrible words through gritted teeth. "My father is dead, and you were not here. I was left to comfort James alone. My father loved you like a son, like you were his own flesh! He was kinder to you than your own father, and you left while he was ill. You were there to bury Noy but not my own father!"

Zeb's mouth fell open, face gray and stricken.

I left before he could say a word.

❖

It'd been years since I'd experienced the urge to flee, years since my world closed in on itself and robbed me of breath. This time, the pressure was unbearable, as my lungs were already constricted from pregnancy and my body was too weak to run into the fields. Instead, I sat alone in my room, leaving James to Naysa's care while I begged Adonai for air.

At night, I held James close, neither one of us able to sleep without the presence of the other. Even as I held my son, I longed for Abba's arms. He'd spread them wide, and I'd burrow into them like I was a girl of nine. He'd capture me against his beating heart and call me Zohar. How could I flourish in my place as wife and mother without the man who had always believed in me so ardently?

"You've been cut from the mother rock and are searching for your new place." As a girl, I'd been jarred loose by Ima's death, and here it was again—another shuddering apart, another desperate hunt.

———— ✦ ————

Zeb's trip had been both successful and disastrous. The meeting with Hiram, Annas' steward, had gone well. He was happy with the quality and had begun negotiating a standing contract. Upon seeing the favorable turn of events, Elazar had drawn Zeb aside and requested a partnership in his new venture. When Zeb indicated that he would need to discuss it with Jonah, Elazar had grown furious, insisting that Jonah was unnecessary and that Zeb should cut him out. Zeb had not complied, and Elazar had responded by charging a fee for the use of his goods. The fee was beyond the profit margin Zeb had brought in, meaning he returned home in debt.

"He is charging no interest and therefore breaking no law, and yet the spirit behind this is shameful. We entered this venture in goodwill, not expecting to be charged a fee." Zeb's hands shook. "I knew him to be shrewd, but not this, not heartless. Will we even see Deborah after this? With her husband treating her family in such a shameful way?"

"I don't understand why Elazar wanted to cut Jonah out. Jonah is a good man. Did you ask for his reasoning?" Jonathan pushed.

"I did, but he gave none. I imagine that he didn't want to split profits three ways."

"It's unfortunate that he put you in such a situation, but when he did, you should have chosen family over friend." Jonathan's voice darkened.

Zeb shook his head. "I disagree. I'd already given my word to Jonah. Elazar is the one in the wrong. After this next delivery, I will pay him the remainder of the fee and then we will never use his services again."

"There are costs to growing a business. We can't afford to funnel our profit to Elazar," Jonathan thundered. "You should not have hesitated when he wanted in on the business."

"What is done is done," Zeb stated firmly. "I suggest that *you* talk to your son-in-law, for he will not reason with me!"

On and on they argued, setting everyone's teeth on edge.

My distrust of Elazar had proven to be founded, and that knowledge mixed with the anger and hurt, hardening into a rock of bitterness within me.

Our marriage had endured anger and disappointment before, but this latest rift was new and unchartered. Both of us sensed it. With tears, Zeb tried to hold me, to apologize, but I couldn't receive it. He'd loved my father. I understood this and observed it anew in the way he wept when he thought no one was looking. His grief should have softened my heart. When it didn't, I was left even more confused.

As I continued to rebuff Zeb's efforts to mend the rift, he grew increasingly sullen and withdrawn, which in turn fueled my own anger, until we were caught in a spiral neither one of us could control.

Thirteen

SPRING 11 AD

"It's too soon!" I moaned as Naysa propped me upright on the bed. "We have another month to go at least!" I clutched at her hand as if she had the power to stop the convulsions in my body. Even as my mind and mouth protested, my body knew that yes, this was happening *now*, whether I wanted it to or not.

My panicked mind skittered to Keturah. *"He was born too soon and only lived for one day."*

"Adonai, please!" I gasped the words, too frightened to say more.

"Babes have their own will, even in the womb." Naysa clucked. "And this one wants to meet you early."

Unlike James' agonizing birth, everything moved swiftly this time as my body remembered what to do and went about it with terrifying speed. Hadara had scarcely arrived before I began to push. As the sun rose and the men returned from the lake, I birthed him—a small, wriggling boy who was barely half the size his brother had been at birth.

"Another son!" Naysa declared as she cleaned him.

Not a girl, but a boy . . . the boy Abba knew I would have. I turned my face to the wall.

"Do not fear, Salome. He is small, but from his cry, I can tell his lungs are mighty. Praise Adonai—he is healthy." Naysa nudged my shoulder, urging me to face her as she nestled the babe in my arms and pressed his searching mouth to my breast.

He was scrawny and bald, his wail thin and grating. When I'd first nursed James, he'd felt like an extension of my own body. But this? This boy felt utterly separate from me, as if someone had plucked him from the sky, thrust him into my arms, and said, "Here. Here he is to love."

But I did not recognize him. I did not know him.

"Love is an unlimited resource." Abba's words were whispers pushing forward through the darkness. I stared at this boy and waited—waited for the love to come—but all I found was my own father's face. All I felt was his absence. All I could think was how this boy would never know him.

"Two strong sons. Salome, you are blessed indeed." Hadara pronounced the very words that had left Abba's lips.

I turned my face back to the wall and wept.

◆

Love for James had poured from me like an underground spring, gushing up with overwhelming abundance. Had I used it all up? Was there nothing left for this, my second son? How could I give what this babe needed when I was so hollow and hungry myself?

When I gave him to Zeb, that hungry hole widened as he held the boy with reverence. He brought him to the window, tilted him toward the light, and studied him with an urgency that twined my soul into a knot. When he looked at me, there was love in his face reaching out to bridge the gap, an expression that said, *I'm sorry. Come back to me.*

I wanted to return but couldn't.

"*You* name him," I whispered one night, lying on my side as I tried to get the babe to suckle. He was so small, and his latch was weak.

Zeb covered the babe's head with a large hand, face thoughtful. I noted pain before he hid it. "John," he declared.

"After your father?" My voice lifted in surprise. "But—"

"God is gracious." Zeb stated the name's meaning. "Even when man is not, we serve a God who is gracious toward us. His name is John." His eyes broke from mine as he left the room.

◆

As difficult as this pregnancy had been, the recovery was much easier. My swollen legs returned to normal size, veins growing less painful. I lost the additional weight quickly this time—perhaps too quickly, for my milk supply diminished until Naysa was harassing me to eat every moment of every day. Even as I worked to increase my milk and my body moved toward a new normalcy, my spirit continued to resist the change to our family, lagging far behind the rest of me.

Everything about John was difficult. I was walking through deep sludge, pulling on each foot, straining to make even the smallest progress.

It shouldn't be this hard. What is happening?

Life as Zeb's wife and James' mother had kept doubt at bay, but now it presented itself in new ways, slithering into every unguarded moment.

No suitable mother struggles in such a way. Do you not love your child? What kind of woman wrestles with loving her own child?

"No," I gasped my resistance, hands trembling as I held John close. "I love him. I *do*." Desperately I called forth the memory of Abba's knuckle beneath my chin, tilting my face, my thoughts, my emotions up, up, up to my Maker.

You believed that James was a sign of God's favor, but perhaps this is a sign that you never should have been a mother.

"No." I wept, swiping tears from my golden eyes. "My Maker knows me, and He would never have given these boys to me if it was a mistake. He will make me a good mother to them. He *will*."

"Motherhood can be a joy, although some days it can feel like a burden." Had *this* been what Deborah meant by a burden?

I began observing Deborah as a drowning man might observe a boat upon the waves. She'd always seen me in a way no one else had. If I brought this to her, what would she say?

Since Elazar's shameful treatment of our family, we rarely saw Deborah and her girls, so one morning, when I exited my room and found her in our own courtyard, I startled and stopped short, gazing upon her with both longing and fear.

"Deborah has come to help with the babe," Naysa explained as she lifted a squirming John into Deborah's waiting arms. "Isn't that nice, Salome?"

The strain between the families was hard on Naysa. She needed this, her daughter back under her roof.

"I heard how fussy he's been, barely sleeping." Deborah began bouncing John. "My eldest was like that—always crying."

"I'm afraid there might be something wrong with me," I blurted.

Both women stopped what they were doing to stare open-mouthed at me. "What do you mean?" Naysa asked.

You cannot state this out loud. They will not understand, and they will view you with disdain. Fear linked arms with doubt. But I was too weary from fighting this battle alone and too desperate to hold back.

"I'm worried that perhaps . . . I don't love John the way I should."

"What are you saying? Of course you love him." Naysa's eyes jerked to mine, confusion embedded in their depths, but Deborah stilled, alert as a gazelle within sight of a hunter.

"I *do* love him, I just . . . I don't know what's wrong with me!" My shoulders slumped. I did not know what else to say, how to put this feeling into words. With James, I had longed for physical contact, had delighted in his skin against mine, but with John, I was happy when someone else took him—preferred it that way. In my heart I knew I loved him, but the feelings refused to make themselves known to me, hiding behind a darkness I couldn't dispel.

"Salome." Naysa drew close and placed a gentle hand to my cheek. "The transition from one babe to two is always difficult, but it will pass. Now that you have more than one child, you must be sure not to choose favorites."

"I'm not choosing favorites." My emotions didn't feel like a choice of any kind.

"You don't have to look past our own nation's history to see that when parents choose favorites, disaster results," Naysa continued. "Look at Jacob and Esau or Joseph and his brothers."

"I'm not choosing favorites," I repeated miserably. "Deborah, you can understand, can't you?"

Deborah was staring at John. He squirmed in her arms while she remained impassive.

"Deborah, please—"

Her eyes drifted to mine, taking detours along the way. When they finally landed upon me, I saw it—an aching, gaping awareness.

"You *do* know what it feels like. With Abigail, with—"

"Enough!" Naysa threw up her hands, voice growing shrill. "Are you rebuking your sister-in-law? She who is more experienced in motherhood than you?"

"No, I—"

"You are trying to say that we are alike," Deborah answered. At her mother's outburst, the raw look in her eye had hardened, giving me nothing but the reflection of my own desperation. "But we are nothing alike, Salome. Nothing."

She deposited John into my arms, the hard look deepening. "Ima is right. I am more experienced than you. Stop comparing your love for one child with your love for the other. Resist the urge to do so, and your sons will thank you later." She left with brusque steps.

"No, no . . ." Naysa muttered, hand reaching to her departing daughter. As the front door closed with a definitive bang, John began wailing in loud, uncontrollable gusts. It was how he spent most nights—crying ceaselessly until I began weeping right along with him.

"What did you do?" Naysa groaned. "She came in goodwill, and you accused her! She won't step foot in this home again." She twisted away, rushing from the courtyard and leaving me alone with an incensed John.

———— ✦ ————

Deborah would be of no help, that much was clear. Any warm feeling I'd harbored over the years toward my sister-in-law now cooled, her response and Naysa's drawing me further inside myself. If they didn't—or wouldn't—understand, they who had birthed multiple babes of their own, then how would others? How would Zeb?

I was hungry for my husband, needed him in a new and frightening way, and yet even as I longed for him, I shrank back, unwilling to return to him in my current state.

In those dark days, Zeb was a bright light, a constant fount of love for our children. Rather than becoming unmoored, Zeb had anchored himself in his role as father. My hurting heart noted it, the bitterness toward him melting.

While he slept in the mornings, I tried to keep the children quiet, but inevitably John would shriek and wake him. Instead of leaving the wailing babe to me, Zeb would exit our room, bleary-eyed, searching for his distraught son, tucking him tightly into the crook of his arm, taking him back into the room with whispers of assurance. John's cries grated on my ears but seemed to have the opposite effect on Zeb. Sensing his father's adoration, John would quiet at the sound of his voice, eyes hunting for his face and stilling when he found it.

In the evenings, Zeb began instructing James on how to fish, spending long hours with him along the shore, teaching him the names and functions of various nets and taking frequent breaks to splash and play. Every night, he put James to bed before leaving for the lake and in the morning was there to welcome his son into a new day. He appeared to be taking his frustration with his own father and letting it turn him into something stronger, sturdier. Lustrous.

Not long after my disastrous encounter with Deborah, Naysa found me in the outer courtyard making bread, James playing by my side while John slept in a nearby basket. She bent over John, one finger dancing along the curve of his brow.

"Savta, look!" James held up a fist. A thin roll of dough sagged from his palm.

Naysa approached James with a broad smile. "What do you have there, my boy?"

"Ima let me play with the dough, and I made a snake." James thrust his hand toward his grandmother. The dough jiggled in the air.

"Oh!" Naysa jerked back and put a hand to her mouth. "Don't let it bite me!"

James shouted a laugh and plopped the dough onto the ground. "Look, I'm only playing. It isn't real." With pinched fingers, he guided the dough snake along the ground, slithering it up Naysa's ankle and down again.

"What a relief," Naysa sighed. "I'm frightened of snakes."

"I would protect you, Savta." James quirked his lips into a smile that appeared much older than his five years. "I wouldn't let anything hurt you."

"I know. I'm fortunate indeed to have such a courageous grandson. Now, do me a favor and go gather sticks for the fire."

James beamed, shoulders straightening as he leapt to his feet. "Yes, Savta!"

"He's so loyal and protective." I watched as James raced out of the courtyard but not before stopping to smack a kiss upon his little brother's forehead. John startled, thin arms shooting into the air before settling back to sleep. "I do believe James would jump in front of a viper for someone he loved."

"Not unlike his mother."

My eyes sought Naysa's, and the affection I found there made me lower my gaze to the dough.

"Salome, I'm sorry."

I began separating the dough into even lumps, flattening each one in preparation for the oven.

"I let pain and worry over Deborah blind me. I was harsh with you and unkind."

Tears flooded my eyes, and my nose grew stuffy with the effort of suppressing them. I sniffed and wiped my face, leaving specks of dough behind. "It's okay."

"No, it's not." Naysa crouched by my side. "Salome, I may not understand what you're going through, but I don't have to understand in order to love you."

With a low cry, I dropped the dough and covered my face with sticky hands.

"I haven't experienced what you described, but I *have* struggled in other ways. I once came to your mother the way you came to me, hurting so deeply I didn't know what to say. I was . . . struggling to love my husband. There is good in my Jonathan, but he is a hard man to live with. I don't have to tell *you* this." Naysa broke the tension with a shaky laugh. "It was hard to admit to someone else. You can imagine my shame."

I bit my lip at the image of a young, distraught Naysa.

"As I tried to explain, I could see that Miriam didn't understand what I was going through. But this one thing she did know—that I hurt inside." Naysa's voice was thick. "Miriam didn't condemn me for my pain. Rather, she hurt simply because I did."

I drew in a shuddering breath and lifted my face.

"Salome, this is what I promise you." With calloused fingers, Naysa picked small clumps of dough from my face, gathering them into a small ball within her hand, gaze tracing my features. "I hurt because you do. And when you heal—because you *will* heal—I will be there to rejoice."

Not long after John's birth, we received a gift that lifted the family's spirits. Having heard of Elazar's unscrupulous dealings, Kadmiel sent funds to cover the entirety of Elazar's fee. In his letter, he praised Zeb's foresight in desiring to move the family to Capernaum and emphasized how impressed Hiram was with Zeb.

"You see how our son has good business sense," Naysa crowed, cupping Zeb's narrow face within her hands. "Making use of family connections and impressing the high priest's steward. Kadmiel sees the potential in our Zebedee. He would not gift us such funds if he did not."

Rather than joining his wife in praise of their son, Jonathan refused to look at Zeb as he grunted, "Swindled by one son-in-law and saved by the other. We are fortunate to have Kadmiel in the family. Now we can capitalize on this opportunity because Kadmiel not only paid our debt but also gave additional funds. We can purchase the livestock and wagons necessary for transporting the goods ourselves."

Zeb had stopped looking for Jonathan's praise a long time ago, and yet I noted how stiffly he held himself after Jonathan's statement. My aching heart moved my hand to his, where I wrapped his long fingers within my own and squeezed. He didn't turn but slowly squeezed my hand back.

With the debt settled, the account with the high priest secured, and Zeb's idea praised from Kadmiel's lips, Jonathan began preparing the family to move.

Capernaum—the bustling village at the heart of the fishing trade. No one moved goods through Galilee without going through Capernaum, which was why Herod had planted his presence there. His troops were composed of mainly Gentile mercenaries, Gallic and Thracian soldiers who held no love for our people, executing the will of Herod with impassive efficiency. And now it was to be my home.

Unease over the move was soothed by the thought that Keturah was waiting for me on the other side. Abba had claimed that place pulled upon a man, but increasingly I found that it was people who exerted the strongest pull. I'd lived my entire life in Bethsaida, but it was not the village itself that called to me, nor the black rocks of the Golan Heights. It was Abba, the humble man who'd lived and loved, worked and died upon this land that tethered me to this place. And now it would be Keturah binding me to the new one.

Life was moving in the direction Zeb had always longed to go, and yet I sensed a new despondency in him and knew myself to be its source. We had never gone so long with untended hurt between us, and it was wearing upon us both.

He began looking at me searchingly, but fear turned my face away. I didn't want him to see how I suffered inside, but perhaps he sensed it. In the listless way I held John, in my sluggish steps and pinched face, did he sense it?

I tried to put on a happy face for Zeb, but also for James, who didn't understand why the new addition to the family wouldn't stop crying.

"Is he sad, Ima?" James wondered, brows gathered into a confused cluster on his brow as he watched his brother fuss.

"No, my love."

"But you're sad," James observed—not a question but a statement.

I gathered him into my arms and buried my face into his curls, unable to respond without tears.

Soon after Kadmiel's gift, I awoke to excited voices in the courtyard. John had finally slept for several hours in a row, and I was disoriented. For a long, confused moment, I thought I was in Abba's workshop. Stumbling from my room, I half expected to see Noy tearing about the courtyard. Instead, as though stepping from my thoughts into the light, there was Keturah. Her face broke open into a generous smile at the sight of me.

I stood rooted to the earth, one hand to my head, the other reaching, reaching.

She clasped me before I fell. With strong arms she caught and held me as I cried her name.

Fourteen

For long hours Keturah simply listened while I talked in a long stream of confused words. At first, I tried holding it back. Who was I to entertain such emotions when she had lost a child? Here I was with arms full and heart empty while she suffered the reverse. But she had come to listen and would not let me remain silent.

We walked along the shore, and when I finished, she stood still and held my hand. "There is no shame in being hurt, Salome." She looked across the lake to a distant mountain ridge. "I know what it's like to face darkness you cannot explain, to be frightened of your own mind."

She broke off, gaze flitting down to her dusty toes. "You begin to feel shaky, no longer able to rely upon the strengths you used to. There is a stripping that happens—like a tree that is felled and shaved of its bark, whittled down and down."

"Yes," I gasped.

"I felt much the same way when I lost Gabriel. So many people needed me, but I was too needy myself."

"What did you do?"

Keturah was silent for a long moment. "I took walks in the heat of the day." She broke off with a slight laugh. "Probably not the answer you were expecting, but there is something about forcing yourself into the light. There is a path in Capernaum that I often took, a footpath through the vineyards. I'd walk that path and pray this prayer."

Keturah closed her eyes, opened her lips, and released the words of King David. "I love You, Yahweh; You are my strength. Yahweh is my rock, my fortress, and my savior; my God is my rock, in whom I seek refuge; my shield, the power that saves me, and my place of safety. I called on Yahweh, who is worthy of praise, and He saved me from my enemies."

"You worshipped?"

"Worship is a powerful weapon."

I shook my head. "You are more righteous than I. Lately, I cannot utter a single prayer. I used to come out here to the lake and pray big prayers to Adonai. I used to feel Him, Keturah. Do you know what it is like to feel the living God with you?"

"Yes," Keturah whispered.

"I miss that feeling." My voice broke. "Does He still see me if I cannot even cry out to Him?"

"You think Adonai only listens when we are loud and bold?" Keturah bumped my shoulder and grinned. "What do you do when James is hurt, Salome? What do you do when he's so hurt, he can't reach for you?"

Her question startled me even as the answer came swiftly. "I run to him and pick him up. I hold him close and tend his wounds."

"And how does James respond when you do this?"

"He cries and clings to me."

Keturah nodded. "And what do you feel toward him in that moment?"

"Love," I murmured, turning my eyes to heaven. "Overwhelming love."

"So it is with me and my boys." Keturah squeezed my hand.

"The deepest moments of connection experienced in the deepest moments of need."

Warmth spilled over me even though the sun was hidden behind a blanket of clouds and the air from the lake was brisk. Still, inexplicable warmth kissed my skin.

"Don't doubt Adonai's presence, Salome. He hears the prayers stuck inside us too."

Love for my friend relieved the ache. "Thank you for giving me kindness instead of condemnation. I've been . . . scared to let anyone see inside me."

"Even Zeb?" Keturah prodded.

"Especially Zeb. There is a barrier between us. He has so much love for our children, and I feel like a spectator on the other side of the wall."

"I think he's convinced that you don't want comfort from him."

I considered this. "At first, I didn't."

"He's the one who sent for me. That man loves you deeply. He's a lot like my Jonah, though—a little lost when it comes to a woman's heart."

"And so he sent you to navigate my heart for him, rather than speak to me himself?" I raised a questioning brow, lips twitching into the beginnings of a smile.

Keturah grinned. "Something like that. It wouldn't be the first time he remained stubbornly silent, though, would it?" She knew the story well, how I had all but insisted Zeb betroth me to himself.

"He's prone to silence, but I can't blame him when I often do enough talking for the both of us," I admitted.

Keturah laughed, a trilling, sweet tone that loosened the mirth in my own chest, causing it to bubble up and out. Together we turned toward home, arms linked.

Darkness made the light more precious. Walking the shoreline with a friend, laughter upon our lips—this was a gift directly from the hand of Adonai, light at the exact moment it was needed.

◆

The night after Keturah left, I awoke so abruptly that my heart galloped like a stallion. I lay on my bed, tense and alert. There was no cry from John, so what had awoken me? A gasp from the corner alerted me to another's presence. Zeb was crouched on the floor near John, who lay swaddled and content while his father wept. With one hand covering his face and the other resting upon our son, my husband wept.

Compassion swelled within me until my body shook with it. *Say something. Reach out to him. Take him into your arms.*

John chose that moment, however, to stir, brows scrunching as his mouth suckled and frustration mounted in his tiny body. Zeb quieted as he noted John's restlessness. He offered the babe a knuckle and as the boy began to gum it, Zeb prayed a blessing over his son. When Zeb began praying for *me*, I stifled a cry.

I'd never heard him like this—so broken and yet fervent and expectant, as if Adonai were in the room while he presented his requests to Him.

John settled beneath his father's prayer, and as Zeb rose and shifted toward me, I kept my eyes closed, too overwhelmed to move.

His kiss lingered on my brow. There was dampness on his chin—the remnants of his tears. When he stood, my heart went up with him, securely in his hand.

◆

The next morning, he found me in the corner of the courtyard with James underfoot as I sat at the loom. With practiced fingers, I worked the shuttle through the warp, weaving a mantle for the winter months. He stopped in front of the loom and peered over the top.

This time I did not look away from his gaze or skitter from his presence. My whole being stilled, lips parting as I held his eyes with my own.

"I've told you that I'm sorry," he stated.

I started to speak the forgiveness that was ripe and ready on my tongue, but Zeb lifted a hand to stop me.

"But I haven't told you what I'm sorry *for*. I was so focused on an opportunity I didn't want to lose that I dismissed your concerns over your father. He was an excellent man. He was . . . an abba to me. I should have been here to bury him. Should have—"

"Zeb, I—" I could hardly say more for the pressure in my throat that pinched off my words. I'd been gifted a husband who cared for me the way my abba had cared for my ima, a man who valued my heart so much that the current strain was destroying him. "Zebedee—"

The wall between us was cracking, and I was ready to do whatever I could to demolish it. "I was harsh with my words. You're not the only one who is sorry, Zeb."

In my own hurt, I'd wounded him. I'd allowed my own fear to keep me away from him rather than working through that fear *with* him. Lifting a hand, I invited him close. He came, moving swiftly around the loom, stooping to take my hand within his own.

"We will be leaving this place, and I want you to have something to remember it by." Slowly he turned my hand over, trailing a thumb across its center before nestling a small, supple leather pouch in my palm. "A gift for you."

I loosened the drawstrings and carefully shook the contents free. Two black basalt stones fell into my palm. Typically a porous stone, these had been worn smooth by the water until they shone. I glanced up to find Zeb watching me.

"To remember your father," he whispered. "And to celebrate our sons."

"I love You, Yahweh; You are my strength."

The midday sun blazed across the lake. Most of Bethsaida's fishermen were still abed and so the shore was quiet. I'd begun forcing myself out into the sun every day, baring my face to its steady beams as I prayed the words of David.

"Yahweh is my rock, my fortress, and my savior; my God is my rock, in whom I seek refuge."

I turned the words into a song, testing them on my tongue. My voice—it was not as beautiful as my mother's had been. Very few were. I tried again.

"I called on Yahweh, who is worthy of praise, and He saved me from my enemies."

John fidgeted at my breast, discontentment radiating from him as I neared my rock. Planting my feet upon its surface, I cast my gaze up to Adonai as I bounced my son.

"Fear is an enemy. Worry is an enemy."

John gurgled and shifted. I bounced him harder.

"Save me from my enemies!" My cry startled John into a prolonged wail.

"Shush, shush. I'm sorry, love." Pulling John from the sling, I pressed his scrunched face into my neck and rubbed his back with the long, firm strokes I knew he liked.

"Look, look at the waves like a blanket of blue. Look at the waves you will ride upon." My words bounced in time with my arms.

Before us, the sun danced its beams across the undulating folds of the lake. Far in the distance, I could barely make out a mountain range in the Decapolis. To the west was the bustling town of Magadan, with all its resources. Behind us was Bethsaida, separated from her neighbors, small and sleepy—unimportant.

John continued to fuss, his warbling cries piercing the hazy quiet of the lake. Everything was calm now, lazy under the blazing sun, but I had seen storms develop in a heartbeat, the strongest of which the fishermen called *sharkia*. Winds from the east would develop quickly, descending from the mountains to whip the lake into an uproar. The storms often arrived in late afternoon, the sky darkening as everyone lashed their boats to the shore and braced themselves for the upheaval. If one were caught on the lake during such an event, death was a real possibility.

I stared at the winking lake. She held life and death within her. Another gurgle rose from John.

"You're as troubled as a sharkia today," I muttered.

John whimpered, the sound throbbing with pain and snapping me sharply into focus. "What's wrong? I just fed you. You should be content." I sat and spread him out upon my lap, attention lingering over the way he curled up his legs and arched his back, his pinched face and wails . . .

"You're uncomfortable. You're hurting, aren't you?"

Gently, I pressed upon his stomach. It was tighter than a drum. I moved his legs, stretching them out to their full length and then back up, again and again. More massages to his belly, more movement of his legs until he released air from both ends at a volume that would put grown men to shame.

The relief that flooded his tiny face undid me.

"John," I gasped, fingers exploring his body. "Does it hurt anywhere else?"

He sighed deeply and blinked at me, contentment relaxing his limbs. With a low cry, I brought him to my face, covering him with a thousand small kisses.

Love was unlimited—like the sun behind dark and roiling

clouds. I held my son and wept, both of us settling into each other, flesh against flesh.

This, then, was how it would be. The darkness, lingering and present, wouldn't be dispelled all in one moment, but rather in a slow encroachment of light.

I would focus upon each and every beam.

◆

The early morning mist hung low, a field of white hovering above the face of the water, obscuring the returning boats. I stood knee-deep in the lake with John snug against my breast and shivered in the nippy air, nose growing pink and numb, bare toes tingling against the slick rock bed. A fish nibbled my flesh before flitting away. Off in the distance, the melodic call of sparrows threaded the sky.

Zeb's boat bobbed against the waves, timber creaking like an old man's bones. My heart stilled at the plop of oar entering water, the sloppy kiss of the waves against the hull as his boat approached.

A splash indicated the moment my husband entered the water to heave the boat ashore. I turned toward the sound as he emerged through the white, head lowered, hard muscles straining as he pulled.

"Zeb."

His head whipped up, eyes widening with surprise, then deepening with pleasure. He released the boat and splashed to me, slowing as he neared.

Bumps spread across my skin, racing up my legs and along my arms, raising fine hair in their wake and jerking me in a sharp shudder.

His hands found me, palms warm on my arms. I gazed into his eyes framed with long lashes, watched his lips tremble into a smile.

"I love you, Zebedee." The words fell off numb lips, landing squarely between us. Zeb closed his eyes, tightened his hold on me.

"I love you." I said the words again, louder, sturdier, but with a break right at the end.

He'd been right. I was fire and stone, ice and heat. When I loved, it was with my whole being in a blaze. But he had shown me the tender underside of love—the part that was quiet and vulnerable, patient and kind.

When Zeb opened his eyes, they were even brighter than my own. He pulled me close, nearly crushing John between us. I shifted the babe, angling into Zeb, resting my head upon his shoulder, pressing up against his familiar, lanky frame.

He dipped his head to capture my lips with his own. His kiss was firm, but I pulled back, softened it into something slow and savoring. He smiled against my lips as he matched my pace, gentle and focused. John let out a squeaky sigh as light streaked the sky. James would awaken soon and come tearing down to the lake to find us.

Zeb's arms tightened about my waist. I placed a palm to his chest above the steady thump of his heart, my own swelling with resolve.

Everything within and without was shaky, but this was firm— the love I held for this man, for these boys—gifts from the hand of Adonai.

Help me. The prayer lifted with the morning mist. *Help me.*

Yes, with Adonai's aid I would rise like a lioness for the ones I loved the most.

I am at rest in God alone;
my salvation comes from him.
He alone is my rock and my salvation, my
stronghold; I will never be shaken.

Psalm 62:1–2 CSB

PART
TWO

PART

TWO

Fifteen

Autumn 27 AD
Capernaum, Israel
Sixteen Years Later

Sounds of celebration swelled into the crisp night, but within my courtyard, everyone was hushed. By my side, Abigail trembled. I took her smooth hand within my own.

The noise drew closer—a clatter of tambourines accompanied by laughter and the rise of masculine voices, raucous with happiness.

"Oh," Abigail breathed, fingers clutching, feet shifting, eyes darting from me to the door and back again.

"Are you thinking of fleeing, dear one?" I murmured. "And where would you go that he would not follow?"

Abigail's cheeks flushed.

"You would welcome his pursuit. Don't deny it." I chuckled, drawing her close. "I was also nervous. I understand. When you are fearful, fix your attention upon him and let everything else fade away."

Abigail nodded and turned her attention back to the door, teeth catching her bottom lip. I peered at her profile through the gauzy veil—this niece who was more than that to me, this woman who was the daughter I'd longed for but never had.

"They'll be here any moment." Deborah clucked and strode over to Abigail, plucking at the veil, running fingers along the bracelets jangling at her daughter's wrist. I stepped back to make room for her picking and prodding, body tensing as I noted Deborah's sharp glances in my direction.

A loud thump sounded upon the door. They were right outside now. Beams from their lamps streaked into the sky. The door groaned open, spilling light and laughter into the courtyard.

James entered first, broad shoulders filling the entrance. Light from the lamps threw shadow onto his face, making his eyes gleam even more than usual. He grinned, lips spreading even wider than his arms as he approached us. "Are you ready?"

Abigail accepted her cousin's arm, and then she was airborne, swooped up onto a canopied chair. She squealed and clung to the sides, wobbling and shifting like a boat upon the waves, borne from the courtyard amid loud whoops, carried away on the shoulders of family and friends.

I became lost within the crowd that danced throughout the streets with lamps lifted high. All of us a current, swift and sure, bearing this beautiful bride to her groom.

◆

For once, he was quiet, eyes wide and serious. At the dumb-founded look on his face, all nervousness seemed to flee from Abigail. She beamed, rocking onto her toes and down again, one brow quirking upward in a teasing look that said, *I caught you. You're mine now.*

And like a fish tangled in a net, Simon was helpless.

"You're pleased with yourself." Behind me Zeb laughed, looping an arm about my middle. "I've never seen such self-satisfaction on your face."

"Of course I'm pleased."

With a swift pull, Zeb turned me into his arms. "And not humble enough to hide it."

I gave him a hearty smack upon the chest. The years had gathered flesh about my hips, but Zeb was as slim as ever. He boasted thinning hair at the crown of his head, a hint of gray at the temple, and extra lines around his eyes and mouth from years of smiling. Tucking me into a snug embrace, he dipped his head to peck my cheek.

"And why shouldn't I be pleased?" I smirked. "When it was I who suggested this match?"

"May Adonai use this union to heal old wounds," Zeb murmured.

Deborah stood across the courtyard, arms tightly clasping herself. As the mother of the bride, she should have been surrounded by friends, but she stood alone with a veiled expression as she observed Abigail's joy.

"Will you go to her?" Zeb urged.

I shook my head. "She won't want my company, not right now."

"You still think she's jealous of your relationship with Abigail?"

"You've had a year to observe it for yourself. She resents me, Zeb. You know this. Any respect she held for me has long been outweighed by resentment."

"Are you sure the resentment is only on her side?"

I averted my face from my astute husband. After John's birth, a door had slammed shut between Deborah and me, and it had remained that way all throughout the years, time weathering past grievances into an unmovable barrier between us.

"I'm simply grateful that she agreed to this union," I finally stated.

"If Elazar was still with us, then this marriage would certainly never have happened," Zeb replied. "Let's hope that Deborah's willingness indicates a softened heart."

As the nearest male relative, Zeb had opened our home to Deborah upon the death of Elazar a year ago. Her two older girls were married and away, but the unmarried Abigail had joined her mother beneath our roof. For the sake of Abigail, whom we both loved, Deborah and I had fallen into civility, but daily I sensed how much she hated being dependent on our family.

"I'm nearly more surprised by Jonah's approval of this union than Deborah's." Zeb nodded toward his old friend and business partner. "He holds on to past grievances, and even though he has nothing against Abigail, I anticipated his refusal simply because she's Elazar's daughter."

"Simon and Abigail love each other." My face split into a smile I couldn't contain. "I saw it before the rest of you. I'm thankful Jonah could see it too."

"Perhaps it's time for you to find our own boys suitable wives."

"In good time. You know they don't like my meddling."

"Most men don't appreciate meddling mothers."

I raised a brow. "But aren't you glad your own mother meddled with us?"

Zeb pressed a wordless kiss into my palm.

A loud laugh drew our attention to where John stood with Andrew. My youngest son was often loud. From youth he had asserted himself over his brother, seeking to dominate in any way possible, and a beleaguered James had endured his antics. Catching Zeb's eye, John gave a mighty wave, urging his father to join him, and with a final peck to my cheek, Zeb did.

Precious little soothed me more than observing John with his father.

Earlier I'd attempted levity over the idea of brides for our boys, but the truth was, I worried. Both sons were consumed by their various pursuits, with little thought to taking wives. My arms ached to hold babes again. For years after John, Zeb and I had waited, until finally the truth became too evident to deny. There would be no more children after our beautiful boys.

I longed to welcome daughters-in-law into our home and fill its walls with the squeals of children. *"Salome, you are blessed indeed. The mother of mighty men."* Abba's words, ripe with joy, still sounded in my head. *"Mother of thousands, of ten thousands."* We had quite a ways to go before reaching Abba's vision of my future.

Hardly a day went by when I didn't think of Abba. He was, after all, so evident in his namesake. James' broad and sloped shoulders, the shape of his eyes, and even the tenor of his laugh all reminded me of the quiet man buried in Bethsaida. James may have inherited my father's features, but he shared Zeb's business mind and passion for fishing—not simply a profession but a calling, not only a livelihood but a joy.

Another laugh, distinct and loud, pulled my attention back to John. A whole head shorter than his brother and with Zeb's wiry build, narrow face, and enormous smile, John was undeniably his father's son. He had, however, inherited my own father's philosophical bent—passionate for truth and eager for the Messiah to come.

He was so earnest with Andrew, both of them drawing Zeb into deeper conversation, hands dancing with their words. They were probably discussing the new teacher they'd discovered, the one in Judea who was gaining momentum.

"Doda!" I was tackled from behind, held and hugged by two strong arms, lifted from the earth with the air squeezed from my body.

"Simon," I croaked as he planted me back onto the ground and faced me with a grin.

"You've always been Doda to me, but now you are in truth." He laughed.

"Let me tell you a secret." I leaned in close, still catching my breath. "That's why I wanted this match. To finally claim you as nephew." I pinched a scruffy cheek. "Selfish of me, I know."

Simon winked. "I'm blessed to benefit from your self-centeredness."

"Are you prepared to expand your household in more ways than one?" I nodded to Deborah. "A wife *and* a mother-in-law under your roof."

"And now I see your other motive." Simon dipped his chin and pursed his lips. "Really, Doda, do you have to be so obvious?"

I threw my head back with a laugh so large it put John's to shame. "It hasn't been bad living with Deborah this past year." I kept my words light, masking the truth.

"She finds me too loud and impetuous." Simon rubbed a hand behind his neck.

"And how does Abigail find you?"

His averted gaze and soft smile said everything.

"Something you need to know about your new mother-in-law . . ." I leaned in close again. "Love is a practical matter to her and shown in practical ways. She is not given to large emotion or tender words." I left unspoken how Deborah could nurse a grudge longer than anyone I knew.

Nearby, Abigail was speaking with a friend, but her gaze never parted from Simon. "Truthfully, this used to bother me, especially since Abigail thrives on affectionate demonstrations of love."

"I will give her plenty of that! Don't worry."

I chuckled. "No one doubts it."

"Perhaps this is why Abigail is so affectionate herself." Simon grew contemplative as he observed his bride. "Praise is always on her lips. The love in her is evident. She is . . . so much better than me."

"Go to her." I squeezed his arm. "Stop talking to your old doda and go be with your wife."

"You're hardly old." Simon captured me with another embrace.

Before he pulled back, I whispered the words I'd been holding on to all evening, the words wrapped in tears in the hidden corner of my heart. "She would be so proud, Simon. So very proud."

He stilled, body tensing in my arms, before his broad shoulders relaxed, words leaving on an exhale. "I know. Six years, and I still carry her with me wherever I go."

My thoughts drifted to my side where the pouch hugged my hip, two black stones nestled within. I knew what it was to carry love and grief as constant companions.

"You bear her memory well." I placed a hand over Simon's heart. He covered it with one of his own.

◆

Capernaum eased along the banks of Lake Gennesaret in a sprawling half circle with harbor walls knifing into the blue. Our home sat next to Jonah's, facing the lake. The years had been full, laced through with goodness and sorrow. Our standing account with Annas had multiplied into more accounts with other priestly families. Nine years ago, when Annas' son-in-law, Caiaphas, succeeded him as high priest, we gained an account with Caiaphas' household as well. With the increase in demand, Zeb had hired help, his vision for the future proving true—an established life with friends we loved.

"He was radiant, Keturah." I spoke the words aloud as I followed her path—the small one through the vineyard, the one I'd come to regularly for six years—ever since she'd gone to be with Gabriel.

"Your boy was radiant and full of love. How I wish—" I broke off, the old ache in my chest threatening to squeeze the air from my body. *Not today.* I took one slow breath, then two, tethering myself to my surroundings until the tightness loosened.

It was not the time for grapes, and the barren vines pushed against my arms as I turned toward home, bearing the memory of Keturah as a warm cloak about the shoulders. She'd left so much light behind her. In Andrew's compassion, I saw her and was soothed. In Simon's exuberance, she lived bright and fierce. Keturah rested within both her sons like embedded jewels.

Later that night I couldn't sleep and so lingered in memory, traveling back to the time when John was little and daily made Keturah laugh with his antics. She'd often caught him lying in wait for the older boys on their way to synagogue for lessons. He'd ambush them with wild whoops, and Keturah would stand by, face alight with fun as she watched him chase the older boys.

But one day Keturah and I had caught John in the act together, and James had been quick to solicit my help. "Aren't you going to punish him?" he'd urged, eyes sparking with anticipation.

"You shouldn't long for someone else's judgment, Gibor." I often used Abba's nickname for him, a reminder of how I viewed him—mighty hero.

"But you let him get away with so much!" James had pouted, pointing to where John rode on Andrew's back, whacking him with a hand as he drove him up and down the street with shouts. "You would never let me act in such a way. This man needs justice, Ima!" James' voice had squeaked with earnestness as he'd jabbed a thumb into his chest.

Behind him, Keturah had doubled over with suppressed laughter, spilling a full pitcher of water all over her feet.

"Whose righteous right hand brings forth justice, hmm?" It wasn't the first time I'd asked him this question. It wouldn't be the last. "Is it yours, Gibor?"

"No." James had hung his head. "The Lord says vengeance and retribution belong to Him."

"That's right. So you can return to your studies rather than taking the role of judge."

As James had left with dark scowls, Keturah had bumped me

with her hip. "You just wanted him to leave before you release the Lord's vengeance upon John, didn't you?"

This woman knew me too well. "I'm afraid John takes advantage of Andrew's patience."

"Andrew doesn't mind. John is like his little brother." The mirth in her face had flickered. "It helps me to see them together."

I'd hooked an arm through hers.

"They complement each other," Keturah had continued, watching as Andrew hoisted John higher onto his back. "John's spirited nature with Andrew's levelheadedness . . . they are good together."

"Like you and me."

Keturah had tipped her head to touch mine. "Like you and me."

Sixteen

The winter months brought change as Deborah and Abigail moved out of our home and our four walls became quieter. In the past year, I'd become used to other women beneath my roof and found the absence jarring. It was time, I decided, to meddle with my boys and find them wives. Marriage had grounded Simon. Daily I witnessed a new steadiness within him and longed for the same, not only for my boys, but also for Andrew, who was as good as my own.

During the month of Adar, we made plans to visit the Holy City to make several large deliveries of salted fish and to meet with another prospective client. While there, we would stay with Kadmiel's family. Simon and Andrew agreed to join us, but Jonah declined, still too disgruntled with Kadmiel to accompany us.

"They couldn't bother to come visit us, so why should I go visit them?" Jonah asserted. "Jerusalem is not so far away, and yet Abigail's own aunt and uncle couldn't bother to attend her wedding ceremony!"

"Don't hold this against them," I exhorted.

"You are right to be offended," Zeb offered. "But you must release the offense rather than dwell upon it."

"Why must I?" Jonah huffed. "Kadmiel did us several favors many years ago, and yet you act like we're forever beholden to him."

"They did send a gift," I reminded him. "The necklace . . ."

"Yes, an extravagant gift to compensate for their offense!" Jonah snorted. "I told Simon to return it but he didn't want to upset his new wife."

"And that makes him a good husband," I soothed, placing a hand to Jonah's arm, but he shook it off.

"You would find a way to help my Jonah, wouldn't you?" Keturah's request lodged in my chest as I gazed upon her sullen husband. Since his wife's death, irritation lurked just beneath Jonah's skin. One prick was often all it took for anger to slip out.

I returned a hand to his arm and held on tight. *"I will never abandon your family—never."*

<hr />

Under the blaze of the midmorning sun, I squinted at Andrew with a tilted head and assessing eye. We stood outside Kadmiel's home along one of Jerusalem's winding roads. I'd hoped that his brother's happiness with Abigail might have directed Andrew's own thoughts toward a wife. We had many connections in the Holy City with established families who had eligible daughters, and I had plans to point a few of them out to Andrew. But no sooner had we arrived in the city than he'd announced that he and John would be spending their time with the new teacher.

"Are you sure this is a good idea?" I drew him close and voiced my concern in an urgent whisper.

Keturah's wise and sensible eyes resided in her second son, eyes that glinted now with understanding, crinkling at the corners as he smiled. "I know the strange location worries you, Doda, but the teacher has many followers. We will hardly be alone."

"I'd much rather you joined James and—"

"*There* you are!" John entered the street, the door banging behind him. Propping a hand on his hip, John appraised me with narrowed eyes, suspicion gleaming from their depths. "I wondered why you snuck out here. You don't want us to go, do you?" It was an accusation. Lately, most things from this boy's tongue were.

"Your aunt expects you to take supper with her tonight, and your brother expects you to help him." I crossed my arms and jutted my chin in the general direction of the high priest's home.

"The teacher has been gone in Perea for so long, but now he's back in Judea. You cannot blame us for wanting to go." John shrugged.

"I don't like the idea of you two out in the wilderness overnight. This teacher's practices are . . . unusual."

"Why did you come out here to share this with Andrew when you could have talked to me?"

My jaw clenched, for I knew the source of his irritation. I often went to Andrew when concerned over John, and he had long resented it.

"I'm a grown man, Ima. I wish you trusted me."

He was sixteen. Indeed, a man, and yet also my boy—my curly-headed, high-spirited boy. "It's not a matter of trust."

"Then let us go." Seeing my continued hesitation, he caught me in long arms, pulled me close, and rested his cheek atop my head. "Ima . . ." All irritation abruptly drained from his voice as it melted into irresistible softness. "Ima, please. This isn't our first time visiting the teacher. All will be well."

John was often like this—accusing me one moment and drawing near the next. At times fiercely independent and other times as loving as a pet lamb. I breathed in his scent—a hint of cassia coupled with the smells of bread from Leah's table.

"Oh, just go." I shoved at him with a scowl. "I'll make excuses to your aunt."

"You're the best mother in all of Israel." John dropped his lips to my cheek, scraggly beard tickling my flesh before he pulled away.

I shot a pointed look at Andrew that said, *Watch over him.*

As the two hurried off, I worried my lip. Shouldn't I rejoice that these young men were eager for truth? And yet the man they so ardently followed held to practices I couldn't begin to understand.

"They're off to see that Baptizer, aren't they?" Behind me, Leah's observation sounded with an undercurrent of reprimand. She stood in her doorway, slender and beautiful, even with the furrow in her brow. "You should speak with Kadmiel. He has direct knowledge of the man."

Her confidence grated on me even while my curiosity swelled. "Is there nothing that Kadmiel doesn't know?" I'd meant it as a jest, but Leah frowned.

"If he was *my* son, I would ensure he stayed away from false teachers." The hard words were accompanied by the scrape of the door as it closed in my face.

◆

The air about Kadmiel's table that evening was stifling, clogged with unspoken grievances. I passed a dish of dipping oil to Abigail, whose neck boasted a beautiful golden chain—the expensive wedding gift from the aunt and uncle who couldn't be bothered to attend the ceremony itself.

In Simon's face, I perceived internal conflict. Most likely he was torn between protecting his wife's feelings and sharing in his father's irritation. He'd planned to be with Zeb and James tonight, who were dining with a client, but had changed his mind due to Abigail's insistence that he dine with her family. Simon's pinched lips showed how much he was regretting his choice.

"Leah says John and Andrew are interested in the Baptizer's teachings." Kadmiel reclined at the head of the table with an affable manner, his sonorous voice commanding everyone's attention.

"Yes, you must excuse their absence tonight." I matched Kadmiel's manner, easy and light, willing to smooth over ruffled feelings. "Whenever we are in town, they are eager to be by his side."

"Understandable." Kadmiel tore off a piece of bread and dipped it in oil. "However, I would give you a word of caution." Nestling the oil-drenched bite into his mouth, Kadmiel chewed for a long moment, wiping his fingers clean on a cloth as he made all of us wait for his pronouncement.

As a teacher of the Law, Kadmiel was well regarded. He taught in the synagogues and spent long hours meticulously copying our holy writings. An erudite scholar whose interpretation of the Law was called upon in many legal matters, he'd risen in estimation over the years, although his greatest desire remained unmet. He had not risen to a placement on the Grand Sanhedrin.

"At the behest of our religious leaders, I went to speak with the Baptizer." Kadmiel finally spoke, a fleck of bread sticking in the corner of his mouth.

At his news, I pushed myself upright. "And? Is he as wild as they say?"

"Wild in appearance, yes." Kadmiel poked at the stuck crumb with his tongue, loosening it and bringing it into his mouth.

"Unkempt," Leah muttered. "Like a madman."

Kadmiel raised a hand to silence his wife. "As I said, wild in appearance but not so in manner. His father, as you may know, was a priest and highly respected. Some of that heritage is evident in the Baptizer's tone and bearing. He was reasonable, knowledgeable, even. We asked him directly if he was the Messiah, and he said he was not."

"But he gathers a following and practices an unusual baptism." I worried my hands in my lap but stopped as Leah noted it.

"Yes, about that." Kadmiel cleared his throat. "He acts entirely unsanctioned by the religious leaders, as if he himself is a priest purifying the people. He holds no such authority."

My unease heightened. "John says some have likened him to Elijah."

Kadmiel nodded. "'I will send the prophet Elijah to you before that great and dreadful day of Yahweh comes.' So speaks the prophet Malachi, and so we asked him, 'Are you Elijah?' Again, he responded that he was not. We asked him if he was the promised prophet spoken of by Moses. Again, no."

"He didn't speak of his identity so much as his function," Admon offered from the end of the table. Kadmiel's son often exhibited a hidden strength that went unnoticed. Doe-eyed and with a round face and slight form, he was unassuming, and yet his voice was deep waters, drawing the listener close. "He quoted from Isaiah and said his work was to prepare the way for the Lord."

"And yet"—Kadmiel lifted a brow—"and yet he did *not* have a reasonable reply as to why he is practicing baptism."

Admon lowered his head in acquiescence and resumed eating. A scribe in training, Admon idolized his father. His twin sister, Affera, looked just like him and had married a wealthy merchant; already she was the mother to a son. Both children a credit to their parents.

"It's his baptism that worries me the most," Kadmiel concluded, motioning to a servant and wiping his hands. "If he is not the Messiah, nor Elijah, nor the prophet, then what is he doing going off on his own, claiming authority he does not have?"

"Do you think he draws unnecessary attention from Rome?" I asked.

"His teachings? No." Kadmiel shook his head, lips curled

downward. "The crowds, though . . . that's another matter. Crowds make Rome nervous. Pontius Pilate has wielded his position for less than a year, and he will be eager to suppress any spark that could lead to a flame."

The fifth prefect to rule over Judea since it fell under Rome's direct control, Pilate was already proving to be a ruthless leader.

"You needn't look so morose." Kadmiel smiled. "The Baptizer's popularity will wane, and when it does, so will the crowds." Clearing his throat, Kadmiel rose and stretched. "Forgive me, but I have an early morning and must retire. I'm glad we've had this talk, Salome. Now you can properly warn both John and Andrew."

"They are men with minds of their own." Simon finally spoke, brushing his hands clean of crumbs. "You are certain of your own judgment, but perhaps my brother has noted something that you have missed."

A strained hush fell upon the table. Color rose in Abigail's face as her eyes darted between husband and uncle.

Kadmiel observed Simon for a quiet moment, unflustered and confident.

"Andrew is young and eager. As was I once. I do not blame his exuberance. Nor do I blame your own desire to defend him. But please take my caution as it is intended. Men learned in the Law have looked long and deep into the Baptizer's words and find him to be a false teacher. Your brother's zeal is admirable, but in this case, it is misguided. I relay this out of love." Briefly, he settled a hand upon Simon's shoulder before leaving, not waiting for a reply.

Simon muttered and pushed off the table as he rose. "It's late, and we should retire for the evening as well." He extended a hand to Abigail. As they left, I released a long breath I hadn't realized I'd been holding. Kadmiel was reasonable, so reasonable . . . but never thought he was wrong. And I sympathized with Simon, for how was one to talk to such a person?

Within the solemn man, I still saw the boy who'd helped pull me from the lake. The boy with the kind smile and bright mind who'd seen my unusual eyes and temperament as differences that made me stronger, who'd been the first to tell me, *"I'm sure you'll make a fine wife and mother someday."*

The years had worked a prideful streak into Kadmiel, but it was a flaw I attempted to overlook. Which of us was without fault? People were prone to various vices, so was it any wonder that a man with Kadmiel's intellect might sometimes tip into pride? That didn't make all of his judgments wrong, and in this matter, perhaps he was right.

As the room began to clear, Leah's eyes caught mine, and any generosity of spirit dried up. My heart was a stubborn mystery, choosing to overlook Kadmiel's faults one moment and rising in bitterness toward his wife the next.

"Your usual rooms are prepared." Her voice was serene and, like her husband's, reasonable.

I bristled and smiled. "Thank you."

———— ✦ ————

Later that night, I lay in Zeb's arms and listened as he recounted his evening. He'd dined with a current client whose household had recently expanded, which meant the client had more mouths to feed and was increasing his order. In the morning, Zeb and James would meet with a prospective client, and if they secured the account, Zeb would need to hire more help.

He pressed a kiss to my neck, and the hair on my arms stood up. "You're quiet tonight. What's wrong?"

"I . . . I don't know."

John and Andrew were still gone, as I knew they would be, staying the night with the Baptizer. My boy . . . somewhere in the wild with a man whom Kadmiel didn't trust.

Naysa, I miss you. Longing for my mother-in-law consumed

me. Hot tears leaked from my eyes, tickling my temple and pooling in my ears. Only months ago, we'd lost her. It had been expected, unlike Jonathan's death after a year in Capernaum.

"Something is wrong." Zeb followed the trail of my tears with his thumb.

"I'm missing your mother."

Zeb buried his face into my hair with a groan, capturing me within his arms. We lay silent, breaths mixing in the dark.

There was a weight that settled about one's shoulders when the generation before you was gone. Abba . . . Naysa. I longed for their wisdom with a ferocious hunger.

Now the wisdom was mine to give.

Adonai, help me.

◆

The next morning, I was slow, rising later than usual to find Zeb had already left with James. I'd barely slept and pushed the heels of my hands into grainy, dry eyes. I left my room to find Abigail pacing nearby, one knuckle caught between her teeth.

"Good, you're up." She sighed.

"What's wrong?" Alarm rose at the look on Abigail's face—conflicted, hopeful, afraid.

"He came back early this morning, while we were still abed."

"Who?"

"Andrew."

"With John?"

"No." Abigail was still pacing, her left hand methodically rubbing the fingers of her right.

"Hold still." I snagged her. "Abigail, where is John?"

"Andrew said he's still with *him.*"

"The Baptizer?"

"No. With—" Abigail bit her lip. "Andrew came to get Simon.

He came to bring him to—" She broke off and began chewing her nails instead of her lip.

"To *who*, Abigail?" It took every scrap of patience not to shake the words from her.

"To the Messiah!" The words finally released. "Oh, Doda, Andrew says they found him. They have found the Messiah!"

Seventeen

"He called you *what?*" I asked, each word pulled out slow and tight like a bowstring. Simon had repeated it twice, but I needed to hear him say it again.

Before and behind us, our caravan stretched, dusty, noisy, nearly drowning out my voice. By my side, Simon adjusted his pace to match mine, patiently relaying the story again. "As soon as he saw me, he called me by name, saying, 'You are Simon, son of Jonah. You will be called Cephas.'"

Cephas in Aramaic. *Peter* in Greek. The meaning? *Stone.*

Defensiveness flared. "Who does this man think he is to be giving you a new name?" The words leapt from my lips, a challenge.

To rename someone was to claim authority over them. Like God naming Jacob "Israel" or Abram "Abraham." When someone received a new name, their life was changed, given over to a higher purpose.

Keturah, something is happening with our boys—with your boy. We'd crossed the Jordan River at a low point into Perea—it added an entire day to our travel north but also bypassed Samaria. And no one was eager to be in Samaria.

"He is the Messiah, Ima!" John turned to me, walking backward with hands spread wide. "I would say he has the authority to give Simon a new name if he wants to."

"If this is true, then why wouldn't he give *you* a new name, my son?"

John shrugged, a sloppy grin splayed across his face. "Perhaps he will."

My harried mind traveled over all I'd been told, the last few days a blur of excitement and fear. The Baptizer had claimed to clear the way for the Messiah. John and Andrew had been eager, ready for it. And then the Baptizer had pointed and named him. *That* one—Jesus from the small village of Nazareth.

"But what has he *done*, John? How do you know? Simply because the Baptizer said it?"

"He baptized Jesus, at which time he saw the Spirit of God come down from heaven and rest upon him, identifying him as God's chosen one," Andrew chimed in.

What good is the word of a man whom the religious leaders deem a false teacher? I kept the thought private and shifted my attention to Simon. He was staring ahead with a set jaw—undecided, it seemed, about this Jesus.

I studied his profile, and a chill ran down my neck, mind racing back to when he was a boy. My belly had still been soft, for I'd recently given birth to James. Keturah was standing with Simon's small hand within her own. Elazar's brother had just run off into the night, following a would-be Messiah.

I shivered, recalling the way I'd held James and wept when the boy had returned a year later, prepared for burial, delivered into the hands of an inconsolable mother.

"Ima, don't fret." John wormed his way between me and Simon, wrapping a sturdy arm around me. "We're meeting Jesus in Cana. You'll soon see. Everyone will."

I tried to smile, but when I looked at John, all I saw was the blinding white of a burial shroud.

The boy . . . he'd looked small wrapped so tightly.

✦

The absence of clouds meant the stars were bright, poking through the darkness, shining like jewels. We were two days away from Capernaum. Our caravan was large and included many families traveling back to Galilee. We formed a circle by the Jordan, fires and tents dotting the enclosed camp. I stood outside the line of safety, alone beneath the stars.

Zeb was withholding all judgment, neither worried nor excited over John and Andrew's discovery. *"When we meet the man for ourselves, then we can decide. You worry when as yet there is no cause."*

I disliked it when Zeb too easily dismissed what I felt.

"Ima! What are you doing out here alone?"

James.

He stood beside me, facing forward as I did, and rested an arm about my shoulders, pressing me to his side.

With my whole being, I loved this young man, knew him like the lines in my own face. With him there was a relaxed ease, both our souls settling upon sight of each other.

"You shouldn't be alone. Come warm yourself by the fire."

"In a moment, Gibor."

He grinned at the use of the old nickname, teeth flashing white in the dark. There was a dimple in his right cheek that formed with each smile, although it was covered now by a beard. As I tilted my chin to gaze at the stars, James did too and then pointed. "I still connect them into shapes, especially on nights when I cannot sleep."

"What do you think about this news of the Messiah?"

James quieted. "It's hard to know *what* to think . . . at least yet."

"A common man from Nazareth? And did anyone else see this Spirit of God descending upon him? How reliable is the word of the Baptizer? Has this Jesus done a sign to prove his identity?"

I often spoke with James in a way reserved for him. More open, perhaps, than a mother should with a son. When he was a youth, he'd never once pushed me away or resisted my wisdom the way John had done. Consistently, he'd come to me, and now, in a great reversal, I found myself coming to him, seeking his judgment.

When I finally paused for breath, he spoke. "I don't know, Ima. I'm not sure what to think. I wasn't there."

"Andrew says Jesus invited Philip to follow him to Galilee. Doesn't that concern you? *Philip*."

I cast my gaze back to the stars. The belligerent boy who'd laughed at Noy's burial had grown up beneath the shadow of an angry father. The mother had died birthing a third babe, and Gideon had been left alone with three boys.

"What kind of teacher would invite the companionship of a man like Philip?" I mused.

James sighed and shifted his feet. "In all fairness, we don't know Philip well."

I cast a sidelong glance at my generous son. "True. We are not close with the family, but women talk, James." I snatched at his beard and gave it a yank. "Tongues wag, and in this case, they all say the same thing. Gideon's sons are insolent."

"Perhaps." James lifted a shoulder. "But John claims he changed after hearing the Baptizer's message. He preached repentance, remember? Perhaps that is what Philip has done—repented. Is it so hard to believe?"

"You're right." I relented, burrowing into his side, head tucked at the hollow beneath his collarbone. Yes, perhaps James was right and Philip was changed. Then again . . . how could good fruit come from a bad tree?

We neared Magadan in the heat of the day. Only a few miles more to Capernaum. Not all of us, however, would continue north. Simon, Andrew, James, and John would cut east to Cana to meet up with Jesus.

Simon enveloped Abigail in his burly arms, but instead of snuggling into his embrace, my niece held herself as still as a length of lumber.

"We'll be back soon, I'm sure." Simon's confident voice wavered.

"Be sure that you are." Zeb clapped a hand to Simon's shoulder. "What am I going to tell your father when I return home without you?"

"Tell him his son has a new name!" John shouted, already halfway down the road.

I tsked. "Not even giving his ima an embrace before he leaves. Look at him—already gone." I snorted, hoping to elicit a laugh from Abigail, but she remained quiet, eyes trained on the empty road.

"I-I'm a little frightened," she confessed. "I don't know what this man wants with my husband, and I'm not sure that I want Simon to go." The words came spilling out, messy and rushed. "Is that horrible, Doda? Does that make me a bad wife?"

With a smile, I pulled her close. "No, dear one. You're simply experiencing what every wife and mother goes through. The love you feel . . . it's so strong that it hurts sometimes, doesn't it?"

"Yes!" With a single wail, Abigail dropped her face into her hands.

I rubbed her back. "Those four young men have good heads. They will not be swayed by a false teacher."

I spoke the words with an assurance I had yet to feel. I spoke the words forcefully . . . for the both of us.

✦

When we arrived home, it wasn't Jonah who was distraught by Simon's absence—it was Deborah.

"Simon is newly married and yet he chooses to abandon his wife to run after a blasphemer?" She threw her hands up in the air.

"We don't know if he's a blasphemer . . . not yet."

"I'm surprised at you, Salome."

"What do you mean?" I fought to keep my voice even.

"I know how you view my daughter." Deborah's chin trembled. "I know you view her as your own."

"Deborah, I—"

"So why doesn't this bother you? I've never known you to sit by the side, especially when it comes to someone you love." Before I could answer, she'd left.

The years had taught me that love was not far from fear. The two were often entwined, blending seamlessly together until I couldn't tell which one fueled me more.

When they return, you must insist they stay home, fear instructed.

They have good heads, but they are also young and eager. Be the voice of caution that they need, love reasoned.

At the very least, you must insist on meeting Jesus. You must look him in the eye for yourself, fear inserted the final word.

For over a week I wrestled, laying down worry one moment only to pick it back up the next. My thoughts churned, but one remained fixed as a stone in a rushing stream.

I must look this man in the eye for myself.

EIGHTEEN

One week bled into two before a messenger arrived from James. Jesus' company had grown, and he was coming to Capernaum. We were to make our home ready for the Messiah.

The Messiah.

My strong and steady son who'd stood with me beneath the stars, murmuring, *"I don't know, Ima,"* was now convinced.

We met them along the southern road to escort them into town. When their large company came into view, Deborah groused, "So many! Simon will have to offer up his home as well."

I scanned the crowd, finding John as he spotted me. "Ima!" Separating from the others, John ran down the road and took me by the hand, half dragging me behind him. "Come with me."

"Slow down," I chided as he pulled me through the crowd. My complaint died upon my lips as we stopped before a man who was watching our approach with eagerness.

"Jesus, this is my mother." John tugged me to his side as if showing off a prized calf.

"Salome." Jesus' face broke into a wide, inviting smile.

His evident sincerity should have sparked a warm response, but I stood tightly alert, meeting his gaze evenly.

He didn't startle at the sight of my bright eyes as so many still did when encountering me for the first time. His were a deep brown, fringed with long lashes. He was not much taller than my own John, although broader in his shoulders. I squinted, assessing his age. Perhaps ten or twelve years younger than me.

"Ima," John hissed from the corner of his mouth.

Quickly, I ducked my head in a bow. "Teacher, I've heard much about you."

"And you are about to hear more!" John crowed. "We've come directly from Cana and have much to relay."

"But first you will eat," Zeb insisted, coming to our side and extending the kiss of welcome to Jesus. "You've traveled far, and now you will rest at our table."

I watched Jesus' reaction to my husband—full of friendliness and gratitude. What had I expected? That he would arrive militantly, striding into our village and demanding Capernaum's sons?

As the evening progressed, our table burst with people and food. The men reclined at the table, freshly washed feet stretched behind them as Deborah, Abigail, and I served with the help of Mary of Clopas, who was Jesus' aunt, and his own mother, Mary, a slender, quiet woman not much older than me. "You are a guest in our home. Let us serve you," I whispered.

"I am happy to help," she replied.

When the wine was brought out, John gave a shout and leaned back on Jesus' breast. The familiarity in the gesture clenched my heart tight. "Tell them, Rabbi. Tell them what you did."

Jesus laughed, the sound bursting with affection. He nodded across the table to James, indicating that he should tell the story.

"We attended a wedding banquet in Cana. The host ran out of drink, and Jesus turned ordinary water into luscious wine— the best I've ever tasted!" James exclaimed. While he talked, the room grew silent. Belief was etched upon many faces, but not all. The men Mary had identified as her other sons wore hard expressions. It was apparent that Jesus' own brothers did not believe this was a miracle.

"Did anyone here witness this transformation?" One of the brothers spoke up. "Or simply the purported aftereffects?" His implication was clear—just because something was *said* to be a miracle didn't mean trickery hadn't been employed. By my side, Mary drew in a sharp, pained breath.

"We weren't in the room when it happened, but the servants were," Simon assured us.

"Peter's right," Andrew affirmed. "No one in attendance doubted that this was a miracle."

I startled, more astounded that Simon's new name had slipped so comfortably from his brother's lips than at the miracle itself. Abigail stared at her husband with a conflicted expression that surely matched my own.

"God's glory was on display," Philip asserted. Philip—the wild boy with a tongue full of insults—was now gazing upon Jesus with adoration. Sensing my attention, he looked up, directly into my face, and flinched.

My breathing shallowed as the urge to speak fell upon me. As the men continued to fill in details of the miraculous event, I tried to capture Zeb's attention. Perhaps he could speak the question burning on my tongue. But Zeb reclined next to Jonah, both of them staring at Jesus with an openness that astounded me.

By now my breathing was so shallow that my head was light. I poured another drink, nearly missing the cup. Even Jonah had nothing to say? No one would ask the question that needed an answer? My chin was chattering, and my lips were numb. The fire inside wouldn't go away.

I turned my eyes upon Jesus and kept them there. He tore into a hunk of bread with his teeth, eyes flitting to mine and holding fast, our attention now mutually riveted upon each other.

"Jesus of Nazareth, what do you want with my sons?" The

question left my lips louder than I'd intended. Everyone quieted into a tense silence.

One heartbeat and then two before John mumbled an embarrassed "Ima."

But Jesus did not look offended. Instead, he eased back onto an elbow as he studied my face. In his eyes was a spark of pleasure, as though he'd been anticipating exactly this moment. His calm flustered me.

"Forgive my bluntness, Teacher, but the mothers of Galilee have seen too many of their sons snatched away by would-be messiahs—men who use our boys for their own end." Hot tears hid within my voice. "Judas of Galilee . . . you are old enough to remember the birth of his movement?"

Gently, Jesus nodded, eyes never leaving mine.

"He was building something, a movement of hate whose repercussions we feel to this very day. Many believe his intentions were good, but still—" My gaze finally broke from Jesus. "Even if he had good intentions, the fruit was rotten, the result disastrous."

"You are concerned about false prophets." Jesus straightened, addressing the entire room. "Such men come to you in sheep's clothing, but inwardly they are ferocious wolves." His gaze settled upon me. "You can identify them by their fruit, that is, by the way they act. Can you pick grapes from thornbushes, or figs from thistles? As you can identify a tree by its fruit, so you can identify people by their actions."

His words were calm and wise. In them, I sensed truth. What fruit had this man produced? If I was to believe the word of my sons, he had abundantly provided for a small wedding in Cana.

"What is necessary to every building?" Jesus spoke the question to the room.

"My saba helped build Bethsaida." James spoke up with evident pride. "Even though he died when I was young, I still remember his workshop." He glanced at me. "I still remember his wisdom. A building is only as good as its foundation."

"Exactly." Jesus spread his arms wide. Even though he was sitting, his presence filled the room. "Anyone who listens to my teaching and follows it is wise, like a person who builds a house on solid rock."

Everything within me stilled. My eyes slid closed, and I was a girl of seven again.

"Why are you taking so long with that stone, Abba?" I perched at his feet, playing with Yakira, my doll made of fabric scraps. Somewhere on the roof, Ima was singing.

"Because this, Zohar, is the cornerstone." Abba tapped the large rock.

"What's a cornerstone?"

"It's the first stone placed in the foundation of a building. It comes first, and then everything else builds on top of it."

"It has to be strong, then," I mused.

"It does," Abba agreed. *"A building is only as good as its foundation."*

I opened my eyes, drew in a shuddering breath. I could still see Abba's strong forearms, corded with muscles that rippled as he worked.

"And what happens when the rain comes in torrents and the floodwaters rise and the winds beat against that house?" Jesus asked.

"It won't collapse." I whispered the answer so softly, I was startled when Jesus turned to me.

"It won't collapse," he repeated. "Because it had its foundation on the rock, but . . ." He raised a hand and paused, all of us awaiting his next word.

Jesus picked up a crust of bread and crumbled it into fine pieces within his hand. "Anyone who hears my teaching and doesn't obey it is foolish, like a person who builds a house on sand." With a quick breath, Jesus blew upon the crumbs in his palm, and they scattered across the table. "What will happen to that house when the rains and floods come?"

"It will collapse, Rabbi," Philip answered.

"With a mighty crash," Jesus finished.

"Sturdy buildings come from solid foundations as good fruit comes from good trees," James summarized.

As Jesus nodded, I realized that he'd answered my question with a story. Fear whispered in the dark about bad fruit and faulty ground, but in his words, Jesus had given me a better, hopeful picture.

The question remained—did I trust his word?

Jesus' mother met me in the quiet of the courtyard before retiring for the night. I grasped her hand, hoping she wouldn't find the gesture too intimate. "I apologize if I came across as impudent in my questioning."

"Oh no." Mary squeezed my hand. "And if I know my son, he didn't find your concern to be impudence. He understands an ima's worry. He's seen it in me many times over."

"You clearly believe in his ability to do these . . . signs. And yet his own brothers . . ." I broke off as I noted pain in Mary's face. "I'm sorry. I shouldn't prod."

"It's all right." Mary sighed and dropped my hand to pull her mantle tightly about her shoulders. A spark of awareness shot through me.

She was lonely.

"There's a special burden you carry when your own family disbelieves." Mary tipped her face to the sky. By the light of the moon, I noted the sheen of tears on her cheeks. She swiped at them swiftly before turning to me. "But your sons . . . the belief in your sons is bright and beautiful to see. You must be so proud."

At my hip, the pouch with the stones hummed. *Proud. Proud.*

"*You* must be proud." I delivered the words slowly, more of a question than a statement.

Something flickered in Mary's eyes. "Yes," she finally whispered. She looked past me to something beyond. "Now that he has shown his power, however, I sense something between us shifting—as it should."

"He loves you dearly. Anyone can see that."

"And I love him, but now . . . now it is my role to follow him." Mary gathered her mantle tightly at her throat. "I bore him under unusual circumstances that have followed me all my life. I knew this day was coming."

The loneliness I'd noted earlier had intensified in her demeanor. I slid a hand to her arm. I understood that small, private feeling of being different—how it shaped you for life. I wanted to communicate my understanding, but the lump in my throat prevented speech, and so I let the touch of my hand be enough.

I wasn't yet sure what to make of Jesus, but I dearly liked his mother.

◆

"John's heart is already in Jesus' hand." I ran a comb through my hair. It snagged on a knot, and I stopped to pick at it with calloused fingers.

Behind me, Zeb undressed for bed. "I think you embarrassed him at the table."

"Any good mother would have asked the same." When Zeb remained silent, irritation flared. He was often unwilling to come right out and speak his mind, leaving me to pick at the hints, try to untangle his meaning.

"I asked John if Jesus is accepting disciples." Zeb eased onto the bed. "After the event in Cana, it sounds like more people are following him. It's one thing for a teacher to gather interested listeners. It's another thing entirely when he begins accepting formal disciples."

"And? What did John answer?" I turned to gaze at my husband, fingers still busy with the knot.

"Ah, Salome . . . you should have seen him." Zeb ran a weathered hand over his face. "John was so . . . sad and happy. Somehow both at the same time."

"He wants to come beneath Jesus' teaching full-time?" I asked with a growing ache in my chest as I recalled the clear friendship that already existed between Jesus and John.

"I think so, but he will never ask. He said that when the time comes, surely Jesus will accept those with more learning."

It was the role of promising students to approach a rabbi and request to come beneath his teaching. As bright as he was, Kadmiel at fifteen would never have dared to approach a rabbi if it had not been for the urging of his instructor. Bethsaida had swelled with pride when the answer had been yes, when one of our own was deemed worthy of such an honor. And now there was a similar hunger in John to come beneath Jesus, to take on his yoke of instruction.

"He's never seen himself as bright," Zeb continued. "No matter what we've told him, he carries old wounds."

My breath caught as I recalled ten-year-old John. *"I'm not smart, Ima!"* He'd smacked his head with a fist. *"My teacher says I have the heart but not the mind for study. When the time comes, he says I won't be able to attend* beit midrash *but will go back to my nets, where I belong."*

I'd rained down fury upon that hook-nosed instructor until all of Capernaum had left their courtyards to see what was happening. To witness John put down in such a way was more than I could bear. I saw so much of myself in him—too much.

"I've never seen John so passionate, and we both know how

significant that is." Zeb barked a laugh. "There's more passion in that young man's right hand than in my whole body."

Quietly, I crossed the room, forgetting my earlier flash of irritation as I settled by Zeb's side. "Both of our sons are convinced that this man has been sent by God. Those who claim to be the Messiah accompany it with a sign. Has Jesus made such a claim?"

"I don't think so. Not yet." Zeb rested a hand on my knee. "But perhaps this miracle with the wine is the sign? It seems a strange way to announce his authority—at a small wedding in Cana."

Everything about this was strange. I had no answers. All I knew was that I did not want my sons to be hurt. John—so full of fire, so like the hopeful girl who'd faltered two steps behind, the girl scrambling for a place, latching on to every foothold, the one who'd hoped for a future that felt out of reach.

Nineteen

Cradling a full bowl of steaming broth in my hands, I shuffled to Jonah's door, pausing outside before entering. How I wished Simon and Andrew were here, but they were still in Judea, still with Jesus.

For a while, after Jesus' visit to Capernaum, life had returned to normal. Every night my boys had pushed off the lake's shore to search her depths for fish. James and Simon had helped their fathers hire more men and renegotiate our contract with Magadan's factory. Life had settled into a familiar pattern . . . except for John. He had been subdued, focusing on the task before him without any exuberance. I'd asked Andrew if he knew what ailed him.

"John can't bear to be parted from Jesus, and I don't blame him. Work has lost its luster now that we've found the Messiah."

But then Passover had neared, and Jesus had arrived, with many followers in attendance this time. My boys had joined him and traveled south ahead of us. All throughout Passover, they'd remained close to Jesus' side. The memory mixed with concern outside Jonah's door, and I took a moment to compose myself.

My sons had spent months with Jesus outside Jerusalem, and

171

if the news traveling north was true, many were flocking to Jesus for baptism. Another teacher in the wilderness with another baptism. More people were asserting that Jesus was a teacher from God with the strength of God within his right hand. If this was true, then I was blessed indeed to have sons by his side. And yet I could not shake the memory of Elazar's mother at the graveside of her son. I could not cleanse my heart of the fear that still whispered in the night.

Many were convinced, but most of our religious leaders were not. Leah's face the last time I'd seen it came blazing into view. She'd been full of warnings before but now appeared smug, lips pursed as she hid a smile. Her children were a credit to her, but mine? Mine were off in the wilderness again with strange teachers.

"Jonah? Are you awake?" I pushed aside Leah's face and entered the room to find Jonah struggling upright. "Here, let me help." Swiftly setting down the bowl, I helped Jonah rise enough to eat. A harsh, scraping cough left his lips. Placing a hand to his brow, I frowned.

"Still raging with fever?" Jonah asked.

"You've been getting better, but we should send for your sons."

"Bah, I'll recover, and they have more important things to do than sit by their father's bedside and watch him sleep."

Ever since we'd returned home from Passover, Jonah had talked of nothing else but Jesus.

"He cleansed the Temple of the booths of Annas by driving out the merchants and money changers with a whip!" Many knew the story, but we had been present. The family of the high priest Annas had long held stalls within the outer Temple courts, stalls that Jesus had overthrown. The clatter of the coins, the bangs of the tables, the indignant shouts of the merchants—it was a cacophony that still rang joyously in Jonah's ear. *"Men arrived from Annas' household to stop him, but Jesus put them in their place."*

"You're smiling." I raised the broth to Jonah's lips. "Thinking of Kadmiel's face again, are you?" My brother-in-law, although not present at the Temple that day, had heard of the scandalous event afterward.

Jonah managed a swallow before laughing. "It was purple. I've never seen a man's face that shade of purple."

"I'm glad his discomfort delighted you," I stated dryly. Jonah might be pleased by the disruption Jesus was causing among the elite, but many of our clients came from that class, and we could not afford to make enemies. How long before Hiram, Annas' steward, discovered our connection to the man who'd driven out his master's merchants?

"You think, then, that Jesus is the one we've been waiting for?" I questioned.

Jonah was weakening. "Peter—" He said Simon's new name with pride before another series of coughs cut him off. I dipped a rag into a bowl of water by the bed, dabbing his brow.

"Andrew brought Peter, and then Peter brought me to Jesus," Jonah rasped. "I've spoken long and hard with that boy, or rather . . . I listened." His breath was growing short, color rising in his face. "Wouldn't it be . . . something . . . if the Messiah came to fishermen first? And why shouldn't he? Why not my boys? Keturah—" He spoke his wife's name on a sob and clutched my hand. "I wish she could have seen this day."

"Me too." Even resigned to his bed, Jonah bore new hope. I could hear it in the way he said Keturah's name—not with bitterness over his loss, but with gratitude for the long years of love between them. The arrival of Jesus into our lives had softened this man, erasing the irritation that had formerly been his companion.

"Is he done with that?" a voice interrupted us.

Turning, I found Deborah leaning against the doorframe.

"The food. Is he done?" Crossing the room, she peered into the bowl and tsked. "How will you ever recover if you refuse to eat?" She plucked the bowl from the table with unsteady hands, sloshing some of the broth onto her mantle.

"Deborah, are you all right?" Her eyes were glassy, red-rimmed, and circled with shadow.

"I'm fine," she snapped, but as she left the room, she moved slowly, as though navigating through shifting sand.

"She doesn't like tending to me." Jonah tried to laugh but was too exhausted for displays of mirth.

Draping a fresh rag across his forehead, I rose. "You rest, and I'll check on her."

As I left the room, a splintering crash hurried my feet, and as Abigail's shrill cry pierced the air, I flew to the courtyard.

Deborah lay collapsed in a splatter of broth, shards of the bowl scattered across the floor.

◆

After Jonathan's death so soon after our arrival in Capernaum, Naysa had grown quiet. With Deborah back in Bethsaida and Leah in Jerusalem, she had turned to me, and I had met her with the open arms she'd always given me.

"*Some lessons are learned too late,*" she'd mused one night, both of us by the fire after putting the boys to bed. "*I wasted many years wishing my husband was different rather than asking Adonai for help in loving him as he was.*"

"*He felt your love. I know he did.*"

"*You're right.*" Naysa had rested her hand over mine. "*But I wish I'd been more generous with my love.*"

I had not understood her regret in the moment, but now, as I stood above Deborah's bed, a deep knowing filled me.

Deborah. Sister.

Her features were twisted in pain, wrestling an unseen foe. I pressed a fist to my mouth.

"I've sent a messenger by horse," Zeb whispered from across the bed. "He will arrive in Judea in a couple days."

"But it will take Simon longer than that to journey all the way home," Abigail moaned. "What if they don't make it in time?"

"We shouldn't worry about what we cannot control," Zeb comforted, offering an embrace to his niece.

The fever gripped Deborah quicker than it had Jonah. While he remained coherent, Deborah tossed deliriously upon her bed, writhing as the sickness grasped her with long talons and glinting fangs, refusing to release its kill.

I stared at the woman before me, this sister-in-law with her blunt tongue. We'd tussled with each other on and off for years— admiration, resentment, and respect warring for footing between us, finally settling into hardness.

I wish I'd been more generous with my love.

Pulling a long drag of air into my lungs, I held it until it burned.

＊

Two days after sending the messenger to Jerusalem, I entered Jonah's room to discover him curled upon his side with a smile on his lips, having peacefully left us in the dead of night.

"You stubborn man! Of course you would do this to us." I sat on his bed, arms crossing my chest, which heaved with emotion. Not since the early years of his marriage had I seen such contentment upon his features.

"You couldn't wait to see Keturah, could you? You didn't consider that we still need you here, did you? What am I supposed to do now, you obstinate man?" My rebuke broke into a cry as I dropped my head to his quiet shoulder.

I'd honored my friend and stood by her husband through both abundance and loss. He'd needed me in the years after Keturah's death, but now I realized how much I'd come to depend upon him.

"You can't go and leave me like this. Your boys still need you. We . . . Zeb and I . . . we need you." I dropped my face to his hand, wetting it with my tears.

My emotion rose up like tumultuous waves beating a shore. But my husband, his emotion pooled in his chest—a hidden pond that was inaccessible to me. With quiet focus, Zeb managed his friend and business partner's affairs. His subdued efficiency contrasted starkly with the raging storm within me. I directed that tempest to Deborah's bedside, where I clenched her hand while reciting portions of the *Shemoneh Esrei*, the ancient prayer at the center of our faith, the series of blessings and petitions that every Hebrew knew by heart. I gripped Deborah's limp hand and imagined Jonah, vibrant and well, holding Keturah's.

"Heal us and we shall be healed; help us and we shall be helped. Raise up full healings for all our wounds, for You are a true and merciful physician."

I rocked in time with the words, desiring the arrival of the Messiah in a new way. "Adonai, we are broken in body and spirit. We need You. Listen to our groaning again. Attend to the needs of Your people."

When the Messiah came, he would bring the power of God with him. Doubt flickered into hope. "Adonai, let it be Jesus. Let it finally be the time for redemption."

On her bed, Deborah moaned, and furiously I squeezed her hand. "Do not leave your brother and me here to guide these young ones on our own." My throat tightened, the weight on my shoulders deepening. "Come back to me, sister."

The day after Jonah's burial, our messenger returned with a hard look in his eye and a bandaged head. He'd arrived in Judea to discover that Jesus and his company had already left for home by way of Samaria. "I attempted to find them, but I was driven from town after town with curses and rocks. No Samaritan dog wants to help a Jewish man locate a Jewish rabbi," the messenger spat.

Samaria had a long, tumultuous relationship with the rest of Israel. Samaritans worshipped not at the Temple in Jerusalem, but on Mount Gerizim. With their own calendar and version of the Torah, they were separated from Jewish religious life, so why had Jesus traveled through their region?

When the company finally returned, I eagerly searched their midst for Jesus, but he'd parted from them at Magadan and was preaching throughout Galilee in the direction of Cana. Our young men came home exuberant—vigorous with excitement over all they had seen. They returned so hopeful and were met with a crippling blow.

I'd once met my own husband in a similar situation, flinging my words like weapons. Abigail, however, met her husband with open arms, and as she held him, she gave him the news, simple and straightforward.

Simon was wrecked. Later that night I heard him, alone in Deborah's room, weeping for his father while draped across his mother-in-law's feverish form. His tears came in long, sweeping gusts, like the brutal eastern winds that lashed the lake into chaos.

TWENTY

"O Lord, the Redeemer of Israel, look upon our affliction and fight our fight and redeem us speedily." I whispered another portion of the Shemoneh Esrei as I gazed across the lake.

A week after their return and Simon had yet to leave Deborah's room. Andrew, however, had spent nearly every moment outdoors. The grief of Jonah's sons finally elicited tears from my husband, who began following Andrew to the water, where they stood side by side on the bank, shoulders touching.

With the words of David, I fed my small flicker of hope. "I am feeble and crushed; I groan because of the tumult of my heart. O Lord, all my longing is before You; my sighing is not hidden from You." When had Adonai ever looked away from pain? I clenched my jaw and gazed hard at the sky. *Adonai, look.*

And then Jesus came.

Cutting through the haze of our grief, Jesus came to Capernaum. The first time he'd arrived, he'd done so quietly, drifting in like a gentle breeze from Mount Hermon. This time, however, his reputation preceded him. Dozens of people traveled miles to accompany him into town. He was so surrounded by crowds that there was no hope of a private word.

"I wish we could get close!" My hungry eyes sought him, but the crowds battered me back.

"We'll invite him to stay in our home again," Zeb assured as we entered the flow of the crowd with our sons.

"Where is your brother? He would want to be here," I asked Andrew as he joined us.

But Andrew shook his head. "He won't even see me, so I doubt he'll show his face today."

It was the Sabbath, and our synagogue ruler invited Jesus to read from the scrolls. We entered the synagogue to find it already packed. In the center of the room was a platform with a wooden lectern. The synagogue ruler wheeled the scroll in on a cart and reverently lifted it onto the lectern.

Everyone hushed as Jesus unrolled the scroll and began to read, the words of Ezekiel pouring from his lips. "Then I will sprinkle clean water on you, and you will be clean. Your filth will be washed away, and you will no longer worship idols. And I will give you a new heart, and I will put a new spirit in you. I will take out your stony, stubborn heart and give you a tender, responsive heart."

His voice stilled me so abruptly that my muscles clenched. He spoke the words of God with an intimacy I'd never encountered before. I'd heard these very words spoken by other teachers who approached the text reverently and delivered it as if offering riches to those listening.

But this was different.

Jesus spoke the text, approaching it not from the outside but from within, as though he embodied it. In offering Scripture to his listeners, he gave us himself.

He looked up from the scroll and began teaching, his words building upon the imagery in Ezekiel. "Very truly I tell you, no one can enter the Kingdom of God unless they are born of water and the Spirit. Flesh gives birth to flesh, but the Spirit gives birth to spirit."

Born of water. Cleansed of filth. What was this new birth Jesus was referencing?

Even in the midst of my own confusion, I could not doubt his authority—no one could. The room was silent as he spoke, his words hushing all inner and outer turmoil, descending upon us like a mother's hand upon her child, warm and heavy, firm and loving.

"No one has ever gone into heaven except the one who came from heaven—the Son of Man."

At this word, murmurs broke out as recognition sparked. Why was Jesus referencing the prophet Daniel's vision? The Son of Man was the only one able to stand before the Ancient of Days. The Son of Man was the one to whom God gave dominion and glory and a kingdom. A *kingdom*.

Up until this moment, my body had been stilled, but now my heart thudded, and I shook with the weight of its rapid beat. Jesus had spoken about a kingdom before. James had relayed the words to me. Jesus had stood in the Judean wilderness, hair whipping in the wind as his words stretched into searching hearts: *"The time has come. The Kingdom of God has come near. Repent and believe the good news!"*

My heart pounded so hard that I could feel its pulse behind my eyes as another portion of the Shemoneh Esrei left my lips on a broken whisper: "Master of mighty deeds, who may be compared unto You? You are the King sending death and reviving again and causing salvation to sprout forth."

A disruption from outside stole everyone's attention, sharp cries that pierced the air with panic. The crowd parted swiftly like the Red Sea. Stepping through their current on dry ground came the man everyone in Capernaum avoided at all costs.

The last time I'd seen him, I'd been walking Keturah's path. His scream had rent the air, alerting me to his presence before he clambered on all fours, barreling down the hill and toward the vineyard, tone ripe with rage. He'd stopped short, breath rushing to and from his body in ragged streams—long pulls in and guttural moans out—before he'd leapt upon a vine and gnashed at a cluster of grapes, juice pouring like blood and coating his lips, staining his chest. His gaze had roamed past me and then he was away, fleeing back to the trees.

His name was Amos—a man made in the likeness of Adonai whom the devil had stolen and sullied, pouring his dark spirits into a vessel meant for light.

I covered a gasp as Amos walked into the center of the room. His torn clothes hung upon his emaciated frame, and yet he held himself boldly, walking with firm steps through the people who shrank back in fear.

He never came within the town limits, the spirits within keeping him at a distance, so what had compelled him into our midst now? I'd never seen him stand so tall. His body stretched like a tree angling for the sky. Had his sanity returned? He pushed through the last of the crowd until there was nothing between him and Jesus. Slowly, Jesus turned, one hand resting lightly on the lectern as he faced Amos.

With a jerk, Amos crumpled to the ground, body pulling inward like dry leaves shriveling before a licking flame. "What do you want with us, Jesus of Nazareth?" The words left his lips in a howl—at once high and low. "Have you come to destroy us? Go away!"

Amos' head whipped to the right, his body following in a fluid motion as he eased along the ground at Jesus' feet with an arched back and grasping fingers. "I know who you are—the Holy One of God!" Amos reared up onto his knees, neck craning backward, so close to Jesus yet not daring to touch him.

Jesus stood quietly before Amos with his hand resting upon the scroll of Ezekiel. His expression reminded me of James when, at the age of eleven, he'd come across a jackal with a bird clenched within its jaw. With great might, James had thrown rocks, young voice cracking with fury as he contended for the bird.

Amos stood and jabbed an accusatory finger at Jesus, body trembling with rage. "Go away!"

"Be quiet!" Jesus released the two words, slow and heavy with authority. "Come out of him!"

At once Amos collapsed in a heap on the ground, accompanied by more startled cries from the crowd. He shook in a series of horrible convulsions, eyes rolling into the back of his head, mouth quivering in a prolonged shriek. With a final shudder, he lay still.

Jesus extended a hand. As soon as it touched Amos' shoulder, his eyes opened and he grasped that hand of welcome, allowing Jesus to lift him onto his feet. Swiping long, matted hair from his face, Amos cast wide eyes about the room. As they skimmed over me, I gasped, for there was clarity within their depths.

When his gaze came to rest on Jesus, Amos fell to his knees, this time compelled by a cry of worship, and then he was weeping—sobs mixing with laughter in a cacophony of joy that squeezed my throat tight.

Jesus bent over Amos' shaking shoulders, dipping his head to murmur into his ear. As commanding as he'd been, Jesus was now equally tender—at once authoritative and intimate.

The Holy One of God.

Only God could command a demon to flee. Only God could free a man from such a bind. Everything in my body loosened at once.

As Amos stood, Jesus clasped him within his arms, claiming him, like a father with a long-lost son, and Amos continued to weep, face hidden within his hands as he allowed Jesus to hold him.

"Who is this? He commands unclean spirits with authority and power, and they come out! Who is this?"

I could not stop shaking as the question filled the air, passed from mouth to mouth. "What is this message? Who is this man?"

He left the synagogue with a restored Amos by his side, all of us parting to give them room. Awe mixed with fear, no one daring to draw near to the man who'd pulled a demon out of a man as swift and sure as yanking a gnarly weed from the earth. One word and the man was free, no lingering root of Satan left behind.

"Who is this man?"

The people asked, but the demons knew.

The Holy One of God.

Awe left me an island, hardly able to register the presence of anyone but this man. He passed me, and I was so shaken I couldn't breathe. The flickering hope I'd nurtured before his arrival now mixed with the realization that I'd questioned him. In my own home, I'd bluntly questioned him! The memory drove a shaft of terror directly into my breast.

Until I recalled Jesus' response to me. Until I remembered the liquid warmth of his eyes as he told me a story about a cornerstone. He'd met me with the same kindness he now directed toward Amos—a kindness that restored rather than condemned.

He left the synagogue, and I followed. On a current of wondering spectators, I was borne from the synagogue out into the dusty streets of Capernaum. None of us dared to approach him. No one but Amos stood by his side.

Until a low cry rent the air. "Master!"

Simon shouldered his way to Jesus. He was unsettled and trembling as though fighting a battle within that finally undid him, driving him to his knees. He bowed his head and spoke to the ground. His loud voice was shaking. "Master, I am not worthy for you to enter my home, but for the sake of my wife, I dare to ask it. Please . . . my mother-in-law, she is desperately ill."

◆

We pressed in tight like fish in a basket, toppling over one another in the dimly lit room. We were hushed and uncertain, still reeling with awe . . . all of us but John, who teemed with energy, bouncing on the balls of his feet as if preparing for a footrace.

I hushed his frantic movement with an impatient hand. "What does Simon expect Jesus to do?"

"The impossible." John grinned and yanked his arm free from my grasp.

Zeb stood nearby, face drained of color as he gazed upon the feverish form of his sister.

Abigail sat by her mother's bed with Simon beside her while Jesus stood gazing upon Deborah before taking her limp hand within both of his own. His lips moved in silent prayer, face tilting to the roof as though looking directly into the face of God.

Hushed expectancy filled the room.

Jesus' lips stilled, eyes closing briefly before he turned to stare hard at Deborah. With firm words, he rebuked the fever. As with Amos, he kept his gaze focused, but his hands were gentle as he cradled hers.

Deborah gasped, her eyes opening, fingers closing over Jesus' hand, clutching at him as if he pulled her from an abyss.

Abigail collapsed onto the bed with a sob, Zeb placed a hand over his mouth, and John laughed—jubilant. Amazement rippled through the room, spilling into the courtyard beyond. As the news spread, people grew restless, daring now to come close, pushing into the room to see the man who commanded not only spirits, but the physical body as well.

In the middle of the mounting excitement, however, Simon remained still, arms loose at his sides, lips slightly parted, eyes resting on Jesus.

The Holy One of God.

Twenty-One

"Your mother was right. You have paradise in your eyes. As if you've seen God's very glory." I startled awake, blinking into the light that filtered through the high window. With a sigh, I curled onto my side and let myself miss my parents.

The dream was an embrace, and I lingered in it, basking in the memory of Ima's song and Abba's hands on my face, his blessing on my head, his confident hope over my future. *"Adonai has good things in store for you, never doubt it."* How could I have known then that my golden eyes, once the source of childish taunts, would one day witness miracles?

Out of every place on earth, Adonai was expressing His power in the middle of Simon's courtyard.

"Jonah," I breathed, recalling Andrew's stricken face as he'd come to Zeb last night. He'd crashed into my husband's embrace, unable to speak beyond uttering his father's name, eyes flooding with tears, wonder, and loss.

Adonai taking the one and sparing the other. Those of us who remained behind were left with the mystery, left to wrestle with joy and sorrow within the tangled web of our own understanding.

Since Deborah's healing, she was undeniably changed, and the evidence was on display in nearly every relationship, especially with Simon. Rather than resenting his mother-in-law for a healing his father was too late to receive, Simon drew close to Deborah as a true son and she to him. Her arms could not get enough of the burly man whom she'd once deemed too loud, and he accepted and returned her affection with eagerness. Abigail was beside herself with joy at the new love that existed between husband and mother.

Word spread like fire, and soon the house was full. The awe that initially drove Capernaum to silence now burst into a flame of desperation. There was a man with the power of God in his hands, and he was in Simon's home. Day after day, people brought their sick loved ones, and Jesus healed them of every kind of ailment. The only time his gentleness shifted was when he confronted evil spirits. And then he ripped those spirits from the people they tormented.

"You are the Son of God!" With screams, the demons identified him and with thunder he silenced them.

The Son of God.

I tended to Jesus as he stayed in Simon's home with a bashfulness that snaked throughout my gut. Every time his eyes fell upon me, I shrank back, too overwhelmed to hold his gaze. *Jesus of Nazareth, what do you want with my sons?* My own question rang in my head, setting my cheeks aflame. With every dish I served him, my heart pounded a wild dance, furious beats that roared in my ears. *My sons, my sons, the Holy One of God is with my sons.*

By now the desire in James and John was so evident, it was painful to see. They stayed close to Jesus and he to them, his eyes resting upon them with evident affection.

He had the hands of my father—the rough hands of a man accustomed to hard work. I learned from those who followed him that he was a *tekton*, a builder by trade. He'd lived most of his life working with wood and, on occasion, stone.

As his hands touched the injured and brought forth healing, I imagined those hands working with raw material to turn it into something good, something useful.

He had the hands of my father—hands eager to draw out new purpose from what was rough and ordinary.

For days he stayed with Simon, teaching and healing. My boys were out on the lake by night, but instead of sleeping during the day, they remained by Jesus' side, weary yet attentive, holding on to his every word like fish drawn close within a net.

✦

He left early in the morning as the boats were coming in. We'd known it was only a matter of time.

"Master, won't you stay?" I'd overheard John speaking in a rare, private moment with Jesus the night before. *"Stay,"* he'd begged, voice rough with emotion that he was too earnest to hide.

"I must go, John. I must preach the Good News of the Kingdom of God to the other towns as well."

Now, as Jesus left Capernaum, he did so via the harbor street. Paved in black basalt, the street ran along the shoreline and was clogged with those eager for Jesus to stay, John's own desire finding expression in their reaching hands.

I stood in our outer courtyard that fronted the lake, losing sight of Jesus in the crowd even as I caught sight of my sons. Their boat was anchored farther down the quay and they were cleaning their nets with Zeb and two of our hired men.

As I approached, John lurched from the boat and pointed to the crowd. "Is that him? He's leaving, isn't he?"

"There he is!" James pointed.

Jesus was entering Simon's boat, which was full of empty nets from a fruitless night of fishing. He motioned for them to row back out onto the lake. As Andrew dropped anchor, Jesus sat down and began to teach the crowds before his departure.

"The Kingdom of heaven is like treasure hidden in a field.

When a man found it, he hid it again, and then in his joy went and sold all he had and bought that field."

Again, the Kingdom of God that Jesus said had come near—this time spoken of in terms of treasure. John and I stood on the quay while James perched in the bow of our boat, nets tangled in a heap at his feet.

The water served to amplify Jesus' voice, ensuring that his words would not be lost among the crowd. Old and young, men and women—they all lined the quay. Children sat with legs dangling over the harbor wall, heels kicking against the stone. Fishermen hunched in their docked boats, cleaning their nets, while women stopped what they were doing, arms full of fish as they listened to the words of the Healer and Teacher.

And in the background . . . soldiers.

"John," I hissed, nodding at the glint of sun off armor.

"They won't stop him. They haven't these last few days. You fret too much."

Biting my lip, I directed my ear to Jesus' message but kept my eyes trained on Herod Antipas' soldiers. Teachers came and went, even those claiming miraculous power, and yet none had performed the undeniable signs of Jesus that extended even to the Gentiles. With shock, Capernaum had watched Jesus heal not only our own, but also the son of a military official.

"Ima," John muttered, glancing at my hand, which clasped his arm like a claw. "They're concerned with crowd control, not his teaching. Relax." He pried my hand off while Jesus continued to teach.

"The Kingdom of heaven is like a net that was let down into the lake and caught all kinds of fish. When it was full, the fishermen pulled it up on the shore. Then they sat down and collected the good fish in baskets but threw the bad away."

Here was an image familiar to us all. Appreciative murmurs spread along the quay. Jesus stood and turned to Simon. He kept his voice loud, intending that we all hear his next command. "Put out into the deep and let down your nets for a catch."

"What is he doing?" Zeb wondered. "The fish will not be active during the day."

"We've fished all night with no success," James added.

By my side, John shifted from foot to foot.

Simon was speaking but kept his voice low, hiding his words from the watching crowd. Whatever doubt he harbored, he still followed Jesus' instruction. Both he and Andrew began rowing back into the lake while Jesus stood in the middle with a hand on the mast.

"They're using a trammel net," James observed, tone matching the disbelief in Zeb's face. "They're using a trammel net in the middle of the morning."

"The fish will see the net." John stated the obvious with a wild grin splayed across his face.

Together, Simon and Andrew lowered the net into the lake. For a moment, all was calm. The two fishermen peered over the side while Jesus remained at the mast, both hands grasping the wooden beam, bracing himself.

A shout from the lake came first, followed by a violent tipping of the boat. Jesus remained upright, while Simon and Andrew nearly tumbled into the water.

"No." Zeb's voice was low, hollowed out, raw with amazement. "No, it cannot be."

"Abba, look! So many . . ." James was scrambling to the prow, nearly trampling the hired men, all of them watching in slack-jawed disbelief as Simon's boat began to sink.

"Help them!" I pushed John, shoving him back into our boat as the cries came from the lake.

"Help!" Simon was waving frantically at us while Andrew leaned across the edge of the boat, half of his body in the water.

With a shout, Zeb began to row. They reached the floundering

189

boat swiftly and began drawing in the net. People ran along the shore to gain a better view, shouts from the quay drowning out the shouts from the lake as more and more fish poured into both boats.

I stood immobile, my feet an extension of the basalt stones as I stared at the distant forms of my sons. John had stripped and was in the water while James pulled from the boat. Light danced upon the scales of countless fish, heaped into writhing piles. Slowly the boats returned to shore, ponderously pushing through the water.

"They're both sinking!" The cry sounded behind me, and I finally moved, stumbling down a pier to the farthest point. Some of the fish were slipping back into the water as the bottoms of the boats sank lower and lower. Timber creaked as the boats finally groaned into the harbor. By now, the piers were crowded with people, hands reaching to help as laughter pierced the air.

"Zeb!" His back was arched, the muscles taut beneath sun-darkened skin as he strained at the oar. He turned, releasing the oar to throw me a rope. I held it fast. More ropes, more laughter, multiple hands helping to secure the boats, pregnant with fish.

Our astonishment was loud, but Simon was louder. He collapsed at Jesus' feet. "Lord! Go away from me, Lord! Go away!"

It was the cry of Amos when confronted by the holiness of God. The words had leapt from Amos' lips as an insult—the fear of the demons finding release in a mocking demand that Jesus depart and leave them alone in the dark.

In the mouth of Simon, however, these words were something else.

He was weeping, broad shoulders shaking as he tried to lift his head. Failing to do so, he crushed his face to Jesus' feet. "Master, please leave. I-I am a sinner. I cannot handle this holiness." Fear nestled deep within the cry.

Jesus stood on the pier, mantle wet, hair wild from the wind, expression kind as he beheld Simon's hunched form. He'd silenced the demon in Amos with a loud voice. To Simon, however, he gave a whispered word, so gentle, those of us watching almost missed it. He placed a hand on Simon's shoulder. "Do not be afraid." It was the quiet hush of a mother, the steadying hand of a father. It was strength bestowed upon Simon, lifting his head.

Jesus drew Simon to standing. Andrew clasped Simon's shoulder as Jesus pointed a long finger at each brother. "Follow me, and I will make you fish for people."

I gasped as Jesus walked down the length of the pier, back to the shore, Simon and Andrew close at his heels. No . . . it couldn't be.

Zeb and James were still in the boat. John stood on the pier, bare-chested and dripping, breath heaving in and out of his body in ragged gulps. Jesus stopped parallel to us, eyes landing solidly on John before sliding to James. "You two, follow me."

John left, brushing past me quickly, not even stopping for his outer garment.

John. I thought I'd spoken his name out loud, but I hadn't. My lips were parted, hands reaching, feet unable to move. *What is happening? John.*

Behind me, James scrambled from the boat, falling into the water before pulling himself up and onto the pier.

"James . . ." His name was a hoarse scrape across my tongue. I clutched at him, fingers catching at his sleeve.

"Ima."

He was breathless, face hovering above mine, eyes bright and so alive. There was a ring of lighter brown circling the black center of each eye as if my own golden color was fighting to push through. He grazed my forehead with his lips.

And then he was gone.

My boys. My boys. My treasure.

Fire seared my throat.

"Salome."

Zeb stood at the very end of the pier. Behind him everything was blue . . . the sky, the lake. He was fighting for words, the swell in his throat bobbing with effort. I went to him, as I had a thousand times before, meeting him on the shore, the two of us caught between land and water.

He opened empty arms, and I filled them, pressed myself up against the curve of his chest, head against his pounding heart.

Only when he held me did I realize I was trembling.

Twenty-Two

Memory is precious . . . and ruthless. A comfort but also a thorn. I spent the days after my sons' calling wrapped in memory, an embrace that at times turned sharp. John, a thin boy of twelve with flashing eyes, determined to dismantle others' harsh judgments of him, to make their hard words untrue. James, equally passionate and yet with a bedrock of steadiness so like his father.

Alone in our storage room, I clasped a jar of olive oil and breathed through the stab of memory. How long had I stood here—trapped? Long enough for Deborah to go hunting. Entering on quiet feet, she closed the door behind her. "Sister."

Never had she addressed me by that title.

She tugged me into her arms, and I eased into her embrace. The hardness between us had softened into a sisterhood that both of us sorely needed.

"I wondered where you'd gone. People are looking for you," she murmured.

"I came in here for oil and then forgot to leave."

"Are you sure you're not hiding from all the visitors?"

"Our home *has* been full to bursting," I acknowledged.

"And you have been smiling and accepting all the well-wishes, but perhaps you still aren't sure what to feel. Perhaps, like me, there is some fear." Deborah pulled back with pursed lips.

"You've always been astute." I laughed. "There's fear—of course there's fear—but this pride is stronger than any fear."

"Follow me." Jesus had not waited for esteemed, promising men to approach him. No—he had gone hunting for his own disciples, and he had selected them from my home.

Adonai, You see my sons. Not since I'd first discovered I was pregnant with James had such overwhelming sureness flooded me. *You see them.*

"Yes—pride outpacing the fear." Deborah sighed. "Peter, my son . . ." She spoke Simon's new name easily. "I've spent long, long years wishing for a son."

"You have it in him." I smiled.

"Yes, his is a temperament I never would have chosen, but it is the one God knew I needed in my life. Salome, I confess that I resented you because of your two beautiful boys. In truth, I resented you for far more than the gift of your sons. You had the respect of my mother. You even had the marriage I wished I had. When Elazar treated your family so poorly, I was ashamed of his actions. I could have extended an apology for his behavior, but bitterness kept me even from this. Forgive me."

This woman had always confounded me, and I'd leaned into that confusion as an excuse for my own hardness of heart. But now, for the first time, I saw her clearly.

"I forgive you." I threaded my fingers through hers. "If you can forgive me? We are not, after all, so different."

Deborah's face cracked open with a smile. "Now I know that Jesus' healing extends to the inner person as well," she exclaimed, eyes lifting to the ceiling, free hand moving upward in praise. "He's healed more than my body. To be with Jesus is to be changed." Her voice dipped into softness as love crossed her countenance, a slowly spreading light that transformed her features. "What an honor for the young men we love to be near him."

"An honor, yes." I sighed. "An honor Zeb and I were never expecting, and now . . ."

Deborah cocked her head. "And now you're wondering how to talk to your husband."

My strained face confirmed her words. After the calling, Zeb had fallen into silence, and we had yet to address all that was occurring within our home.

"I've never known you to be hesitant, Salome." Deborah smirked. "Especially when it comes to that quiet brother of mine. Instead of hiding in the storeroom, you might go and find him. Bring him some of your pride and joy."

———— ✦ ————

He was by the shore where our boys had left him days before. His head was bent over a net as he picked out debris, two of our hired men working steadily with him. A surprising twist of nervousness halted my steps. Deborah was right—when had I ever hesitated in speaking my mind to my husband? And Adonai had blessed me with a man who welcomed and valued my thoughts. But this was new, and I did not know how to discuss the miraculous events unfolding in our family, nor the new, strange loneliness nestling within, side by side with the joy.

"You've barely been home these last few days. Hiding out here, are you?" I teased. "I was doing the same in our storeroom. Our home has been swarmed with neighbors, all coming to congratulate us. They've been asking after you."

Zeb glanced up with a grunt before returning to his work.

"Deborah and Abigail are preparing to travel to Chorazin to meet up with Jesus and our sons. I've been thinking of joining them."

At this, Zeb paused, although he kept his face averted. "Do what you must."

When he began working again with nothing more to say, I playfully yanked on the net in his hands, masking my concern with a jest. "Zebedee, won't you look up at your wife and talk? Or is that net more engaging than I am?"

Zeb's hands stilled as he shook his head. "You will *always* be more interesting than fish, Salome." He glanced up with a spark in his eye that swirled a small eddy in my stomach.

"Then talk to me."

With a low sigh, Zeb nodded to the hired men to leave, and as they did, he muttered, "Formal discipleship. We are looking at formal discipleship."

"I know! Think of it—out of all the men in this village—in *Israel*—this man chose our sons!"

"Full-time discipleship." Zeb resumed work, plucking twigs from the net and tossing them aside.

"Remember when your father crowed over Kadmiel? But it is *you* who now bears the greater honor!"

Zeb remained silent, long fingers moving swiftly over the net.

I sat and placed a hand to his thigh, searching his face. "You are quiet, but I need to hear your thoughts."

"And you are loud, but I need to think."

"Zebedee!" Rearing back, I gave him a mighty shove.

He rocked onto one hip with a loud laugh. How long since I'd last heard that sound? Quieting, he tucked stray hairs behind my ear, dancing fingertips along my jaw.

"I am not like you, wife. You want to talk rather than letting things lie for a moment, but I need to think."

"You take too long to think."

Zeb hung his head to study his hands—the calloused, bronzed hands that had once rocked a restless John and lifted a happy

James up onto his shoulders. "I understand this is an honor, but it is also a loss."

His words resonated within the lonely space I was suppressing. No, I did not want to hear this. Swallowing hard, I shifted to gaze out across the lake. "So you do *not* want our sons to follow after this man? The man who miraculously healed your sister? Who commands demons to flee and fish to jump straight into nets?"

"I did not say that."

"You would have our boys look Jesus in the face and say no?"

"Salome! That is not what I'm saying."

"You yourself noted the longing in John."

"Yes, but—"

"Words can inflict lasting wounds. John has long pushed against his first instructor's careless words, but now . . . oh, Zeb, the brightness on that boy's face when Jesus called him is a light I will hold on to for the rest of my days."

"Salome, you want me to talk, but you aren't even listening!"

Crossing my arms, I swiveled to face him. "Okay then, I'm listening."

Zeb swallowed hard, eyes jumping to the sky, the ground . . . anywhere but me. His lips parted, but no words left. He appeared to be searching for them in the surrounding scenery.

"Zeb?" I prompted.

Dragging his eyes back to my face, my husband groaned, and I saw the ragged grief he was trying to hide. "Jonah is freshly buried."

"I know," I whispered, body releasing its tension.

"My friend is gone, and now his boys . . ." Zeb's lips thinned into a line, hand shading his face from me.

My heart thudded with compassion. "I know what it's like to miss a friend, but think of how proud Jonah would have been."

"I have a responsibility to Jonah's sons."

My breath caught.

"Would you help watch over my boys should anything happen to me?" Keturah across a late-night fire, James' hair pooling in her lap as she told me of Gabriel.

"It's important we focus upon the honor of this moment." My voice shook. "Keturah's sons are beneath the teaching of a rabbi who performs miracles!"

"And now they are away—gone!" Zeb exclaimed.

"Gone with *him*," I clarified.

"You're only focusing on what you *want* to feel, but there is more here than honor, Salome!" Zeb pushed to his feet. With agitated strides, he paced the shoreline. "Why do you not see it? How can I explain? I feel a weight for Jonah's legacy. I have a responsibility to the business he helped me build."

At Zeb's expressed fear, my own leapt in response. I clenched my jaw and tamped it back down. "Now is not the time to focus on our business when a man sent by God has called your sons to follow him."

Zeb flung an exasperated hand in my direction. "*This* is why I did not want to speak of it right now."

"What is *that* supposed to mean?" I scowled.

Zeb merely muttered in a surly tone that was so like Jonathan that my next words poured out before I could stop them. "Do not be like your own father, Zebedee bar Jonathan!"

Silence stretched between us, pained and tense, until Zeb broke it in a hollowed voice. "Why would you say that?"

Lowering my head, I gazed at my lap, mortification mixing with frustration. "For a moment, you sounded like him. He overlooked you, Zeb, and it hurt me to see it. He suppressed your desires and thoughts, and I don't want you to do the same to our sons."

Zeb came to my side but didn't touch me. I gazed up but couldn't see his face. The sun was behind him, shrouding his features in shadow. "I am not like my father," he stated, slow and firm.

"I know. I—"

"I am wrestling, Salome. I am overcome with pride and . . . *grief*! Let me mourn this. I have worked my entire life to build this business and have just lost my oldest friend. I am proud of our work and the lives we have built. I am so proud of my sons that I have a hard time talking about it. I . . . I love them, Salome. They are my life. They are my future. If they leave, then what do I have? If they leave, then where does my business go? My whole life's work . . . given to my hired hands?"

"Zeb . . ." I was undone and covered my face with my hands so he wouldn't see.

"This is not a small thing. This is not a small moment. I understand exactly what this is. My boys called away from one life into another. You see the honor, but I see the cost. Salome, of course I am proud, but let me mourn."

He departed on swift feet while I remained in the echoing silence he left behind him.

TWENTY-THREE

The next morning, I departed with Deborah and Abigail for Chorazin, but not before seeking my husband. The years had taught me that clinging to my own pride within our marriage was costly and that choosing love sooner paved the way to peace. Our words on the shore sat heavy between us, a conversation that must and would be continued. For the moment, however, I simply needed to see him and be seen in return.

He stilled at my approach, wary and distant, but I held him anyway. Standing on tiptoe, I linked my arms about his neck with the unhindered affection we'd shared in our youth. He rocked back on his heels with a surprised grunt, for a moment stiff and unyielding in my arms before loosening in a rush, melding his body to mine in a brief, deep embrace.

The journey to Chorazin didn't take long, for it was only a handful of miles away. When Deborah, Abigail, and I joined Jesus, we could see that his company had increased. Many remained close to his side, but only a few had been formally called. James, John, Simon, and Andrew had been the first, but when we arrived, we discovered that Philip had been added to that number, along with a man from Cana named Nathaniel.

"What do you make of it?" I whispered to Deborah. "James

and John both believe Philip to be changed, but I confess that I'm less certain."

Deborah squinted. "If he is anything like his father, then perhaps the best place for him to be is by Jesus," she mused. "Who are we to question his choice?"

She was right, and yet I struggled. Was it because I doubted Philip? Or resented his father?

"To be with Jesus is to be changed." Daily we witnessed Jesus' transformative power. He stretched out a hand and touched a leper, a man who defiled anything he contacted. But under the hand of Jesus, the man became whole and restored. Transformation—it was inevitable wherever Jesus went.

From Chorazin down to Magadan and back up to Gennesaret, Jesus traveled with a company that grew day by day. In Abigail's face I saw my own awe—pride mingled with confusion. Each of us wondered, *How can this be?* A disciple's role was to become like their rabbi—to walk so closely to him that the dirt kicked up from his sandals covered the disciple in dust. The goal was to become like him, in word and deed, but how? Daily we watched Jesus do the impossible and quietly questioned. How would the men we loved emulate such a teacher?

"Not everyone who calls out to me, 'Lord! Lord!' will enter the Kingdom of heaven. Only those who actually do the will of my Father in heaven will enter."

Jesus often talked of true discipleship and of a kingdom. If there was to be a new kingdom, then how would it come, and what role would my sons play in its arrival? I could see now that Jesus of Nazareth was nothing like Judas of Galilee. Judas had preyed upon Israel's sons, forming them into insurrectionists who saw themselves as God's sword, but Jesus brought life wherever he went.

"When you pray, pray like this: 'May Your Kingdom come soon. May Your will be done on earth, as it is in heaven.'" Jesus connected the will of God to the Kingdom of God and in doing so seemed to align himself with the Pharisees, who saw adherence to the Law—not a violent uprising—as ushering in the messianic age.

"You're worried," Deborah observed. We stood along a road while Jesus taught beneath a tree. "You worry about what will be required of them," she whispered, gaze resting upon Simon.

"Jesus says he's come to fulfill the Law, but how can one man do that?" I whispered back. "Does he mean to fulfill the Law for us all? I wish I knew how his Kingdom plans to come." My eyes flitted to James. He had Zeb's height, towering over those gathered. I stared hard at him until he turned.

The smile on his face was too beautiful to look at for long.

◆

We arrived back in Capernaum as the sun was setting. Jesus was staying with Simon and Andrew, and my boys lingered behind with them while I returned home. We'd been gone for weeks, and I was hopeful that now Zeb and I could talk.

The lamps were lit, the courtyard glowing in the growing night, casting pools of shadows into the corners. Several dark forms crouched about a fire, and I approached them with an outstretched hand.

"Zeb, we're home." I let love dominate as my fingers brushed a shoulder. "I missed you."

The form turned, and my body tensed.

"It's good to see you, Salome." Kadmiel smiled, easy and wide, eyes glinting in the firelight.

◆

With my own hand, I served Kadmiel his morning meal. He and Admon had arrived from Jerusalem a couple days ago. Given the late hour the night before, there had been only small talk. But now, well-rested and with a plate overflowing with bread and salted fish, our guest was primed to speak.

Kadmiel sank his teeth into a round of bread drizzled with honey. Swiping a sticky finger on a cloth, he pointed at me and spoke around the bite in his cheek. "Where are your sons? Won't they break their fast with us?"

"I believe they're already next door." I gave Kadmiel a tight smile and offered Admon a cluster of grapes. Behind me, Zeb entered the courtyard from a night of fishing. Plucking up a piece of bread, he tore into it while his other hand caressed the back of my neck in welcome.

"News of this Jesus continues to spread in Jerusalem. As soon as we heard that this man was performing miracles in your very town, we knew we had to see it for ourselves." Kadmiel jostled his son, who nodded amicably. "Zeb informs me that your boys are close to him."

"Our boys are not simply *close* with this new teacher." I threw a glance to Zeb, who was studying his bread like it was a ledger full of complicated figures. "Our boys are his *disciples*."

Kadmiel sucked his lower lip in thought, gaze shifting from Zeb to me and back again. "His disciples?"

When Zeb didn't answer, I jumped in. "Some of his very first. He chose them."

Silence reigned until Admon spoke up. "Well, it doesn't surprise me that Jesus would do things differently. A rabbi choosing his disciples!" He laughed but stopped at the sight of his father's pinched face. Ducking his head, he tore off a bite of bread.

Kadmiel frowned. "I came to assess the man for myself rather than relying on secondhand knowledge. I didn't meet him when he came to Jerusalem, but as you yourselves know he created quite the stir in the Temple courtyard. The lingering talk of him is not all positive. My colleagues asked him directly by whose authority he could do such things, and his answer was cryptic and delusional."

"'Destroy this temple, and I will raise it again in three days,'" Admon quoted.

Zeb dusted the lingering breadcrumbs from his hands and drew himself up. "It's well-known that the money changers charge exorbitant fees from those coming to worship."

"That is not against the Law."

"Still . . . it doesn't seem right." Color hinted at Zeb's neck as he tried to untangle his next words, but Kadmiel's were smooth and confident, cutting him off.

"Jesus is showing a pattern of disregard for the religious establishment."

"But . . . is he breaking God's Law?" Zeb managed to ask, color deepening along his throat.

Kadmiel raised a brow. "He healed on the Sabbath."

"He healed my sister on the Sabbath," Zeb retorted, this time quickly, the color moving to his cheeks. "*Your* sister-in-law."

"On the Sabbath," Kadmiel emphasized.

The mounting anger in Zeb was apparent as he shifted from foot to foot.

"Whose law is that breaking?" I dared to ask. "God's Law? Or man's interpretation of that Law?"

Instead of answering, Kadmiel offered another pronouncement. "He is disregarding authority. That should at least give you pause. He calls himself a rabbi, but he has no formal training. Who has he studied under?"

Suspicion clawed at my mind. Was Kadmiel . . . *jealous*? My lips parted, but for once no words came.

"A reputable teacher will position his teaching beneath another rabbi. He will reference that rabbi so that the people might have confidence in the instruction they are receiving. You know this!" Kadmiel shook his head in a woeful gesture that unfastened my tongue.

"Perhaps you should withhold judgment since you have not yet sat beneath his teaching."

Zeb flicked me a warning look, but Kadmiel seemed unoffended. "Wise words, Salome. And that is why I am here."

As the morning had lengthened, the sounds from outside had increased, and a sudden disruption drew our attention to the door. Shouts filled the air. Running to our door, I swung it wide and gasped at the crowd of people in the streets.

"So many." Zeb was behind me, hand at the small of my back.

"They're destroying it!" a woman yelped, finger pointing in the direction of Simon's home.

Pushing out onto the street, I rose on tiptoe to see. A group of men stood on Simon's roof, hacking at it with axes, hard muscles straining, bodies glistening with sweat.

"What are they doing?" Kadmiel shoved past me, face aghast.

"The teacher is inside, but there's no way to get in," a man answered.

No way but through the roof.

"Let me through." Kadmiel's voice was heavy with authority. When his command didn't produce the desired effect, however, he clapped his hands, raised them high, and boomed, "I said, let me through!"

Heads turned in our direction. Upon seeing Kadmiel's long robes and exaggerated tassels that marked him as a teacher of the Law, people began to mutter and shift, creating a tight passageway for him. He pushed forward, Admon close behind. I followed snugly at Admon's heels.

Shouts rang from the roof, followed by the crash of debris. Ahead of me, Kadmiel began shoving people who weren't moving fast enough. When we finally neared Simon's door, I was out of breath.

A man was suspended on a pallet in the middle of the room, dangling in the air. Jesus' gaze roamed the young man, lingering on his emaciated legs, and then, with a grin, he peered up at the hole in the ceiling. A cluster of sheepish, hopeful faces plugged the hole. Jesus' grin spread into a smile, and the smile opened into a laugh, deep and rumbling from his belly. "Have courage, son, your sins are forgiven."

Kadmiel grunted deep in his throat. Immediately, Jesus' eyes jerked up, gaze lingering on Kadmiel for a long moment before he moved. Swiftly and surely, Jesus skirted the pallet that still hung in midair and walked right up to Kadmiel.

"Why are you thinking these things in your heart?" Jesus' brow furrowed as he placed a hand upon Kadmiel's shoulder.

Kadmiel cleared his throat but didn't speak.

"Is it easier to say to this man, 'Your sins are forgiven,' or 'Stand up, pick up your mat, and walk'?"

Sickness within and without—Deborah was convinced that Jesus could reach both. We had seen the visible healing. Was it any wonder that Jesus could also heal the invisible?

Admon was staring at Jesus with parted lips and flushed cheeks. I could not see his father's face, but I could see Jesus, and the sadness in his eyes showed me the hardness in Kadmiel's own.

"I want you to know that the Son of Man has authority on earth to forgive sins." Jesus leaned toward Kadmiel. And then he turned with an outstretched arm and a loud voice. "Stand up, pick up your mat, and go home!"

No one spoke a word as the young man slowly eased his legs over the side of the suspended pallet. His bare feet hovered over the ground, toes wiggling, testing the waters before entering them. Then he jumped. With a hearty leap, he left the pallet, feet landing hard and sturdy upon the ground. He nabbed the pallet from the ropes, rolled it up tight, slung it over his shoulder, and walked out of the room.

Kadmiel watched him leave, jaw clenched. Behind him, the ropes dangled, loose and empty in the air.

Twenty-Four

Sliding curious fingers over the intricate carvings on the door-post, I paused before entering the home most of Capernaum despised. For years I'd passed by here, never imagining that one day I would enter this place.

"Ima." John jerked his chin, indicating for me to follow him deeper inside. Hesitantly, I followed.

Situated along a major trade route from Damascus to the Great Sea, Capernaum was a prime spot for a customs office. For the past decade, one man had held the position of tax collector, efficient in his dealings and thoroughly despised. I glanced at my opulent surroundings and grimaced.

"I know, Ima, I know." John slanted a wry look at me. "But try a little harder to hide your feelings."

"Speak with more respect, brother." James approached, cupping my elbow with his large hand. "This is unexpected for all of us, and you know it."

"I was jesting!" John frowned. "Why must you be so quick to rebuke?"

Before James could answer, our host entered the courtyard.

"Welcome!" He spread his hands wide, a smile splitting his face in two. This face—so familiar, but never in a festive setting.

The last time we'd seen this man, we'd been handing him an exorbitant amount of money, knowing that some of it was padding his own pocket and funding this indulgent home.

"Rest yourselves and let my servants wash your feet. Tonight, we celebrate!" our host boomed, approaching Jesus with open arms.

As Jesus clasped Matthew by the shoulders, I realized that Jesus was welcoming the embrace of a man whom Judas of Galilee would have slaughtered on sight.

⁍

Matthew served us himself, bringing in dish after dish, alongside his own servants. Never had I seen such humility displayed in the man who regularly consorted with Herod's troops. A Jew by birth but viewed as a traitor to our people, Matthew had spent the last ten years collecting taxes that funded the construction of Tiberias, Herod's new capital city.

Black hair streaked with silver, eyes a somber gray, Matthew was typically quiet and withdrawn, but tonight he exuded unbridled joy.

"More wine, Salome?" Matthew asked, lips forming a smile that infused life into his eyes.

I lifted my cup and studied the man. Almost immediately after healing the paralytic, Jesus had called this man to follow him—had invited him out of the old life in a tax booth and into a new life by his side. The light in Matthew reminded me of the paralytic. Something dead and withered had been brought to life.

Straightening, Matthew continued down the table, offering more sumptuous food and wine to his guests.

"Uncle would not approve of such a banquet, would he?" James leaned close, delivering his dire observation into my ear.

"He most certainly would not." I gnawed at my lip as Matthew

poured wine for a known prostitute. She sat next to Nathaniel—
the respectable reclining next to the outcast.

After his encounter with Jesus, Kadmiel had grown quiet. *"He saw what you were thinking, Abba!"* Admon had whispered, urgent and excited. *"If he can heal a man—inside and out—then surely he can discern what is in the heart."*

"He discerned nothing," Kadmiel had refuted. *"It hardly takes the power of God to understand the proper reaction to such an event. Everyone knows that only God can forgive sins. To claim otherwise is blasphemy, so no, my son—he did not miraculously see what I was thinking. He knew his own blasphemy and so knew that I, as a man of God, would detect it."*

"But the man got up and walked." In Admon's face there was belief—belief he was trying hard to hide from his father.

"A hoax or, worse yet, a work from the devil."

"I wish Abba had come," James muttered as he scooped a bite of stew into his mouth.

"We have guests who are leaving soon. He is being a good host." I left unspoken the growing tension in Zeb the longer Kadmiel stayed—irritated with him one moment and smoothing over ruffled feelings the next.

At the head of the table, Jesus reclined in the position of honor. On his left and on his right were other tax collectors—the only friends Matthew had.

"Does this . . . bother you?" I asked, observing James' profile. "Seeing who he is calling?" First Philip and now Capernaum's tax collector. It was enough to make my head spin.

James sighed as he watched Jesus. "It would bother me . . . if I didn't trust Jesus," he finally answered, still focusing on the man himself. "In my own mind, yes . . . yes, it confuses me, and that confusion would fester and turn into bitterness if I let it. Because if he calls a tax collector—a man who makes a living betraying our people—then what does that say about my own appointment? I would like to think—" James flushed and looked at his hands.

"To think what?" I nudged him with my shoulder, urging more of his honesty.

"I suppose I would like to think that I am righteous and that is why Jesus called me. But—" James broke off to look at Matthew. "But I'm realizing that I could never be righteous enough for a man like Jesus, and that perhaps . . . in his choosing, he is showing us this fact. None of us could ever be righteous enough."

"And so you trust him," I murmured.

"If I can know *him*, then I can be at peace not knowing much else." James laughed.

Love and pride pooled in my breast. I slid my fingers into James' hair and gave a playful yank, tugging a smile right out of him before he shook his head at me with a grin.

One of Matthew's servants approached James. "There is someone at the door for you, sir."

"Who?" I questioned.

"He didn't say, but he asked for both James and John, and he was insistent they come immediately."

With alarm, I rose to my feet and motioned to John, who sat across the table.

"You don't have to come," James whispered as he stood.

"I'm coming," I stated firmly. As the servant led us to the door, I sensed Jesus' attention like a swift caress. Turning, I found his eyes upon me.

Had he really seen inside Kadmiel's heart, unearthing the thoughts he'd left unspoken? If that was the case, then what did he discern in me? Perhaps he saw what was better left buried, the worries that still clutched tight. Perhaps he also saw the love for my boys that raced through my body like blood.

Ducking from the room and away from Jesus' inspection, I followed my sons to the front door, where three men waited, faces obscured by shadow. As we neared, one strode forward. "I hardly believed it when Zeb told me where you all were." Kadmiel's face twisted into a grimace. "What could possibly compel you to come *here*?" He waved a hand about our lush surroundings. Matthew's wealth showed in the elaborate furniture and plush textiles filling his large home—wealth pilfered from his fellow Jews.

"Jesus called Matthew as he called us." John's voice was too loud, for my youngest did not know the meaning of discretion. "Matthew wanted to host a banquet to honor him."

"No respectable rabbi would dine in such a home, let alone call such a man to be a disciple." Kadmiel stabbed the air for emphasis.

To share table fellowship with someone was to align oneself with that person. And what respectable Jew aligned herself with tax collectors and prostitutes?

"I understand your hesitation." Placing a firm hand on Kadmiel's arm, I infused my voice with charity. "But you needn't worry. Matthew is changed."

Was he? Certainly, it was too soon to tell. I crushed the bothersome thought. Perhaps I didn't yet trust Matthew, but wasn't it enough that I trusted Jesus?

"I *must* worry." Kadmiel swept my hand from his arm. "These are my nephews. My name is linked to yours in Jerusalem." He jabbed a finger into Zeb's chest. "Or did you forget that I helped secure your largest accounts? Your business with Annas and Caiaphas is thanks to me."

"You would hold that over us?" My cheeks warmed. "That is disingenuous of you."

"Salome, please remain calm." Zeb lifted tired eyes and covered Kadmiel's hand with his own, easing it from his chest.

Me remain calm? When Kadmiel was the one lobbing veiled threats? Heat simmered beneath my skin.

"Perhaps it's best if we all go home for the night," Zeb continued.

"Yes, you two, come with me." Kadmiel commanded James and John with a brusque flick of his hand. "You should not be eating and drinking with tax collectors and sinners."

I expected John to erupt, but it was James who spoke. "We will not come away, Uncle. Not while Jesus is here. Our place is by his side."

"But why?" Kadmiel pressed. "Why would you stay in such a home?"

"Who needs a doctor?" We all turned at the question to find Jesus in the doorway of the dining room, one hand resting on the wooden frame as he observed us.

"What do you mean by that question?" Kadmiel drew himself upright, hands folded and hidden beneath the wide hem of his tunic.

Jesus pushed away from the frame and crossed the courtyard. "Who needs a doctor? The one who is healthy? Or the one who is sick?"

"The one who is sick, Master," Admon replied.

"The one who is sick," Jesus affirmed.

Kadmiel stepped closer to Jesus, blocking Admon. "Disease spreads, sir. Impurity defiles what is holy!"

"Go and learn what this means: 'I desire mercy, not sacrifice,'" Jesus exclaimed. "I have come to call not those who think they are righteous, but those who know they are sinners."

With a sharp hiss, Kadmiel stepped back and brushed his hands, cleansing them of filth. "I exhort you all to come with me, away from this table of thieves and harlots." Turning on his heel, he did not wait to see who would obey.

"Zeb—" I whispered as he began to follow Kadmiel.

"He leaves in the morning, and I would try to repair the relationship before he departs." Zeb hung his head, avoiding my face. It'd been years since I'd seen him so weary.

As Zeb and Kadmiel left, I braced myself to face Jesus. Did he think poorly of my husband for leaving? If he could indeed discern my thoughts, then perhaps he knew Zeb was an upright man who simply needed time—time to embrace this new life.

Jesus held my gaze with his deep eyes. It was an ordinary face but for the effect it had upon those he encountered, drawing devotion from some and fury from others.

"Rabbi, I must apologize." My fingers fluttered about my face, tucking stray strands of hair back into place. "My brother-in-law, he . . . he has a hard time accepting anything outside of what he knows."

"He is patching an old garment," Jesus stated. "But he leaves an even bigger tear than before." Quietly, he gestured for James and John to return with him to the table, but before leaving, he lingered. His eyes paved an open road straight to Admon, who fidgeted, chest rising with rapid breath as he shuffled one pace back, then two. Jesus waited a moment longer and then left.

As my boys left with Jesus, I tarried, heart softening toward my nephew, who had backed up almost to the door. "You could stay, Admon," I urged. "He is producing good fruit. In following him there is wisdom. His words and teaching are solid enough to hold you. Why don't you stay and see for yourself?"

Admon shook his head vigorously, but as he stumbled from the home, there was longing embedded in his eyes.

TWENTY-FIVE

"What did you say to him?" I questioned Zeb as I folded an extra tunic within my pack. Kadmiel had left, still upset but not nearly as incensed as he'd been in Matthew's home.

"Does it matter?" Zeb sat on our bed, preparing to sleep even as I readied to leave with Jesus. The midmorning sun slanted into our room, highlighting the deep lines on my husband's face.

Straightening from my task, I placed a hand on a hip. "He was rude, Zeb. He was unbearably rude to our sons and to Jesus. I am fond of Kadmiel. I appreciate him and all he has done for this family, and yet to speak to us in such a way? As if we were ignorant people in need of his instruction?"

"I know, Salome, and yet what would you have me do? Reprimand him? You realize that he has the power to make our lives difficult."

"They think they are better than us."

"Who?"

"Leah and Kadmiel . . . they always have. But it is our boys, Zeb—*our* boys—who have been chosen as the Messiah's disciples! Perhaps Kadmiel speaks more from jealousy."

Zeb was silent, back arched as he slowly unlaced his sandals, slid them from his feet, and then kneaded his brow.

"Admon . . . he seems to understand Jesus' teachings. I'm sure he would join our sons in following Jesus but for his father. Kadmiel is keeping his own son from the Messiah! Zeb, what can we say to convince him?"

My husband sighed, slid the sandals beneath the bed, and hung his head, leaving the messy knot for me to untangle alone.

At his silence, loneliness reared upright. "Zeb, I—"

He glanced up sharply. "What?"

I shook my head, unable to articulate what I felt.

Zeb stood, clasping me in a quick embrace before returning to the bed. "I need to sleep, and you need to be on your way. Be safe on the road and give my love to our boys."

"That is all you have to say? Our extended family is torn over Jesus and you have no help to offer?" My voice crackled with unshed tears.

"What would you have me do, Salome? What else do you want me to say?"

"*Something!*" I spluttered. "I know I can talk too much, but . . . it's how I come to know my own mind, to find a way forward when I don't know what to do. When you are so silent, I have a hard time—" I broke off and bit my lip.

Zeb stared at the ceiling, brows drawn in concentration. Finally, he patted the bed in invitation.

Part of me wanted to stomp from the room and leave this man alone with his impenetrable thoughts. Another part wanted to curl up by his side and sleep the morning away with my head against his heart.

I perched on the very edge of the bed with a rigid back.

"You are direct and bold, something I've long admired about you. But with certain people, that approach is flint to stone." Zeb rested a hand over mine.

"You would have us cower and demur?"

"I would have us be circumspect. We cannot force truth on anyone, Salome."

"We cannot remain silent either." I turned my hand palm up to thread my fingers through his.

He squeezed hard before propping up on an elbow and facing me. "Wisdom is needed when navigating uncertain waters. We must be careful that when we speak it is not from hurt pride."

"Perhaps, but we must also not confuse caution with fear."

Zeb looked at me long and slow before grazing my lips with a kiss. "I don't know what will finally crack Kadmiel's hardened heart, but I sense it won't be from you and me prying it open."

———— ✦ ————

Autumn 28 AD

As the hazy months of summer passed, Deborah, Abigail, and I continued to travel on and off with Jesus' growing company. The love between Deborah and I continued to deepen as together we sat beneath Jesus' teaching and observed growth within the young men we loved. But one morning, I entered Simon's courtyard ready to leave for another trip only to find Deborah unprepared, face apologetic, hands balancing a tray of food.

"What are you doing? Where's your pack?"

"I won't be going this time. Abigail is unwell. I've been trying to get food down her all morning. Nain is too far of a journey, so I'll remain behind with her."

Thirty miles southwest of Capernaum, Nain was indeed a long, arduous walk. "Nothing serious, I hope."

Deborah suppressed a large smile. "Serious, yes, but in a good way." She clamped her lips shut, brows lifting, inviting me to infer what she was leaving unsaid.

Understanding dawned, and with a gasp, I dropped my pack. "Where is she?"

"Lying down—"

But I was already hurrying from the courtyard to Abigail's room, joy fueling my flight.

Abigail lay on her bed with a hand to her forehead. Upon seeing me, she tried to rise, but I stayed her with a swift hand.

"Don't get up. Ah, my girl!" I swooped to the bed, planting myself by her side and smoothing stray hair from her face. "You didn't tell your doda yourself?" I clucked my tongue.

"I told Ima not to tell you until I did." Abigail laughed.

"I *didn't* tell her," Deborah defended from the doorway. "Can I help it if your doda is perceptive?"

Gently, I probed Abigail's belly, observing her pale, pinched face. "How far along? You aren't able to eat? Why didn't I notice this for myself?"

"Still early, and Peter doesn't know."

Peter—how easily the new name of her husband slid from her lips, ever since her mother's healing.

"Shouldn't you tell him before he leaves?"

"I'd rather wait until he returns. If I tell him, he may not go, and he must . . . he needs to be with Jesus as much as possible." Abigail's tired eyes flamed with certainty.

Jealousy tumbled through me, surprising and unwelcome. I stiffened, urging the emotion away.

"I understand, but don't wait too long." My smile was weak. Swallowing hard, I tried again, nudging the smile into my eyes. "One of my dearest memories is Zeb's face when I told him I was pregnant with James."

We were so young! Adonai, we were so young and had no idea what You had in store for us. My breath was gone, swept away by the memory of Zeb on his knees, face to my belly as he spoke to our unborn babe. He'd been all light and happiness, and I had loved him lavishly, with the abandonment of youth.

Capturing Abigail's hands in my own, I imagined a babe— Simon's babe—nestled in her arms. Again, the jealousy came, this time as a whispered thought. *Deborah will be a grandmother.*

Blinking hard, I refocused on Abigail. "I . . . I'm happy for you, dear one."

"I knew you would be. Oh! Don't weep." Abigail raised a hand to lightly tap my cheek, soaking up the tears I didn't realize had escaped. "You've always been like another mother to me," she whispered for my ears alone, love shining from her eyes.

Sniffing hard, I kissed her face. My tears wet her cheek, a benediction. But who were they for? Did I weep with joy for her? Or sorrow for me?

◆

We traveled the thirty miles to Nain, collecting more people as we went, a mixture of men and women from every walk of life. Up ahead, another Simon walked, a new addition who still made me squirm like insects were crawling up my spine. When James had introduced him to me, he'd done so by name only. It had been Simon himself who'd shared his former identity—Zealot.

Like Matthew leaving his tax booth behind, Simon had said the word as if it were something wrapped up in his past with no bearing on his future, and yet I'd taken a large step back without even meaning to.

He strolled ahead of me now with John, his thick neck, broad shoulders, and strong build all denoting him as someone trained for physical combat. John had to walk briskly to keep up.

What was it my wise son had said? I regarded James, who ambled next to me. *"It would bother me . . . if I didn't trust Jesus. If I can know him, then I can be at peace not knowing much else."*

James glanced at me from the side of his eyes and grinned. "Admiring the view, Ima?"

I snorted.

"You've been quieter than usual," James continued. "What are you thinking about?"

"Nothing that concerns you, son."

James gnawed at his lip. "I thought perhaps you were thinking of Abba."

"Your father?" I linked my arm through his.

James sighed heavily. "He's been so quiet lately."

"He's often quiet; you know this."

"I told him we would be back within two weeks to help."

"He has plenty of help, James. You don't need to feel guilty." My eldest had a keen sense of duty and an ingrained desire to defend. If it was hard on Zeb to watch his boys leave, it was equally difficult for James to go.

"You are where you should be. Your father knows this."

"Still, I know what this means for our family, the cost that Abba is paying."

The honor and the cost—every single one of us cradled both within our hands. I thought of Abigail lying weak upon her bed and yet alight with conviction that Simon needed to be near Jesus.

At the thought of Abigail, my eyes sought her husband. He walked with Andrew, both of them near Jesus toward the head of our group. Something Simon said sparked mirth in Jesus, who tipped his head back with a booming laugh.

The jealousy I'd experienced at Abigail's bedside reemerged, demanding I confront it.

Simon has a new name and yet you haven't used it. Why? Could it be that you cannot bear to call him Stone?

In my pocket, the pouch nestled heavy with meaning. Sometimes I poured the contents smoothly into my palm, played them about in my fingers. My two strong boys—mighty men.

"You are Simon, son of Jonah. You will be called Cephas."

Why was I experiencing this unsettling feeling toward Keturah's son, the boy who was as good as my own? Years of love stretched between us as I'd watched him grow, and when Keturah had passed, that love had deepened.

Jealousy twisted my attention back to myself, repeating the

thought that'd plagued me earlier. *Deborah will be a grandmother, not you. Deborah, the mother of thousands, of ten thousands. Abigail a mother. Simon a father.*

Peter. His name is Peter.

I pressed my hand to the pouch hugging my hip.

His name is Peter.

Ahead of me, Simon turned to walk backward, gesturing to Nathaniel with arms stretched wide, unaware that he left a pregnant wife at home.

"Ima, are you okay? Do you need me to get Peter?"

"What?" I blinked up at my concerned son.

"You said his name." James frowned. "Ima, what's wrong? You're shaking." My arm was still threaded with his, hand resting on his forearm. He covered it with a large palm. "Do you want to speak with Peter? I'll go get him."

"No, I . . . no. I don't need to speak with . . . Peter."

"Let's stop. You need water. You don't look well. Here, take a drink." James released my arm and urged his pouch into my hands, nudging it to my lips.

I swallowed long and deep, more to satisfy him than my thirst. Wiping drops from my chin with the back of my hand, I focused on James in order to silence the jealousy, but it lurked, waiting, biding its time until I was alone and unguarded.

"There." James returned the pouch to his belt. "You look better already. Don't scare me like that, Ima." He pulled my arm back through his. In his eyes, I caught a frightened look—one that I recognized. It was the strong love that bound itself up with worry. A bond so deep it was frightening. An expression that said, *What would I ever do without you?*

Twenty-Six

Our feet were sore, backs aching as we neared the small village of Nain. Nestled against the slope of Mount Moreh, it was a small farming village a few hours' walk from Samaria and only eight miles south of Jesus' hometown of Nazareth. Instead of stopping in Nazareth, however, we'd bypassed it.

I'd heard how those in Jesus' hometown had attempted to kill him, driving him to the edge of a cliff in order to throw him to his death after he'd claimed to be the fulfillment of Isaiah's prophecy.

"Who do you think you are? You're the carpenter's son!" Words of fear and confusion as they'd surrounded Jesus . . . before he'd miraculously walked through their midst without a single person touching him.

Privately, Mary disclosed how hard it had been to live in Nazareth since Jesus' ministry had started. More and more, she took to the road with her son, away from the judgment and disbelief at home. Ahead of me, she walked with Mary Magdalene, a young woman from Magadan who had been in a worse state than Amos. Formerly controlled by seven demons, she now kept company with Jesus' mother, the two in earnest conversation.

As Nain came into view, a loud wail pierced the air. A long line of mourners was leaving the village. Four men shouldered a pallet bearing a tightly bound body. Trailing behind the body was a woman screaming as though her heart was being torn from her.

She was the mother. I knew it immediately, for I understood the pain in her cry—the searing, unbearable certainty that her world had been shattered.

I clutched James' hand. He responded by entwining long fingers with mine. *God be with that poor woman. Be with her.*

Ahead of us, Jesus stopped in the middle of the road as the litter approached. We were close enough that I could hear Jesus groan. It emanated from his core, and as the woman drew near, he stopped her, halting the progression of mourners on their way to the grave and extending his arms to the woman.

She stared at him, shock and hesitation all over her face as Jesus grasped her shoulders. "Oh, don't cry. Don't cry." Jesus' voice as I'd never heard it before—impossibly tender. Like Zeb as he cradled a flailing John, promising peace and safety wrapped up in his presence. "Don't cry."

He tugged her into an embrace so gentle, I ached. She was stiff, unmoving, but the longer he held her, the softer she became until she'd melted into his arms, face to his shoulder as she wept, quietly this time.

Jesus drew a long breath, easing the mother from his embrace and turning to the litter. His gaze swept along the body before he placed both hands upon the bier and bowed his head.

"Disease spreads, sir. Impurity defiles what is holy!" Kadmiel's outcry thundered in my head as Jesus become ceremonially unclean in the presence of this grieving mother.

Jesus lifted his head, and with a loud voice spoke directly to the body. "Young man, I tell you, get up!"

Immediately, the body sat upright. "Ima?" His muffled voice was young. It was the cracking voice of a boy becoming a man. "Ima, where are you?"

The woman was facedown at Jesus' feet, crying so hard she

rocked, hands raised in worship while the long line of mourners began shouting and dancing.

Some in the crowd began unwrapping the young man. Jesus helped, throwing aside loose strips of linen, assisting the boy onto his feet, presenting him to his mother. She couldn't stand and so Jesus lifted her up and into her son's waiting arms.

"Ima—" James' face was ravaged with wonder, hand shaking within my own. "How? Did you see? Did you see it?"

"I saw it. I saw it," I rasped.

"Surely God has visited His people today!" The mourners mingled with the disciples as the cry spread. "A mighty prophet has risen among us!"

Impurity had not defiled Jesus. No, his holiness had cleansed the impure.

Something new swelled in my breast, new and unnamed. I clung to James' hand and stared at Jesus, the blood draining from my head. He looked up—briefly but intentionally—directly into my marveling face. Jealousy was silenced as I beheld him, as the new emotion settled into a name.

Love. It was love. A deep and devoted love for the Messiah who had stopped to heal the heart of a hurting mother.

◆

Should I feel pride or abject terror that my boys were following a rabbi who could raise the dead? It was unseasonably dry and hot in Nain, the air sparking with heat, the ground cracked and ready for rain that refused to come. I stood in the marketplace and shivered hard, chin trembling, hand unsteady.

We were overwhelmed, all of us. The comradery from the road had morphed into speechless awe. John, usually so eager to be by Jesus, now hung back by my side, eyes wide and riveted to the man who had undone death.

"How . . . ?" he muttered.

"How what?"

But John simply shook his head, lashes moving in rapid blinks to clear his vision.

My mind jumped to fill in what John left unsaid. How could my boy walk in the footsteps of such a rabbi? How was he to become like him?

"I wish your father had seen it," I whispered.

"We can describe it to him," John whispered back. "But . . ."

But how to describe the indescribable?

The entire village had poured into the streets, following Jesus as he made his way to the synagogue. I'd lost track of James but kept a hand on John, the two of us a small part of a large current of people streaming after Jesus.

As we neared the synagogue, we could see it was undergoing repair. Jesus ascended the front steps, stopping by a pile of stones neatly gathered by the door. As he so often did, Jesus drew upon his surroundings when he taught. He motioned to the stones and then out to the gathered crowd.

"If you want to be my disciple, you must, by comparison, hate everyone else—your father and mother, wife and children, brothers and sisters—yes, even your own life. Otherwise, you cannot be my disciple."

His words rippled across my mind, disruptive and confusing. "He gave a woman back her son and now he tells us to hate our own family?"

"By comparison, Ima," John muttered back, eyes shifting between Jesus and me. "Not to actually hate our own flesh and blood."

"Count the cost!" Jesus gestured to the pile of stones. "For who would begin construction of a building without first calculating the cost to see if there is enough money to finish it?"

"*You see the honor, but I see the cost.*" Zeb's anguished words soon after Jesus called our boys.

I'd known. All along I'd known that there was more here than honor, but I hadn't wanted to feel anything other than pride over my boys.

"Count the cost! For if you lay the foundation and are not able to finish it, everyone who sees it will ridicule you, saying, 'This person began to build and wasn't able to finish.'"

I studied my hands. Calloused fingers worried the hem of my headdress. Certainly the honor of coming beneath the yoke of such a teacher far outweighed the cost, but . . . what if it cost me grandchildren?

What kind of lives would my boys now lead? Would James ever be a father? Would John? I shot a furtive look at my youngest. His life would no longer be the one I once envisioned—a quiet life in Capernaum, working with his brother and father. Me, finally having daughters beneath my roof who bore my boys strong sons. The vigorous life of discipleship left little room for matchmaking. My boys had shed the old life for a new one that was still unfolding in strange and unprecedented ways.

I had been too eager to smooth over Zeb's turmoil. He sensed it might cost him our business, but now I wondered . . . would it also cost us a legacy? Who would carry Zeb's name forward if our boys had no children?

"Those of you who do not give up everything you have cannot be my disciples."

Everything?

My eyes lifted in time to catch Jesus' gaze. I blinked golden eyes and fought for the love and awe to keep a firm place in my heart. He was worth it. Surely he was worth it. Yes, he was.

Jesus tilted his head. The compassion that had infused his tone with the mother on the road now entered his voice again as his eyes held mine. "Anyone with ears to hear should listen and understand!"

He was tender toward mothers. He had held that woman's

pain like it was his very own before he transformed her life from darkness to light. She had not even known him, had not even understood the power that was before her. But I understood. I had seen it over and over again.

Consider the cost. Consider into whose hands I was giving my sons. Consider that Jesus was tender toward me.

TWENTY-SEVEN

"Will you come?" Before each trip with Jesus, I asked the same question of my husband. "This time, will you come?" And with each request, he gently declined.

"Who would run the business if I left? We've contributed to the ministry financially, and perhaps we can give even more, but how can we give if we have no income?"

Zeb was supportive, but from afar, and the longer he remained removed, the more I witnessed James battle with guilt.

"He's hired more help," James noted, hand kneading his brow. "We're so often away that he's been forced to hire more help."

"It's inevitable, my son, and doesn't reflect poorly upon you. Remember what Jesus said about the plow."

"'No one who puts a hand to the plow and looks back is fit for service in the Kingdom of God,'" James quoted. "I'm not looking back, but it pains me to know that Abba is spending long hours on the lake with men bound to him by coin, not blood."

I began bringing some of my worries to Mary, who had quickly become a dear friend. "Zebedee believes. I know he does. He serves Jesus' ministry by sacrificing so we can be on the road, but I wish he'd come and witness for himself all that Jesus is doing."

"You think that would alleviate some of the weight James feels," Mary observed.

"I don't know. Perhaps?"

"Zebedee is an excellent man." Mary smiled. "He reminds me of my Joseph, quiet and steadfast."

"You miss him." I opened a hand in invitation.

Tucking her hand into mine, Mary whispered, "Every moment of every day. Don't despair over your husband, Salome. With remarkable callings comes remarkable grace."

Every year during the month of Chislev, as the temperatures dropped and the rains increased, Zeb took our family back to Bethsaida to visit my parents' grave on the anniversary of my father's death.

With great care, Zeb ensured that Abba's memory stayed alive in his grandsons. *"Here lies a great man."* He would touch the stone that covered the family tomb. *"He was kind and gentle and loved you very much. If you are half the man he was, then you will do mighty things in your life."*

When the boys were young, they would fidget, wanting to tumble and play, but as they grew older, they would settle and listen, placing their own hands on the tomb, honoring those who rested within. Every year we came as a family, but this year, Zeb and I came alone.

I stood out on the rock I had run to as a youth. The rock on which I'd sat with James, staring up into a star-studded sky, tracing patterns, speaking hope for the future. I stood alone upon the rock and stared across the lake in the direction of my boys in Capernaum.

"We'll join you in two days, Ima," James had assured me. *"Jesus is traveling that way in two days. We'll be there."*

"A place and a purpose. You've given my boys a place and a

purpose by the side of Your Messiah. Now hear my prayer and help my husband. He feels alone, and I don't know how to help him. Adonai, help him . . ." The rest of my words were too stuck to come out and so I closed my eyes and simply let my heart cry, knowing Adonai heard this prayer too.

◆

On the night before our boys came to meet us in Bethsaida, Zeb woke me with a strong shake. "What is it?" I mumbled, rolling over with a groan.

"A storm is coming."

Blinking awake, I struggled upright. "It's the season for storms."

"No . . . a big one." Zeb's brows were knit together as he threw off the blanket and pulled on his outer garment.

The wind howled outside our walls, emphasizing Zeb's dire words. "How big?" I questioned. Zeb stood by the door, peering out. The frightened look upon his face drove fear into my belly. Zeb had grown up on this lake, was more familiar with her than with his own face. If *he* was frightened, then this was serious indeed.

"James said they often cross the lake at night to avoid the crowds. Perhaps when they saw the storm they waited?" My voice was small.

Zeb shook his head. "Normally there are warning signs, but this storm came quickly."

"Do you think . . . they're out there? Right now?" I threw on my mantle to join him at the door. The winds were steadily increasing, pounding on the walls with gusty fists. Instead of answering my question, Zeb pushed from the door and out into the wind, arms shielding his head.

"What are you doing?" Gathering my mantle about my frame, I pushed out into the night after him. The wind drove the rain like daggers to the earth. We exited the home to find the shore writhing with waves that swept across her banks in tumultuous sheets. Wave after wave pounded her shore.

"Sharkia!" Zeb shouted the word as I huddled by his side.

Bethsaida was still the sleepy village I remembered. She didn't boast a fine harbor like Capernaum. Instead, her boats were anchored close to the shore or pulled up onto the bank. Numerous fishermen dotted the shore, hauling their boats farther onto land, lashing them down with ropes to keep them from being swept out into the waves.

"Surely no boats are out in this!" I yelled.

But some were. Through the thick rain, we could make out numerous sparks of light, flickering in and out of focus among the swells. My entire body grew heavy, eyes straining toward those lights.

Zeb began to pace along the ridgeline, hair whipping about his face. "They're out there!" he shouted.

"Perhaps not!"

But Zeb was convinced. He paced away and then back, looming before me, eyes joining briefly with mine. Fear was a fire deep in his gaze, consuming him. Snagging his arm, I held on as a gust of wind battered at my back and drove me hard against him.

Adonai, if our boys are out there, then they are also with Your Messiah. What if something happens to all of them?

Zeb broke from me and began running parallel to the lake. I ran after him. "What are you doing?"

"A boat! I need a boat!" Zeb's words were whipped away by the wind as he darted down the embankment toward the lake.

"You cannot go out in this!" Fear over my boys curled into panic over my husband. One by one, he approached others along the shore, who waved him off. No one would dare go out in such a squall, and certainly no one would give a crazy man their boat.

A wave at least eight feet high crashed onto the bank near Zeb, obscuring him from my sight. When the water receded, I could no longer see my husband. Panic turned into something deeper that gripped my chest and squeezed the air from my body. Tearing down the rocky embankment, I slipped and fell, landing hard on my hip and scraping my hands. Pain throbbed dully, arcing into my back, but I hardly noticed it as I scrambled upright and screamed Zeb's name.

My feet landed on the shore. The stones were slick with water as I clambered to the spot where I'd seen him last. Another wave came, not as big but still strong. I jerked out of its way and fell hard on my knees, tumbling sideways onto an elbow, yelping with the pain that now spread to new areas of my body.

I cannot lose him. I cannot lose him. The one thought was stronger than the winds, surer than the waves. It pounded through my body—an erratic, pulsing heartbeat. The thought became audible cry as another wave came and washed over me, beating my body into the ground, sucking at my frame. I clung to a rock and sputtered, gathering battered legs beneath my trembling frame, preparing to stand.

"Zebedee!" It was a shriek. It was fire in my bones.

Eyes hunting the water, I stumbled along the shore. A distant shout filled me with hope.

"Salome!" Farther down the shore, a dark form waved.

Relief left me weak. I toppled forward, catching myself before falling completely. Another wave came, driving me to my knees, which screamed with pain. When it left, I hugged the embankment, slowly making my way toward the voice that was calling my name.

He was in a small alcove in the embankment, nestled within the earth, sheltered from the winds. With long, aggressive pulls, he was tearing ropes off a small boat.

"Zeb—" I tumbled to his side. He turned and I grabbed him, pushing him back against the boat, anchoring him into place with my full weight as I shoved my face to his breast.

He pushed me back, ripping himself from my arms, whirling to pull at the ropes. "I almost have it loose!"

"What are you doing?"

In another moment, the boat was free. It was a small boat, meant for a couple men. As Zeb began dragging it out of the alcove, I ran to him and screeched, "Zebedee bar Jonathan, what do you think you are doing?"

He stopped, blinking rapidly, perhaps seeing me for the first time. "They're out there," he stated simply.

"You cannot save them." Fisting his tunic, I pulled him close. "Zeb, you cannot save them."

"I can try." He set his jaw and turned, violently yanking the boat from the alcove and out onto the bank.

"This is madness." I whispered the observation as Zeb hauled the boat closer to the seething water. One wave would undo him. It would take only one wave to shatter this small boat and suck Zeb out into the current. He was a strong and steady swimmer, but even he would be unable to navigate waves of this magnitude.

Scrambling to Zeb's side, I grasped his arm. "Look at me! Look at me!"

He pushed at me, turned to the water.

I jerked him back, so insistent he was forced to stop. His eyes were glazed, wild. Framing his face with my hands, I shouted, "You cannot save them! You will only destroy yourself."

He blinked hard and focused upon me. "But they're out there. My boys—"

I yanked him into my arms. "I know. I know."

He shuddered and finally his arms released the boat and found me. I drew him away from the shore and back to the alcove.

How many times had I met him on this very bank? Countless moments caught between rocky shore and lapping sea. But never had we experienced such a desperate moment. We stood in the alcove and stared out at the roiling lake. Zeb captured a sob with his hand. With widened eyes and covered mouth, my strong husband stood helpless before the furious wind and relentless waves.

Air hung in my body, unable to move into or out of my lungs, which began to throb in protest. *Breathe! Breathe!* But how could I breathe when my boys might be in peril at this very moment?

Time slowed to a stop until I could no longer detect its passing. I bowed my head and opened my lips. "Adonai, please, please . . ." I lifted my head and blinked.

As quickly as the storm had begun, it stopped—and all was violently still. The quiet slap of a rocking wave sounded against the bank and, in the distance, the hopeful trill of birds.

"What?" Zeb strode quickly from the alcove and down to the water, where he jerked to a stop, eyes casting about on land and sea, hunting for a place to drop anchor, to ground himself, to make sense of what had happened.

I followed, placed a hand on his back, and pointed.

Out on the lake was a boat moving steadily to shore some distance south of us. Without speaking, we ran in the direction of that boat. Zeb's breaths thundered from his body as he quickly outpaced me. My hip throbbed with pain, my knees scraped and bloody, and yet I stumbled after him.

The clouds eased away from the moon. Her beams caressed Zeb's head and shoulders, pouring silver light over his long frame, which ran and ran as though he were a youth of twenty again. The boat was coming to the shore, and Zeb was nearly to the boat. I gasped for air, shoved a fist to the pinch in my side, and ran as fast as my battered body could go.

A heron swept low over the water, large wings starkly black against the curve of the moon. In the long rushes of the lake, the warbling voices of toads joined with the other night sounds. *All is well*, they sang. *All is at peace.*

When I caught sight of James, standing tall by the mast, I

stumbled to a stop, planted hands upon my knees, and drew in a long breath. The boat was full of men, all disheveled, wet, and silent—all of them turned toward the bow.

Even before the moon slanted her light across his face, I knew him. Jesus stood calmly facing the shore, while behind him the men's ragged faces told us all we needed to know. The boat nudged to shore, delivered by a loving hand. No one moved, all eyes were riveted upon Jesus, and not a voice broke the calm . . . until Zebedee.

With a loud cry, he plummeted into the lake to meet the boat, sloshing through the shallow water and grasping at the bow as it neared. Jesus leapt easily from the boat to join Zeb in the water, where he clapped a hand to my husband's shoulder. For a long moment, the two men faced each other until Zeb collapsed, crumpling straight down. Crouching in the water, Zeb caught the hem of Jesus' robe, tethering himself to the *tzitzit*, the tassels tangling between his rough fingers.

Jesus rested his hand upon Zeb's head, fingers disappearing into the wiry shock of hair, his gesture and demeanor as gentle as the moment outside Nain, the moment in which he'd seen a mother before restoring her son. At Jesus' touch, Zeb released a deep, earnest cry, and in his broken voice, I heard it—the unmistakable sound of worship.

Twenty-Eight

The morning after our boys' rescue, I sensed an emptiness. Hand rushing to my pocket, I searched for it. Heart racing, I hunted through our belongings, but it was absent. In the lazy morning sunlight, Zeb slumbered in an exhausted sprawl upon the bed while I flew about the room in a fruitless search.

Retracing my steps from the night before, I ran to the shore. Scattered across the shoreline were thousands upon thousands of stones, but it was two in particular that held my heart. With a dreadful, mounting certainty, I searched for what I knew to be thoroughly lost.

A small leather pouch with two smooth, black stones.

◆

On the first day back home in Capernaum, Zeb approached me as I prepared the day's bread. "We need to talk." Without waiting for me to clean my hands, Zeb pulled me to standing and into his arms in a strong embrace.

My arms hovered in the air, two birds startled into flight, flour falling like feathers. "Zeb, I'm a mess." I laughed.

He pressed me close as though he couldn't get enough of this mess.

Slowly, my arms drifted downward, coming to land upon his back, hands tracking white across his tunic as I clasped him in return. The years had weathered us into a pattern meant for each other, every line of my body meeting comfortably with his.

"Our boys are following a rabbi who can calm a sharkia with a single word." There was no hint of mournfulness in my husband's voice, not anymore, only a newly birthed awe.

Settling my cheek against his breast, I traced the divot of his backbone.

"I let practicality overtake me and was not as expressive of my support as you have been. Did I ever tell you what your father said to me the day we married?"

Wordlessly, I shook my head.

"He told me that you had a big spirit. He said he knew I was the one to marry you because I also saw and appreciated that spirit."

I pressed a kiss into Zeb's chest.

"Our boys are blessed to call you mother."

My husband's beautiful words were a canopy above us, and we rested comfortably beneath it.

"You're quiet," Zeb murmured.

"I'm thinking."

Zeb chuckled, easing back with a broad grin. "What's happened to us? Me doing the talking and you embracing silence?"

I cast my eyes upward in playful exasperation. Years of habit drifted my hand to my side. The delicate gift of that ordinary pouch—it represented everything in this life that was dear to me. Although it was gone, the love it represented remained, and yet I itched to play the stones between my fingers.

"Oh, Zeb, I rushed past your worries because I didn't want to feel them. Pride and fear—honor and loss. I'm slowing down to see both. I'm thinking that there is indeed a cost to following Jesus."

My husband ran a large hand up and down my back. "What

are we to give to God other than our whole selves? Like Abraham offering his son, we hold nothing back from God. Some things are worth the cost."

He cupped my face within his hands and gave me one of his long and slow looks. I held his gaze before tilting up onto my toes to brush his lips with mine. Whatever was to come, we would face it together.

SPRING 29 AD

Usually it was Judea that swelled with visitors. Not only Jerusalem, but all of the surrounding Judean villages saw an influx of pilgrims three times a year during the annual foot festivals. In a great reversal, it was now Galilee that welcomed a steady stream of guests.

Crowds typically made our political leaders nervous. The crowds that Jesus drew, however, were composed not of zealous revolutionaries, but of broken men and women who needed what Jesus was offering—healing and hope. Unlike Judas of Galilee and others before him, Jesus' influence extended to both Jew and Gentile, both lowborn and highborn. Joanna, a noblewoman from Herod's own court, had benefited from Jesus' healing and now offered monetary support to his ministry.

"Joanna says that Herod is eager to meet Jesus," Mary Magdalene relayed to us.

"That cannot be good." Matthew shook his head. Recently, Herod had executed the Baptizer in the dungeons of Machaerus, and we were all still reeling from the news.

"Jesus does not directly address our political leaders the way the Baptizer did, nor does he incite unrest," I mused.

"And yet he speaks of a kingdom," Mary Magdalene whispered. "For now, Herod is curious, but Joanna worries that his curiosity will take a dangerous turn."

Matthew grimaced. "The outcome of political resistance is seared upon this region's memory, and Herod will not want Rome's attention drifting north."

As Jesus continued to travel, he avoided the larger cities, keeping to the villages. "A prophet arises from Galilee?" One incredulous voice sounded after another, for Jerusalem was the center of all intellectual thought. No one looked to upper Galilee when it came to learned teachers of the Law. Perhaps no one understood this better than Kadmiel.

After his encounter with Jesus in Matthew's courtyard, we heard little from Kadmiel but wondered if he'd made good on his veiled threat.

"Is it true that your family follows this new rabbi? The one causing so much disruption in the Sanhedrin?" a client questioned us.

"Yes, it is true" came Zeb's quiet answer.

A week later, that client closed his account with us.

"Count the cost." Again and again, Jesus' exhortation echoed in my head. *"Count the cost."*

It was with some surprise when, soon after the miracle upon the lake, we opened our front door to find Admon outside. I cast an anxious gaze behind him into the street.

"Abba is not with me . . . not this time."

"And does he—?"

"He doesn't know I'm here." Dark circles shadowed Admon's eyes.

I ushered him inside and, as he settled before an open fire, pushed food upon him.

He ate in silence until Deborah arrived. "Where is my nephew? He was seen slinking into town like a lost puppy. Aha!" Swiftly she closed the distance to pull Admon up into a mighty embrace before grasping his chin to study his face. "You are changed."

"I am weary," Admon amended.

Deborah quieted. "I don't suppose you've brought my sister with you? I have yet to see Leah since—" She broke off. Not once since Deborah's healing had Leah come to Capernaum or sent a word of celebration, and that distance was a thorn piercing Deborah.

"Travel doesn't suit Ima." Admon's brief explanation fell flat. "Besides, I didn't want Abba to know where I was going, and if Ima knew, then she would certainly tell him."

Deborah sighed heavily.

"Where is your Jesus?" Admon questioned.

"He's away praying on Mount Eremos. Welcome, cousin!" James' strong voice boomed as he crossed the courtyard to pluck Admon from Deborah's arms into his own.

Admon coughed against his cousin, attempting speech when James released him. "Your rabbi goes away to pray alone on mountains? That doesn't seem safe."

"He has command over nature." James grinned. "Believe me. I have seen it. Peter and Andrew are with him this time."

"It's an unusual rabbi who frequents desolate places rather than our nation's centers of learning," Admon mused.

"Come to critique, did you? Is that why you're here?" John darkened the doorway. "Collecting information for your father?"

"N-no." Admon flushed, averting his face.

"Your uncle doesn't even know he's here," I assured John, who brushed my words aside.

"Then why *are* you here?"

"I was curious and wished to see Jesus without Abba knowing."

John pushed from the doorway into the courtyard, eyes leveled upon his cousin. "People do not light a lamp and put it under a bowl, do they? Light goes on a stand, Admon. Or do you think you can follow without anyone knowing?"

"Do *not* use Jesus' words lightly, brother!" James faced John with fire in his voice. "We bear his teaching upon our shoulders. Do not be so quick with his words. You wield them as if they're a weapon rather than life itself."

For a moment, John frowned up into his brother's face, starkly reminding me of the boy who was prone to push against his big brother, convinced he knew better. But then something in John's face shifted, a softening that cracked him open and made room for truth. His eyes cut to Admon, flooding briefly with regret before he ducked from the room.

✦

In the morning, Andrew came with news. "Jesus is calling all of his followers to join him at Mount Eremos."

"Did he say what he wanted?" Zeb questioned.

"No, only that he spent all night in prayer and now had important news to relay."

Word spread easily through the neighboring villages. The mount was a few miles from Capernaum, and yet travel was slow, for hundreds came.

"All of these are his followers?" Admon asked.

"Some come to question him while others merely marvel at his works," John stated. "Not everyone is a true follower. Not everyone stays."

What should have been a short journey lengthened as we gathered more people and progress slowed. Eventually, the gently sloping shoulders of Mount Eremos rose before us. She stretched luxuriously along the lake, green against the blue sky, overlooking the waters that had churned with fury at her feet not long ago.

Jesus stood a short distance up the mount. We spread down the slope, a blanket of people. John began pushing to get close, but Zeb put a hand on his shoulder. We were close enough.

When we'd gathered, Jesus spoke, his voice traveling loudly over rock. "I am here to appoint twelve of you as my apostles."

Those who were close repeated his words. The announcement rippled behind us, a current of wind ruffling a sheet. Anticipation mounted throughout the crowd. *Apostle*—one who is sent out. I threaded my fingers through Zeb's, heart slowing to a dull throb in my throat.

By our side, Admon shifted on impatient feet. "Twelve—the number of authority. What is Jesus establishing?"

In my body was a beat, three words in a pounding rhythm, both prayer and plea. *Keep them close. Keep them close.*

Some strained now, shoving themselves forward so they could hear Jesus better. My hands grew slick with sweat, Zeb's palm warm against mine.

Adonai . . . keep all four close.

When next Jesus opened his mouth, Simon's name was on his tongue, Andrew's name right after.

This was good—Keturah's sons by Jesus' side—but then Jesus paused, and my toes curled within my sandals as doubt and jealousy tried to crawl into the moment and ruin it.

I trust him. Whoever he chooses, whatever he does . . . I will trust him.

Restlessness crept up and down my legs, making them itch for movement even while my knees locked as I held myself in place—waiting, waiting.

"The two sons of Zebedee—James and John." Jesus' eyes hunted the crowd, landing upon Zeb and crinkling with a smile.

I collapsed against my husband, air leaving me in a rush as I caught a laugh with a shaking hand, relief pouring throughout my body, leaving me weak-kneed with gratitude.

"What does that mean—apostle? What is being required of you, cousins? Where is he sending you?" Admon babbled his confusion, but my mind barely discerned his words.

Everything inside me was smooth and supple, warmed by the knowledge that these four men would remain by Jesus' side. Satisfaction flowed from my lips in the form of a shaky laugh. I leaned into my husband, who was watching our boys as they neared Jesus, his own face an endless well of wonder.

Twenty-Nine

I stood on the shore at some distance from Capernaum's harbor as the sun dipped to the horizon and red streaked the night. Fishermen pushed out into the water beneath a brilliant sky bursting with ruddy colors, but my son did not have the eyes to appreciate it. In front of me, John squatted on the bank, swatting at the rushes with a stick. I'd followed him out here and now stood, uncertain and tense, behind him.

"Tell me again what he said to you. Tell me again the directions he gave," I asked.

Without looking at me, John straightened and tossed the stick, watching it tumble through the air and enter the water with a distant splash.

"He said . . . he said that he was giving us the power and authority to drive out all demons and cure diseases." John threaded shaking hands behind his head.

Terror gripped me so strongly I stopped breathing and had to remind myself to start again. I wanted to hold him but resisted the urge. What did he need from me in this moment? What would he welcome, and what would he refuse?

I held myself still and spoke to his back. "We know *Jesus* can do these things. We've seen him do it time and time again."

"Yes, but only Jesus." John's voice cracked, and he coughed to clear it. "Now he is sending twelve of us out, giving us the authority as well."

The urge to be near him was too great to resist. I approached as one might a skittish colt and slipped a hand to his shoulder. "You once wondered how. How were you to follow in the footsteps of such a rabbi? My son, this is how."

"You saw me use Jesus' own words to shame Admon." John shifted so that my hand fell away. "I'm still learning, Ima! Sometimes I'm afraid that I'm too quick and angry to be his disciple, let alone—"

"Don't you think he knows you? He knows the kind of men he's called. And if he can calm a sharkia, then surely he can calm *this.*" I placed a hand on his chest. "If he says he is empowering you, then he is doing so. Certainly this is an easy thing for him."

My words were firm and confident, but inside I shook as hard as my son. *Adonai, he is only eighteen.* I traced a finger down his stubbly cheek, felt a muscle twitch in his jaw. The youngest of the group . . . and the feistiest. Also the one who made Jesus' eyes light up. The one often by his side.

"I thought Jesus would send me out with James, but he's paired me with Peter." John avoided my gaze. "Peter is often first. Jesus seems to single him out. After all, he did give him a new name. Do you think he paired me with Peter because he wants him to keep an eye on me?" In his voice was a restless uncertainty.

I clasped John by the arms. "I've often treated you as though you needed tending, haven't I?"

John's brows lifted in surprise.

"And it's true. I've often looked to the older boys to watch out for you, but, John—" I clenched my jaw and refused to weep. "It has never been for lack of trust but because you are—"

The tears, they were coming. I yanked John into my arms and

let them fall onto his mantle. "You are precious to me beyond words, but you are even more precious to *him*."

"I . . . I don't want to fail him. I can't fail him. I would sooner die." John's voice cracked again but this time kept splitting, wider and wider, the fear becoming apparent until it tumbled right out of him, bringing him to his knees.

On the banks of the lake, I hovered above my son, this passionate young man who'd spent most of his youth pushing against me, as strong and persistent as the current lapping onto the shore. In showing me his vulnerability, I knew he was inviting my wisdom.

"Oh, my son, my son." What could I say or do for my boy who was the Christ's apostle?

John covered his face as my hand hovered above his shoulder, landing with a brief caress. "This new future feels foreign to you," I finally whispered. "Foreign and intimidating. There is a lot I don't know and so I won't speak empty promises. Rather, I'll share the one thing I *do* know."

Crouching beside him, I prayed that my next words would be a seed burrowing deep within him, where it would one day bear fruit.

"My son, you can trust Adonai to form you into who you need to be."

◆

"*Do not go among the Gentiles or enter any town of the Samaritans. Go instead to the lost sheep of Israel. Take nothing for your journey, no staff or bag or bread.*" Jesus' instructions were clear.

"No money, Mary," I wondered aloud. "Jesus explicitly told them to take no money for the journey. Not even an extra shirt!"

"They will have to trust in God's provision." Mary raised a brow, threading an arm through mine. "Perhaps that is the point."

Two by two, the newly appointed apostles left Capernaum

with instructions to continue Jesus' ministry of teaching and healing.

James was paired with Philip, the two of them traveling back to their hometown of Bethsaida.

"Where will you go?" I asked John on the morning he was to leave with Simon.

John shoved a raisin cake into his cheek before answering, words garbled around the mouthful. "West to Sepphoris and then perhaps south to Nazareth. They were hostile to Jesus before. We'll see how they treat his apostles."

I looked to Admon. "And you will go home?"

"He'll travel with us to Sepphoris before returning to Jerusalem," John answered for his cousin, tone remaining neutral.

A clatter at our door signaled Simon's entrance. "What are you doing still sitting around? It's not as though we need to pack." He shouted a laugh. Behind him, Deborah stood in the street with a pregnant Abigail, who had a hand to her back, the other resting on her rounded stomach. She appeared to be fighting hard for the smile on her face.

Past Simon's exuberance was a tender core, emotion he was trying to mask. Leaving Abigail this time would be hard on him.

Most of Capernaum poured into the streets to escort Simon and John out of town. As we neared the western edge, the crowd behind us grew agitated, until a cry pierced the air.

"Wait!" A man pushed his way through the crowd with a large bundle upon his back. "I'm searching for the rabbi Jesus and was told he was here." He drew close, eyes rimmed with red, hair tousled and unkempt.

"Jesus departed Capernaum a few days ago," John stated regretfully.

"Do you know where I can find him, then? I've traveled all this way from Arimathea. I'll travel even farther."

Before anyone could answer, the bundle upon the man's back moved. "Abba?" a garbled, thin voice emerged.

The man eased the bundle to the road as a young boy's head poked from the pack. "I need to find Jesus . . . it's urgent." The man choked on his words. "My son fell to the ground, not responding or seeing, and when he came to himself, he was paralyzed on one side. Please help me. He can barely talk or eat."

Sympathetic murmurs rose from the crowd as everyone clustered around the boy. He gazed up at us and offered a smile that moved only one side of his mouth. It was evident that half his body was immobilized, making it impossible for him to stand.

If Jesus were here, he would lay his hand upon the boy and restore him immediately. We did not have Jesus, but—

I glanced at John where he stood rooted to the road. His face was ashen, hands clasped tightly before him as Simon stepped forward. "Jesus has given us his authority to heal."

The man studied Simon, reservation lining his face. I could understand his skepticism, for Simon was a fisherman through and through. Even after all this time following Jesus, his roots remained evident in his work-roughened hands and demeanor. He was a man of the lake, and yet what had Jesus told him? *"Follow me, and I will make you fish for people."*

"If you indeed have such authority, then please use it for the sake of my son," the man pleaded.

Simon stepped forward and crouched before the boy, cupping his contorted face within large hands. "Look at me, child."

The side of the boy's body that still had movement was trembling, but he did as he was asked, eyes fastening upon Simon.

"I have no power in myself. It is only in the name of Jesus Christ of Nazareth that I command you to be healed."

Tears shone in the boy's eyes as he smiled once again . . . both cheeks lifting this time in a beautiful, full expression of joy.

The father dropped to his knees and pulled the boy to standing, placing him upon his feet, where the boy jumped with a laugh. Weeping, the father crushed his son to his chest while the people around us gasped their astonishment. No one was more surprised than Admon, who jerked back as if confronted by the brilliance of the sun.

John, however, was standing still and quiet, as immobilized as the boy dancing before us used to be.

THIRTY

SUMMER 29 AD

As our sons traveled throughout Judea and Galilee, Zeb dealt with a rapidly shifting business as three long-standing clients closed their accounts with us, claiming they had found lower prices elsewhere. "What price?" Zeb pushed. "Let's discuss and see if perhaps we can rework your contract."

But the doors closed with no room for negotiation. "My master chooses to buy from God-fearing men whose heads remain unturned by false teachers," one steward stated with a curl to his lip. The accounts with both Annas and Caiaphas, however, were intact, although for how long remained to be seen.

A year ago, the loss of these accounts Zeb had worked so hard to build would have destroyed him. Now, however, he remained stubbornly hopeful. "My boys are fishing for people," he often said, eyes alight. "I raised them to follow after me, but now they follow after the Messiah! Isn't this every man's desire? To see his offspring instrumental in the coming of the Christ's Kingdom?"

Jesus' newly appointed apostles came and went, bringing reports back to Jesus and resting briefly at home before starting out on another mission. The time for listening and learning had transitioned into a time of doing and going.

On his first return home, James pulled me aside, weariness evident upon his face. "Ima, your heart would break to see it."

"See what?"

"The unbelief in Bethsaida." James scrubbed a hand over a stubbled cheek. "Jesus was rejected in his own hometown, and Philip and I—" He swallowed hard. "It was the same for us, Ima. People who remembered us from our youth scoffed at the message we bore. They thought we elevated ourselves above them."

"Did *any* believe?" Dismay lowered my voice into a rasp.

"Perhaps some, but they would not come out and state it openly."

"And Philip's family?"

James shook his head. "Philip is grieving. He tried sharing Jesus' message with his father, but Gideon wouldn't listen. Gideon took one look at me and said he wasn't surprised I was running after a blasphemer, given my . . . parentage. He blamed me for misleading his son."

A slow burn began in my belly.

"Philip understood the slight and defended not only me but also you and Abba. His words incensed his father. Gideon said that even with your bright eyes, you are blind."

I gritted my teeth until my jaw ached.

"And that's when Philip followed Jesus' direction."

"What direction?" I could hardly speak through the tangle of anger.

"'If anyone does not welcome you or listen to your words, shake the dust off your feet when you leave that house.' Philip did so, and as we left, Gideon told him, 'Never come back here.'"

As quickly as the anger had burned, sorrow rushed in, accompanied by a sinking realization. I'd been holding Philip's parentage against him, the way Gideon had James'. But what had Jesus said?

"*You can identify them by their fruit, that is, by the way they act.*"

With swift steps, I went next door to Simon's courtyard, where Philip was warming himself by a fire with Nathaniel and Matthew.

"Philip bar Gideon!" I stood in the doorway with a hand on my hip as all three men swiveled in surprise. Philip's eyes jerked away from mine.

"Come here." I softened my stance as the young man approached. He stood before me with hesitation written on every line of his face—the face that looked so much like his father's. Behind that face was a man whose life was bearing good fruit.

I opened my arms in invitation, half expecting Philip to refuse, but he entered my embrace with shocking eagerness. In his ear I whispered four words. Four words to combat the last four hurled at him by his father.

"I'm proud of you."

Change—it was evident in Philip, in my sons, in all of these "sent ones" as they journeyed across Galilee and down into Judea with the power of Christ in their hands and upon their tongues. Adonai was indeed shaping them, leading them into a rooted dependence upon Himself.

Having begun his journeys harboring fear, John now exuded a growing courage, each trip home unveiling yet another layer of maturity. The youngest and shortest of the group, John was growing in confidence *and* height. The thought of John on the road bearing Jesus' own authority even while his young body continued to change and stretch into manhood made my heart unbearably tender. When it became too much to handle, I would press at my breast with a trembling hand—hard and then harder, hoping that ache would lessen enough for me to catch the next breath.

I began walking Keturah's path each day and the lake at night, recalling the moment Jesus had calmed the sharkia. Again and again, I replayed it in my mind. The chaos had calmed in a single moment. "He's worth the cost." I spoke the words aloud, reminding my heart of what I believed. The future was still murky, not nearly as straightforward as I'd once envisioned. If I let it, all the unknowns would pull me under, and so I walked Keturah's path in the heat of the day and spoke truth into the sky. "I trust him. I trust him with my boys—with *all* of them."

And yet some thoughts came sneaking in from the side, entering on quiet feet with whispered questions.

But can you trust him with yourself?

◆

Abigail was on the shore, helping me sort the night's catch, when she jerked upright with a gasp.

I was on my feet, hand to her belly. "Have your pains started? Is it time?"

Abigail shook her head, face pale. "No, it's . . . the water . . ."

My heart dropped as I lifted her tunic. Her legs were slick with fluid and still more was coming. "You need to lie down. We don't want too much escaping before the pains begin."

But with every step toward home, more fluid came until Abigail began sobbing against me with fright. Deborah met us at the door, face instantly graying. Together we lay Abigail down upon her bed.

"Peter isn't even here," Abigail moaned as Deborah and I gathered the necessary items. Clean cloths, the birthing stool, and warm water, oil, and herbs to induce her labor. When all was assembled, I sat by Abigail's side. "Your mother and I, we are here, and we will help you. You are strong, Abigail, and you can do this."

She nodded shakily and then groaned as the first of her pains came. "Oh, oh, oh!" Alarm flooded her face.

"This is good," I soothed. "This is right."

"We want the pains to come now that your water has broken." Deborah settled on Abigail's other side.

All throughout the day, Abigail labored and then into the night. Exhaustion lined her face as we did everything in our power to make her more comfortable. But her body was learning what it meant to deliver new life, and it resisted, making her progress slow.

"Your body will hold on to this memory," Deborah encouraged. "And then the next time, it will be easier."

She continued to labor well into the following morning until all three of us were bleary-eyed with exhaustion. "I think it's time." I lowered Abigail's tunic. "She's ready to push."

How many births had I witnessed? How many times had I helped life into this world? But none could compare to this moment as I witnessed Abigail's strength and determination. The labor had been long, but the moment the babe's head crowned, he was coming. In a rush of blood and water, he came, delivered into my waiting hands.

"A son! You have a son!"

A beautiful, bawling boy with Simon's thick black hair plastered over his brow. Swiftly, I cut the cord and began cleaning the babe, rubbing him with salt and then soothing him with oil, my hands remembering what to do, going through the motions while my eyes took him in.

Behind me, Abigail wept her husband's name, laughed, and then wept again.

I was shaking as I checked every limb and counted every toe while his gusty cry pierced the room. Perfect—utterly perfect. And he looked just like Simon . . . the same broad brow, the same flare in the nostrils.

"Keturah . . . you have a grandson." I whispered the words as I held the babe in my hands, missing his grandmother with a fire that stole my breath away.

"Salome—" Deborah's voice cut through my mind, severing my attention from the boy. She was looking at me with a furrowed brow.

"Yes?"

"The babe." Deborah motioned to my arms. "Give Abigail the babe."

"Of course, of course. I was just cleaning him." I glanced down in surprise, for he was swaddled and nestled tightly against my breast. With a lump in my throat, I crossed the room to Abigail.

"Thank you, Doda," she gasped. "Thank you." She extended her arms for her son.

With great effort, I made myself release the babe into his mother's eager embrace. Instantly, I was cold. Taking a large step back, I stared at the beautiful scene before me—Deborah bent over her daughter, lips pressed to her grandson's head. Abigail's smile directed between her mother and newborn son. So much love. So much light.

Like an old acquaintance too long ignored, jealousy took on a more definitive form, pushing off the wall and slinking to my side. Even employing all the effort in the world, I could not stop her, not after holding that beautiful boy. She knew it and came, wrapping long, long arms about me, holding me close.

In my weakness, I didn't even want her to let go.

THIRTY-ONE

SPRING 30 AD

*"I tell you the truth, unless a kernel of wheat falls to the ground
and dies, it remains alone. But if it dies, it will produce many new
kernels—a plentiful harvest of new lives."*

Every farmer knew that death preceded life—from the surrender of the one seed came the growth of a harvest.

*"Those who love their life in this world will lose it, while anyone
who hates their life in this world will keep it for eternal life."*

Like his teaching on true discipleship, Jesus was calling us to
a greater love. Not to despise the breath within our lungs, but to
love the Maker more than the breath He gave.

I watched Keturah's grandson grow into bright-eyed wonder-
ment, taking in every new face with enthusiasm, his hiccupping
giggles and toothless grin leaving me full of love and yet also
hollow and achy.

They'd named him Jonah.

Zeb's eyes had glowed as he'd bestowed a kiss of blessing on
the forehead of his friend's namesake. I'd watched with a painful
lump in my throat.

Could I love Adonai and His plans more than the gifts He gave . . . or didn't give?

———— ✦ ————

The message came on a cold night, the dire words biting harder than the wind.

> *Stop this madness. You're following after a man whom the Sanhedrin condemns. Whether or not your Jesus holds political aspirations, our religious leaders will portray that he does in order to goad Rome into involvement. If our leaders must crush Jesus' blasphemy using Rome's fist, they will. There will be far-reaching damage afterward, and I don't want your family destroyed in the aftermath.*

Worry settled in the bottom of my stomach as I considered the genuine fear evident in Kadmiel's warning. The other day, some Herodians had questioned Jesus in depth, no doubt wondering if he would draw more than curious people north. Would he also draw Rome's ire? If Kadmiel was to be believed, the Sanhedrin would ensure that he did.

"Should we share this with James and John?" I asked Zeb.

Zeb shook his head. "They have enough on their minds. They know the risks. We all do. Kadmiel is blinded and so he does not understand that Jesus is worth the risk."

If Jesus was *not* the Messiah, then Kadmiel's words were wisdom. Compassion for my brother-in-law crashed through my body like wave to shore. He did not know. He did not see. He could not share in the courage so evident in my boys the longer we all loved and served Jesus. Self-proclaimed messiahs had come and gone, all failing because they were false. But Jesus was truth, and he would not fail.

Adonai, unveil Kadmiel's eyes.

✦

Once consumed with guilt over leaving his father, James now walked with him shoulder to shoulder along the road. For months, Zeb had traveled with Jesus' company, leaving the business in the capable hands of our hired men. The joy within James was palpable, and my heart was well pleased even though Kadmiel's warning still sounded in my head.

We'd set out early in the morning, before even the birds were awake to sing. Uncertain how long we'd be gone, I'd packed as much food as I could. Ahead of me Simon walked, quiet and subdued. Abigail was staying behind with Jonah, and before leaving he'd spent long hours cuddling the boy, who was now eight months old with rolls of fat lining his thighs. Fatherhood suited Simon, and I'd told him so. Through hidden tears, I'd told him, "You are a good father."

Increasingly, I harbored a persistent desire—this cost we were paying *must* be worth the sacrifice. The dangerous path we walked, it *must* result in the redemption of Israel. My boys lay heavy upon my mind, thoughts tangling with hope, expectation, and worry.

John sidled up to me. "I ate the last of my raisin cakes five miles ago. Do you have any more in your pack?"

"I have some dried figs." Edging to the side of the road, I moved my pack to the ground, located the figs, and passed them to John, who threw them all into his mouth at once.

"Don't choke," I admonished. "Honestly, how did you ever manage without me when you and . . . Peter were on the road?" I fumbled the new name. How long until I stopped doing so?

"It was trying." John winked, cheeks bulging.

As we rejoined the group, John took a long swig of water to wash down the figs. Wiping the back of his hand across his mouth, he glanced at me. "You're quiet. Is it because of what happened in Jerusalem?"

During their last trip to the Holy City, crowds had tried to seize Jesus in the Temple. My sons had been in the thick of it.

"They almost stoned him, John."

"I know." John quieted.

"Right there in the Temple courts." I tried to keep my tone light, knowing how much John disliked me fussing, but this time he met my concern with seriousness, arm brushing mine as he drew close.

"I won't deny that it was unsettling to see rocks in the hands of our scribes as they cried out, 'Blasphemy!' It was a miracle, Ima—nothing less than a miracle—that we escaped their grasp."

"Stop this madness. There will be far-reaching damage."

I shook my head to clear it of Kadmiel's words. "A miracle," I sighed. "Why doesn't that surprise me? Do you know how I sleep at night?"

John raised a brow and shook his head.

"I sleep because I know you are with *him*." I nodded to where Jesus walked with Andrew, an arm slung across his back. "Lately, he churns up conflict like foam from an agitated sea. There is a storm about him, but we've seen what he can do with storms." I hooked a hand through John's elbow. "He has proven his power ten times over."

"Even so, many don't understand that his life is in alignment with our Scriptures. If they would draw close and look—"

"For some it is easier to withdraw and judge." I sighed, thoughts drifting, once again, to Kadmiel's urgent message. "Regardless of what our religious leaders say, I'm proud of you, and I've noticed how Jesus has begun singling you out. He often takes three of you with him when he goes off to pray. You, James, and—"

"Peter," John finished, eyes hunting for his lifelong friend. "Yes, I was discussing this with Peter the other day. Jesus seems to be focusing his efforts in smaller and smaller circles. He often teaches just the twelve of us and sometimes—" John broke off, studied his hands. "Sometimes just the three of us," he finally whispered, voice hushed with awe. "Ima, I don't know why Jesus has chosen to love me the way he has. I am so bullheaded and yet he keeps drawing me close and teaching me. He's so patient with me. I do not deserve such devoted focus."

"Son, look at me."

John obeyed, face open and vulnerable.

"When you were five, you asked me, 'Why are your eyes so strange, Ima?' Do you remember what I told you?"

"That Saba said you have paradise in your eyes. That you were extraordinary."

"And you said, 'Well, then, I must not be special at all because my eyes are as dark as mud!'" I laughed aloud at the memory. "You were so indignant! And so certain that you were destined for misery because your eyes are as brown as everyone else's." My laughter squeezed into silence, the mirth tangling in my throat.

"I remember what you told me." John stared at Jesus. "You told me that Adonai has good things in store for me and that I should never doubt it."

Grasping John's chin, I tugged his face to mine. "He has chosen to love you. Accept it as a gift. You are John—the one who is beloved by the Christ."

His chin trembled within my hand, and I sensed that never had my words found such impact.

"We're almost there." James' observation broke John's eyes from mine as he and Zeb lingered in the road, waiting for us to reach them.

"Caesarea Philippi." I frowned. "Why such an idolatrous city?"

Many miles north of Lake Gennesaret at the base of Mount Hermon, Caesarea Philippi had a long, sordid history of idolatry and was renowned for its temples erected in honor of the Greek god Pan.

"Look." Zeb nodded ahead to where Mount Hermon rose

into the sky. The road became more crowded as we neared the intersection with the international highway connecting Mesopotamia and Egypt.

Rather than turning onto the highway, Jesus continued straight, drawing us closer to Mount Hermon and the atrocities at its base. Evening was approaching, and the sun was low in the sky. We'd walked all day with only a few brief stops. Weariness mixed with caution and a growing unease until most in the group fell silent.

Ahead of us, Jesus stopped and motioned for everyone to gather close. We were on a low ridge, the path continuing downward to where multiple temples were cut into the mountain base. The largest temple had been built into a cave that was believed to be the gate to the underworld. Despicable acts of fornication and sacrifice happened within that dark cave.

I shuddered, eyes traveling up the rock face, which was hewn with large shelves housing more idols and offerings to Pan. Springs poured from the mountain, surging south, feeding into Lake Gennesaret and all the way down the Jordan before emptying into the Dead Sea. It all stemmed from this spot, this mountain pockmarked with idols.

We huddled about Jesus as if seeking warmth from a fire, confusion lining everyone's faces. Jesus stood quietly for a moment, observing the scene before us. The sun cast orange across the rock face, the idols glinting beneath its rays.

"Who do people say I am?" Jesus turned with an earnest, sun-streaked face.

The unexpected question rippled through us. "Some say John the Baptist," Andrew answered.

"Some say Elijah, and others Jeremiah or one of the other prophets," James added.

Jesus nodded, gaze drifting among us, landing on person after person. "But what about you? Who do you say I am?"

"You are the Messiah!" Simon stepped forward. His face reminded me of the moment he'd been called on the shore—open awe. And yet . . . the expression was accompanied by a new attitude, one that stood upright and firm rather than crumpling in abject fear. Simon strode toward Jesus as he spoke the answer again, louder this time. "You are the Messiah, the Son of the living God."

Jesus' somber face broke open in a smile as Simon neared him. "You are blessed, Simon son of Jonah, for this was not revealed to you by flesh and blood, but by my Father in heaven." Jesus settled his hands upon Simon's shoulders. "And I tell you that you are Peter."

Jesus turned to the rest of us, the last of the light bathing him, throwing shadows into the planes of his face. He extended his hands, palms down, pressing. "Upon this rock I will build my church." Swiftly he pointed to the temple that covered the gaping mouth of the cave. "And the gates of hell will not overcome it!"

An *ekklesia*, a church, a called-out group of people who would withstand and overcome the evil represented at the base of Mount Hermon. Never had Jesus stated his purpose so directly.

Self-proclaimed messiahs had come and gone, and Kadmiel expected Jesus to do the same—to rise and then fall because the foundation was false.

From their cliffside nests, a thousand lifeless eyes winked beneath the waning sun while before us the Son of the living God declared his intention to build a church that would endure.

THIRTY-TWO

For six days, we lingered in the region of Caesarea Philippi as Jesus taught in the smaller villages and people traveled for miles to hear him. After his declaration of Jesus' identity, Simon had withdrawn from the others, and when we began the journey home, he fell near the back of the group.

Keturah, if you could see how far he's come, your heart would sing. I flicked a glance to my nephew, then back to my hands, where they worried the hem of my headdress, his mother's wisdom ringing in my ear.

"Someone else's joy doesn't diminish our own."

Yes, good gifts, no matter whom they came to, were worth celebrating. Adonai had given my nephew such good gifts—a wife, a son, a new name that spoke strength. And yet he hovered at the edge of the group, morose and silent.

I twisted to glance at Simon again. He kicked aggressively at a clump of grass at the side of the road. There he was—the large-spirited, sunburned boy I had loved all his life. Moving to his side, I bumped his arm lightly with my shoulder. "You are alone and quiet—unusual for you."

Simon's lips lifted in a wry smile. "Ah, Doda. I fear no one *wants* to be around me right now."

"Why do you say that?"

"I've been singled out twice in a few days, and it's making everyone—including me—uncomfortable."

"Twice?"

Simon kicked at a clod of dirt, sending dust into the sky. "I forgot. You weren't there when I rebuked Jesus yesterday." At my mortified expression, he gave a hollow laugh. "He was speaking of suffering and death as if these things were in his future, but how can that be since he is the very Son of God? Didn't God miraculously protect him in Jerusalem? Stones ready to fly and yet he walked through them unscathed. I spoke my mind, Doda. I'm too quick with my tongue. I always have been."

"I know a thing or two about loose tongues myself. Sometimes the tongue is faster than the mind. It takes an extra effort of the will to slow it down."

Simon brushed past my words, his own tongue racing to condemn himself. "He rebuked me, and rightly so. At Mount Hermon, Jesus said I was blessed, that what came from my lips had been revealed to me by God, and then I act like *all* my thoughts are God-breathed!" He huffed a mirthless laugh and shook his head.

"Peter." I said the name that was still so slow to come from my wayward lips. "Ah, Peter, you're hiding away in your shame, but Jesus wouldn't want that." I extended a hand, but he shifted away.

Ahead of us, Mount Miron's lush sides rose into a darkening sky. We were now over halfway home and would need to make camp soon before nightfall. Jesus raised a hand to command attention. "We'll camp at Mount Miron!" His words traveled easily over the quiet group.

When I turned back to Simon, I found that he'd lagged behind me and shifted to Nathaniel's side.

As we neared the base of Mount Miron, Jesus indicated that

he would continue up the mount for the night. "James and John, come with me."

As my sons obeyed, Jesus looked through the crowd, hunting for someone. "Simon Peter, where are you?" Jesus used both of Simon's names—the old and the new pressed up together. A tense hush entered our midst, a taut cord that the slightest word might break.

"Here, Lord." Simon stepped out from behind Nathaniel.

Jesus quieted, eyes gentling before he tipped his chin in Simon's direction, signaling for him to follow. Turning, he made straight for the heavily forested mountain with my sons, Simon jogging to catch up.

A strained silence fell over the group as we busied ourselves making camp for the night. I wasn't the only one to notice Jesus' continued selection of those three. The observation filled me with pride, but it appeared to cause disquiet in others. I began to unpack while nearby Andrew tried pitching his tent. Without the help of his brother, he was obviously struggling, but he shoved away all those who attempted to help. Until Zeb came.

Gently, Zeb stilled Andrew's jerky movement, easing a pole from his hand and securing it himself before gathering the cloth and stretching it over the frame. Andrew watched Zeb before handing him a tent peg, both men quiet and steady, humbly working side by side.

❖

The next morning found us ready to be on our way. Capernaum was ten miles southeast, and we were eager for home. As we broke camp, someone pointed with a shout, drawing our attention to the mount, where four figures emerged from the trees. As they drew close, murmurs spread through our group. Simon, James, and John appeared ashen. We awaited an explanation for the gravitas on their faces, but none came. Instead, Jesus simply motioned for everyone to follow him as he returned to the road heading south.

"What *happened*?" Andrew voiced the question on everyone's mind.

Simon glanced sharply at James and John before answering. "We . . . we can't say."

"What?" Andrew reared back. "Why not?"

"They've seen something," I whispered to Zeb as I searched my boys' faces. "Something that has shaken them."

All three seemed shocked into silence. Simon shifted his walking stick from hand to hand, wiping one palm and then the other on his thigh.

"Brother—" Andrew pleaded as he fell into step with Simon.

"Jesus explicitly told us not to say anything," Simon explained. His words ignited everyone's tongues.

"He's kept things from the crowds before," Nathaniel stated. "But he's never kept something from all twelve of us. Are you sure those were his instructions?"

"This is not . . . easy on me either," Simon mumbled.

Nathaniel snorted. "Not easy on *you*, Simon Peter?" As he repeated Jesus' use of Simon's two names, the jab was evident.

Simon whipped around, eyes igniting, lips parting, but holding back speech at the last moment.

"I . . . I shouldn't have used that tone with you." Nathaniel sighed. "But Jesus keeps singling you out. It's not easy—"

"Would you rather he publicly rebuke you, Nathaniel?" Simon retorted. "Call you blessed by God one moment and an instrument of Satan the next?"

"No," Nathaniel muttered. "Perhaps if you were slower to speak, you wouldn't find yourself in such situations."

A growl rumbled in Simon's throat.

"You may feel left out, Nathaniel, but recall what Jesus said the moment he saw you." Philip joined the group. "I was there and remember it well. Jesus called you 'a genuine son of Israel' and said you were 'a man of complete integrity.'"

"And yet listen to him now . . . jealous and petty," John cut in.

"It's easy for you to talk!" Philip retorted. "You who rush to his side at every meal. Perhaps one of *us* would like to sit by him for a change! You're like an eager pup at his feet."

"I'd rather be a dog at the feet of Jesus than a prince in the kingdom of darkness!" John declared, finger jabbing toward heaven for emphasis.

Silence followed before Matthew quietly stated, "All of us—every single one of us—wants to be near him, John."

"If we trust him, then why begrudge whom he favors?" James asked.

"Whom he *favors*?" Matthew's calm voice elevated in pitch. "You put yourself above us?"

"No!" James flushed. "And yet . . . isn't this why we're arguing? Jesus singling the three of us out?"

Mile after exhausted mile, the bickering continued, at times simmering beneath the surface and at times breaking out into whispered arguments. In their heatedness, they'd let Jesus get ahead of them, everyone trailing behind.

When we finally entered Capernaum, Jesus headed straight for Simon's home, Deborah meeting him at the door with open arms.

"Rabbi! Welcome home."

Jesus smiled, hunching over to allow Deborah to gather him into her arms.

"You must be weary and ready for rest after such a long journey." Deborah gestured for everyone to come in as the restless cries of Simon's son emanated from the home.

"We'll leave you to your family," Nathaniel muttered.

Simon cast his hands upward. "Oh, just come in, Nathaniel, come in. You know you're always welcome."

We piled into the home, but I snagged James before he could follow. Zeb saw it and lingered with us in the street.

"What was that all about?" I asked.

"We're tired and confused. We all want to be of use to him—to be valued."

"No." I swatted a hand. "I meant, on the mountain."

James quieted, studying my eyes. I gazed back with confidence. He had never withheld anything from me—ever. In the press of my hand and encouraging nod, I reminded him of that fact.

"Ima . . ." He exhaled. "I love you dearly, but there are some things I cannot tell you." He touched his forehead to mine. "I must obey *him* above everyone else." He grinned and winked. "Even above my ima."

I scowled and scrunched my nose at him, both irritated and proud.

As James entered the home, Zeb waggled thick eyebrows at me. "Rebuked by our boy, eh?" he crowed. I slapped at him, but he caught my hand and drew it to his lips, planting swift kisses along my knuckles. "You're holding on tightly, Salome. Like all of those wonderful men in there who are trying to hold on to their positions."

"What, exactly, am I holding on to?" I huffed.

Zeb moved my hand to his chest, flattening my palm against his heart. "That's for you to answer."

Everyone reclined in Simon's courtyard around the fire. I helped Deborah serve wine and bread along with platters of roasted nuts and dried figs. Having covered so many miles in such a short amount of time, everyone was weary, and a few were beginning to nod off.

Jesus popped a fig into his mouth, chewed slowly, and then

with a long sigh, he leaned forward, resting his forearms on his knees. "So." His voice was bright, conversational. "Tell me . . . what were you discussing out on the road?"

Uneasiness fell upon those gathered. Nathaniel, who'd been dozing, snorted awake, while Andrew shoved an entire round of bread into his mouth to prevent himself from speech.

"Hmm?" Jesus prodded. "Come now, what were you arguing about?" He raised his brows with an openness and expectancy that only caused more agitation. Eyes fell to the ground, the fire, anywhere but Jesus' face. Andrew began quietly choking on the bread until Deborah handed him a cup to wash it down.

"No one?" Jesus waited one heartbeat and then two.

Simon's mouth opened but closed quickly, doubt and guilt evident upon his face.

Jesus took a deep breath, holding it captive for a long moment before pushing off his knees with a sharp exhale. "Listen closely. Whoever wants to be first must take last place and be the servant of everyone else."

Matthew's wide eyes jumped to Jesus, while others began shifting in their seats. Jesus *knew*. Of course he knew.

"Where is that dear child?" Jesus turned, hunting for Simon's son.

"Abigail is feeding him," Deborah answered.

"He's finished," Abigail announced from the door. She entered the courtyard, Jonah curled contentedly against her shoulder, face nestled into the crook of her neck. "He's a hearty eater . . . like his father." She raised her brows at Simon.

Jesus extended his hands, and Abigail deposited Jonah into Jesus' arms. He planted the child on his shoulder, rubbing his back with firm strokes until Jonah released a large belch, breaking the tension in the room and inciting chuckles about the fire.

Grinning, Jesus settled the child in his lap. Jonah startled, one hand flailing, hooking onto Jesus' finger before he settled into a contented sleep. Jesus lightly danced his finger while Jonah clung tight, his chubby arm dancing in time with Jesus' movement, tracing invisible patterns in the air. With his other hand, Jesus cupped the child's head, large curls poking through his knuckles.

Across the fire, Simon watched his Lord, tears evident on his face.

"Look at this child," Jesus murmured. "All of you, look at this beautiful child."

With welling eyes, I obeyed, heart resting upon Keturah's grandson.

"Anyone who welcomes a little child like this in my name welcomes me, and anyone who welcomes me welcomes not only me but also my Father who sent me."

Silence reigned as Jesus drew the child up to his face and placed a kiss of blessing upon his forehead before giving him back to his mother.

"So, you want first place?" Jesus turned back to the disciples. "Take the last place. Be the servant of all."

The admonition hit home. Faces softened as the tight emotions from the road slowly unfurled before the fire, the sharp feelings of competition easing into comradery and repentance. Everyone seemed more at peace. Everyone, that is, except John.

Across the fire, my boy fidgeted. His face was flushed, a sheen of sweat on his brow. With long, impatient strokes, he wiped his palms across his thighs while his eyes flitted from the child in Abigail's arms to Jesus and back again.

"I've prepared several rooms upstairs," Deborah announced. "Zeb, can some stay with your family?"

"Certainly." Zeb stood, and others followed, everyone preparing to retire for the night.

"Wait!" John's cry stilled our movement. He had his hands on his knees, both legs jiggling with pent-up energy. "Teacher, I . . . I need to confess something to you."

People began sitting back down, faces flooding with curiosity.

John sighed, head hanging low between his shoulders. "When you sent us out in pairs, Peter and I witnessed something during our second trip that greatly disturbed me at the time."

Understanding dawned on Simon's face, and he came to John's side, placing a hand on his shoulder.

Jesus nodded, encouraging the honesty that was clearly pushing to get out.

"You say that anyone who embraces even a little child *in your name* embraces you, and not only you but God Himself! Well, I . . . I openly rebuked someone for casting out a demon in your name." John heaved another sigh and jerked to his feet. "He was using your name, Rabbi. He was using your name to cast out demons, and I told him to stop because—"

John sat back down, shoulders slumped. "It was Admon. Peter and I both saw him in Jerusalem. The demons fled at the name of Jesus in Admon's mouth even though . . . he isn't a part of our group."

Shock slithered through my body as I imagined Admon casting out demons—gentle, quiet, timid Admon. "Was Leah there? Kadmiel?"

John shook his head. "I'm sure they have no idea. And that's part of my frustration. Admon adheres to your teaching, Rabbi, but what has he given up to follow you? Nothing! You once said we needed to love you so much that the love for our parents was like hatred in comparison, and yet Admon is so troubled over his family that he cannot openly follow you." John groaned, fighting the dark feelings inside him. "And then to use your name . . ." His voice broke, one hand kneading his brow. "I told myself that I was worried over the misuse of your name, but now I realize that I was far more concerned with my own pride. Perhaps . . . perhaps I should not have stopped him after all."

Jesus extended an arm, inviting John to his side, and immediately my son obeyed, leaning into him the way he used to do with Zeb as a little boy. Jesus draped an arm across John's back, anchoring a hand on his shoulder, sheltering him against his side with the same tenderness he'd held Simon's son.

"Do not stop him." Jesus finally spoke. In his voice there was evident love—for John, but also for Admon. "No one who performs a miracle in my name will soon be able to speak evil of me. You recall what I told the Pharisees who accused me of driving out demons by Beelzebul?"

John nodded against Jesus' shoulder. "You said a kingdom divided against itself will be ruined."

"And that whoever is not with you is against you, and whoever does not gather with you scatters," Simon added.

"A tree is recognized by its fruit, and the mouth speaks what the heart is full of," Nathaniel added, eyes holding Simon's. Perhaps asking forgiveness for his own words along the road.

Jesus placed a strong hand on John's back. "Anyone who is not against us is for us." Glancing around the circle, Jesus addressed his next words to the group. "If anyone gives you even a cup of water because you belong to the Messiah, that person will surely be rewarded." Jesus moved his hand to the back of John's neck and squeezed. "Do not stop him, John."

THIRTY-THREE

AUTUMN 30 AD

The month of Tishri brought fluctuating temperatures as summer came to an end and the early rains of autumn swept across the land. As the Festival of Tabernacles neared, many wondered if Jesus would dare go to Jerusalem. With sneers, his own brothers prodded him. "Leave here and go to Judea, where your followers can see your miracles! You can't become famous if you hide!" The devastation on Mary's face was horrible to witness.

Jesus turned the other cheek, refusing to speak back harshly, refusing to rise to their baiting. When his brothers left without him, he turned to his disciples. He would go quietly to Jerusalem with them instead.

"Do you think this wise?" Andrew worried to Mary. "It's volatile in Jerusalem. Our religious leaders are too conflicted over his identity, and some still want to kill him. If the charge of blasphemy stands within the High Court, they may even seek to arrest him. He should remain in Galilee for the time being, but he won't listen to us."

"Perhaps he'll listen to you," Philip added.

"You think his ima can change his mind?" Mary shook her head. "I've had to learn many things over the course of Jesus' life. Some of those lessons have come hard and slow, and some lessons I'm still learning. But one thing I do know is that I cannot stand in the way of his purpose. Believe me, this ima would like to direct him toward safety, but he is not in my hands. He is in his Father's."

Her soft words were a sword, piercing me to the soul. *"You're holding on tightly, Salome."* Zeb's observation mixed with Mary's own words. Didn't every good ima guard and guide, counsel and protect?

"He is not in my hands. He is in his Father's." Mary's gentle words, sharp and biting as a blade.

◆

The company traveling south with Jesus was small, with only a handful of family members in attendance. I kept close to Zeb, Deborah, Abigail, and Simon—all of us taking turns with a fussy Jonah, who'd recently begun to walk and did not want to be strapped to a back.

We expected to cross the Jordan River at Scythopolis, a city north of Samaria. In this way, we would travel south into Perea before cutting west, back over the Jordan and into Judea. Two days into our journey, however, James came to me with a tight expression on his face. "He says we're to stay the course through Samaria."

"He's passed this way before with no problems, hasn't he?"

"Yes, but Jesus is more . . . infamous now," James worried. "They may not take kindly to an infamous rabbi traveling south to Jerusalem. I encouraged him to travel through Perea instead, but he is set upon this course."

"Instead of trying to direct him, perhaps we should simply follow him."

James settled at my words. "I know you're right, Ima. You usually are."

As we neared the border of Samaria, Jesus sent Judas and Thomas ahead of us to Salim, a small village five miles south of Scythopolis, with instructions to prepare the village for our arrival. The sun was low in the sky as we neared the Jordan Valley. Below us we could see the sprawling lights of Salim.

"They're returning at a run!" Andrew called our attention to the two figures sprinting down the road as if dogs nipped at their heels, their urgency evident even at this distance. They heaved to a stop before us.

"Turn back," Judas wheezed.

Thomas hunched over, hands on his thighs as he gulped in air. "You will find no welcome there!"

"What do you mean?" James questioned, pushing to the front, alarm highlighting his face.

"As soon as they heard Jesus' name, they began to mock us, saying, 'How dare you ask us to house your rabbi on his way to your Holy City. You view us with disdain and yet expect us to shelter your false Messiah.'"

"They would not even fill our skins with water," Judas added, lifting his empty pouch for emphasis.

Thomas straightened, face flushed. "You will find no welcome there, Rabbi. In fact, you may find bodily harm."

John pushed forward next to his brother. "It is late in the evening and they would turn us away in such a fashion?"

James shook his head. "I know we share no love with the Samaritans, but this is outrageous."

"Rabbi, in this very region, didn't Elijah call down fire from heaven against the forces of evil?" John turned to Jesus.

James nodded. "'If I am a man of God, let fire come down from heaven and destroy you and your fifty men.' These were the words of Elijah spoken over the evil soldiers of King Ahaziah. Not once, but twice, and it was done!"

"Did you not say that those who give us a cup of water because we belong to you are blessed? Well then, what shall be done to those who deny us much more than water?" John pulled his hands into fists.

"Tell us what to do, Rabbi." James was quieter than John but no less fervent. "Tell us what to do and we will do it."

John pointed down the slope to the sleepy village in the palm of the valley. "Do you want us to call fire down from heaven to destroy them as Elijah did?"

"*Fire?*" Jesus' eyes flew wide. He followed John's pointing finger to the pricks of light in the valley. "Fire from heaven, James and John?" His voice dipped into the beginnings of a rebuke.

What had my boys done? They'd asked for fire, but it was already blazing bright in both of their chests, an unfettered flame they wanted Jesus to sanction. I recognized the desire behind it—had seen it over and over again throughout their youth. James' strong sense of justice coupled with John's fierce love made them ardent in their devotion. But to ask to be instruments of God's wrath?

It was the request of a Zealot.

My heart flopped like a fish, heat climbing my face as I stared at Jesus.

Do not think poorly of them. Please, please.

The zeal in my boys' faces was dimming, slipping into uncertainty the longer Jesus lingered over their fervent question.

With a rumbling sigh, Jesus shook his head before placing a hand on each of my sons' shoulders. "You don't realize what your hearts are like, the manner of spirit you harbor. Have I been with you all this time and yet you still do not know what I am about?"

John ducked his head, but Jesus placed a knuckle beneath his chin, urging him to receive his words. "The Son of Man has not come to destroy people's lives, but to save them. Remember my teaching that it is the thief who comes to kill and destroy. But I have come that people may have life and have it to the full."

Jesus grabbed ahold of the scruffs of their necks as if they were eager pups he was training into usefulness. "Oh, you passionate men, you Sons of Thunder!" He pulled their heads together as if to knock sense into them. He was shaking his head again but this time his shoulders also shook, and I realized he was suppressing laughter.

"Tell you what to do and you will do it? Rather than decimate this village, we will simply go on to the next. Aenon is only two miles away." He released them, along with a low chuckle, and led the way around Salim.

That night I lay motionless on my back, painfully alert in the upper room of our host's home in Aenon. All around me the soft breathing of the other women in our company indicated that they were enjoying rest, but there could be no rest for me. Again and again, I replayed the moment above Salim, the fire in my boys and Jesus' rebuke.

Nearby, Jonah woke with a cry. Abigail was up in an instant, shushing and placing him to her breast. John had been like that— perpetually hungry and up in the night. Restless, irritable . . . thunderous.

"You passionate men, you Sons of Thunder!"

I shifted onto my side, missing Zeb's warmth. There hadn't been enough room in the home for our whole group, so he was next door with some of the men in our company. Before separating for the night, however, I'd pulled him aside. He'd noted the distress on my face. *"I'll speak with them tonight if I can find a private moment,"* he'd assured me.

"Don't shame them, but . . ." I'd bit my lip, still disturbed that our boys' passion had compelled them to seek violence.

"You saw Jesus with them," Zeb had encouraged. *"Eager to redirect and instruct. He loves them, Salome. Sometimes I realize he*

might even love them more than we do. His love . . . it's unsullied, perfect. We can trust him with our boys' bullheadedness."

He'd grinned. "*You know it's a fitting name. Don't deny it.*" When I'd pouted, he'd laughed. "*I've always said you were formidable, so is it any wonder that James and John are Sons of Thunder?*"

I rolled onto my back with a sigh, surprising Abigail, who looked at me questioningly. Swiftly, I closed my eyes to avoid conversation. Without realizing it, my hand slipped to my side in search of the pouch.

How long before my hand ceased its hunt for the gift that had been my comfort all these years? I'd lost the pouch, but I still had my sons, and surely their futures would be bright in Jesus' Kingdom.

Will your sons continue to be a part of Jesus' inner circle, though, now that they've shown how zealous they can be? Doubt wondered.

He knows them, I reasoned. *He's gentle with their stubbornness and is working with them. It's like I told John—he has chosen to love them. That choice will not change.*

He called Simon a rock . . . something sturdy and dependable. But your boys? They are as volatile as rolling thunder.

I fell silent after that.

Thirty-Four

Booths dotted the Judean landscape as pilgrims from all over congregated in and around Jerusalem for the Festival of Tabernacles. Rather than staying within the Holy City, we constructed shelters in the Garden of Gethsemane, east of Jerusalem across the Kidron Brook. Daily we journeyed to the Temple to witness the lighting of the lamps in the Court of the Women and the outpouring of water, which priests carried from the Pool of Siloam in a golden pitcher. They emptied it at the altar, commemorating the water God had drawn from stone in the wilderness. Miraculous provision poured out upon a stubborn people.

Everywhere Jesus went, speculation followed, grumblings that stirred beneath our feet.

"He's a good man."

"He's the Messiah!"

"No, he's nothing but a fraud who deceives the people."

The division of ideas over Jesus' identity thrummed all throughout the festival, but no one spoke their thoughts too loudly.

"He's long held the attention of the scribes and Pharisees, but both Caiaphas and Annas are beginning to take note," Zeb shared privately with me when he'd returned from a visit with Annas' steward.

"I'm surprised we still hold those accounts when we've lost so many others."

"Hiram is sympathetic toward Jesus." Zeb sighed. "He won't come out and state his support directly. He, along with many others, is too afraid to do so, but I see it. He asks me for news of Jesus with eagerness. He won't bring our connection with Jesus to Annas' attention."

For his part, Jesus moved quietly about the rumblings . . . until the seventh and final day of the celebration. We gathered in the Court of the Women after the water libation as the Levites led the people in song. Beneath the glittering lamps, we raised our voices to the accompaniment of the harp and lyre, pouring out a song of David:

> "The stone the builders rejected has become the
>   cornerstone;
> Yahweh has done this, and it is marvelous in our eyes.
> Yahweh has done it this very day; let us rejoice today
>   and be glad.
> Yahweh, save us! Yahweh, grant us success!
> Blessed is he who comes in the name of Yahweh.
> From the house of Yahweh we bless you.
> Yahweh is God, and he has made his light shine on us.
> With boughs in hand, join in the festal procession up to
>   the horns of the altar."

A hush fell over the crowd. Every day for seven days there was this hush—a holding place for memory. As the echoes of the music danced off the temple stones, Jesus strode to the circular steps outside the Nicanor Gate and turned to address the people.

"Let anyone who is thirsty come to me and drink!" His invitation reverberated through the crowd, as arresting as the crash of a cymbal. Directly behind Jesus lay the Priests' Courtyard and the altar. The crowd was stunned into a deeper silence as Jesus continued in a loud shout, "Whoever believes in me, as Scripture has said, 'Out of his heart will flow rivers of living water!'"

The whispers over Jesus' identity erupted into loud exclamations.

"This man is the Prophet we've been expecting!"

"He *is* the Messiah!"

"But he can't be! Will the Messiah come from Galilee?"

The crowd began jostling one another in an effort to draw closer to Jesus. Near the East Gate, a contingent of Temple guards stood at the ready. Calmly, Jesus descended the steps and walked directly toward the guards while we all scrambled to keep up. I barely had time to pray for his protection, but worry became amazement as the guards parted and allowed Jesus through.

——— ✦ ———

As we'd done each night of the festival, we withdrew to our *sukkot* booths in Gethsemane. Jesus' words pounded in my head. *"Let anyone who is thirsty come to me and drink!"*

"It's not the first time he's referenced living water," John confided. "He reminded me, Ima. As soon as we crossed the Kidron, he looked at me and I knew . . . somehow, I knew what he wanted me to remember."

Tears pooled in my son's eyes. "In the very beginning, he told someone that he was able to give living water. In plain terms, he said that he was the Messiah and that those who drink of his water will never thirst again. His water would become a fresh, bubbling spring within them." John shaded his face with a hand. "He gave these words to a woman . . . a *Samaritan* woman."

Right in front of me, John's heart was cracking open—achingly wide.

After Jesus' rebuke at Salim, both my boys had quieted, but instead of withdrawing from Jesus, they'd pressed nearer, and despite my earlier fear, Jesus continued to invite them into his intimate circle. In my sons' demeanor I sensed a renewed desire to learn, to follow their rabbi even closer, to cover themselves in the dust from his feet. They wanted to be with him, to be like him, and that desire was a fire no rebuke could snuff out. Rather, Jesus' redirection had served as fuel for that flame.

"Jesus is somber, quieter than usual," I observed to James. "Do you think it's due to all the speculation? Or the concern that they will confront him with stones rather than words?"

"We have seen Adonai protect him, and surely He will continue to do so," James answered.

Nearby was a large tree close to the garden grotto where olives were pressed into oil. Nightly, Jesus had gone to this tree, one hand anchored to the trunk, head bowed, praying. Nightly, James, John, and Simon went with him, standing at a distance, surrounding him with their presence.

"He seems to be preparing for something," James continued. "So many people don't understand who he is or what he teaches. I'm still learning, Ima. I want to be someone he can rely upon—sturdy, dependable."

"Unshakable," I breathed.

James bared his face to the sky.

I joined him, slipped an arm about his waist, and peeked up through thick branches, searching for those pinpricks of light beyond.

"'He determines the number of the stars and calls them each by name,'" James quoted the psalmist.

God's provision and knowledge spread across the sky. We stood quietly together beneath it.

---- ✦ ----

The day after the Festival of Tabernacles was a Sabbath, after which Zeb and I would travel home.

"Jesus is determined to stay," Andrew told me. "Despite all of the hostility, he's directed his attention to Jerusalem, and I don't think he will return to Galilee anytime soon."

For over two years, I'd witnessed Jesus' transforming work and watched my sons change beneath his teaching—at times growing bold and confident, at other times falling into stillness and reflection, but always moving, hearts shifting closer to the Messiah. Was it time for his ministry to change? For the promised Kingdom to come?

As he'd done every day since arriving in Jerusalem, Jesus taught in the Temple courts. He didn't need to announce his presence, didn't need to go and gather a crowd. People came. Like sheep seeking shelter in their sheepfold at night, they huddled about Jesus and hung upon his every word. Outside the ring of listeners, however, a different crowd formed. I stood beneath the southern colonnade with Zeb and pointed to the scribes and Pharisees.

"Their faces trouble me," I whispered. "Still so much hatred."

Zeb scanned the crowd. "Neither they nor the Temple guards interfered yesterday. Let's hope that the interest of the crowd is enough to stay their hand."

"And their stones," I muttered.

Jesus stood near the treasury. With a long arm, he pointed above our heads to the lampstands that still burned from the previous night. "I tell you, I am the light of the world. Whoever follows me will never walk in darkness, but will have the light of life."

"Ha! Here you are, appearing as your own witness?" someone scoffed behind us. "Your testimony is not valid." A Pharisee pushed through the crowd.

Jesus answered the outcry in an even voice. "My testimony is valid even though I'm testifying about myself. For I know where I came from and where I am going." Jesus strode toward his accuser. "But *you* . . . you have no idea where I come from or where I am going." Jesus pointed up and then down, each firm gesture driving his words home. "I stand with the Father, who sent me! Your own law says that if two people agree about something, their witness is accepted as fact." Jesus thumped a hand to his chest. "I am one witness, and my Father who sent me is the other."

The Pharisee remained silent for a long moment, lips pursed. When he finally spoke, each word was clipped. "And where is your father?"

"You do not know me or my Father," Jesus replied. The fire in his voice grew soft with sadness. "You are blind guides—blind guides! If you knew me, you would know my Father also."

"You dare to call *us* blind? Who do you think you are?" another voice shouted.

My stomach sank low. Compulsively, I fumbled for Zeb's hand. He caught it and squeezed.

The voice came again, loud with indignation. "Well? Who are you?" Kadmiel shoved his way forward to join the Pharisee.

All throughout the festival, I'd wondered if we would see him. There was a time when we would have celebrated the festival *with* Kadmiel and Leah, but that time was long gone. Memory piled upon memory as I recalled our boys playing with Admon and Affera on Kadmiel's roof. It was the one time of the year in which Leah's children seemed to welcome mine, the sukkot booth serving as a peaceful meeting place for the cousins who were so different from one another.

This year we had not even sought our kin, knowing we would find no welcome. Tears gathered in my eyes as Kadmiel demanded an answer to his question.

"Who am I?" Jesus repeated as he drew close to the Galilean scribe who'd followed his ministry with skepticism. "I am what I've been telling you from the beginning." Turning, he addressed the crowd. "You are truly my disciples if you remain faithful to my teachings. And you will know the truth, and the truth will set you free."

"What do you mean 'set us free'?" someone called. "We are descendants of Abraham. We aren't enslaved to anyone."

"Everyone who sins is a slave to sin. If the Son sets you free, you are truly free. Some of you are trying to kill me because there's no room in your hearts for my message." Jesus turned back to Kadmiel with an extended hand of invitation. "You aren't listening to my words but are following the advice of your father."

Kadmiel snorted. "Our father is Abraham."

"No!" Jesus dropped his hand and took a large step back. "No, for if you were really the children of Abraham, you would follow his example. Instead, you are trying to kill me because I told you the truth. No, you are imitating your real father."

"Real father?" Kadmiel's face was inscrutable, but I'd known him my whole life and could see the storm that was brewing within. "You speak as though we are illegitimate children! God himself is our true Father."

"No, you are the children of your father the devil."

A frenzied sharkia of offense and accusation whipped through the Temple as voices rose in protest.

"You Samaritan devil!"

"You're possessed by a demon!"

"Salome, look." Zeb pointed. A group of men were handing out stones.

"No," I gasped. "Not again. Not again." My hand flew to my mouth, heart thundering as I searched for Jesus, but he was nowhere to be found. "Where is he?"

Jesus was gone, and some of the disciples with him. Fear propelled my steps, and I dragged Zeb behind me. "Where is he?"

Instead of locating Jesus, I found James standing near the South Gate. He caught my eye and began pushing his way toward me as Zeb's hand was wrenched from mine.

Startling, I turned to find Kadmiel clutching Zeb as he shouted at him, "Where is he? Where did he go?"

Around us, the crowd swelled and surged like rolling waves. Some rushed from the Temple in search of Jesus, while others cast their stones aside in exasperation.

"How did he disappear?" Kadmiel cried.

"Release him!" James shoved his way to Zeb's side. "Uncle, release him."

Kadmiel faced James. "You heard him, all of you. He said we were children of the devil! Surely now you see him for what he is—a blasphemous man with no regard for the Law or its teachers."

"No, Uncle, I'm afraid it's you who are blinded." James' voice was gentle, and in its quiet timbre I heard the echo of Jesus' own sadness. "To deny Jesus is to deny God Himself. What else is such denial if not demonic?"

Kadmiel observed James with disbelief before turning to Zeb. "I've had enough. In his blasphemy, this Jesus not only leads people astray but also taints those connected to Galilee. Do you know how hard I have worked for the role I now enjoy? I have pushed through years of prejudice, and now because of this Jesus' obnoxious claims, those in the Sanhedrin are openly mocking Galileans."

"Do not let your own pride and ambition stand in the way of truth, Kadmiel," I urged, but he refused to acknowledge me.

"*Why shouldn't I aim high?*" Through the twist of anger on Kadmiel's face, I glimpsed the beautiful boy along the shores of the lake who felt out of place. Too bright for Bethsaida. Too provincial for Jerusalem. Caught in a stranglehold of his own thwarted ambition.

"I made excuses for your family," Kadmiel stated. "To my friends and colleagues—and even some of your clients—I made excuses, but no more. I will not tolerate such blatant apostasy

285

within my own family any longer. Through my warnings, I'd hoped that you would take action, but now I see something more drastic than a warning is needed."

"What are you saying, brother?" From the moment Kadmiel had accosted him, Zeb had remained quiet. He spoke now with evident pain, and I understood that he was mourning a loss.

"I am saying, *brother*, that unless you deny this Jesus, I will go to your clients—straight to Caiaphas himself—and demand that they drop your accounts. You will never do business within this city again."

James stilled, body tense as he gazed at his father.

All around us, people searched for Jesus and argued over his words, but in our small circle of four people, there was silence, a painful pause—a bruising that went deep.

"Kadmiel, please—" My voice broke along with my heart. The shaggy-haired boy who'd pulled me from the lake had been weathered into a man I didn't recognize. My mind traced the years of our relationship, all the help and encouragement he'd given Zeb, the way he'd stood by him when Zeb's own father had been skeptical and aloof. And now . . . it had come to this. I gazed steadfastly at my husband and waited.

Zeb stood erect, back slightly arched so that he angled toward the sky, eyes closed, demeanor peaceful. His face was darkened and rough from a life lived beneath the blazing sun. He invited that warmth now, let the rays kiss his work-worn skin.

All he knew was the lake. All he knew was life lived for the day's catch and then the next. Year after year, I had watched him pour all of himself into that work, and I had seen God bless the fruit of his labors. I slipped my hand into his, threading our fingers together, giving him my presence, my love. Years of giving him that love, choosing it time and time again.

Zeb nodded, a small, nearly imperceptible dip of the chin, accepting something. When he opened his eyes, they were bright and resolute.

"You can dismantle my business, client by client. You can undo years of my labor and ensure that I never trade within the Holy City again. You can speak ill of me to the high priest himself, but I will never renounce the truth I have witnessed."

"You would throw away your life's work for this lunatic?" Kadmiel ground his teeth.

Zeb smiled softly. "I would surrender my life's work to the Messiah. I trust him and what he is building. I believe it to be worth whatever the cost. Go ahead and do your worst, but my lot is with Jesus and there it will remain."

Quietly, Zeb led us away from Kadmiel, James brimming with pride.

Later, in the quiet of the night as we lay in bed, I held my husband's hand, resting the other in the hollow of his cheek.

In that moment, I had never loved him more.

Thirty-Five

We returned to Galilee with Deborah and Abigail while our loved ones remained in Judea. It was only a matter of time before we suffered the repercussions of our encounter with Kadmiel. Sure enough, two weeks later, we received a missive from Caiaphas' household canceling our account. The loss came with immediate consequences as we were forced to release some of our hired help.

"God willing, our account with Annas is secure. Hiram will see to that." I attempted to soothe my husband, but his smile was tight, eyes unsure.

Nightly, Zeb stood on the shore of the lake, thinning hair tousled by the wind as he watched other fishermen push out into the water.

Instead of pressuring him to talk, I let him think. On occasion, I went with him to the shore, standing in the shallow water while the waves licked our ankles.

As our large, successful business dwindled into a small livelihood, some of our neighbors watched in open confusion.

"Why suffer such loss? Where are your business partners, Zebedee? For that matter, where are your two sons? Are they still following Jesus even though the Sanhedrin condemns him? They should be here to help build up your business."

But Zeb merely shook his head. "They are building something more important. They are fishing for people."

I confided my fears to Deborah. "He mourns not only the business but also a brother."

"It's the second time he's had to do so," Deborah sighed. "Zeb has been treated poorly by not one but two brothers-in-law."

"Do you think Leah condones her husband's actions?" I asked.

"I doubt we will ever untangle *that* mystery." Deborah's words were clipped.

News traveled north, and we knew our sons to be in the center of it. Jesus continued to heal and often on the Sabbath, directly in sight of the religious leaders, whose anger still simmered with violence. As we'd witnessed in the Temple courts, his speech was becoming more direct, his claims so intense that there could be no middle ground. One was either for him or against him. Living water, bread of life, light of the world, Son of Man—he was either a lunatic, as Kadmiel claimed, or exactly who he purported to be.

The Feast of Purim came, and with it the ferocious winds of winter. We would travel south soon for Passover. I had woven two thick cloaks for my boys and would take them with me.

"Why does Jesus linger in Judea when they clearly do not welcome him there?" I worried to Zeb. "When will he return to Galilee?"

"Is the welcome any warmer here?" Zeb wondered, and I recalled Jesus' rebuke. *"Woe to you, Chorazin! Woe to you, Beth-saida!"* After all of the miracles he had performed on and around this lake, many still chose unbelief, their hearts chasing after his miracles while denying his authority.

As the month of Adar ended and our thoughts tipped toward the new year and Passover, unusual news rattled Capernaum.

Jesus had raised a man from the dead.

"I've seen him do this before!" I exclaimed, recalling the moment outside Nain—the mother devastated, weeping, and Jesus with compassion that seared my soul.

"Yes, but this man was four days dead when Jesus resurrected him—four days!"

The words he had given were just as astounding as the miracle: *"I am the resurrection and the life."*

The life. This wasn't the first time Jesus had called himself by that name. I shivered hard as my mind unraveled its meaning. Jesus as life. Jesus restoring someone so thoroughly gone while under the very shadow of Jerusalem, so close to Passover.

As the festival neared, many decided to leave early, to see for themselves the man who'd been brought back to life. We left early too, with an equal measure of eagerness and uneasiness. The last time we'd seen Jesus, he was causing a stir in the middle of a major festival, so what could we expect during Passover after he'd so dramatically shown his power?

SPRING 31 AD

Ephraim was a small village in northern Judea, perched on a hill with a view of the Jordan Valley. A quieter location than the villages surrounding Jerusalem, Ephraim bordered Samaria and was a day's journey away from the Jordan River.

"Is Jesus returning north?" I asked James. "After everything you've described, it would make sense." We stood outside in the sharp evening air. I shivered, and James wrapped an arm about my shoulders.

"No, he'll remain in Judea." He took in the stretch of wilderness before us. Shadows moved against the rough terrain as the sun slipped behind the clouds.

"Will he go to Jerusalem for Passover?" I prodded.

"I'm not sure. Peter has urged him to remain here for the time being, but you know as well as I that Jesus will not be swayed once he's directed his mind toward a goal."

At the mention of Simon, I quieted. These last few months had been a hard separation for Abigail, and by Simon's reaction upon our arrival in Ephraim, it'd been hard on him as well. He'd scooped the growing Jonah into his arms with profusive kisses. "And how is my nephew?"

"Pensive and loud, which is an irritating combination." John joined us, his mischievous grin softening his words. "Did you ask her?"

"No . . . not yet. Although, I'm still unsure—"

"Ask me what?"

"Before your arrival, a wealthy young man sought Jesus—a member of the Sepphoris Sanhedrin!" James said. "Even here, Jesus cannot hide, for the man found him and wanted to know how to receive eternal life."

"But he would not give up his wealth and comfort to follow Jesus," John added. "After he left, Jesus said it would be hard for the rich to enter his Kingdom."

James sighed, face pinched. "I suppose I've thought . . . this whole time, Ima . . . I thought that our sacrifice now would result in benefit later. We have sacrificed everything for Jesus' sake. Ima . . . you and Abba have sacrificed so much." James' voice shook. John placed a steadying hand on his arm.

"You've sacrificed material wealth for the sake of his Kingdom. We've noted it, Ima, and so has Jesus," James continued.

"It is only what true disciples do," I assured him.

"Yes, and so Peter asked what we were all wondering. We who have given up so much, what will we receive?"

"He asked that directly?" I gaped.

"You know Peter." John smirked. "Of course he did. I believe his exact words were 'What will *we* get?'"

I clucked my tongue. "That seems presumptuous, even for him."

James shifted his feet. "If you think *that* was presumptuous, then I'm not sure how you'll respond to our idea."

"We've talked about this," John muttered with a frown. "It makes sense. Ima will agree."

"Will someone just ask me? The last time you were this nervous, you'd wrecked a neighbor's boat."

"No boyish scrapes this time, Ima." James grinned.

"In response to Peter's question, Jesus promised us something grander than we'd first imagined." John grew serious. "He said that when he sits upon his throne, we who have been his followers will also sit on twelve thrones, judging the twelve tribes of Israel."

The breath hung suspended in my body. "Thrones?" I managed to croak, hand clutching at my throat.

I'd held the weight of their futures in a tightly-bound bundle that now burst into a glorious, new vision that left me speechless. My two sons . . . sitting on thrones as judges. It was beyond every hope I'd cherished, more brilliant than my mind could have conceived. My head was spinning as I breathed the word reverently. "Thrones."

"Like the twelve tribes of Israel—twelve pillars in the new Kingdom." John's smile split his narrow face in two.

James settled a hand on my shoulder. "You and Abba have given up so much, and Jesus told us, Ima . . . he said everyone who has given up houses or family or property for his sake will receive a hundred times as much in return. How I long to see that—you and Abba with a legacy." Tears seeped from his eyes.

I lifted a hand to his wet cheek, a bit breathless and dizzy from the news. "But this is . . . wonderful! Why do you weep?"

"Did you ever imagine it, Ima?" James smiled against my hand. "I never could have imagined such a thing. God choosing twelve men to establish His Kingdom like He did when building this nation. Your sons sitting on thrones."

Fire spread through my body, clearing my head. "No one could have imagined all that we have seen these past three years. No one could have been ready for what you boys have witnessed and done yourselves. And yet . . . here you are, the two of you some of his closest companions. If he says he will give you thrones, then he will also give you the right to sit on them. When Adonai purposes to use someone, He does it!"

I grasped James' chin. "Almighty God has purposed to use you." With my other hand, I snagged John's own scruffy chin. "*Both* of you. Two fisherman's sons. And I am . . . I am so proud." The fire erupted into tears. I dropped the hold on my sons' faces to catch my own in my hands.

"Ima . . ." John sighed, pulling me into arms that reminded me so keenly of Zeb's that I wept harder. Those two long, sinewy arms hugged me tighter.

"You've grown," I murmured. "My head used to come up to your nose, but now—" My face was planted squarely in his chest, which, I realized, was broader than I remembered.

John said nothing, merely waited until I'd sniffed myself into calm. "We have an idea, and we want your help. You've traveled with the group and are like a mother to many. Jesus will listen to you."

"We want to ensure not only our future but your own," James added. "You've given your sons to Jesus. You and Abba . . . giving him your very future." His voice grew stronger, surer. "John and I honor that sacrifice, and now we want you to ask something of Jesus, something on our behalf."

◆

As a young woman, I'd learned to pray bold prayers. Like Hannah petitioning the Lord through a storm of tears, I'd learned to bring big things to the God of our ancestors.

Jesus, in his teachings, had encouraged us to approach God with relentless tenacity—to ask, seek, and knock with the confidence of a child approaching her abba. And yet when my sons relayed their request, I hesitated.

"Didn't he instruct you to choose the last place?" I questioned, recalling Jonah in Jesus' lap.

"When serving others, yes, but this is about the establishment of his Kingdom. *Someone* has to sit by his side," John urged.

Yes, if there were to be thrones, then someone would be by his side in the positions of intimacy, power, and authority. I stared deeply into my sons' eyes, finding none of Kadmiel's hard arrogance. Instead, there was a yearning that matched the throb in my own breast.

It was not uncommon to petition a person of honor by involving the family, and gently James reminded me of that fact. "We don't want to approach him by ourselves. The last time we made a request of Jesus, it was rash, impulsive. We will not make the same mistake again of speaking before thinking. If this comes from you and has your sanction, Jesus will know how seriously we are taking his word, how determined we are to remain by his side and to be of use in his Kingdom."

I had seen mothers advocate for their children for far less than thrones. Would I deny my sons when my involvement might grant them success?

◆

The road from Ephraim snaked down a craggy hillside before looping south toward Jerusalem. I walked that path with my sons during the afternoon heat, sweat forming into beads on my brow. Ahead of us lay a rocky field dotted with sprawling acacia trees.

"There." John pointed.

Beneath the largest tree was a lone figure, seated and facing south toward Jerusalem.

"I don't want to disturb him if he's praying," I whispered.

"You won't be disturbing him," James assured me. "Besides, we need to approach him alone, and lately that's hard to do."

As I focused on the man ahead of me, my knees grew weak. This was bold. Then again . . . who better to approach him boldly?

Two things I knew: There was no better place to be than at the hip of Jesus, and there was nothing I wouldn't do for my boys—nothing. Slipping a hand to my waist, I fingered the empty pocket where the pouch used to rest.

As we approached Jesus, a mixture of love and uncertainty swirled itself up into a mess within my stomach.

He heard us and turned. His eyes were bright with unshed tears, catching me by surprise and staying my feet. But at the sight of us, his somberness lifted, and he stood, arms spread wide in welcome. "Friends, come join me."

The acacia was a shorter tree with a broad canopy, not an ideal resting place for one distinct reason. Ducking under a branch, I glanced up through thousands of thorns, each one longer than a grown man's finger.

Jesus noted my caution. "Careful." He extended a hand to help me pick my way under the prickly bough. At the touch of his hand on mine, I began to tremble. It was this hand that had raised people from the dead. This hand that now guided me over a gnarled root had once stilled a sharkia and delivered my boys safely to shore. He'd empowered James and John with his own authority, and now . . . now he had promised them thrones.

I believed him. I knew his word to be true, his power undeniable, and I wanted my boys by his side—always.

I stumbled, and Jesus' grip tightened. The kindness in his touch was too much. With a low cry, I tugged my hand from his and sank to my knees before him. "Lord, I come to you today with a request."

The presence of my sons flanked me from behind as I dipped

my head in reverence. "A request on behalf of my two sons. They ... they are the light of my life. My joy. My great pride." My fingers were claws digging into the earth, heart roaring its love within my ear.

"What is it you want?" Jesus asked softly.

I tried to look up but couldn't, the desire within me so intense that surely it had leaked out all over my face. I kept my head bowed, eyes trained to the ground.

"In your Kingdom, please let my two sons sit in places of honor next to you, one on your right and the other on your left." I had ceased to breathe as I awaited his response, fingers clutching, holding on tight and then tighter.

There was a long, heavy pause during which I could hear my sons' breath even while my own remained trapped. The tension in my body was so great that the muscles in my legs began knotting.

A whisper of a touch on my head and then another—an invitation. I lifted my head but stopped midway. He caught me beneath the chin and urged my gaze to his.

Understanding pooled in his eyes as he studied my own. Three years of following him. Three years of sacrifice as he transformed my boys, and in all that time, had I ever looked him directly in the face for longer than a few moments?

As I held his gaze, my heart quickened into a burst of flutters. *He sees you. Look away. Run.* Fear was a goad, prodding me away from him.

"Salome." He said my name—my common name—but in the mouth of Jesus, it was specific. Releasing my chin, he rested a finger briefly on the corner of my eye.

He sees you. He loves you. Rest. Truth was a spring, fresh water bubbling up; a solid rock, sturdy beneath the feet.

"Salome," Jesus repeated. "You can let go."

Let go? I blinked once, twice. My throat ran dry at his unexpected words.

Jesus lowered his gaze to my hands, which were still crushed to the earth. My knuckles shone white. He covered them, urging my fingers to relax. "You can let go," he whispered.

Slowly, I released my hold upon the ground and lifted my hands. My grip had been so tight that small pebbles were embedded within my palms. Gently, Jesus picked them out, until all that remained in my hands were his own.

Wrapping long fingers around mine, he drew me up. As we stood, the afternoon sun slanted through the boughs, highlighting the ruddy undertones of Jesus' dark hair. He straightened to his full height, hair catching in the thorns of a low-hanging branch. My hand in his was warm and snug as he gazed past me to my sons. When he spoke again, his voice was weighed down by thick emotion.

"You don't know what you are asking. Are you able to drink from the bitter cup of suffering I am about to drink?"

John stepped forward. "Yes, Rabbi! Yes, we are able."

Jesus groaned deep in his throat. "Yes," he finally answered, eyes brimming with a sorrow I couldn't understand. Releasing my hand, he clasped James by the shoulder. "You will indeed drink from my cup, but to sit at my right or left is not for me to grant. My Father has prepared those places for the ones He has chosen."

My boys dipped their heads, all of us quiet after Jesus' somber words. Without explaining further, he ducked under the boughs and left us.

We stood silent beneath a canopy of thorns.

THIRTY-SIX

"You will indeed drink from my cup." I tossed on my bed, sweat dampening the sheets.

"You don't know what you are asking." Air, I needed air, but I couldn't make my body cooperate.

"Are you able to drink from the bitter cup?" A moan escaped my lips. My eyes fluttered. There was light. It must be morning.

"You will indeed drink from my cup." With a gasp, I lurched upright, clinging to the sheets, the wall, anything I could find.

Next to me, Zeb shifted, but even his familiar presence could not drive away the panic.

What cup? What cup would my boys drink?

Think upon his words to you, Salome, I urged myself.

As my husband slowly awakened and the morning light brightened the room, my body relaxed as I rested my mind upon Jesus' other words—the quiet ones he'd given me as he cradled my hands.

"You can let go."

"Our boys know which parent to go to when they want something!" Zeb released a large, incredulous laugh.

No one else was laughing.

"You would involve Doda in this?" Simon railed against his lifelong friends. "I would never have asked her to do such a selfish thing."

"You sought to elevate yourselves above all of us? We who have been through so much together?" Andrew added in disbelief.

The brothers had overheard James and John discussing the conversation with Zeb, and their indignation was so loud that soon the entire group knew what had transpired.

Not unlike the moment Jesus had named them Sons of Thunder, my sons were abashed, although this time it was mixed with defensiveness. "I don't believe for a moment that none of you thought to ask the same thing! I saw you after Jesus promised us thrones," James argued. "You wanted the same thing as us, so you have no room to judge."

On and on the bickering went until Jesus cut through it with a firm command. "Whoever wants to become great among you must be your servant, and whoever wants to be first must be your slave."

Silence descended at the stark image of someone willingly lowering himself into the position of a slave. There was reproof in Jesus' voice as well as exhaustion. He tired quickly these days. Even with the decreased physical activity of remaining in one place, Jesus seemed constantly tired.

When he gathered everyone close, they came with remorse evident on their faces. "The rulers of this world flaunt their authority over their people, but not so with you!" he told them. "Remember my words. Take the last place. Be the servant of all. For even the Son of Man came not to be served but to serve others and to give his life as a ransom for many."

A ransom—the price paid for redeeming captives. Jesus' words about a ransom mixed with the image of a bitter cup, throwing themselves deeper into my dreams, where the cup pressed to my sons' lips, brimming with blood.

◆

If ever there were a moment for Jesus to go north, then this was it. We waited with him on the outskirts of Judea, and in his disciples' faces was the desire to go home. At night, they muttered to one another.

"We can be in Perea by nightfall tomorrow!" Matthew whispered. "We are less than four days from home."

But although the men desired it, no one would suggest it to Jesus. In their somber observation was a deference that, at other times, had been missing. They'd learned and were now continuing to learn what it meant to wait.

When Jesus received an invitation to attend a banquet in Bethany honoring both him and Lazarus, the man he'd raised from the dead, he turned his face south. Silently, we all did the same. No one opposed him. We would travel toward Bethany via Jericho, even though doing so would put us within the shadow of the Holy City.

"Whether or not your Jesus holds political aspirations, our religious leaders will portray that he does in order to goad Rome into involvement."

Kadmiel's missive sat in a drawer at home, but the contents rested firmly in my mind, mixing with the image of large rocks in the hands of our scribes. They'd been ready to crush him with stones, and yet he'd escaped by the hand of Adonai.

"If our leaders must crush Jesus' blasphemy using Rome's fist, they will."

Seeing as stones hadn't worked, would they attempt something larger? Each step south was one step closer to a brewing storm whose developing winds continued to confuse and alarm me.

I combated every fearful thought with the memory of my hands securely planted within his.

◆

The host of the banquet in Bethany was a Pharisee whom Jesus had healed of leprosy, and he had spared no expense. The tables sagged beneath mounds of sumptuous food. When people found out that Jesus had arrived, they swarmed the home, hoping to touch the man who'd once been dead and to encounter his healer for themselves.

I stood in the back of the dining hall with Mary. Her eyes were trained upon her son, who reclined next to the host in the place of honor. "He's going to Jerusalem, isn't he?" I asked.

"Yes," Mary whispered. She fumbled for my hand, and I took it within my own, recognizing her pain. It was the same ache from my dreams, the same hollowness as I watched my boys' lips touch a cup.

Although the room was spacious, so many were present that people pressed against the wall and spilled out into the courtyard. All about me was joyful commotion.

"Look at me, harboring mournfulness at a celebration." Mary shook her head. "Perhaps you understand, though."

For the moment, my sons were laughing, but sorrow hid behind the joy, a tension they held close. "There is nothing stronger than a mother's love," I whispered to Mary. "My mother said this to me, and I've lived it a thousand times: A mother is like a lioness. She will do anything for her young."

"Yes," Mary sighed. "Yes, she will . . . even if it means letting them go."

I glanced sharply at my friend. "What did you say?"

Mary studied our joined hands. "The hardest thing a mother can do is to release her children to Adonai, to let *Him* contend for them." She smiled through a sheen of tears. "After all, He is stronger than any lioness ever could be."

"How?" The question came out strangled. "How do you let them go?"

Mary tilted her face to the ceiling. When she finally spoke, the words were steady, and I knew them to be wise words learned over many hard years. "You accept Adonai's purpose for your sons. You elevate that purpose above your own, trusting that His hands are strong enough to bear their future and that He Himself is good."

There was a slender cord of strength evident in this woman that held her together. How I wanted that strength. "If I let go, then I fear I'll fall apart," I admitted.

"That's why it's not enough to let go. One must also cling. Cling closely to Adonai, who is our strength. And lest you think I don't need this reminder myself, I do." Mary looked at Jesus. "Every day is a choice to let go and cling. Every day a fresh choice."

I mulled over Mary's words as someone jostled me from behind.

"Pardon!" Martha, Lazarus' sister, brushed past me for the tenth time that night with a platter full of nut cakes in her hands. "These are his favorite." She smiled a quick apology before making a direct line to Jesus and offering him the sweet. He popped one in his mouth and then took two more, eyes focused upon Martha. She flushed with pleasure, love emanating from her like light.

As she rushed past us on her return to the kitchen, there was worship etched all over her face. Her worship eased my worry, unfurling it, making more room for peace.

◆

The next morning, we climbed the Mount of Olives in the direction of Bethphage, a small village at its peak. "This, then, is how he will enter Jerusalem," I observed. "With all of Bethany at his heels."

"It would seem so," Zeb agreed.

Jesus had sent Simon and John ahead into Bethphage and soon we saw why. They returned with a colt, assisting Jesus as he mounted the young animal. He would enter the Holy City not on a horse but upon a common donkey, a lowly beast of burden—the entrance of a man of peace.

Shouts rose in the distance, and before my wondering eyes a swell of people ascended the slope to meet us at the top. Many waved palm branches, a symbol of victory. Their words spread bumps across my skin and poured fear and excitement into my breast.

"Blessed is he who comes in the name of the Lord!"

Someone thrust a palm branch into my hands. I turned to see Mary, Lazarus' younger sister, with an armful of fronds. "They've come from Jerusalem to escort him in!" She was urgent with joy. "Here, take more. We will join them!" She shoved more fronds at Zeb before darting off in the direction of a grove.

I clasped my palm branch tightly, its leaves poking at my face. Zeb pointed. "Look!"

Ahead of us, Lazarus' head soared above the crowd as men carried him upon their shoulders. He bobbed like a boat upon the waves, his wide eyes and pale face indicating that he wanted down, back onto solid ground.

Zeb tugged on my hand, urging us forward. He pointed again, this time to Jesus. People were throwing their cloaks upon the ground and waving their branches with such energy that I was shocked the colt didn't spook. Instead, it ambled along demurely while its rider smiled and held the gaze of one person and then the next.

With a loud shout, Zeb pulled us closer. He glanced back at

me, as full of joy as Mary had been. I stumbled awkwardly behind him with a mounting dread.

Jesus was smiling . . . yes, he was smiling, but I could see more upon his face. There was love and joy but also sadness wrapped tightly about him, close as skin—so close no one seemed to see it.

But I did.

It was the same softness I'd noted beneath the acacia tree. The same look that'd both alarmed and comforted me as he'd held my hands and gazed upon my boys.

"Are you able to drink from the bitter cup of suffering I am about to drink?"

"Zeb," I gasped. "Zeb, wait, I—" I needed to stop. To stand still for a moment. To think. Something was happening, but what?

"It's happening!" Zeb shouted and lifted a palm branch high.

The cries grew more intense. "Blessed is he who comes in the name of the Lord—the King of Israel!"

The King. The thrones. The cup.

If this continued, Rome would notice. The Sanhedrin would not need to fabricate political aspirations if Jesus entered Jerusalem accompanied by these cries, even riding an animal symbolizing peace. The cries of "King" carried the signal of change, and whatever was about to happen, James and John were in the center of it.

"Where's Mary?" I shouted.

"In the grove gathering more branches? I don't know!" Zeb shouted back, releasing my hand to wave two palm branches.

"No, not Lazarus' sister!" It was Jesus' mother I wanted. Dread twisted in my stomach, coiled and ready like a snake.

John was close to the colt, one hand on its neck while he tried to clear the way before the animal. I strained to catch sight of James but instead saw a cluster of Pharisees. They moved as a group to stand in the road, blocking Jesus' path. Now it was I who tugged on Zeb. Not waiting to see if he followed, I sprinted toward John, reaching him as the colt stopped.

"Teacher, do you not hear what these people are saying?" One of the Pharisees pointed aggressively to the crowd.

"What are you going to do about it?" another shouted. "We demand that you rebuke your followers for saying such things!"

Kadmiel stood within the throng of Pharisees, silent and scowling. John saw him the same moment I did.

The crowds were still surging about Jesus. Before us, the road continued down the Mount of Olives before slicing through the Kidron Brook. The Temple Mount was in full view, and lamb after lamb was streaming through the Sheep Gate into the Temple compound.

"Well?" the first Pharisee shouted. "Rebuke your followers!"

Jesus swept a hand over the crowd. "I tell you, if they kept quiet, then even the rocks would cry out!" He pointed a firm finger to the ground before urging the colt onward.

The Pharisees parted, and as we passed, Kadmiel's eyes locked with mine. I jerked my gaze away and then back. His eyes were steadfastly pinned on me, unmoving, unblinking. I pushed past him and down the slope of the Mount of Olives.

"Even the rocks would cry out."

With great trembling, I tried to lift my voice in praise, but nothing would come. No song left my lips.

Sing, Salome. If even the rocks would cry out, then you can too.

I was jostled away from the colt, away from John, buffeted about, loose and disoriented as we entered the Garden of Gethsemane.

Sing, Salome. He is worthy of your song.

Pushing off the gnarled trunk of the tree Jesus had frequented during the Festival of Tabernacles only months before, I joined the crowd entering the Kidron Valley. There were so many people that most splashed through the water rather than cross the bridge.

My feet entered the stream as a jarring cry rent the air, so unlike the sounds of praise that it stopped me in my tracks.

"Wait! Wait!"

Chills spread across my flesh as I recognized the voice even before she said my name. "Salome, wait!"

Leah sprinted down the hillside. She splashed after me into the water, so out of breath that her words came in pieces.

"Admon . . . where . . . seen him?"

"Why would I know where your son is, Leah?" I steadied her as she stumbled against me. "Your husband, though . . . I saw him a moment ago in a group of men confronting Jesus."

At the mention of Kadmiel, Leah's face went white. "I need to find Admon before my husband does. If he finds him first, I don't know what he'll do to him!"

Thirty-Seven

Leah had lost vitality. Her round cheeks were sunken, and shadows lurked beneath her eyes. Always a slender woman, she now appeared too thin, the bones at her wrist so delicate, they might snap with firm pressure. She caught me staring and offered a wan smile. "Thank you for coming with me," she whispered before facing the woman by my side. "And thank you . . . sister."

Deborah dipped her head in acknowledgment of Leah and moved closer to me so the back of her hand brushed mine. This was hard on her, and she knew that I understood her struggle.

Leah turned from us to our hostess, a widow named Mary who lived in the modest home in the Lower City with her only son, John Mark. "Thank you for opening your home. I didn't know where else to go."

"My son often mentions Admon. I'm honored you thought to come here. I'm sure they will find your son soon," Mary assured her. "And when they do, he is welcome to stay as long as he needs."

"Mark is a friend of Admon's," Leah explained, worrying her hands. "They studied together and have known each other for years."

"Between him and Zeb, they'll find Admon," I soothed.

After catching me in the Kidron Valley, Leah had offered little by way of explanation, not even to Zeb, whom we'd located with Deborah soon after. Upon sight of her brother, she'd wept, pleading for him to find Admon and bring him to Mary's home.

"Mark has proven to be a good friend to my son." Leah bit her lip. "Perhaps because he believes in Jesus' claims the way Admon does." Her voice became a hushed whisper, eyes darting to the door leading into the noisy street, as if Caiaphas himself were outside with a host of Temple guards.

"And you?" Deborah questioned. "Do you believe?"

Leah avoided her sister's question, focusing on her own hands, fingers twirling a ring up and over a knuckle and down again.

"You can choose belief for yourself, no matter what Kadmiel thinks," I urged.

"A submissive wife will not oppose her husband," Leah muttered.

"A righteous wife chooses truth." I extended a hand, but Leah didn't take it. "And truth sets people free. A righteous wife may even lead her husband to that truth."

"You don't know what it's like. You haven't had to make such a choice!" Leah's eyes jumped to mine, and my jaw slackened as I recognized an emotion I'd never thought I'd see on her face. Jealousy.

"We have made many sacrifices, Leah, and continue to do so." I tucked my offered hand back to my side. "But in this you are correct. I have not had to choose between the truth and my husband."

"I . . . I know you have sacrificed much, and for that I am sorry." Leah ducked her head. "I love my husband, but I hate some of the choices he is making. I could explain away those choices at first, but now . . ."

"I know what it's like," Deborah abruptly inserted, surprising us all. She stepped close to her sister. "Leah, I know what it's like to wrestle with your husband's choices."

Leah's chin trembled as she studied her sister's face.

The tightness of Deborah's jaw indicated bitterness trying to poke through—the old stubbornly pushing against the new, the new finally rising above the old. "I have experienced the miraculous from Jesus' own hand, transformation that only he can bring. Kadmiel is stumbling in the dark. Do not leave your husband alone in that place. Embrace the light and bring it to him."

"You speak of miracles and change." Leah sniffed back tears. "A year ago, I would have scoffed at the very idea, but I've seen that change for myself . . . in Admon. He's kept his devotion quiet, but a mother knows. A mother hears what is left unsaid."

Leah shivered, drawing her mantle tighter about her slender frame. "I began following my son without him knowing. I saw for myself how he healed others in the name of your Jesus. I didn't know what to think, what to do. Things are different here than in Galilee. Here, it is dangerous to follow your Jesus." Again, Leah's eyes darted to the door as her words lowered into an urgent hiss. "Our leaders have declared that anyone who publicly acknowledges your Jesus as the Messiah will be put out of the synagogue."

"It's true," Mary confirmed. "Many who were once outspoken have grown quiet. Although now that he's entered the Holy City so publicly, perhaps—" She broke off with a hopeful look. "What will our religious leaders do when so many herald his coming? They cannot ban the entire population from the synagogue!"

"Even so, it is far from safe. I do not want to see my son ostracized. This is all my fault, all my fault," Leah moaned.

"How is it *your* fault?" Deborah asked.

"When Admon heard that Jesus was coming into Jerusalem for Passover, he wanted to join the crowds leaving to meet him. I tried to change his mind, but I was careless in my worry, loud in my fear, and Kadmiel overheard me. Admon left, and my husband insisted I tell him everything I knew of Admon's connection to Jesus." Color flooded Leah's face. "I was frightened that Admon's adherence to Jesus' teachings would become public, so I allowed myself to believe that Kadmiel would respond in love. I hoped he'd help me protect our son from unwanted scrutiny, so I relayed all I knew—all of it!"

Leah dropped her flushed face into shaking hands. "I didn't think Kadmiel would become so outraged! I didn't know . . . I didn't know . . ."

Deborah slipped an arm about Leah's shoulders, lending her strength to continue.

"Instead of responding in love, Kadmiel swore to confront Admon and place before him a choice—to renounce your Jesus, or he . . . or he . . ."

"Or he would renounce him as son." Deborah finished the words Leah could not bring herself to say.

"I sense you fear your son's own strength," Mary observed.

Leah jerked toward Mary.

"Yes." Mary nodded thoughtfully. "You fear the strength of your son's conviction. You sense that when the moment comes, he will stand resolute in his faith."

With a low wail, Leah cried, "I'm wretched and torn. I should be proud of my son, but all I can feel is terror."

I averted my face, understanding Leah's emotions in a way that was too immediate.

"If he is so convinced and I myself have seen the evidence, then perhaps—" Leah's face was a mess of tears, despondency, and hope. "Then perhaps he is right about Jesus," she rasped. "And if he is . . . then what do I do?"

A sound from outside arrested everyone's attention. We stood alert as the door shook. "Ima!" a voice I didn't recognize cried out.

"It's Mark." Mary sighed, shoulders easing downward as she

unbarred the door. Her son entered swiftly and motioned to others behind him.

Zeb entered, more disheveled than the last time I'd seen him, but it was Admon who seemed the most rattled. Tentatively he entered the courtyard with a haunted look.

Leah pushed past us to gather her son into her arms, clinging to him as though never to let go.

———— ✦ ————

Not long after Jesus reached the Temple, he retired to Bethany for the night. Deborah returned to the village with Abigail, both desiring to be with Simon, while Zeb and I remained in the Holy City. Mary invited us to stay with Admon in her home. Despite Admon's urging that Leah stay too, she left with promises to come back the next day.

"Abba will only press her for my whereabouts," Admon groaned, slumped before a fire, the night air prickling our flesh.

"She is strong enough to resist," Zeb comforted.

"The chief priests have given orders that anyone who finds Jesus' location should report it so they might arrest him," Mark shared. "It's not as simple as pride. There's real fear behind these threats."

It was no secret that Rome had its hand in the high priesthood. Those at the highest levels of authority held their power as long as they were cooperative with those who'd placed them there.

"A new king means a new form of government and a new priesthood," Mark continued. "These men are frightened."

A new form of government . . . perhaps involving twelve thrones? Swallowing hard, I stared at the grooves on my palm, tracing their arc with a thumb.

"After the miracle with Lazarus, the chief priests' alarm has intensified. If things continue to progress, they fear everyone will follow after Jesus. Then the Roman army will step in to control what the priests allowed to flourish. They will be viewed as incompetent and be replaced."

I shuddered. The last time Rome had intervened, executions had followed. It was never good for our people when Rome initiated action.

"Jesus is aware of the danger," Zeb stated. "After today something will change."

I watched the fire, eyes jumping with the flame. Yes, I sensed it too—pressure increasing like the swell of new wine in an old skin.

------- ✦ -------

More pilgrims arrived by the hour from all over Israel and beyond, uttering the name of Jesus in every language as speculation flourished. Rather than staying away and letting the talk die down, Jesus returned the next morning and headed straight to the Temple, where he drove out the money changers. We heard the news from Mark, who relayed the song the children sang as Jesus healed the blind and lame within the Temple courts.

"Hosanna to the Son of David!"

Leah arrived the next day with a bleak report. "Your father searches relentlessly for you," she said to Admon. "Especially after Jesus' display in the Temple."

"I cannot avoid him forever, Ima. Sooner or later, I will have to face him."

Leah's tight expression revealed her unspoken plea. *Not yet. Not yet.*

But in Admon's face was a fire that for too long he had banked. "Tomorrow I will go to the Temple to see Jesus. I have followed him in secret, but if he can enter our city with such boldness, then I can name him with equal boldness."

As we left the next morning, Leah met us at the door. "I won't let you do this alone." She smiled up at her son, meeting his resolve with her own small, flickering spark.

We joined a throng of people on their way to the Temple, a crowd that swelled the nearer we came, thick and close as flies on honey. As we mounted the Southern Steps, we encountered Andrew and Matthew outside the Huldah Gates, tense with alertness.

"*There* you are!" Andrew welcomed me with a huge embrace before addressing Admon. "Jesus is teaching in the Women's Court by the treasury. Your father is in there, along with many others who have come to test Jesus. We're keeping watch for any sign of disturbance from the Temple guards."

Admon turned to Leah, but she was already bowing her head in acceptance. "Do what you must. You are right . . . you will have to confront him sooner or later, so perhaps it is better here, in God's house, than elsewhere."

We followed the rise of voices to where Jesus taught, a large group of chief priests and elders forming the innermost ring around him. "By what authority are you doing these things? And who gave you this authority?" Kadmiel's question rang throughout the courtyard, as did Jesus' reply.

"I will also ask you one question. If you answer me, I will tell you by what authority I am doing these things. John's baptism— where did it come from? Was it from heaven, or of human origin?"

"Kadmiel always said that John was a false teacher," Leah whispered. "But he won't dare state this publicly."

Sure enough, after a long pause, Kadmiel replied, "We don't know."

"Neither will I tell you by what authority I am doing these things," Jesus cried. "John came to show you the way of righteousness, and you did not believe him, but the tax collectors and the prostitutes did. And even after you saw this, you did not repent and believe him."

The ring around Jesus was growing restless, and his next words ignited their agitation. "Have you never read in the Scriptures: 'The stone the builders rejected has become the cornerstone; the Lord has done this, and it is marvelous in our eyes'? Therefore, I tell you that the Kingdom of God will be taken away from you and given to a people who will produce its fruit. Anyone who falls on this stone will be broken to pieces; anyone on whom it falls will be crushed."

The chief priests began dispersing to mutter together in small groups.

"You!" Kadmiel broke away from a cluster of elders to stride toward Zeb. "I should have known my son was with you. You've encouraged him to follow this madman. You heard Jesus claiming to be the stone from Daniel—the rock that crushes other kingdoms and endures forever. How do you not see his insanity?"

"Because we have seen his miracles. We have seen the power of God at work in him and in us," Zeb responded calmly.

The veins in Kadmiel's forehead stood out, his face red as he fought to hold on to something that eluded him.

Admon grasped his father's arm. "If you would stop to honestly entertain his claims, to examine them next to Scripture, then you would see too, Abba. The closer I've looked at Jesus, the truer he becomes."

"Enough!" Kadmiel shook his head. "If you persist in this heresy, then you are no longer my son and no longer welcome beneath my roof."

By my side, Leah suppressed a cry with a trembling hand.

Kadmiel barely seemed to notice his wife's distress as he gazed at his son with challenge.

To my surprise, Admon turned to me. "You once told me that Jesus' words and teaching are solid enough to hold me. I've not forgotten that. A building is only as good as the ground beneath it." Tears glazed Admon's eyes as he faced his father. "If Jesus says he is the cornerstone, then far be it from me to reject him. If he is the firm foundation, then that's where I must build."

Dismay and disbelief lined Kadmiel's face. "Think carefully about what you do in this next moment, for there will be no going back."

"I know." Admon nodded swiftly. "I've counted the cost." Leah softly wept as Admon broke from our group to stride toward Jesus.

Even from a distance, Jesus saw him coming, and as Admon pushed his way forward, Jesus did the same, parting the crowd with an eager arm, meeting Admon in the middle with a cry of welcome and a warm embrace. Tears streaked my cheeks as my nephew threw himself down at Jesus' feet, one hand clinging to his robe.

Thirty-Eight

Passover dawned warm and windy. Having spent the night in Bethany, Jesus returned to the city to share the Passover meal with the twelve.

"He is drawing them near," Zeb observed. "The closer we've come to Passover, the more he's gathered the twelve about him."

"But they'll be in the same district as the high priest." I worried. My heart traveled to my boys, hopeful that they would remain safe in the shadow of Caiaphas' home.

We spent the evening with Admon, Mark, and Mary, sharing a small table and sweet fellowship. Sorrow lurked behind Admon's eyes, especially since Leah remained away, but threaded through the grief was a settled joy that was tied to Jesus.

The unease I'd experienced along the slope of the Mount of Olives was present that night as I lay alert in Zeb's arms. My thoughts flew to Leah, who must be mourning alone, scared and uncertain of the future. I prayed for my sister-in-law, my request becoming tangled up in earnest words for us both.

I'd fallen into a fitful sleep when a pounding at Mary's door startled me awake. Zeb was already up, mantle about his shoulders. We entered the courtyard as Mark opened the door. Nothing could have prepared me for the sight of my son collapsed against the doorframe, panting as though he'd run a great distance. I flew to him as he stumbled inside. With a low groan, he collapsed into my arms, sobs racking his large frame. I clutched him with all my strength and gasped his name. "James!"

His teeth chattered as he sat by the fire. Despite the flame and the blanket draped across his shoulders, my strong son could not stop shaking. We all gathered about him, but I pressed close, hip to hip.

"They came for him with swords and clubs like he was a criminal. Judas led them straight to Jesus . . . and kissed him," James rasped. "They arrested Jesus, bound him as though he was an insurrectionist with an army at his command, and took him away."

Betrayed by a brother. Judas was one of the twelve and had exhibited years of apparent faithfulness, even being trusted with handling the group's funds. Shock left me numb. "Where did they take him?"

"I don't know." James shook his head furiously. "We all fled . . . all of us. I don't even know where John is!" His shoulders bowed in defeat. "I failed Jesus so many times tonight. Before they came, Jesus asked me, John, and Peter to stay with him while he prayed. He was so distraught. I've never seen him like that. He was weeping and so sorrowful that none of us knew what to do. We tried to keep watch while he prayed, but sleep overcame us. When he woke us, there was—" James stopped, unable to articulate his next words.

"There was what, son?" Zeb settled on James' other side and placed a steadying hand on his back.

"There was blood on his face," James moaned. "We thought he'd been injured, but it was like sweat coating his brow . . . red and dripping . . . I-I've failed him so deeply." James' teeth were chattering so hard he couldn't continue.

"*I want to be someone he can rely upon—sturdy, dependable.*" James' own words in the garden tore through me. I gathered him into my arms as Zeb jerked to his feet and began to pace.

"Do you suppose they took him to the Sanhedrin?" Zeb asked.

Mark shook his head. "They can't hold trial at night."

"It hardly sounds as though they are following the Law!" Zeb strode in and out of the light, agitation hurrying his feet. "Where else would they have taken him at this hour?"

"Perhaps to Annas?" Admon suggested, face ashen. "To hold him until morning?"

Zeb stopped and raised a finger. "Yes. I will go there myself and talk with Hiram, see if he's heard anything."

My own emotions were sluggish, weighed down by grief, but at Zeb's suggestion, sharp panic pierced through. "Are you sure? Is it safe? I don't want anyone to see you, to question you."

"I'll be careful, but I need to go. We need to learn more and—" Zeb's voice faltered. "And we still don't know where John is."

As Zeb hurried off into the night in search of one son, I held the other in my arms. *Adonai, what is happening? Jesus is not like those who've come before. He comes from You, so he cannot fail. How can he reign if he is captive?*

I gazed into the sky and noted the stars. I held on to James, listened to him weep, and counted as many stars as I could find.

Zeb returned early the next morning with the horrific news that Jesus was being passed about by the religious rulers. The soldiers took him first to Annas, then Caiaphas, then the full Sanhedrin, before finally bringing him to the Roman authorities.

"I spoke with John briefly," Zeb shared. "I found him near Caiaphas' home. He was present for the hearing with Annas, having begged Hiram to give both him and Peter entrance. According to John, the first hearing was brief and mocking. They are not searching for the truth, only for grounds on which to condemn Jesus."

"Are they still with him? And what of Mary—" I couldn't say more, think more. What must my friend be experiencing?

Zeb hung his head. "Everyone is dispersed. I don't know where anyone is."

The close-knit group surrounding Jesus was shattered like a jar dashed to pieces. My heart was fragmented, journeying a thousand different directions to all the hurting people I loved.

"I told John to come here," Zeb continued. "But he's determined to follow Jesus at a distance."

"It isn't safe!" The trembling inside my body dipped toward nausea. "What if they arrest him too? These trials . . . they are illegal. If our leaders are willing to break the Law in such a way, then what else might they do? We need to find John. We need to keep our family together."

"He was resolute, Salome."

"Then I will go to him," I insisted past numb lips.

"And do what? Compel him to leave?"

"I-I don't know."

"Salome—"

"I will go, Zeb!" Rearing upright, I threw a wild look at my husband, feeling as desperate and resolute as he'd once been dragging a small boat into a sharkia. "Where is Jesus now?"

He studied me quietly. "You can't save John from whatever is about to happen."

I pressed my lips closed in a wordless cry as I recalled the moment Jesus' feet had hit calm waters, my boys safe by his side. My boys secure in his hands. But now that he was captured and bound?

"Where is Jesus now?" I repeated dully.

"The last I heard, he was being passed from Herod back to Pilate," Zeb answered. "I'll go with you."

"Stay here . . . please." I glanced past my husband to an inner room, where James had wept himself into a dead sleep while I sat by his side. "When James awakens, I want his father to be the first thing he sees."

"Very well." Zeb anchored my face within his hands and gave me the long, slow look he reserved just for me. I rose to my toes and pressed my trembling lips into his.

———— ✦ ————

"May all your enemies be soon cut off, and speedily uproot the haughty. May we not come to shame, for we have trusted in You." Outside the praetorium in the brisk morning air, I stood beneath a misty sky and whispered the Shemoneh Esrei. "Hear our voice, O Lord our God, spare and have mercy on us."

I stood within a crowd outside Herod's Palace compound built into the western wall of the Upper City, near the Gennath Gate. My silence contrasted sharply with the jeers surrounding me. They'd given the sentence as I'd arrived but my mind could not comprehend it.

"Crucify him!"

The words were a sickness in my gut—festering, spreading. The horror was all-consuming and my thoughts pushed against it. No, this was impossible. How could Judas of Galilee's fate be the fate of Jesus? All around me, the crowd shifted, increasing by the moment as they waited for Jesus to exit the praetorium.

My head swam, and I swayed, eyes pinned on the closed door as I recalled the last time I'd seen him, speaking passionate words in the Temple about a cornerstone. I'd watched him clasp Admon in a vibrant embrace. And now—

This cannot be the bitter cup. It cannot be. My thoughts came in snatches. How could the bitter cup be death if Jesus had promised us a Kingdom?

The door to the praetorium groaned open, and a Roman guard

appeared, carrying a long pole with three signs affixed at the top. Each *titulus* was inscribed with a name and a crime. I could not read them but didn't have to, for the guard shouted the words aloud as the crowd quieted.

There were two names I did not recognize, each followed by their crime—revolutionaries who'd attacked Roman convoys, men of zeal and violence. Once I'd worried that Jesus was such a man, that he would lead my sons down a violent path. That was before I had come to know him, trust him, love him.

"Jesus of Nazareth, the King of the Jews!"

My stomach dropped. It was as Kadmiel had feared. The Sanhedrin had latched on to Jesus' teaching of a Kingdom in order to use Rome's might.

"If our leaders must crush Jesus' blasphemy using Rome's fist, they will."

Here we were, and they were doing it. But how could Adonai allow it? "You saved him from stones, now save him from this." I rocked with the prayer, the words coming in sharp gasps.

The guard shouted the names and the charges again as he slowly descended the steps leading into the street. Behind him, more guards followed, and then stumbling to the top of the steps was Jesus.

A cry lodged in my throat as I fought for air. Until this moment, my mind had refused to accept the verdict, but I couldn't deny what was before me.

Blood streaked his face, one eye was swollen shut, and his beard was torn out, the remaining hair in ragged, bleeding patches.

On his head was a crown of acacia thorns.

"Careful." Jesus' gentle word as he'd led me beneath an acacia tree, moments before he'd cradled my hands in his.

Jesus! My heart cried out to him as he swayed at the top of the stairs.

Two guards exited behind him, bearing a broad wooden beam between them. One kicked Jesus behind the knees. He dropped like a felled tree, and the men hoisted the beam onto his shoulders. As the beam landed heavily upon him, Jesus cried out in pain.

They'd whipped him. My breath came in short bursts as I imagined the leather thongs full of bones lacerating his back.

The guards wrenched Jesus' arms up and slapped his hands upon the crossbeam, tethering him to the wood with rope before goading him back onto his feet. As Jesus stumbled down the broad steps, the other condemned men exited to receive their own crossbeams, more guards taking up position behind them.

"Jesus of Nazareth, the King of the Jews!" The guard in the front called out the charges again, leading the way, while the crowd jostled to make room and fell in step behind the procession.

"They should change the sign to read, 'He *said*, I am King of the Jews'!" a priest spat.

"I will bring it to Pilate's attention," another agreed and hurried off.

It was not enough to hand him to Rome? They would alter the wording to sate their own pride?

Many in the crowd mocked, but some wept. I stumbled after the procession, attempting to keep Jesus within view. The progress was slow, partly due to the crowd, but also because the men were weak, barely able to remain upright. I pushed through the crowd in time to see Jesus fall. His tunic clung to the open wounds on his back, blood seeping through the wool. I could not get close enough for him to see me, since the crowd was a current that kept driving me back. I pushed against them as a guard yanked Jesus upright and we came within sight of the Gennath Gate.

A stream of pilgrims was entering the city, coming up against the gruesome procession and stagnating our progress. Jesus fell again, and this time it was clear he could not rise, not beneath the weight of the beam. The guard closest to him shouted for aid, and a group of them formed, muttering to one another. No Roman would bear a crossbeam for a condemned man, and no Roman would ask an innocent Jewish bystander to do so for fear of the resulting riot.

As the progression stalled and the guards gathered around the fallen Jesus, I tried to push closer but was snagged from behind. "Ima!" John whirled me about. I had one brief look at his ravaged face before he crushed me to his chest.

"John! John!" Even the relief over his safety could not pierce the horror that enveloped me. "Your father said you were determined to follow Jesus. That everyone else is gone, but that you and . . . Peter—" I broke off. "Where is he?"

John's grief was apparent in the red splotches on his face. His eyes were swollen and dry, evidence that he'd spent countless hours in tears and now had no more to spend. At my question, he lowered his gaze. "Peter has fled, along with the others."

And yet John was here.

"I came to find you." I lifted a hand to his cheek, fingers sliding through his scruff. "I came to find you and bring you back to your brother."

"I will not leave him again." John was firm, eyes casting forward to where the guards were unlashing Jesus' arms from the beam. "I ran from him once in the garden. I will not run from him again."

"John, I . . . I . . ."

"You will indeed drink from my cup."

My thoughts, which had been tied up in grief, now raced with panic as the guards transferred the beam from Jesus to a bystander, the man's complexion denoting him as a foreigner.

"Everyone has left him to suffer alone, Ima." John choked out the words. There was no condemnation in his voice, only a howling emptiness. "I once asked him for a prominent place by his side, for a throne right next to him in a place of honor."

The guards had secured the beam upon the bystander, but even with the relief of his load, Jesus could not remain upright. Instead, two guards bore him forward, half dragging him between them. As the crowd began to move again, John turned to me.

"How can I leave my Lord now? If I was willing to be by his side when it meant honor, how can I then leave his side when it means shame? I cannot do it, Ima. I cannot leave him alone in his suffering!" John wept the last words. As his face crumpled, I could see the frightened boy inside the resolute man.

"Every day is a choice to let go and cling." This choice had been easier when thrones were within sight, when the honor outweighed the cost. But here was Jesus, being stripped of his throne right before our eyes. What, then, could my own son expect? Certainly not a throne. Hopefully not a cross. Could I still let go with the future so uncertain?

The crowd was surging around us, and the front guard was already through the Gennath Gate. John was teeming with urgency to be near Jesus, but I held on, fingers tangling in his.

"Salome, you can let go."

I do not want to let go! Adonai, not my boy. Not my own dear son! If he goes all the way to the cross, what will become of him?

I could not bear to release John, but I could not bear for Jesus to suffer alone. Would I really encourage my son to walk away?

Let go. Release him. Cling to Adonai's strength.

"My son." I wept the words and captured his young face within my hands. "You are loyal and fight for your own to the end. When you love, it is with your entire being—body, mind, and spirit. I am proud of this. I am proud of you."

John studied my face through watery eyes, his tears seeping into my hands.

"You have been by Jesus' side from the very beginning. Far be it from me to keep you from his side now. You must give him the comfort of your presence, your loyalty . . . to the end."

THIRTY-NINE

An abandoned rock quarry stretched along the western road that led from Jerusalem to Emmaus. Golgotha, place of a skull, was so named because the craggy hill resembled a face. Partially excavated, several openings gaped like empty eyes. Numerous rifts were etched into the sides, ledges carved by stonemasons whose hammers rang out across the landscape years ago. The Romans had repurposed the quarry, turning it into one of several execution sites around Jerusalem.

Quarries—ugly places, fit for the feet of a restless girl who chucked stones down their sides while she wept inside for her mother. They were dark and lonely places, so it made sense that the Romans had chosen a quarry as a place of death, affixing rows of vertical beams into the ledges.

Outside the Gennath Gate, I'd found Mary. She'd extended a trembling hand, and I'd crushed it in my own. What else could I give her but my presence? We stood across the road in a tight cluster of women, eyes roaming the rocks, jagged and foreboding.

How many times had we passed this very spot on our way into the Holy City? How many times had we seen these very beams, standing erect and waiting, never knowing that one day we would be here, helpless and watching while hope died?

The Roman procession was spread along the road. They'd led the three men to a ledge near the ground, where they would be raised above the gathered crowd but still low enough to receive their insults, the very spit from their mouths.

They affixed the tituli to the upright beams for all to read before stripping the men of their clothes. As wool pulled away from their shredded backs, their cries reached us, and we cringed. I could see it now . . . the ribbons of flesh on what used to be Jesus' back. Each man was laid out on the ground, arms extended along his crossbeam.

"You do not have to look," Mary of Clopas whispered hoarsely. She held Mary's other hand tightly to her breast.

"I will look." Mary's eyes never strayed from her son.

As the guards drove long iron nails into the base of Jesus' palms, he screamed, and still Mary stood rigid, so tightly wound I feared she might shatter. My flesh crawled, bile rising in my throat as one by one, the guards hauled the crossbeams to their corresponding trunks. They affixed the beams before driving nails into the heels of the men's feet on either side of the trunks.

At the sight of Jesus splayed naked on the cross, Mary collapsed straight down to the ground as though a sword had run her through. The hand in mine shook as her sorrow turned violent, tearing through her body, rapid and devastating. She convulsed with hard, shuddering gasps. I hovered over her, as did Mary of Clopas and Mary Magdalene, all of us attempting comfort when there was no comfort to be found.

Jesus was lifted onto the cross at the third hour, during the time of the *tamid*, the daily morning sacrifice.

As the guards began casting lots for Jesus' clothing, I gazed up to where he hung, back arched in agony, his ragged, pained gasps audible even from a distance. I wept his name as I beheld him suspended between earth and sky.

And on his left and on his right . . . a cross.

◆

Pilate kept the charge as it stood, refusing to alter it to please the chief priests.

"Jesus of Nazareth, the King of the Jews." Those passing by on the road laughed. "So he is the King of Israel, is he? Let him come down from the cross right now, and we will believe in him!"

As the insults continued, it was John who brought Mary the most comfort as he gathered her into his arms with the tenderness of a son. His young face had aged. There was a new seriousness that marked him as he held Mary to his heart.

She cried out, arm clasping him about the neck as he buried his face into her hair, murmuring gently for her ears alone before looking back up to his Lord, a world of love and devastation on his face.

While many came and went, a few of us remained. As the crowd shifted, and we remained steadfast, it became clear that our group was with Jesus. As John held a weeping Mary, love for my son mixed with a mounting terror.

Two thousand crucifixions. When Judas of Galilee had taken Sepphoris, Rome had lined the roads with crosses, mile upon mile of gruesome death. Jesus' peaceful entry into Jerusalem was nothing like Judas' violence, and yet they were killing him all the same. Would more crucifixions follow? What might our religious leaders think of a young man so devout that he would stand at the foot of his rabbi's cross? Rome might not perceive the profound loyalty of one disciple as a threat, but the priests might. And if they involved Rome once, they could do it again.

The role of a disciple was to become like their rabbi, to step in his very footsteps. Would it be *my* son next? My boy's twisted form splayed upon a cross? The thought came with images too gruesome to handle, and I took a step back, trembling and clasping my arms for stability.

"You will indeed drink from my cup."

I backed up a few paces more and bumped into Mary of Clopas, who looked at me with a furrowed brow. Ignoring her questioning look, I took in the scene before me. John near Jesus' cross with Mary in his arms. John standing a mere two paces away from the Roman guard who had driven the nails into Jesus' palms. The guard was looking at John. What was he thinking while he watched my son?

My own words returned to me, heavy as ripe fruit ready to fall. *"You must give him the comfort of your presence, your loyalty . . . to the end."*

Each moment beneath this cross presented a fresh choice to let go.

Turning, I retched onto the ground. When I straightened, my face was clammy, chin chattering, nose streaming.

"Here." Mary of Clopas offered a cloth. Gratefully, I swiped at my face. She was gazing at me with understanding. "This is hard on you . . . with your son," she whispered.

"I . . . I shouldn't be thinking of myself in this moment. Not with Mary . . . not with *him*—" I broke off as my body began to shake.

I gazed up at the man who had spent years loving my sons, countless moments shepherding them toward righteousness, molding their very lives with his truth. He was slumped, a wilted branch on a bough. With a groan, he pulled himself up just enough to draw in a quick gasp of air before collapsing back down upon the *sedile*, the small, pointed seat that served both as support and additional pain.

"Mary's sorrow is unimaginable. Mine is a pale shadow in comparison. For her sake and for Jesus' sake, I am glad that John is here."

Mary of Clopas rested a hand on my shoulder. "Love keeps

you *both* here to honor Jesus' life even though the world would seek to slander his name."

"Salome, look." Mary Magdalene pointed to where Jesus was gazing down upon his mother, mouth opening and closing, straining to utter words. He couldn't speak in a slumped position and so painstakingly he pulled himself upward. Each small movement was rife with agony as the wood of the trunk scraped across his raw back; his elbows flexed, and his feet pushed until he'd gained enough ground to speak.

"Dear woman," he gasped, eyes holding Mary's, "here is your son." With a groan, he crumpled back onto the sedile.

Mary wept and clung to John, while Jesus began working his way upright again, slowly pushing and pulling until he held himself up, entire body quivering in a momentary suspension so he could deliver his next words. "Here is your mother." He locked eyes with John in a searing look before sinking back down.

John bowed his head and turned his face into Mary's hair. Jesus could have entrusted his mother to one of her other sons, but he hadn't. He had given her to *my* son.

Certainty roared to life—a growing, living thing. *He is Yours!* Ragged words from my heart to Adonai's ear. *He is Yours. I see it. I see it. John is Yours.*

As Jesus gasped another breath and rested his eyes upon John and Mary, there was love mixed into the pain, a thin thread of sweetness among the bitter gall.

I touched a hand to the hidden place where the pouch used to rest. For the first time, I sensed no loss, only an emerging conviction. Both of my boys—my two greatest gifts . . .

They are Yours. Adonai, they are Yours.

⁘ ◆ ⁘

The world went dark at noon. The sun had been high in the sky, and yet instantly everything was shrouded in darkness. The guards at the foot of the crosses cursed and muttered as they lit torches. Light from their flames glinted off their armor and cast their already severe faces in deep shadow.

I glanced up for the stars that had often been my comfort, but even they could not combat this oppressive darkness.

"What is this?" I gasped my question and jumped as a hand touched my arm. I jerked away, but the hand captured my elbow.

"It's just me, Ima. It's me."

I couldn't even see John, though he stood close. "Surely this is God's hand," I whispered. Would the stars fall upon us next with streams of fiery judgment?

As the guards lit more torches, it began to rain. Their curses grew louder as they sheltered their flames.

I pulled my headdress tighter, eyes adjusting enough to see Mary upon a boulder. As I settled next to her, she leaned close. Without the warmth of the sun, the air quickly turned cold. John draped his mantle about our heads and shoulders but even so, both of us shivered as rain wet us from above and cold nipped at us from below.

Hours passed, during which time the night creatures came out, appearing to be as confused as we were. As the rain lessened, a distant howl spread bumps across my arms. Moments later, another howl, but closer and joined by others. By the light of the torches, I saw a large, dark form fall from the sky. "John!" I yelped, pointing, but he had seen it too.

"Birds of prey," he rasped.

Two dark forms perched on the crosses. John raced toward the guards, voice urgent. They laughed and shoved him, unwilling to clear the crosses of the birds. John tried to push past them, but they shoved him again, and he fell hard onto the road.

I surged to my feet as the centurion on duty intervened. The guards hung their heads in deference to their superior as he hauled John back to his feet before turning and thrusting a spear at the birds. They cried out with loud voices, wings spread like angels of death before easing into the sky.

How long could this horror last? As the shrill yips of jackals pierced the unnatural darkness, Mary shuddered against my side. *How long, Lord? How long?*

After hours of darkness and cold, hours of jumping at every sound, a new sound rent the air.

"My God, my God, why have you abandoned me?"

Mary lurched upright and stumbled toward Jesus, the rest of us following. It'd been hours since he'd spoken last, since he'd been able to hold himself aloft for more than a quick gasp. Even the guards took note, for men near the end often went silent or became unconscious. Indeed, the forms flanking Jesus had gone still, but as we stood beneath the wavering light of the guards' torches, we could see Jesus pull himself up, this time flinging his face to the sky, lips parting to shout a single word.

"*Tetelestai!*"

The word tore through the quarry, resounding off stone. Tetelestai—it is finished, paid in full.

Jesus' eyes remained fixed upon the sky, voice clear and strong. "Father, I entrust my spirit into Your hands!" With a deep moan, he slumped back down upon the sedile and was still.

Mary rocked, both hands covering her mouth.

"It's over," John stated in a dull voice.

I dropped my face into my hands, eyes wide and unblinking as the ground beneath my feet began to quake.

Mary of Clopas stumbled hard against me, driving us both to our knees. I grasped at the ground as it continued to quiver with a deep, grinding growl. Beneath my splayed fingers, the earth was restless and roving, tumultuous as the sea. I sank my fingers into the dirt, trying to find purchase as before my startled eyes, the rocks split apart, opening themselves up to the darkened sky.

FORTY

"There is nothing more promising than a quarry." Abba picked his way among the rocks with his tools snug at his waist.

I leapt from boulder to boulder like a goat and scoffed. "Quarries are ugly!"

"Ah, you nearsighted girl!" Abba laughed. "Only seeing what is on the surface and not the riches beneath."

I paused my climb to dig at the ground, scraping a stone free from the earth, breaking my fingernails in the process. "Rocks are hardly riches." I tilted the one in my palm before slinging it across the hillside.

"In the right hands, they are." Abba chuckled. "Open those bright eyes of yours, Zohar, and you'll see it. Glory under the grit and grime."

The scent of myrrh still clung to my skin as I sat next to Zeb in Mary's courtyard. It was the Sabbath day, a day of rest, but what rest could there be when everything in Jerusalem and within our souls was in an uproar?

Rather than languishing in a mass grave, Jesus had been laid to rest in a new tomb. Joseph of Arimathea and Nicodemus, two prominent men who were secret followers of Jesus while he was alive, now came forward in his death to claim his body. I had spent hours with Mary of Clopas and the other women preparing spices and perfumes for the body. Our efforts, however, were cut short by the Sabbath.

The death of Jesus was only the beginning, as the religious rulers worried that his message would linger. At their insistence, Pilate placed a Roman seal on the tomb and stationed a guard.

In a corner of the courtyard, James sat with Mark, the two in close conversation. I had relayed all that had happened, and with each word, the shame had deepened in James' eyes. *"How can I face my brother? How can I ever face any of them again?"*

James wasn't the only one in hiding. Some of the disciples were staying in the upper room, where they'd shared the Passover with Jesus before his arrest. Still others were scattered throughout the city.

We had cast our lot with Jesus, and now that he was dead, so too was our future. It was unimaginable that the rabbi who had raised others from the dead, who had called himself the life, was now residing in a grave.

Our already struggling business would certainly collapse after this. Our boys were known comrades of Jesus, and now that he had publicly died in the most shameful of ways, what would happen to the good name of my sons? Those who died on the tree were cursed, so our writings said. How were my boys to show their faces as disciples of a rabbi whom the world deemed cursed?

My thoughts traveled to Admon and all those who had been forced to choose between Jesus and family. What would happen to them now? What lives did they have to go back to?

It was midday on the Sabbath when a knock sounded at the door, startling us all. Mark rose and opened the door partway to peer hesitantly outside, as though the chief priests themselves were on the other side, ready to drag the rest of us before the Sanhedrin. But it was John, urgency radiating from him.

James jerked to his feet, all color draining from his face as he stared at his younger brother. John looked at him but made no move to draw near, instead directing his words to me. "Ima, I need you to come with me."

"Come where?"

"It's Peter. It's bad, Ima. I've never seen him in such a state."

"We are all in a bad state," James whispered.

"You were not there, James, and so you did not see," John murmured. "Peter followed me to Annas' house. I gained entrance for us both, but Peter remained in the courtyard by the fire. When directly asked if he was a follower of Jesus, Peter said no. Three times he said no, as Jesus had predicted."

Shame and fear had drawn circles of isolation about the disciples, even from brother to brother. As John spoke, James averted his face, sitting back down, folding in upon himself. "Isn't that what all of us have done? Deny him?"

"You know Peter," John said. "The first to speak and act. All of us ran from the Lord in his time of need, but he is the one who first stated that he never would. Ima, I beg you to come with me. You've known him his whole life." John scrubbed a hand through his ragged hair. "And right now, I think he needs you."

◆

John guided me through the narrow streets of the lower city to a small room at the back of a bakery. "The owner is . . . *was* a follower of Jesus," he explained. "Peter couldn't bear to return to the others, and so I suggested he come here. Deborah and Abigail are with him."

"But no one else?"

"No one," John affirmed. "Only a few know where he is, and I think he wants to keep it that way. He doesn't even know that I went to you, but Deborah insisted I do so. He's too ashamed to let Abigail comfort him, and Deborah has tried her best."

As we entered the shop, the calming scent of bread enveloped us, contrasting sharply with the disquiet within me.

Keturah, what words can I give your boy? What can I expect to bring him?

Placing a hand to the wall, I stopped and bowed my head. *Help me.* I needed Adonai's strength to love those in my life in a way that honored the memory of Jesus. *Help me.*

We entered a room to find Deborah pacing outside a closed door. She clasped me in strong arms, asking on an exhale, "How's James?"

I shook my head, unable to describe the despair in my son.

"How is . . . Peter?" I managed to ask.

"I've given him what comfort I can, but you are the one who has loved him longest. Perhaps you will succeed where I have failed."

"And Abigail? Where is she?"

"Asleep with Jonah. Peter has drawn away from her in his shame, and it's hurting her."

"He's in here, Ima." John opened a door, revealing a quiet interior starkly reminiscent of a tomb.

The room was windowless and dark but for one feeble light on a table. By its flame, I could make out my nephew. He crouched on his knees in a posture of supplication, and at the sound of our entrance, raised his head. My tenseness released into a pool of warmth at the sight of his forlorn face.

Here was the freckled boy with the large laugh, the ruddy young man who was always ready with a word of encouragement for my sons. Here was the boy at Keturah's hip, the youth who'd adored his ima and wept bitter tears upon her death. Here was Abigail's husband, a new father who was still learning what it meant to shoulder the mantle of manhood. Here was a man quick to speak but also quick to repent, a man who acted and then thought, but all under the banner of an impetuous love that saw the best and wanted the best in everyone.

When he saw me, Simon uttered one word on the end of a sob. "Doda!"

I went to him swiftly, arms spread like wings, sheltering his large frame as a hen with her brood. He turned his face into my shoulder and wept. Not even at his mother's grave had Simon expressed such grief.

"I'm a coward," he moaned. "Unworthy to bear the name of Jesus."

"You were frightened," I soothed. "We all were."

"When they took him in the garden, I cut a man's ear off!" Simon exclaimed. "And when that same man's relative questioned me later, I answered him with curses, fearful that he would avenge his relative. I thought only of my own welfare while Jesus . . . while he . . ."

"Peter, look at me!" I used the name Jesus had given him with a confidence and forcefulness that had previously evaded me. Slipping my hand into his hair, I said it again and yet again with none of my former hesitation. "Peter. Peter."

"Do not call me that!" Peter looked up swiftly, devoid of emotion. I had never seen him so empty.

"Jesus named you Peter and so you are. So you shall be called."

"I am not worthy of the name!"

"Worthy or not, it is the name given you. It is not the quality of the stone that matters but the skill of the mason's hands."

"How am I to be a rock, to be steadfast, when I am clearly so changeable, so prone to run?"

"I don't know," I answered truthfully. "I cannot pretend to know what the future holds, but I do know that he gave you this, Peter, from the very beginning. He claimed you and named you. Hold on to that name and in doing so, honor him."

As Peter's sobs quieted, I placed a hand to the back of his

head. "You've received a strong blow and now you are in pain, but I will pray, Peter."

Fighting through the pain still present in my own breast, I whispered, "I will pray that on the other side of this, you will be stronger."

FORTY-ONE

"I wish it had never happened!" I spat the words, delivering them with fury so I wouldn't cry.

"And what is that, Zohar?" Abba questioned with a grimace. He was perched on his workbench stool, roughened hands braced upon his thighs as he battled through a wave of pain.

"The accident." I choked back tears, which gathered in my nose, clogging it. "I wish your accident had never happened!"

Abba was silent for a long moment as he breathed deeply, in through his nose and out through his mouth. Finally, he straightened, resting calm eyes upon me where I stood angrily hugging myself in the corner.

"What if it had to happen?" he finally asked.

The question was shocking, and I gaped at him. "What do you mean?"

"I wish a lot of things too, Zohar. I wish your mother had not died. I wish I had not turned to drink afterward, leaving you alone in your grief. I even wish, like you, that the accident had not happened and that my foot was whole. And yet—"

He reached a hand to me in invitation, which I accepted after a few slow, obstinate steps forward, finally tucking my hand into his.

"And yet what if those things had to happen?" Abba studied me.

"What if they had to happen in order to accomplish something we cannot see?"

"Wouldn't that make God cruel?"

"No, Zohar, no. He is above all things and so He sees what we do not. He understands what is necessary in order to accomplish His purposes, to form us into who we need to be. What if pain is part of producing something good?"

◆

Waking before the birds, I sat up, immediately alert. Zeb slumbered by my side, snores emanating from deep within his chest. I dressed in the dark, lips trembling as I observed my husband.

I couldn't see a way forward. As if Adonai had tied me to His hip and I was forced to His pace, to rely upon Him even though everything within me cried, *Now! I need answers now!*

Gathering my supplies, I slipped from Mary's home to meet Mary of Clopas by the Gennath Gate. Together we would meet Mary Magdalene by the Towers Pool, a water reservoir outside the gate. Only days earlier, I'd followed this same path as Jesus stumbled beneath his crossbeam. Only days earlier, I'd watched them mock his kingship. But now? Now we would honor him with the choicest perfumes, sparing no expense. My arms were fragrant with frankincense, myrrh, and aloe—scents of royalty.

The sun was still abed as I neared the gate. A dark form eased from the shadows, bearing her own load of spices. "Salome." Mary of Clopas grasped me in a one-armed hug, and together we left the city for the Towers Pool.

A shiver jerked through my body, from the cold air and the knowledge of what we were about to do. I'd been present when Joseph of Arimathea had taken the body down from the cross. Present, too, when they'd laid him in the tomb. But I had not touched him myself.

No wonder Mary had remained in the upper room with some

of the disciples. Could a mother bear to see the marks of torture upon her child? For that matter, could I?

We were nearly in sight of the pool when I stopped, overcome by the thought of touching the deep trenches carved into Jesus' back, the scarred brow from the thorns, and his hands—

Pivoting from Mary of Clopas, I leaned over my spices, inhaled their heady scent, and let the tears drip from my nose. What I wouldn't give to have my hands in his once again, the tenderness of that grip that drew me up and out toward courage. How could I still have courage with him gone?

Mary of Clopas stood close to my side, shoulder brushing mine. I sniffed and nodded, urging us forward. As we neared the pool, we saw two forms hunched upon the ground, and the closer we came, the clearer we heard the guttural wail.

"It's Joanna," Mary of Clopas whispered.

Mary Magdalene hovered over the young woman as Joanna continued to weep as though someone held her heart in a clenched fist.

"Poor girl," I breathed, understanding the desperation in the cry, the fierce certainty that nothing could ever be right again. Joanna's tears incited more of my own as we waited, giving the two women privacy.

When Joanna's grief quieted, Mary of Clopas and I approached.

Joanna blinked swollen eyes as she rose shakily to her feet. "How will we find the tomb?"

"We followed Joseph that night. We saw exactly where he was laid." Mary Magdalene kept a strong arm about the younger woman's shoulders as we took to the road headed north.

As we reached the intersection of the western road to Emmaus, my eyes lifted to Golgotha, that craggy, dark quarry. Abba had spent so much of his life in quarries, pulling hope from the ground.

The words of the psalmist rang in my head. *I lift up my eyes* to the hills. *Where does my help come from? My help comes from Yahweh, the Maker of heaven and earth.*

My gaze lingered on the quarry, recalling each moment of agony experienced at its base. *What help do You have for us, Adonai? David said his foot would not be moved because You do not slumber.*

The upright beams would still be standing. Blood would still be evident upon them. *Adonai, we are more than moved—we are shaken apart! How will Your help come?*

The garden was peaceful as we entered, and my thoughts jumped ahead to the quiet tomb and the one nestled within it. There would be guards—perhaps some of the very men who'd been present for Jesus' death. Would they be willing to help us remove the stone to honor the body inside?

Swallowing hard, I recalled the soldiers at the foot of the cross—their laughter as John begged them to clear the crosses of the birds of prey, how they'd shoved him to the ground.

My eyes drifted up to the silver underbellies of the leaves, up to where the stars blinked within the sky, giving off the last of their light before the sun's entrance. *Adonai, honor our desire to see him one more time. Somehow grant us favor in the sight of these guards. Do the impossible.*

We neared the corner of the garden where he'd been laid, and a tingling spread across my skin, beginning at my scalp and traveling down my back in a rush. "The . . . the stone—" I gasped.

Joanna was speaking, but her voice was distant. All that filled my senses was disbelief as I beheld a broken Roman seal, globs of wax still evident on the sides of the tomb's entrance, the rope sprawled useless across the dewy grass.

Shock stole my breath, but panic returned it. Gulping in air, I gazed wildly about the garden. "Has someone taken him?"

"Isn't that why they posted the guard?" Joanna asked. "To ensure that very thing wouldn't happen?"

The guards. What would they think if they found us like this? To break a Roman seal was a capital offense, blatant denial of Roman authority that was punishable by death. "Where *is* the guard?" I whispered as if they were hiding around the next tree, ready to catch us at the site of the crime. "They would never abandon a post—never!"

"Someone has taken him. Someone has robbed his grave." Mary Magdalene's panic mirrored my own. "Peter," she gasped. "I must go and get him."

"Do you know where he is?" I whispered my question as Mary Magdalene transferred her spices into my arms. "John is with him, but Peter is in such a fragile state—"

Mary Magdalene nodded firmly. "He will know what to do. I'll run as quickly as I can. I know where he's staying. I'll bring him back."

Her confidence in Peter warmed me even as I worried for my nephew. *Would* he know what to do? Or would this be the final blow that truly undid him?

Mary Magdalene hastily scrambled away, leaving Mary of Clopas, Joanna, and me alone before the tomb. If the guards had indeed been nearby, then they would have been alerted to our presence and confronted us by now. When all remained quiet, panic slowly melted into curiosity.

"It must have happened sometime this morning. No Hebrew would rob a grave and become unclean on the Sabbath," Mary of Clopas stated slowly, each word brimming with questions.

"Perhaps it wasn't a Hebrew." As soon as the suggestion left my mouth, I recognized its improbability.

"What reason would Rome have to do such a thing?" Joanna wondered.

What reason indeed? The centurion who had come to John's aid had later looked upon Jesus' still form with awe. *"Surely this man was innocent!"* As the ground had split open beneath our feet, his cry left the lips of others. *"This man truly was the Son of God!"* The sorrow that had been my constant companion at the foot of the cross had entered the faces and voices of those who'd nailed him there.

Even in his death, Jesus' power to transform lives had been evident. But no Roman would have done this. No guard would have laid down his life to empty this tomb.

"We should wait for Peter," Mary of Clopas suggested.

But I couldn't wait, not one moment longer. The desire to find Jesus mixed with a new, horrifying thought. "What if—what if the robbers were interrupted and he's still in there?"

Joanna gasped at the suggestion. "I hate to think of his body mishandled . . . dishonored even in death."

No, we would not rest until we found him. The mockery ended here. No one would tamper with and dishonor his body, not while I had air in my lungs and strength in my limbs. He had endured enough and deserved peace. "Let's enter and see," I exhorted, my feet already moving with purpose toward the gaping mouth of the tomb.

It had been cold outside, but it was frigid within, the space so empty I ceased to draw air. When I finally did breathe, it was in a deep pull that sent prickles of pain to my lungs.

"Look." Mary of Clopas pointed.

Before us was a shelf, the space where they had laid him. It was empty, the strips of linen in a pile, mixed with spices still strong and heady.

"If someone took him, they wouldn't have *unbound* him." Joanna's voice echoed throughout the chamber.

I moved toward the bench, fingers dipping to touch the *sudarium*, the linen cloth that had covered Jesus' face. It was folded in a tidy manner. My fingers traced each careful crease, the curiosity in my breast breaking open.

The ground beneath my feet moved, like a person before dawn

shifting in their bed. I turned as a bright light flashed before me. The impact of that light in the middle of darkness was blinding, and I stumbled back against the ledge as a voice filled the tomb. There was no echo, for his voice filled every bit of the air around us—swelling to the point of impossibility. I could hear nothing else as he asked in a loud, commanding, yet intimate voice, "Why do you search for the living among the dead?"

My hands were splayed behind me, buried in the strips of linen on the ledge as the forms of two men became distinct, both exuding indescribable beauty. How was I still standing? My arms began to tremble, no longer able to sustain my weight. I slid to the ground, unable to look away.

"Do not be afraid," one of the men said. His countenance was soothing and terrifying all at once. He delivered his next words in a somber yet jubilant voice. "You are looking for Jesus, who was crucified. But he is not here. He has risen from the dead!"

I was crouched upon the ground, incapable of movement. The man turned his glorious eyes—far, far brighter than my own—upon me and delivered his next words while holding my gaze. "Now go, tell his disciples. Tell Peter."

———— ✦ ————

Long, loose laughs eased from my chest and into the sky, mixing with the birds who announced the new day. Inside the tomb, I was weighted and trembling, but now I could run for miles and not grow weary. I could shout and never faint.

Pressing a hand to the stone that had been unable to contain him, I turned to Mary of Clopas with a shout. "We need to tell them—now!" My heart was stretched open, and so was my face, into a smile that made everything ache.

Spices and perfume lay in a fragrant sprawl across the ground. We would not be tending his body this day.

Like seed flung from the sower's hand, we ran into the garden with trembling urgency, our paths crossing in a dizzying blur. I laughed in a breathless, heady rush that threaded through the trees. I could hear the others, their gasps of joy, shock, and terror mixing with mine into a whirl of awe.

I paused near a large tree to draw breath—one gulp and then two before I fell apart into thundering sobs. The earlier vigor in my limbs now melted away, leaving me swaying and overwhelmed. Blinded, I pushed off the tree, rounding its gnarled trunk, nearly colliding with a solitary form on the other side.

Our eyes locked and held fast. My mind could not register what I was seeing . . . not until he said my name.

"Salome."

I crashed straight down with a sharp cry, throwing myself upon his feet as I declared him for who he was. "Master!"

But how could this be? For hours I had watched him die by small, painful degrees. I had seen the spear enter his side—the rush of blood and water and the utter silence of the tomb as his lifeless body was placed inside. And now—

I touched my lips to his warm feet, crying out as they found the hole where the nail had entered.

"Salome." He bent and extended his hands to me, palms up.

Immediately, I clasped his hands, clung to them as he drew me to standing and gazed upon me with absolute delight. He rested a finger upon the curve of one eye and then the next while behind him the sun bathed his hair in brilliant gold.

He held me steady, and I was unshakable within his hands as I stared directly into the glory of God.

◆

The ones I loved the most were nestled in the city, weary and waiting. I would go to them. I would go to them with a shout and wake them up. The air was brisk, sawing impatiently in and out of my lungs as I spilled from the garden and onto the road, Mary of Clopas and Joanna with me. My tunic tangled about my legs until I yanked its long folds up within my hands so I could run.

So many years of running. I had fled from fear only to find it following after me. I had held on tight to anything good in my life as a way to quiet the clamoring voices that sought to shame and intimidate me. But I had nothing to prove and everything to receive.

Approaching the crossroad to Emmaus, my eyes flew to Golgotha—the quarry where rocks had split open when Jesus had died. And now . . . another rock had opened, and he had walked out on scarred and beautiful feet.

My laughs turned girlish, the wonder releasing in giggles until I was breathless. *"Glory under the grit and grime."* I had seen it. I had looked Glory in the eye.

Ahead of me was the Gennath Gate, and beyond it were my husband and our boys, treasures I'd kept close in my hand. As the fields flew by in a whir of gold, I lifted my eyes to the hills and praised the one who'd made them and fashioned me.

Cut from the mother rock, I'd been searching, hunting for my purpose in God's good gifts when all along it was to be found in Him alone. There was no other foundation strong enough to bear the weight of my life. No other ground that was solid enough to remain unmoved through life's storms. Whatever might happen next, this one thing was clear: *He* would be at the very heart of it.

FORTY-TWO

ELEVEN DAYS LATER

Tonight, the lake he'd calmed was beautiful, wreathed in moonlight. I stood on its shore, hand skimming Zeb's. "What have we gotten ourselves into, Zebedee bar Jonathan?"

He did not hesitate, not for a moment. "Something wonderful." His fingers caught mine.

Before us, our boys labored next to Peter, Andrew, and a handful of other disciples, readying a boat for the waves. Eleven days of a new life and yet we could hardly speak of it without tears, without questions, without more and more wonder.

"*Don't be afraid!*" Jesus' exhortation in the garden while Joanna, Mary of Clopas, and I held on to him with tears thick on our cheeks.

And he'd laughed; with the unhindered delight of a groom collecting his bride, he'd shouted his joy. It'd spilled from him like light.

"*Don't be afraid! Go tell my brothers to leave for Galilee, and they will see me there.*"

Back home, back to the place where it'd started, back to the town where I'd first met him along a dusty road, wary and afraid.

We'd been here for only a day—waiting. But Peter was a man of action and could not sit still for long. "Let's fish," he'd told his brothers.

Back to the familiar while we awaited the new, hearts wrapped up in expectation but also uncertainty.

James separated from the group to lope down the shoreline in our direction. Eleven days of watching this young man rise up from shame.

"Will you come?" he asked Zeb, eyes shimmering beneath starlight.

"You go." Zeb rested both hands on his son's broad shoulders. "I'll keep your ima company."

"You don't have food." I clucked and glanced toward home. "Let me gather a few items."

James shook his head. "We're ready, and Peter won't want to wait."

"Then go." Zeb anchored a hand behind James' neck, pulling him close, murmuring into his ear.

My son listened with a bowed head, then looked his father full in the face, studying every weathered line. "Thank you," he whispered, voice hoarse. "Thank you, Abba."

As James rejoined the rest, I settled into Zeb. "What did you say?"

"I gave him words I wished my own father had given me." Zeb pressed his lips to the top of my head.

With a splash, the men were in the water, pushing the boat out into the night.

◆

Eleven days ago, I'd returned from the tomb to a room full of men speechless with disbelief. At the time, they'd looked upon me as if I'd lost my mind as I told them what had occurred.

Even Zeb.

I could not hold it against them, for certainly I would have reacted the same way if I'd not been the one touching his feet, hearing his voice, feeling his breath upon my wide-eyed face.

"Salome."

My name upon his resurrected lips was a gift I would carry for the rest of my days.

John had been the first to believe me, pulling me aside, just the two of us. "I ran with Peter and saw it. I *saw* it, Ima. The wrappings, the sudarium. As soon as my feet touched the floor of the tomb, I heard his voice within my ear. 'The Son of Man must suffer many terrible things. He will be killed, but on the third day he will be raised from the dead.'"

John had shaken his head, hand trembling in mine. "All this time our understanding has been dim, but in that tomb I blinked awake. I . . . I don't know how else to describe it. Words wrapped in mystery became clearer."

"Like a babe being born," I'd murmured. "Taking in the world for the first time, searching for a face."

"Searching for a face," John had repeated, eyes probing mine eagerly. "I didn't . . . but, Ima, you . . . you *saw* him."

We'd been together at the foot of the cross, and now, in this brief and breathless moment, we stood together in this—in the knowledge that Jesus was no longer dead.

Fear of the religious leaders had compelled the men to gather behind locked doors in the same room where they'd last dined with him. The darkness of fear had been strong, binding, but Jesus had not left them there. He'd come after them in their fear and shame, stepping into a sealed room on scarred feet, presenting himself in the flesh, inviting us all to lay down fear for faith.

"Peace to you! Touch me, and see . . ."

And there was the same waking up in the others, the same searching hunger that found fulfillment in one face.

"I am going to send you what my Father has promised."

Power from heaven. Grace to walk out this new life. For years he had taught us and now his words returned, brimming with meaning that had eluded us.

"I will not abandon you as orphans—I will come to you."

The promised gift from God, the Comforter and Advocate.

The joy of being with him again was a soul-deep balm that up-ended our sorrow, reorganized our thinking into startling clarity that only continued to grow brighter. All the fear I'd experienced at the foot of his cross was consumed by delight that death could not hold him. What, then, did that mean for us who followed him? Multiple times he came to us in Jerusalem with the same invitation to believe, and I wondered . . .

I wondered what it meant for a disciple to follow his rabbi's footsteps into a grave and back out again.

———— ✦ ————

I was up early, rummaging through our storeroom, loading baskets with food, when a commotion outside stopped me short.

"Salome!" Zeb burst into the inner courtyard. "Come! Come!"

"The food. They'll be hungry. I was just—"

"Come!"

I followed my husband to the outer courtyard fronting the lake, to the ridge where the ground sloped to the water. Deborah and Abigail were there, Jonah propped on his mother's hip.

Deborah pointed, but I already saw it—the boat sharply angled with a tangled net full of fish. The last time I'd seen a catch this big . . .

"It's Peter," Abigail gasped. A figure thrashed to shore, dark head pushing through the water, strong arms tearing into the lake, swallowing up the distance between him and . . .

"Jesus," I whispered.

He stood in the shallows, crouched, arms spread wide beneath a gently rising sun as though ready to catch the burly man swim-ming toward him.

Out on the water, John was waving at us and pointing, but we saw it. All of us saw it.

Zeb threw me a look of unhindered joy, and then all four of us were running down the slope and to the man who was pulling a sopping-wet Peter up into his arms.

◆

The charcoal fire flickered as Jesus poked it with a long stick. We rested with full bellies, the remains of the fish and the bread near the fire. No one spoke. He had fed us himself, with the hu-mility of a servant, and we'd sat quietly to receive it.

I held Jonah in my arms. He would normally be toddling about the shore, but he was cozy in my embrace, content to suck upon his fingers, his hooded eyes growing heavier by the moment.

And so were we—content in the presence of Jesus.

Behind us was the catch, a net full to bursting. The men had secured it upon the bank. God's provision in and around us.

Most of those gathered were watching the flames, but I studied the man across the fire from me. He glanced up, one corner of his mouth lifting with a smile that threw light up into his eyes, which danced as they held mine before lowering to the bundle in my lap.

Jesus studied Jonah with a slowly deepening seriousness that softened every line of his face. To his right sat Peter. Without turning, he spoke to the father while gazing upon the son.

"Simon son of Jonah, do you love me more than these?"

More than these? My throat tightened. More than those gath-ered about the fire—everyone who was dear to him in this life? More than the nets and boats—all that was familiar to him? More than the chubby boy with the dimpled cheeks snuggled within my arms?

Or did Peter love Jesus more than the rest of us did?

"Even if everyone else deserts you, I will never desert you." Peter's fiery words of faith before he'd run away in fear, before he'd denied his Lord three times over a different fire.

Peter seemed to understand the question in its entirety. He took a long, steadying breath, staring at the flames.

"How am I to be a rock, to be steadfast, when I am clearly so changeable, so prone to run?" His words from the dark room and my own hopeful response. *"I will pray that on the other side of this, you will be stronger."*

Anything from which strength was required had to be tested. I had witnessed the process in Abba's workshop, how he'd tapped the stone with a hammer, listening for the clear ringing tone that indicated soundness.

"Listen, Zohar. A dull thud indicates that there are flaws that need to be found and dealt with. You want a sharp, resounding song."

Peter's eyes were bright, reflecting the flame as he answered. "Yes, Lord, you know I love you."

"Then feed my lambs." Jesus faced Peter, cupping his shoulders with the work-roughened hands of a builder, hands that now bore signs of a cross. "Simon son of Jonah, do you love me?"

Peter's eyes sparked as he twisted to face Jesus. This time his answer was firm and loud. "Yes, Lord, you know I love you."

"Then take care of my sheep." Jesus' voice dipped into softness as he asked for the third time, "Simon son of Jonah, do you love me?"

Peter studied Jesus' face, brows knitted in a growing distress. "Lord," he rasped, "you know everything. You know that I love you."

Slipping his hand to Peter's neck, Jesus squeezed. "Then feed my sheep. When you were young, you were able to do as you liked, you dressed yourself and went wherever you wanted to go."

With suppressed tears, I recalled the independent boy who'd

been born loud and squalling and hadn't quieted since. "A forceful son" who'd brought immeasurable joy to Keturah.

"But when you are old, you will stretch out your hands, and others will dress you and take you where you don't want to go."

At the somber words, my heart leapt to my throat, where it pounded in painful, trapped thuds. *What does this mean?* My eyes flew to Peter and then to my own sons, who looked equally unsettled.

Blood drained from my head, eyes jerking to Abigail, who sat by my side with trembling lips. She slipped a hand to my knee and gripped hard, eyes trained upon Jesus.

What does this mean? My lips parted to utter the question burning on my tongue, fire mounting in my chest with throbbing pressure, begging me to speak, to ask for the meaning of these hard words.

Swiftly, a firm hush entered my spirit. *Listen.* I stopped and stilled, took one breath and then two beneath a heavy, warm calm. *Listen, child.*

Across the fire, Jesus released Peter's neck and placed a palm to his chest, covering his heart as he gave Peter three words— three words that I understood were meant for us all. "Keep following me."

The silence was palpable. Peter swallowed hard, eyes casting to the sky, which was streaking with light, to the water that lapped contentedly to shore, and finally to my son, the young man sitting on Jesus' left, the young man I loved, but whom Jesus loved even more.

The sobering glimpse into Peter's future found expression in the tense question "What about *him*, Lord?" Peter nodded to John, and in the query was a plea, an itch to understand, to figure out, to find some semblance of assurance in the people surrounding the fire. But Jesus yanked Peter's attention back, securing it firmly upon no one other than himself.

"If I want him to remain alive until I return, what is that to you? As for *you*, follow *me*."

Abigail pressed into my side as I covered her shaking hand with my own. How were we to live forward from this moment? *"Every day is a choice to let go and cling. Every day a fresh choice."*

Jesus' hand was still upon Peter's chest and now my nephew covered it with his own, rooting his gaze upon his Lord.

"Keep following me."

One by one, we all rested our gaze upon Jesus. How were we to follow our rabbi into a grave and back out again?

It would be with eyes and hearts remaining fixed upon the face of the one we followed. It would be by his power and not our own.

✦

In two days, we were to meet Jesus at Mount Eremos. Word had spread among his followers, and now our home was full as more and more of us gathered and waited with hearts that cried, *Show us what is next!*

He'd given us a taste in Jerusalem. *"You are witnesses of all these things. As the Father has sent me, so I am sending you."*

And now we were to gather at the mount where Jesus had first named my sons apostles—sent ones.

Leah was coming, and so was Admon. It would be the first time in years that Leah had stepped foot in Galilee, and the joy in Deborah was beautiful to behold.

Beauty, yes, but also pain, so much pain. Wife and son were now alienated from Kadmiel, whose heart was too hardened to join them in belief.

I stood on the shore, memory traveling back to some of the first words I'd heard from Jesus, words that landed upon me now with deeper meaning: *"I will take out your stony, stubborn heart and give you a tender, responsive heart."*

Yes, he could do this. Certainly this was an easy thing for him.

"Are you coming?" Zeb called from the embankment, face highlighted by the setting sun. "Our guests are asking after you."

"In a moment!" I answered as a gust of wind slapped my back.

Zeb propped a hand on his hip and examined the sky. "It's going to rain! Don't linger too long." He turned his enormous smile upon me.

Let it rain. Let Adonai's provision come and let me be caught beneath it.

As Zeb left, a large boom echoed in the darkening sky and I turned to greet it, eyes hunting the distant shoreline in the direction of Bethsaida.

On a whisper, I offered up a portion of the Shemoneh Esrei as light flashed behind a canopy of dark and billowing clouds.

"Rock of our life, Shield of our help, You are the same from age to age."

Like the roaring voice of Yahweh from Zion, another rumble of thunder sent waves of movement through the ground.

"We thank You and give You praise, for our lives that are delivered into Your hands and for our souls that are entrusted to You."

The wind kicked up, but it was gentle. Not the tearing wind of a sharkia but a welcoming wind bearing life.

"I love You, Yahweh; You are my strength."

Another jagged streak of light, another low-throated boom. I turned toward home as the promised abundance came.

The rain fell, and I opened my mouth to sing.

As you come to him, a living stone—rejected by people but chosen and honored by God—you yourselves, as living stones, a spiritual house, are being built to be a holy priesthood to offer spiritual sacrifices acceptable to God through Jesus Christ.

1 Peter 2:4–5 CSB

Together, we are his house, built on the foundation of the apostles and the prophets. And the cornerstone is Christ Jesus himself.

Ephesians 2:20 NLT

author's note

"Promise . . . that these two sons of mine may sit, one on your right and the other on your left, in your kingdom" (Matthew 20:21 csb). We remember the mother of the Sons of Thunder for this singular, startling moment—her one verbal exchange with Jesus Christ, in which she asks for the places of honor for her boys. In comparing the Matthew account with the one in Mark (10:35–40), we see that this request was a group effort with James and John most likely serving as the masterminds who then involved their mother.

What do we know of this bold mother and her family? We know her husband, Zebedee, owned what some scholars believe was a fairly lucrative fishing business in Capernaum. Mark tells us that Zebedee had hired servants (1:20), and Luke tells us that his family was in partnership with Simon Peter (5:10). We know from John 18:15 that the apostle John (and presumably his family) was known to the high priest. We don't know the exact nature of this connection, but some scholars suggest a business relationship.

What of Salome herself? Some scholars suggest she was the sister of Mary, the mother of Jesus, making her Jesus' aunt and

James and John Jesus' cousins. The evidence, however, is not concrete and in constructing this story, I decided against a familial connection. The first time Salome is directly referenced in Scripture, she's making her request at Jesus' feet. But this certainly isn't the last time we see her or the first time she's been with Christ. She was one of many women who followed Jesus in Galilee, caring for his needs (Matthew 27:55; Mark 15:41). Matthew places her at the foot of the cross (27:56) and from Mark we learn both her name (15:40) and the fact that she was eyewitness to the empty tomb (16:1). Salome was present, then, from the early days of Jesus' ministry all the way to his empty grave.

When we consider *when* Salome's sons encountered Christ, we realize just how early she came to know Jesus. From John 1:35–42, we see that Andrew was a disciple of John the Baptist who then followed Jesus after the Baptizer identified him as the Lamb of God. Most scholars agree that the other unnamed disciple in this passage is the author himself, which means both Andrew and John eagerly followed Christ at the word of John the Baptist.

John 2 records not only Jesus' first miracle in Cana turning water into wine, but also a fascinating trip to Capernaum during which he does . . . nothing. "After this he went down to Capernaum, with his mother and his brothers and his disciples, and they stayed there for a few days" (verse 12 ESV). This little trip to Capernaum right before Jesus makes a ruckus for the first time in Jerusalem seemed like the perfect moment for a ferocious mother to come face-to-face with the Messiah.

In placing John next to the other Gospels, we see a progression in the stages of the disciples' calling. By the time Jesus called the two sets of brothers along the shores of the Sea of Galilee in Luke 5, they had already been following him. They did not drop their nets for a stranger. They knew this man and had witnessed his power both at Cana and Capernaum itself. Their discipleship up to this point, however, was informal.

In Jesus' day, a boy's education typically ended at age thirteen, after which he would enter his father's occupation or begin an apprenticeship. The brightest students, however, entered a second phase of education at the *beit midrash*, the house of study, and the most promising would go on to learn beneath a rabbi as a full-time disciple. In this last stage of study, young men would approach a rabbi and ask to take his yoke (or teaching) upon themselves.

As rugged fishermen with no formal training, it's highly unlikely that James, John, Simon, and Andrew would have made such a request of Jesus. They most certainly had not been to beit midrash and would not have imagined a future in which they entered formal discipleship beneath an esteemed teacher. Rather than waiting for eager young scholars to approach him, however, Jesus chose his own disciples, and he did so from an unexpected area.

At the time of Jesus' ministry, no one looked to Galilee for learned scholars, for it was viewed as the home of hotheads and revolutionaries with a bloodied history of resistance that was seared upon the nation's memory. After the death of Herod the Great in 4 BC, Judas, the son of the insurrectionist Hezekiah, briefly seized control of the Sepphoris royal armory and launched a guerrilla war throughout Galilee. Numerous scholars claim that this Judas is the same man as Judas of Galilee, whom Josephus names as the founder of the "Fourth Philosophy" and whose brand of piety was intrinsically connected to national purity. The Roman census in 6 AD exacerbated the unrest, and even though Judas was captured and killed, his influence would be felt for decades to come and serve as the foundation of the Zealot party. This means that at the time of the apostles' births and childhoods, the nation was undergoing a seismic shift whose rumblings would only continue to spread.

In depicting Salome's family of origin, I chose to place her in Bethsaida, just six miles south of Judas' own hometown of Gamala. We know that Peter and Andrew were originally from this village (John 1:44), having moved to Capernaum at some point before Jesus' ministry, most likely for economic reasons. I imagined, then, that the business relationship between the two families began with a simple friendship back in Bethsaida.

Because Salome's family was with Jesus from the beginning, it was impossible to touch upon all they would have experienced throughout his ministry. Therefore, in structuring Part Two, it was necessary to be highly selective in which events to cover. For example, in depicting Jesus' first miracle of healing, I focused upon Peter's mother-in-law. Some believe her healing to be the first while others claim it's the account of the official's son in John 4. For the purposes of this story, I chose not to depict the John 4 account. Another example surrounds the Transfiguration. When Jesus, Peter, James, and John come down from the mountain, they are met with a large crowd and a desperate father whose son was possessed by a spirit (Luke 9:37–43). In my treatment of the Transfiguration, I chose to focus upon the ensuing arguments between the disciples and Jesus' instruction with a small child (Luke 9:46–48) rather than the encounter with the demon-possessed son.

Even though it was necessary to be selective in my depictions, I attempted, to the best of my understanding and ability, to remain chronological, accurately representing the order in which biblical events occurred. I also took careful note of *where* such events took place. For example, traditionally, the location of the Transfiguration is identified as Mount Tabor, but we don't know for sure, and other sites have been suggested, including Mount Miron and Mount Hermon. I went with Mount Miron because it's between Caesarea Philippi and Capernaum and makes sense both chronologically and geographically.

When depicting Jesus calming the storm, I stuck with the direction of travel described in Scripture (west to east) but took creative license in the landing of the boat. Directly after the miracle on the water, both Mark and Luke record Jesus driving out demons from a man into a herd of pigs in "the region of the Gerasenes"—or, as Matthew records it, "the Gadarenes." Matthew seems to suggest that the miracle with the pigs happens upon landing on the other side (8:28), whereas Luke's timing is more ambiguous (8:26). The exact location of the miracle with the pigs is debated, but regardless, it was certainly not in Bethsaida, which would have been farther north. Therefore, I took some liberty in imagining the boat first docking near Bethsaida before heading south to the region of the Gerasenes, and in so doing allowed Zebedee to have his fictional encounter with the returning boat.

Location was also important leading up to Jesus' crucifixion. I decided against the Antonia Fortress as the beginning of Jesus' walk to Calvary and instead placed him in Herod's Palace on the western side of the city. The Gospels mention a "praetorium," which refers to the residence of a Roman official. History shows us that Pilate often used Herod's lavish palace rather than the smaller, fortified barracks of the Antonia Fortress while staying in Jerusalem. Scholars believe it likely that Jesus appeared before Pilate in this palace and that he left the city through the Gennath (or Garden) Gate.

Just outside the gate, along a major road, archeologists found the remains of an ancient quarry beneath the modern-day Church of the Holy Sepulchre. At some point, this abandoned quarry was filled in to create a garden, but a rocky outcropping remained that was used as an execution site. The evidence for Jesus' crucifixion occurring here is compelling, and so I chose to depict this abandoned quarry as the site of Jesus' passion.

How poignant that Jesus, our Cornerstone, might have been crucified upon a quarry! And how beautiful that zealous John, likely the youngest of the apostles, who indeed rebuked someone for casting out demons in Jesus' name (Luke 9:49–50) and sought to call down fire from heaven to annihilate a town (Luke 9:54), then stayed by his Lord's side to the bitter end (John 19:26). John would go on to become a spiritual father to countless believers. Salome's two strong sons, mighty men . . . they bookend the apostles as the first to die (Acts 12:2) and the last (Revelation 1:9). And we, as living stones, build upon their legacy above an unshakable Cornerstone.

In creating this fictional account of a remarkable woman, my heart was to remain true to the Word and the One it points to— our beautiful Savior. My fallible words and imagination cannot compare to the infallible story. Go and dip your hand within its depths. Find your strength and stability in the One who holds you fast.

acknowledgments

This book is the most emotional story I've written to date. Every time I worked on it, I wept, and even now I cannot speak about it without choking up. How does one approach writing the story of the mom of Jesus' best friends? With a tremendous amount of prayer, and yes . . . tears. I made it through this journey surrounded and supported by a host of amazing people.

To my team at Bethany House, I'm forever grateful to be partnering with you! My editors, Rochelle Gloege and Jen Veilleux, continue to be a strong bedrock of support. Thank you for brainstorming with me and encouraging me every step of the way. This story is so much better due to your keen insight. Hannah, Jenny, Raela, Emily, Rachael, Anna—from sharp copyediting, to brilliant covers, to marketing strategies and beyond . . . you're a dream team! Thank you for your tireless efforts for these stories.

My agent, Cynthia Ruchti, is a fount of wisdom. Thank you for not only guiding me with my writing but also for your care and compassion for me as a person. Jesus shines brightly in you, and I'm so thankful for your mentorship.

Thank you to my church family for being some of my strongest supporters and cheerleaders. To my parents, siblings, and all my family and friends who are there through every high and every low. Your consistent support means more than you know.

I'm thankful for the kindness and encouragement I've received from other authors who share advice, help brainstorm, provide accountability, and celebrate every milestone. What a gift! And to my readers . . . I can never thank you enough for spending time with me in story. Thank you for picking up my books, recommending them to your friends, and taking the time to bless me with notes of encouragement. When weariness sets in, God brings you to my mind to strengthen my heart.

Andrew, my husband and friend. I based Zeb's love for Salome on your love for me—quiet and steady. Thank you for your humble, tireless service to me and our family. You balance and ground me in countless ways.

Tristan, Seth, and Caira—my three treasures. Part of the reason this book was so emotional to write is because I felt every word of it as your mama. The love of a mother is indeed strong, but the love of Your Heavenly Father is even stronger. It's my deepest desire to see you embrace and grow in His love for you. And it is my biggest challenge and profoundest joy to continually surrender you into His hands.

Abba, I hardly have words to thank You. Throughout the writing of this book, I have felt so tied to Your hip. And when my heart galloped ahead in worry or flagged behind in fear, You were kind to tug me back to Yourself. Thank You for patiently guiding me, for being the steady Rock beneath my feet. You are worthy of my heart, my life, my song.

discussion questions

1. Salome's father plays a significant role in her life. Which piece of advice from Abba did you find the most compelling? How do we see Salome embrace his words?

2. Deborah and Salome's relationship undergoes many changes. The "delicate scale . . . precariously balanced between resentment and respect" eventually turns into friendship. Discuss their reconciliation. What other female relationships impact Salome?

3. Salome aspires to be like a lioness who will do anything for her young. How are her views developed and challenged throughout the story?

4. Discuss Kadmiel's character arc from ambitious boy to an opponent of Jesus. Did you find him to be sympathetic? Do you think he will come to belief?

5. At first Zeb and Salome have different reactions to Jesus' calling of their sons. Did anything about their reactions surprise you? How do they each learn from the other throughout the story?

6. Which miracle of Christ do you wish you could have witnessed? Which miracle depicted in these pages

touched your heart the most? Even with all of the miracles performed in their midst, many still chose unbelief, their "hearts chasing after his miracles while denying his authority." How do we see this playing out in our world today?

7. Salome realizes she's been unfairly holding Philip's parentage against him. Discuss the various prejudices displayed throughout the story. How does Christ challenge our prejudices?

8. Salome walks Keturah's path and turns to prayer in moments of distress. Share passages of Scripture or worship songs that are your "go-to" in times of worry. Are there practical things you do to remind yourself of truth?

9. How do we see jealousy, pride, and ambition play out in the story? Who lays down their pride and who doesn't? How does the teaching and life of Christ confront our pride?

10. Discuss the significance of Jesus calling his own disciples rather than the other way around. What can we learn from the first-century understanding of the disciple-rabbi relationship? How does this add depth to calling ourselves disciples of Christ?

11. Mary encourages Salome that "Every day is a choice to let go and cling." How do we see Salome wrestle with this advice? Has there been a time when you've been challenged to "let go" of something or someone and cling to Christ?

12. Read 1 Peter 2:4–10. Trace the theme of "stone" and "stability" throughout the story. Discuss the significance of the title *On Living Stone*.

Heather Kaufman is the author of multiple books, and her devotional writing has appeared in such publications as *Portals of Prayer, Open Windows, YouVersion,* and *Guideposts.* Her novel *Up from Dust* was a Carol Award finalist. An editor-turned-writer, Heather worked eight years in the publishing industry while earning her master's degree and spinning tales late into the night. When she fell in love with studying the Bible through a cultural lens, the words of Scripture came springing to life, and Jesus became even more astoundingly beautiful. Now she delights in crafting stories that highlight the goodness of God and compel readers deeper into the Bible. When not reading, writing, or accumulating mounds of books, Heather can be found exploring new parks with her husband and three children near their home in St. Louis, Missouri. Learn more and stay in touch at HMKStories.com.